PRAISE FOR MARY BLAYNEY'S
Traitor's Kiss/Lover's Kiss

"Taut and daring, an emotionally charged tale that satisfies from beginning to end. *Traitor's Kiss* will steal your heart!" —GAELEN FOLEY

"Reminiscent of Regency masters Putney, Balogh and Elizabeth Boyle . . . [Blayney's] consummate storytelling completely involves readers." —*Romantic Times*

"Danger, deception, and desire blend brilliantly together in these two deftly written, exceptionally entertaining Regency romances." —*Chicago Tribune*

"Mary writes with a quiet beauty and great confidence."
—Risky Regencies

"These two exhilarating Pennistan family Regency romances are well written, filled with plenty of action and star great courageous lead characters. . . . Fans will enjoy both super tales." —Midwest Book Review

"This beguiling pair of novels from author Mary Blayney delivers a double dose of romance and intrigue."
—Fresh Fiction

ALSO BY MARY BLAYNEY

Traitor's Kiss/Lover's Kiss

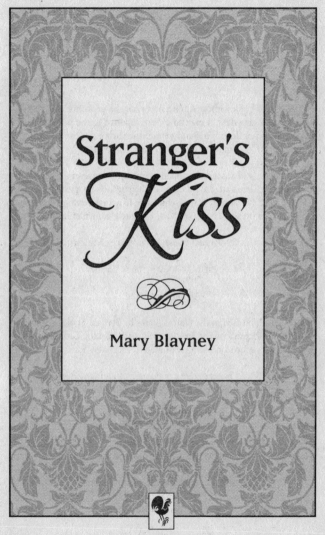

Stranger's *Kiss*

Mary Blayney

BANTAM BOOKS

NEW YORK

2009 Bantam Books Mass Market Edition

Copyright © 2009 by Mary Blayney

Published in the United States by Bantam Books,
an imprint of The Random House Publishing Group,
a division of Random House, Inc., New York.

BANTAM BOOKS is a registered trademark of Random House, Inc.,
and the colophon is a trademark of Random House, Inc.

ISBN 978-0-440-24428-8

Cover art: Alan Ayers
Cover design: Lynn Andreozzi

Printed in the United States of America

www.bantamdell.com

2   4   6   8   9   7   5   3   1

For Diane Gaston
and
Julie Halperson:

Thank you for your friendship, inspiration, and
laughter

Stranger's Kiss

Prologue

London
January 1818

THE DUELING PISTOL lay heavy in his hand. Lynford Pennistan, the Duke of Meryon, counted off the paces with his second, staring at the ground as if each blade of grass mattered.

"Have you decided?" Lord Kyle asked.

Meryon didn't answer. Kyle's practical question belied what was at stake. *Kill the bastard or let him live.* Meryon knew his hand was steady, but his anger burned white hot.

"Lyn, please, you're a better shot than Bendas. He doesn't have a chance."

Kyle's hands were clasped behind his back, a gesture that Meryon recognized. His friend wanted to do something physical, most likely beat some sense into him. "He is the Duke of Bendas." Kyle came close to pleading. "There will be consequences."

"You handle your role as second with honor, but you will not talk me out of this." He reached twenty paces but Meryon kept his back to the field.

"Can whatever happened between you be worth this risk?"

"Yes. It is." Meryon took the cloth that Kyle offered and wiped the barrel and the grip one last time. He owed Kyle this much at least. "Bendas tried to ruin my sister so that she would have no choice but to marry his grandson." Meryon could still see the bruises on Olivia's neck, the way fear shadowed her for weeks.

"He did what?" Kyle straightened. "Lady Olivia . . ."

"The end was better than anyone could have wished. She is happily married, not to his grandson, and she is safe." Meryon narrowed his eyes. "This is not a story I want broadcast."

"Of course not. I have sisters. I know how precious a woman's reputation is." Kyle shook his head, still incredulous. "But why, Lyn? Why would Bendas do something so medieval?"

"For land. He thought his empire more important than Olivia, or his grandson." Meryon gave Kyle his full attention. "What would you do to Bendas?"

Kyle drew a breath. "All right."

With a sharp nod, Meryon faced Bendas.

Kyle stepped in front of him. "One more thing, Lyn. Dueling is not illegal, but *murder* is." Without waiting for an answer, Kyle moved to the sideline.

Meryon watched as Bendas's second handed him the pistol, and with a profound bow he, too, moved to the side of the field.

Kyle spoke to the man who would be counting, someone both seconds seemed to know. How odd, Lyn thought, that his life was in the hands of one man he did not know and another man he hated.

Lyn buried the thought and concentrated on the moment. The ground was softening, filling the air with an earthy scent, carrying the first hint of warmer days. One deep breath told him that it might still be winter but spring would come. He heard the jingle of the horses' tack and the sound of the groom's words as he tried to quiet them.

"Your Graces," the man called out in a strong voice, not turning toward either one of the duelists. "My name is Carstairs. Mr. DeBora and Lord Kyle have asked me to officiate. A physician is present, should there be an injury." He waited a moment. "I will count to three and on the count of three you may shoot at your discretion."

Forty paces away, the Duke of Bendas stood still as a stone gargoyle. *To kill him or not.* The answer came to Meryon as he concentrated on the pistol. Death was too easy. Bendas deserved to suffer in this life. He would burn in hell soon enough.

"Your Graces, are you both ready?"

Meryon gave a slow nod without taking his eyes from Bendas. His hand was steady.

Bendas's expression was more guarded than arrogant, as if recounting the stupidity that had brought him to this.

"On the count of three."

Meryon nodded again.

Carstairs coughed and after a beat called out, "One!"

Meryon did not want to leave his children orphans, but if he died, surely his wife would be there to meet him.

If he went to heaven.

Meryon drew a breath to steady his arm.

"Two."

He raised his pistol for the count of three as an explosion assaulted his ears and a bullet grazed his coat sleeve at the shoulder, too close to his heart to be an accident.

Astonishment held him still long enough for two thoughts.

Bendas had shot before the count of three.

And missed.

The caller counted, "Three!"

Bendas stood still as a statue, awaiting Meryon's volley. Did the man want to die?

"The duke thought three numbers had been counted." DeBora's confusion showed his shock.

"I missed." Bendas dropped his arm to his side, smoke curling from the barrel of his pistol, an odd smile twisting his mouth. "Are you just going to stand there, Meryon? Take your shot."

Bendas wants me to kill him. It would be easy enough to do. The man had no heart, so it would be best to aim for his head.

"The groom is dead, Your Grace! He's dead!" The hysteria in John Coachman's voice reached him before the words made sense. Lowering his gun, Meryon abandoned the field and ran to the fallen man. The physician reached him first, felt for a pulse, and shook his head.

The boy lay on his back, shot in one eye, the other

wide open, as if stunned to find himself the center of attention.

"It was an accident, a mistake." DeBora took one look at the dead boy, then ran toward the woods. Retching sounds reached their ears.

Lynford Pennistan, the third Duke of Meryon, kneeled down beside the dead groom, put his pistol on the grass, and closed the boy's undamaged eye, straightening his arms and legs. Except for the ugly seeping hole in his face, the groom, whose name Meryon had to ask for, looked as though he slept.

The duke's hands shook as misery consumed him. *To say I am sorry is woefully inadequate.* Despair overcame anguish and he clenched his fists. Why did God allow this? Joshua was an innocent with his whole life before him. His eyes filled. Just as Rowena had been too young, much too young.

Ignoring the chaos around him, Meryon prayed for Joshua Kepless. He commended his soul to God. And to his wife, Rowena. Surely she would embrace this boy. One more who had died for the Pennistans.

Rising to his feet, pistol in hand again, Meryon felt years older than he had five minutes ago. The coachman was crying, but tried to compose himself while Meryon waited. When he raised his head, Meryon met his eyes.

"Take Kepless up in the carriage. I will ride home with Lord Kyle. Find out about his family and come to me immediately. The majordomo will direct you to my study."

John Coachman touched his hand to his head in a gesture that was as old as any dukedom. "As you wish, Your Grace."

Meryon shifted his pistol to his right hand and walked to Bendas. DeBora, pale as smoke, stepped between the two.

"The death of the groom was an accident," DeBora insisted.

Bendas elbowed his second aside. "I aimed for your heart, Meryon. This gun's balance is off." Bendas sneered at his second. "That is your fault. Your sole task was to make sure the guns work and I had the better of the two."

Bendas tossed the pistol to the ground. "It's your shot, Meryon. If you are done grieving for a groom."

Bendas's disdain was enough to merit a death sentence. Meryon raised his pistol, aiming it at Bendas's eye. Bendas stood still, waiting. Rage clouded Meryon's judgment, he knew that, but it was impossible to ignore the way it burned through him, demanding action.

Demanding justice.

"Your death will be a blessing to your family, king, and country." Meryon set the trigger.

"Please, Your Grace, a word." Kyle stood next to him as he spoke.

Reason cooled his temper. Yes, Bendas was willing to die. Because it would mean Meryon's ruin. If he killed Bendas, he would have to leave the country, his children, his world.

A renewed surge of fury burned through his trigger finger.

He fired.

DeBora screamed as Bendas fell to the ground. Meryon waited, finding some pleasure in Bendas's white face as he lay blinking on the dew-covered grass.

"I missed." Meryon used Bendas's words and then added, "But I missed on purpose." He handed the pistol to Kyle, whose hand, he noticed, was not quite steady. "Stand up, Bendas, you son of a bitch."

DeBora helped Bendas to his feet. Meryon grabbed the other duke by the lapels and pulled him up so they were face-to-face.

"You are a disgrace to your title and your name. My sister almost died because of you. And now you've killed a boy with as little thought as a man brings down a stag."

"I am the Duke of Bendas."

"And your house is the poorer for it, you bastard." Meryon tightened his hold, coming closer to strangling Bendas, then let go of him with enough force that Bendas staggered.

"I will see that justice is done, Bendas. I will destroy you. In the end you will wish you had died here today."

Meryon nodded at Kyle, who picked up the second pistol. They made their way to Kyle's carriage. Meryon's breathing evened a little.

Ruining Bendas would take more of his time than the man deserved, but this was one task the Duke of Meryon would see to himself.

I

*London
Before the Season
March 1818*

MY DEARS, STOP chatting or you will miss everything! The Duke of Meryon has arrived."

A group of the ton's finest gossips clustered near the entrance to Mrs. Harbison's ballroom. Something interesting had happened.

"Meryon is here?"

"Where?"

"He looks like he's still in mourning."

They paused as one as they considered that even without a smile the Duke of Meryon was worth watching.

"Poor Rowena."

"It has been every bit of a year."

"Is this his first social outing since she died?"

"What else would he do of an evening?" one of the dim-witted asked.

The ladies laughed at her naïveté. The gentlemen added gruff chuckles and considering glances.

"How long before he marries again?"

"He has an heir. Why would he marry again?"

The whispers bit into Meryon like the tip of a sword, reminding him that his wife's death had changed his world forever. But these very gossips were the reason he was here tonight.

"Those women are idiots." His hostess tried to steer him away from the crush of people, her too-tight grip a measure of her indignation.

Meryon halted their progress and bowed over her hand. "Nevertheless, I will speak with them."

Letty Harbison took his arm again. "You will not speak to them alone, Your Grace."

"I can handle The Gossips." He smiled down at her. "I have plenty of experience with backbiting in the House of Lords."

"But this is my house, Meryon, and I want to hear every word."

He laughed out loud and could not recall the last time he had. "What a delight you are, Letty. Does Harbison know how lucky he is?"

She tapped his hand with her fan and faced The Gossips, assuming a look that Meryon could only describe as condescending.

"Good evening, ladies and gentlemen. Your Grace, I am sure you have met *all these people*." He would not laugh. She had neatly insulted them and they had not even noticed, thrilled to have a duke in their midst.

Mrs. Harbison turned to him, including the others in their conversation. "I am so happy to see you among the ton again, Your Grace."

"Oh yes," one of the ladies echoed. "I know it has been a difficult year for you."

"And for all of Rowena's friends," another added.

"But having you with us will remind us of what we loved most about her."

"That she was a duchess?" He raised his eyebrows and smiled to cut his insult.

The wisest of The Gossips laughed. "Of course not, Meryon. We loved her because she made you happy."

"Yes, she did," he said, smiling at the memory, impressed with this one woman's insight.

A long silence followed. Meryon waited it out, squeezing Mrs. Harbison's arm when she would have spoken. The Gossips would not abandon their place by the door but seemed at a loss for words with one of their favorite subjects in their midst.

Meryon waited until they were nervous with embarrassment and then offered his tidbit of news. "Does anyone know why the Duke of Bendas's grandson has taken rooms at Albany this Season?"

The Gossips fell on the question like hungry kittens, discussing the subject with such enthusiasm that the casual listener would think they actually knew the answer. When the ladies began to speculate on whether Lord William would ever marry, one of the gentlemen brought up the subject Meryon had waited for.

"Have you seen the Rowlandson cartoon of the Duke of Bendas, Your Grace?"

"Bendas? In a cartoon?" Of course he had seen it. He'd sent his coachman to Rowlandson with the story. Meryon's task had been to find a way to have everyone talk about it. This group would make that happen.

"You should see it, Your Grace. It shows Bendas blindfolded and with rags in his ears while fighting a duel in which he shoots the wrong person."

The group sprinkled the story with dismay and relish and gobbled it up.

"Rowlandson ridiculed a duke?"

"No one is off-limits to the cartoonists. Look what they have done to Prinny."

Meryon listened.

"But Bendas is so powerful, so formidable."

"He is so insistent upon being shown the proper deference."

"That's what makes it so delicious. I must find a copy."

"My husband will have to add it to his collection."

"It does give credence to that rumor of a duel."

"I suppose that a duel could be the reason that his grandson is not staying with the family?" Meryon asked.

The gaggle stopped chattering.

Before any one of them was brave enough to ask if the rumored duel was true, Meryon bowed to them, offered Mrs. Harbison his arm, and withdrew. The chatter began again, busily weaving a story worthy of the Minerva Press.

"Bendas was in a duel? That's shocking, Meryon. Are you not appalled?"

"Appalled, but not surprised. Bendas thinks he is a

demigod, if not a god. He is old and failing and has convinced himself that his rank sets him apart from the laws of man."

"But who would challenge a duke?"

Meryon thought about his answer. "Someone with a good reason."

"I cannot believe it, Meryon."

"It happened. And Bendas's bullet killed an innocent boy."

"Dear God, that is awful. You know this for a fact?"

"That question, Letty, is why I find your conversation infinitely more tolerable than that of The Gossips. And yes, I know it for a fact."

"But I invited Bendas tonight. I hope he does not come. Surely he feels some regret?"

"None," Meryon said sharply. "He as much as said that women and servants exist to do his bidding and have no value beyond that."

"My God, Meryon." She stopped their progress to confront him. "How do you know all these details?"

He could see she had almost guessed. "Because I'm the one who challenged him. The one he meant to kill."

Mrs. Harbison raised a hand to cover her mouth, agape at the admission. Her eyes were wide with shock. "Meryon! You challenged him to a duel? Why?" She waved her hand in front of her face. "No, I did not ask that. I promise you I will tell no one."

"Thank you, Letty, but the duel, if not the reason, will be common knowledge soon enough." Meryon glanced back at The Gossips, who had most likely begun to ask that question among themselves.

"No one will hear it from me!" With that, she composed herself and they began to move through the crowd with endless curtsies and bows.

Meryon sighed gently. Well, he had accomplished what he came to do, but to leave so abruptly would distract The Gossips from their discussion of Bendas, so he allowed Letty to escort him around the room.

"Meryon!" Jack Forbes greeted him with a bow and a clap on the back. "Good to see a familiar face. I've been in Scotland for near on two years. The weather was foul but the fishing was superb. How's the winter here?"

"The duke has recently returned from France, Mr. Forbes."

"Bet the duchess made you buy her a dozen dresses, eh?"

Mrs. Harbison froze. Meryon made himself relax his fisted hand and hoped it seemed that he could answer the question as easily as any other. "Jack, I am sorry to embarrass you, but Rowena died more than a year ago." He spoke very quietly, stepping closer to this longtime acquaintance.

"Oh, my God, Meryon, I am sorry. She was a sweet lady and I am ten times a fool. I must start reading the paper." Forbes bowed, his expression stricken, as he backed into the crowd.

"I am so sorry, Meryon."

"No apology is necessary, Letty. I expect it."

"That no one remembers their manners?" She was annoyed, but then laughed a little. "Of course we have no manners when something *interesting* happens."

"What empty lives they lead if my return to the social scene excites more than passing interest."

"Duke or not you would be noticed." She tapped his arm with her fan again, which was as close to flirting as her husband would tolerate. "Tall and good-looking never goes unremarked. But add a dukedom to those good looks and you become as fascinating as . . ." Mrs. Harbison paused to try to come up with an appropriate example.

"As fascinating as a three-eyed horse," Meryon finished for her.

She laughed out loud and people nearby turned to look at them. Letty Harbison pressed her lips together and swallowed the rest of her laughter. "More fascinating than a gamester on a winning streak."

She closed her fan and held out her arm. "Please do invite me to dance, Your Grace. You are the most charming of partners. Is it all that fencing that makes you so elegant when you dance?"

He led her to the dance floor, well aware that the Harbisons' ball was not much more than a training ground for the Season's endless soirees. As he moved through the reel his partners blushed, tripped, and counted the steps out loud, and several would not even look up at him.

Meryon found if he smiled they grew even more confused, except for the one bolder than the others. With a seductive look she brushed too close. She could not have been more than seventeen, but when they passed again she whispered, "I can make you happy, Your Grace."

It said something about his age, or the fact that he had a baby daughter, that his surprise mixed with sympathy for her parents.

By the time the set ended, and he bowed to Mrs. Harbison one last time, he felt he had done his duty. He said as much to Letty and she nodded. "Yes, any more time on the dance floor would find The Gossips speculating about which young lady has caught your interest."

Before he could answer he could see she was distracted by something in the hall.

"If you will excuse me, Your Grace, I must welcome this guest personally. It is her first social event since coming to England after the death of her husband. I'm sure you understand."

"Of course." Meryon bowed. "Thank you for the dance."

The orchestra began the next set with a waltz and Meryon watched several couples take to the floor. He added the waltz to the list of a dozen selfish reasons why he missed Rowena. She had liked to dance as much as he did. He had noticed it the night they met. Their delight in dancing together had never faded.

Grief swamped him without warning. His eyes filled and he knew he must find a quiet spot for a moment. If The Gossips saw his eyes water they would talk about it for days.

Meryon went down the nearest passage. The sounds of the waltz faded and the air grew less cloying.

The first door he opened was filled with card players. He raised a hand to the group, but they barely noticed him.

He found a quiet spot on his second try. The dark room was well aired, with an underlying scent of lemon oil polish, which was all he wanted for company.

Avoiding the furniture, little more than hulking shapes in the dark, Meryon found a chair near a fire screen that hid the empty grate. He sat down, relieved beyond reason.

These days his life was equal parts a search for justice and the burden of sorrow, with only the children for relief from his dark thoughts.

Settling into the comfort of the velvet-covered chair, Meryon stared at the embroidered fire screen and did his best to make his mind a blank.

Minutes passed in a haze of memories that he pushed out of his mind as soon as they appeared. His brothers' silence, knowing no words that could console him. His sister's sadness even once she was beyond tears. Michael Garrett's words, so atypical of the vicar he was: "God is a puzzle to me in this and faith is a weak comfort."

The children. He curled his hand into a tight fist. Rexton's constant "Where is Mama?" despite being content enough with his nurse. Alicia's crying as though she knew Mama was gone, inconsolable for days.

All those months in France had done no more than delay a grief that he had been unwilling to face. He'd filled his days with artists, diplomats, government officials, and the occasional visit to the demimonde of Paris.

Tonight proved that time and distance had not enabled him to forget what he'd lost. *Rowena.*

Do not think of her. Do not let the memories in. Even as he commanded it, he remembered one night: Rowena wearing her favorite golden evening frock, asking him to be sure that her glorious pearl necklace was fastened securely.

Burying the memories, he crushed them into a tight ball that settled near the stone-cold place he called his heart.

Meryon stood up. He would find Letty Harbison, give her his thanks, go home to Penn House. The children would already be abed but he could work on his bill for Parliament. He should start on the wording, list those likely to support it, and examine the calendar for a likely opening for the first reading.

He would also see what his secretary had unearthed about Bendas and if John Coachman had anything to report after this week of spying on the old fool.

When he was halfway to the door, someone opened it from the other side. Stepping close to the wall, out of sight, Meryon remained perfectly still, annoyed that even here he could not find privacy.

Surely they will not stay when they see a dark room. Unless it's a couple looking for a quiet spot.

Meryon had grown used to the dark. He could see well enough to make out the furniture, if not any details. He searched for another door.

He'd sat near the fireplace and saw no door on that wall. Facing the fireplace, he identified a settee. A game table and chairs filled the other half of the room. He saw no door on that wall either.

If it was a couple fumbling with the door latch between kisses, he would have the upper hand. No one wanted that kind of gossip spread.

He waited, curious, impatient, and just a little amused to see who had found his hiding place.

A woman came in, alone. Her fragrance announced her presence, roses with a hint of musk beneath, more alluring than sophisticated.

She wore a gown of gray taffeta with an iridescent quality that caused it to glimmer in the light from the passage. A Juno rather than a fairy, the upswept hair emphasized her height. He could not see her face but wondered if it was as fine as her figure.

Elegant came to mind first.

Distraught second.

She remained silent, her breathing ragged, the very air between them filled with her distress. She closed the door and leaned against it, staring at the floor.

"Oh, Edward." She breathed the name, then stumbled to the settee that faced the fireplace, not more than six feet from where he stood.

She sat down, covered her face with her hands, and began to sob. Not quiet tears, but the kind that railed against fate. Lyn completely understood her barely suppressed scream of desperation.

He recognized grief, especially a woman's grief. She had lost a lover or a husband, perhaps not to death but lost as surely as if he had died. Each uneven breath drew one from him, each sob made his own heart hurt until he had to swallow against an answering lump in his throat.

Why could women not grieve in silence? Their voluble sensibilities always left him uncertain. A feeling that made him as uncomfortable as their tears did. With Rowena, his attempts at comfort had always made things worse.

Escape. He took a step away from her. He needed to escape. She wanted privacy. She could have it.

Meryon took another step toward the door.

She looked up at the ceiling and still did not see him.

"God, oh God, please give me the strength . . . Edward, please help me. I feel so alone."

She whispered the prayer, speaking as softly as her tears would allow. When she drew a deep breath, he could tell even without words that she had done with crying.

All at once, the woman straightened and stood. When she saw him in the shadows, she gasped and raised a hand to her heart.

He had been discovered.

2

"I BEG YOUR PARDON, madame." Meryon stepped out of the shadows and bowed. "I am neither Edward nor God, but you are not alone."

"Yes, yes. I can see that. What are you doing here?" Asperity laced her voice.

"The same thing you are," he said, smiling a little. "Though I suppose I could have been waiting for someone or hiding from a man who wants to sell me his horse."

"Is that so?" Interest replaced her brusqueness.

Now he had started a conversation. God help him.

"If you are doing the same thing I am, then you must be either grieving or hiding." The woman leaned forward. "Or perhaps both."

Meryon did not answer immediately, trying to identify her. Not one of The Gossips and definitely not the too-forward girl from the dance floor. This woman had left childhood behind a delightful number of years ago.

"Ahh." Her voice sounded all-knowing. "You want to hide, even from me. I am so sorry to have intruded. I will find another room."

"You do not owe me an apology. I will go. You need the privacy more than I do." He moved closer to the door, had his hand on the latch before the woman spoke again.

"My husband died almost eighteen months ago." She spoke quickly. "One moment he held his violin, practicing Mozart. The next he lay at my feet, dead."

She sat down, as though the truth had drained her.

"I am sorry." Meryon turned back to her. "So very sorry."

"Thank you for your sympathy, sir." She spoke the perfunctory phrase without obvious emotion, but in the deep quiet he could hear her trying to control her tears. She blew out a sharp breath of annoyance, a singularly inelegant gesture.

"I will leave you alone, madame," he tried again.

She reached a hand out, not quite touching him. "No, please stay. For a few moments more."

Meryon could count a number of reasons why a woman would want to speak to a gentleman in private. The obvious did not apply, for surely a woman her age, and a widow, would know that she could not trap him into marriage with a game as old as this.

"I thought I had finished with the tears," she explained, "and then tonight I heard someone playing a violin. He had too much talent for the orchestra and did his best to play down to their level. It reminded me of so many things, but mostly of Edward. I needed to cry." She tried to smile, but it was a miserable failure.

Her words made him feel a fool. The whole world did not live to trap him, to catch the Duke of Meryon in some peccadillo. Garrett had the right of it. His brother-in-law insisted that grief distorted all sensibilities.

He relaxed. Then the Duke of Bendas came to mind. Once the bastard felt the web of ruin tighten around him, Bendas would try for retribution. Could he have already figured it out? Was she part of his retaliation?

Meryon stared at the mystery woman. "I do understand the need to grieve, madame, and I *am* sorry." He moved closer. "My wife died a year ago."

"Oh." He heard new tears in the single word as she reached out again and this time touched his arm.

In that touch he could feel the confusion of her heart: warmth, sincerity, sympathy, pain, hope. If she was acting, it was a brilliant performance wasted on an audience of one.

"I hear heartache in those words, sir. You have my deepest condolences."

"Thank you." He sat down beside her, near the spot she patted with her hand. They sat quietly, she with her eyes closed. In the frail light from the street he studied her profile. The dark lashes resting on her cheeks, her full lips, the rise and fall of her chest as she grew more composed. She had the face of a Madonna, of a grieving princess of some European country, lush, lovely, and not quite a part of this world.

"Cry if you must, madame." Meryon recognized a kindred spirit with a gaping wound where the heart should be. The pain had brought a wisdom that he would have been happy to live without: that life was filled with opportunities he'd ignored, thinking he had forever.

"It is a weakness to cry now. It has been so long." She shook her head, her pretty earrings swinging with the motion. "It will hurt my throat."

When she turned to him, her composure seemed fully restored. "Edward insisted that tears made everyone uncomfortable. I am impressed, sir. Few men tolerate crying with such equanimity."

"I had practice. When my wife was increasing she was inclined to tears."

Her smile of understanding drew one from him.

"Were you in town when the princess and her infant died last November?"

"No, I was in France until recently. My sister tells me that everyone mourned; tears and sober clothes were the order of the day everywhere, even in Derbyshire, where she lives."

"Yes, I heard this too." She paused. "And yet, sir, it is less than three months and she is forgotten, or at least no one mourns." Her sorrow had disappeared, replaced by anger. Or was it disgust?

"It is what the Regent wants. He himself held a soiree in February. And I cannot fault him, madame. He must give his brothers time to marry and beget an heir. Of all people his daughter would understand."

She was silent again as she considered his words. How rare that was, at least in his experience of women. "It could be. Men are more practical than women."

"That is obvious flattery, madame. My wife would insist that I never gave a thought to what was involved in even the simplest request." Meryon smiled, not meaning to sound cynical. "As for the prince, we both know there is more to it than that. He does not wish to face the truth that he too will die someday."

"That is what I think as well! Though I have not met him and have only heard stories of his excesses."

"I have been in his company more than once, madame, and, from what I have seen, he surrounds himself with as much pleasure as he can as though that will make up for what is missing in his life." Meryon stood and looked away. That was not the wisest thing to have said about a man to whom he pledged allegiance.

"Yes, I see we think the same in this. It's as though he is armoring himself against a devil that beats at his door, not realizing that pleasure is the devil's finest ally."

Meryon's raised eyebrows were his only comment.

"Oh dear, you think I have spent too much time among Papists." She tossed off the comment without sounding either apologetic or embarrassed. "You may be right. You see, I have lived in Italy until recently."

"Ah, yes, and Italy is full of Roman Catholics. It would be hard to avoid them." He spoke through a laugh. "But that is not why I kept silent." He sat next to her again. "In essence I agree with you. Prinny thinks he will find what he needs by sharing his wealth and living extravagantly, wasting money that could be used more wisely."

"But, sir, whether it is used well or not, money cannot buy what he needs most."

"Your gown is not made of sackcloth, madame."

She laughed. "How kind of you to notice. But," she faced him with a rustle of her skirts, "you will also notice that neither one of us is among the crush on the dance floor, seeking entertainment while we look for that ever-elusive quality called happiness."

"Ever elusive describes happiness perfectly. I have found contentment, but happiness has proved too much to hope for. I've never liked the social whirl, the Season," he admitted. "Now I like balls and parties even less."

"I would rather practice the harp for hours, and I do dislike the harp, than watch men and women meet, mate, and think that will guarantee happiness."

"You do not believe in happiness?" He had yet to meet a woman who denied it.

"I believe in happiness. Too much so, sir." She sighed. "I had it in my marriage. But the loss of it is so very hard to bear."

"But loss is a blow that one can recover from," he said.

"You think so?" For the second time their eyes met and held. She stared into his and did not look away.

"One *can* recover?" she asked.

"We have to believe it, or how could we go on?"

"Yes." She lowered her head. "Yes, I suppose we can. It merely requires that we lie to ourselves."

Silence fell again. Meryon heard the ticking of a clock somewhere in the room.

The quiet was companionable, but filled with sensibilities he had avoided for too long. She stared at her hands; he watched them too, not surprised when a tear or two fell on her fingers.

"The truth is that one moment all is well, as well as it can be," she whispered and raised her head. "Then death puts an end to the effort."

"For me Rowena's death was a mix of nightmare and relief together."

"Was your wife ill for a long time?"

Thank God she'd misunderstood his relief. To admit that it had been a relief to stop trying to understand Rowena was more honest than he needed to be. "She died in childbirth."

"Aha, like the dear princess."

"Yes, except my baby, a girl, survived."

"Oh, sir, such bitter and such sweet." She raised her hand to her mouth and then dropped it back into her lap. "Your daughter lived."

"Yes, now my son has a sister. Her mother wanted me to name her Alicia. It was the last thing Rowena ever asked of me." Meryon stared at the ceiling and waited until his eyes were dry. "Alicia started to walk this week."

"You are so lucky to still have that much of your wife with you." She stared over his shoulder. "Sometimes I think I should not have come to London. I have no memories of Edward here."

"Memories are not always a comfort."

"You may say that aloud but your heart knows." She spoke with conviction. "Why else would you have sought out a quiet place to sit?"

"I had decided I made a mistake and was about to leave." Read that truth, he thought, and looked at her with challenge. She did not abandon the debate.

"I am glad that you did not. Perhaps we are each to

the other a gift from God because now we are able to speak of our loss to someone who understands."

I do understand. He did not have to say the words aloud; she read his expression as surely as he read hers.

"I decided months ago that I must do my best and take care of those still living. Use my love of Edward to inspire me. It sounds so presumptuous to voice it aloud."

"Not presumptuous, but perhaps too noble."

"How else can I prove his death did some good somewhere?"

"Why should it? Madame, I do believe you must be the kind who tries to find good in the worst of situations."

"You sound cynical," she said on the smallest of laughs.

"I beg your pardon, madame."

Her laugh proved she had a share of cynicism herself.

"Beg my pardon all you wish, sir, but admit that I am right and that cynicism is the easiest way to end a discussion you would as soon avoid."

"Yes. Yes, it is" was all Meryon would allow.

He could end the discussion one more way. It would guarantee that neither one of them would remember what they had been discussing.

He could kiss her.

3

KISS HER? Meryon decided that insane idea came from his roiling sensibilities, plus the absence of a woman in his bed these last months.

She permitted the silence for a minute more, oblivious to his thoughts. The ambience of two burdened souls settled around them again.

"How long were you married?" She asked the question so suddenly that, if he had not been watching her, he would have jumped.

"Rowena died a month after our eleventh anniversary."

"Edward and I were married for nine years—seven of which were truly happy. The other two were miserable. The war kept us apart for a year. He thought I had gone home, and I feared he would find a lover he preferred to his wife. It took us another year to reestablish the trust which is at the heart of a good marriage."

"Rowena and I always trusted each other." He never doubted that. Meryon thought of his mistress. He'd paid Eliza to fill a need, trust hardly a factor. At least not in the way this woman meant.

"What did you like the best about your wife?"

He smiled. "Her enthusiasm. The way she looked at me as though I knew everything." *The way she willingly risked her life to make sure the Meryon dukedom would go to my son.* He kept that one to himself. It led straight down the endless road of guilt.

"Is that all?"

"I think it's quite enough to have someone build their world around you." *Too much.*

But he thought a moment and went on. "The way she loved her dog. The animal irritated me no end in those days. Now I talk to the dog because she looks so lonely." He sat back and closed his eyes.

"Does her dog answer you?" A smile came with the question and he answered in the same silly spirit so that she would keep smiling.

"Sometimes she does, in her own doglike way, and the amazing thing is that she always says exactly what I want to hear."

"Which is the wonder of pets, is it not?"

Her smile mesmerized him, drew him closer. She tilted her head and nodded a little. With a short, sharp sigh, she went on.

"I loved Edward but he was hardly perfect. He annoyed me, too. His striving for perfection, a perfection that only he could hear. The way he would roam through the house shouting for his valet when we had servants who would have been happy to find the man. I hated the way he would express his dislike of a dish even when he was the guest at a dinner party. Still, we would embrace those petty annoyances in a moment to have them back with us, would we not?"

"Yes," he said and for a minute he could feel Rowena beside him. "If she were still alive, I would do better, try to make her happier." Had he said that aloud? This woman's honesty compelled him to speak the truth. Or had she cast a spell over him?

"Oh, yes. I know exactly what you mean. If I had Edward back, I like to think I could be always what he needed, never, never lose my temper, never complain."

"To talk of what we wish we had done is a sure road to madness. I am so sorry I cannot ease your heartache."

"Please, sir," she begged through fresh tears, leaning across the small space that separated them. The tears trickled down her cheeks, but she was not embarrassed by them anymore. "Tell me that someday this pain will end. That something will heal my heart."

Meryon leaned closer and in a motion that felt as natural as it did right, he raised a hand to cradle her neck and kissed her. Pressed his lips to the bowed pink perfection of hers, tasted the tears in the corners of her mouth, felt the sweetness of her, the warmth of her skin under his fingers, the pulse at her throat. He felt the passion there, buried beneath the anguish. He wanted to feel that passion in more than a kiss, for longer than a moment.

But the instant the kiss became more than comfort, he drew back.

His eyes had grown used to the dark and he could see more of her, as if another of a dozen veils had been lifted. Her full mouth with a pronounced dip in her upper lip, a strong, straight nose. Her brows dark arched wings.

"Thank you." She said the words but he heard more. *Do you really think that was enough?*

Not enough, the kiss made him realize that this accidental rendezvous had gone too far. How incredibly stupid it was to kiss a complete stranger.

"So we will each struggle in our own way and find comfort where we can," she added softly.

Should he consider that as an invitation? Meryon wondered. He could not see her expression; she was staring at her hands again.

"What we had is so rare, given and earned by so few. At least my Edward and your Rowena knew how much we loved them."

Her words shattered the camaraderie. Did Rowena know she was loved? He could not ever remember saying the words "I love you" to her. Not until she closed her eyes for the last time. She had smiled. Surely she had heard him. Please, please God, she had.

Meryon stood up. "Good evening, madame. My apologies for the kiss. It is proof that we have been together too long and are begging to be discovered."

"Stop. Wait." She followed him to the door. "What did I say?"

"It was nothing you said." The lie came easily. "I prefer no reminders of what I have lost."

"But you must remember," she insisted.

"No, I do not. I bid you good evening." Meryon bowed and left the room.

ELENA VERANO WENT back to the settee and sat with a graceless thump, her fingers pressed to her lips. He *must* have taken offense at something, but she could not imagine what. They had seemed so *simpatico*. When he spoke, he gave voice to her very thoughts.

That most tender of kisses had proved to her that her heart would heal, the pain would fade, if only because his one kiss had not been enough, not nearly enough. But then the best of kisses always left one wanting more.

Elena stood and circled the room, pausing at a window that looked out onto the street. It was quiet, except for the coachmen talking in clusters.

Waiting, waiting. That was how she had felt since she came to England. She had been waiting for her world to right itself, to move forward with a new sense of purpose. Now, she thought, this meeting might be the beginning of that change.

He had a bearing that spoke of wealth and privilege, like that of her brother when she last saw him. Her shadowed companion was naturally solemn. Even though she could not see his eyes, if eyes were the mirror of the soul, then she knew his would be filled with unhappiness. His continued mourning made that an easy guess.

With a deep breath, she calmed herself and began the series of exercises of both mind and voice that would make this first appearance in England a pleasure rather than a torture. She had yet to decide exactly what to sing of the songs she had practiced.

There was a tap at the door and for the barest of seconds Elena thought he had come back. But he would not knock.

"Elena?"

She knew that voice. "Yes, William. Come in."

Viscount William Bendasbrook entered the room, bringing with him a burst of sound from the party and his own exhausting energy. At something less than five feet tall he somehow managed to carry the air of a man to be reckoned with.

He made no comment about the dark, but stood beside her.

"I knew when you asked for an empty room that you wanted to be alone for a while. Then it occurred to me that you might need some cheering up. Besides, it's almost time for you to sing."

"No. I have at least another twenty minutes. I will prepare my voice and then join you."

He ignored the hint to leave. "So now we are alone together. Are you worried about your reputation? Shall I light a candle at least?" He found a flint and lit a candle on the mantel.

"As if one lit candle would make a difference to The Gossips." She moved back to the settee. "You are a rogue, William, but I will risk it."

"We could tell the truth, Elena." William sat beside her.

"That you are my nephew?" She shook her head. "If I admit that, it will open up old pain that is better forgotten." It would hardly be moving her life forward to claim a familial attachment that neither side wanted to acknowledge.

"Do you really think that no one will guess that the Duke of Bendas is your father?"

"How could they? I was fourteen when I was sent away from home, all arms and legs and stick thin, nothing like I look today. Not even the servants would know me."

William conceded the point with a slight nod.

"I had never been away from home, so who would recognize me? Even my name is different. Who would connect Signora Elena Verano with Lady Ellen Bendasbrook?" She turned to him with a sudden thought.

"I can prove it. Tell me, what is Rogers doing here? Does he move among the ton now? Mrs. Harbison introduced me to him. And, William, he did not recognize me."

"He is allowed because he is the duke's assistant. More than a secretary. Rogers accompanies him everywhere these days, or goes ahead of him to make sure they are prepared for his presence."

"Oh, I see, like a lady's companion."

William laughed.

Then a more disturbing thought occurred to her. "Does that mean the duke will be here this evening? I thought he never went out at night anymore."

"No, no. Do not distress yourself. Rogers told me that there were too many stairs and too big a crowd. But he attends smaller gatherings. You will have to face him sometime."

But not tonight, she thought with relief.

"Did you hear me, Elena? You will have to speak to him sometime. He is your father."

"I have not thought of the Duke of Bendas as my father since the day he made me leave home."

"I am sorry." William took her hand, patting it as if apologizing for his insistence. "But at some point you will have to decide if you want to acknowledge the duke or not."

"Why? Unless he does something untoward, I have no intention of so much as acknowledging his existence." Elena paused. "William, if he was considering attending tonight, do you think he wants a reunion?"

"Rogers is always nattering on about the duke's legacy." William's expression turned so cautious that Elena was afraid of what he was going to say. "Elena, what could it hurt to allow a reconciliation?"

"I will not allow myself to be dictated to by him, by any man, ever again. He did his best to destroy my life. He told me that I would end up in a whorehouse. I was fourteen years old, William." She was on the verge of shouting and with a heroic effort she modulated her voice. "I was terrified." Her eyes filled with tears. "If it were not for my godmother I might well have ended up exactly as he predicted. All because I would not sing the song he wished to hear."

"He has not changed."

"Then there is no point in even discussing a reconciliation."

William appeared to study the pattern in the upholstery as he debated his next words. "Elena, I must ask you something." Still he hesitated. When Elena was about to snap at him, he began.

"There have been a number of rumors circulating of late. Rumors about the Duke of Bendas. One is that he killed an innocent bystander in a duel. Another that he is no longer sane and should not be handling the estate. That he has attempted to acquire land in an illegal manner." William raised his hand, interrupting himself. "That last I know is true, but very few know the whole story."

"I do not really care what stories are abroad." Elena would have covered her ears if it would not have looked so childish. "I have always thought him mad. What else can you think of a man who believes anything is justified when he feels insulted, or if it will add wealth to the name? What does it have to do with me?"

"Do you know who started these stories?" He spoke quickly and seemed to regret the words as soon as they were said.

"No!" Amazement robbed her of speech for a moment. "I told you I want nothing to do with him." She stood up, all feeling of amiability gone. "William, how could you even think I would be involved in something like that?"

"I'm a Bendasbrook. Machiavelli is required reading." When she showed no appreciation for his attempt at humor, William went on. "The rumors started directly after you arrived in London, Elena."

"You know me." Elena wished he had thought longer before accusing her. "You know me better than any other relative and better than most people. How could you think that?"

William stood on the cushion of the settee, which enabled him to look her in the eye. "I know you have a temper, but are much more likely to throw something or slap someone than plot out a more diabolical retribution."

"That is hardly a compliment." She took a step back. "William, I imagine at least a thousand people arrived in London the same week I did. Dozens of them probably have some grudge against Bendas. Why not question them?"

"Do sit down. I am sorry. I should have trusted my first instincts and not even mentioned it. But there is another reason you should know what is happening. You may hear some of it when you join the party. Someone went out to find the cartoon and it is being passed around." He sat down after she did and explained the caricature, ending with, "Obviously someone wishes the ton to believe that Bendas's faculties are failing."

"I assure you, William, that I have not said a word to anyone about the Duke of Bendas. No one even expects me to know him. Tell me that you believe me and will no longer consider me the rumormonger."

"Of course I believe you."

"Thank you, William, and I will thank you even more if you never bring the subject up again."

"Never. My apologies for mentioning it at all."

"Yes, well, I have read Machiavelli, and I have lived in Italy most of my life. I suppose you had to ask, but let us leave it at that."

"Como lo desidera, signora." He stood up, bowed to her and kissed her hand.

"Thank you again. My wish is to be known as Elena Verano." She kissed his head. "As enlightening as this interlude has been, my twenty minutes has dwindled to a few." She stood up. "I need privacy so I can practice for a few moments."

"Have I upset you too much? How thoughtless of me." William slapped his head.

"Not at all. A bit of temper will make my singing better."

"Good. Good," he said with real relief. "I will go to the ballroom and find the perfect vantage point." He hurried to the door.

"I would think you would be looking for a woman who is not married."

"As would Grandfather. But I do so enjoy defying him even in absentia." With a wave he left the room before she could comment, which was just as well as there was nothing to say that would change the truth that his grandfather found him an embarrassment. It made as little sense as her father's unreasonable anger over a piece of music.

Elena dismissed worries from the trivial to the significant and began the exercises that were as much a part of her performance as the songs she sang. When she finished, she opened her mind. To her dismay it was the shadowed stranger she thought of first, the unknown man who had shared his hurt and his heart and the sweetest of kisses.

It happened sometimes that someone other than Edward would be her inspiration. With a *"Ti amo sempre"* to her husband, Elena left the room to make her first singing appearance in England.

4

WALKING PURPOSEFULLY down the passage, intent on leaving, Meryon did his best to control his annoyance at being dragged into such a personal discussion with the woman. And to kiss her!

Meryon could not lie to himself. He knew how that had happened. When she looked at him, her eyes filled with tears, a voice begging for comfort, he could not resist the invitation. It was definitely time to find a mistress.

Once he crossed the back of the ballroom, Meryon had to slow his pace. As usual, people clustered near the entrance. Besides The Gossips, every guest paused after they were announced, some to look for acquaintances, others to wait for a spouse.

Meryon could not make his way to the door without stopping to greet people. Even as he listened to their welcome and their worries, he realized that his inclination to leave immediately was misguided. He should wait until he could identify his companion in the dark, only because it made sense to know in whom he had confided.

Her rose perfume, her soft mouth, her lovely voice tickled his memory. All right, Meryon admitted to himself. There was more than one reason he would wait to see what she looked like.

If she did not return to the ballroom he could always ask Letty to name her.

As he listened to concerns about the state of agriculture, the general unrest, and a number of other subjects that were less than cheerful, Meryon watched the passage. He counted four ladies come into the ballroom, none of them tall or elegant enough to be his companion.

Twice, he was drawn into meaningful discussion. Everyone had an opinion, some better voiced than others. But none of them had solutions. Apparently they counted on Parliament to come up with a way to solve the problem they considered most urgent. Each left him with a bow and an expression of appreciation for his consideration. One annoyed him.

"How is it, Your Grace, that Parliament agreed to the suspension of habeas corpus, and, in less than a year, removed the suspension?" DeBora spoke in a loud voice, deliberately, to attract notice.

"I was absent from London last year and away from the country for the last six months, Mr. DeBora. I cannot speak for the actions of Parliament." Meryon spoke with a cordiality that took some effort. It occurred to him that DeBora served as Bendas's second in more than dueling.

"Yes, and we understand your bereavement." DeBora's perfunctory words pushed Meryon's temper up a notch. "You were absent, but half the seats from Derbyshire are under your control. Surely you still consider violent dissent a real threat."

"I did and I still do." Meryon had explained his stand a dozen times at least. "But that is no reason, nor has it ever been, to deny men their rights." He could speak on, but then he would sound too much like a Jacobin. He held his temper and made to turn away.

"Your Grace, that is easy to say when you live in a castle and are protected night and day."

There was gasp from a woman nearby who had been eavesdropping.

DeBora was trying to insult him, to make him lose his temper. Meryon knew exactly who was behind that.

"The only protection I need is from fools like you. What do you know of threats to your safety?" He ignored DeBora and addressed the people who were listening. "Would you have us behave like the French, who do not think that you need a reason to put a man in prison? Believe me when I tell you that you can pay too high a price for security." He gave them all a curt nod and the group dispersed, as he intended.

Meryon then gave this Bendas lackey his full attention, speaking in a voice so quiet that no one but a complete idiot would miss the challenge in it. "Tell Bendas that he is a coward to send you to do his work." Meryon relaxed his fist. "I am not that easily gulled. Leave my sight, or I will find you at Jackson's and we will fight with our fists. I guarantee it will hurt more than words."

Even the goddess of all beauty and grace was not worth conversation with DeBora. Without waiting for an answer and determined to ask Letty to name a guest who had lived in Italy until recently, Meryon turned and found his friend Kyle looking anxious.

"DeBora is a fool." Meryon loosed some of his temper with those words. "He wouldn't be allowed in the room if he hadn't married the daughter of a marquis. Bendas put him up to this. DeBora cares no more about habeas corpus than I care about women's shoes."

"You and Bendas?" Kyle shook his head. "When will this feud end, for God's sake?"

"This 'feud,' as you call it, will end when Bendas is ruined." Meryon had never said that aloud before, but Kyle needed to understand there was no halfway.

"Ruined?" Kyle's expression showed more confusion than distress. "The duel was supposed to end your retribution."

"Bendas fired early and admitted that he wanted me to die. The duel, as defined in the Code Duello, never happened." Before Kyle could answer, Meryon went on. "I know you live to debate any issue, my friend, but you cannot sway me on this. Not tonight. Or tomorrow."

"The thing is, Lyn"—Lord Kyle tugged at his cravat as though it were choking him, keeping him from speaking— "to seek revenge is unworthy of your rank. Revenge diminishes you as a gentleman."

"You misspeak when you call it revenge. I want justice for Kepless and his family." Meryon gave Kyle a deliberately intent stare.

"I've always hated that 'off with your head' look."

Meryon could not help but laugh at Kyle's impertinence. "There are times when your French heritage shows through. The guillotine is not used in England."

"Madame might be ghastly, but the blade is quicker and cleaner than what you are doing." Kyle raised his hand when Meryon's smile faded. "Never fear. I'll protect your back. I always will."

"I never doubted you would." Did Kyle give any thought to how this vendetta would affect him if it played out badly? He would save that discussion for another day. "Will you be at Jackson's tomorrow?"

"I've been there when you allow yourself to lose your control." Kyle patted his shoulder. "I will be no more than a spectator."

"The Gossips are trying to determine what we are so intense about. Laugh, or they will begin to weave a story worthy of one of Georges's melodramas."

"Georges's plays are beyond belief." Kyle did laugh. "At least The Gossips almost always have some bit of truth buried in their tales."

"You've been to a performance."

"My sisters insisted they must go see one." Kyle leaned closer as though ready to confess. "Frankly, Georges's fables are amazing tales. I have seen three and each one is more incredible than the one before it. And the actresses are quite, quite lovely. Georges knows how to attract an audience. If Bonnie were not bright, beautiful, and so sweetly generous, I would know where to look for a new mistress."

"I'll take that as a hint and see if I can make up a party to attend."

The music stopped and the dancers began to drift to the edges of the floor, ending their private conversation and now effectively trapping them between ballroom and hall.

"I am determined to have a word with Mrs. Harbison and be off before the next set forms or someone insists on talking politics again. Tell me, Kyle, if we come to these galas to escape the pressures of Parliament, why do so many want to talk about what goes on there?"

With a laughing slap on the back, Kyle bid him farewell and Meryon searched the area for his hostess.

"Good evening, Your Grace."

Meryon looked to his right and then down at Viscount William Bendasbrook, a strange little man of wit and intelligence. Meryon liked him, but he did not trust him. Lord William's grandfather was the Duke of Bendas.

"Lord William." Meryon acknowledged him and began to move on. At that moment, the orchestra played a chord, demanding their attention, and the viscount grabbed his arm, keeping it in a bruising hold.

"You cannot leave, Your Grace. You must hear this woman. She is amazing."

"I am not interested in hearing anyone sing." Meryon jerked his arm, but Lord William would *not* release it. The duke turned his sharpest gaze on him.

The viscount remained unfazed. "I will not let go, and think how ridiculous it would look for you to be seen dragging me out of the room behind you. Trust me, Your Grace, you will enjoy this."

Harbison's announcement precluded further discussion, much less an escape.

"This evening I will introduce to you a lady whose reputation is not yet fully appreciated here in England. None other than the renowned concertmaster and teacher, Signor Ponto, has declared her voice to be one of the finest in all of Europe." With a gesture to the woman standing below him, Harbison announced, "Signora Elena Verano."

The viscount had not let go of Meryon's arm, but Lord William could not stand still, constantly bouncing up and down on the balls of his feet. Meryon caught his eye and Lord William stilled, dropped his hand, and climbed onto a nearby chair for a clear view over the crowd.

The silence lengthened. Meryon turned toward the stage, where he found the Signora looking at the crowd, smiling, waiting for complete attention.

She had his. Before him stood the woman he had just met and already kissed, one of the loveliest women he had ever seen.

Even though she stood on the other side of a noisy, crowded room he could not take his eyes off her any more than he could stop watching a beautiful sunrise.

Of course, her husband, Edward, must be Eduardo Verano. His mastery of the violin was legendary. Meryon had heard him years ago, before the war, when youth had kept him from fully appreciating Verano's talent.

Leave. Leave now. Meryon did not want to hear the song, or rather her voice. It was too easy to imagine it, powerful, evocative and, above all, too filled with emotion.

He stayed as if rooted to the spot.

With a gesture to the orchestra, she began. Signora

Verano's voice was not what he expected. It did not have the power for an opera hall, but in a space like this it reached every ear and every heart.

The last of the whispers stopped as the first notes floated out, but he might as well have been alone with her in the room. She sang with her eyes closed but he still felt her singing to him, only him.

Although she sang in Italian, Meryon needed no translation. Her voice gave the words all the meaning they needed.

Passion filled the air. Promise poured from her, mixed with a happiness—no, more than that—a *euphoria* that spoke of intimacy so complete that his whole body responded.

Meryon felt as though she were continuing their conversation, assuring *him* life would go on, even more fully than before. Joy now enriched by experience. Loss gave a deeper meaning to passion.

Her voice made his kiss a weak and tentative consolation. Oh, how he wanted to show her what a kiss could be.

Her husband had written this, surely. After they had made love. The music filled the air with such exuberant satisfaction that he could only imagine what they had shared.

When she finished, the room exploded into applause. Meryon joined them, glancing at Lord William, who was cheering and applauding with an enthusiasm that announced he knew her better than most. Lord William flashed a grin at Meryon, who raised his hands, still clapping, acknowledging her excellence, even as he wondered how the Signora and the viscount had met.

Signora Verano curtsied a little, smiling and appreciative, with an air of apology for having sung a song of such intensity in public, relieved they were not offended.

The next song began with an orchestral introduction. It was a joy-filled air that intrigued the listeners as it was so at odds with Signora Verano's expression. The orchestra stopped playing and he watched her draw a breath before continuing *a cappella*.

Leave, he commanded himself. *Leave, before she breaks your heart*. Looking neither left nor right, Meryon stepped away and into the now empty hall before her voice could draw him back.

5

ELENA SAW HIM leave the room. How could he? He had recognized her; she knew he had, as she had known him.

Her voice faltered for a second, a terrible failure, but it came on the exact note when the mood of the song changed and seemed to add to the moment rather than distract from it. The analytical part of her decided she might sing it that way in her next performance.

She dismissed the thought and concentrated on the words, losing herself in the music, which drove her sensibilities, coming from her heart and mind.

At first her world was free from care, oblivious to the future. The blithe first phrases gave way to shock, loss, desolation, and confusion. There were tears on her cheeks as she held the last note. The audience stood silent, transfixed. They understood.

She smiled an apology for subjecting them to something so painful, as glorious a smile as she could manage. If they thought everything was all right and they need not worry, it was exactly what she wanted them to believe.

With an audible sigh of relief the audience relaxed and applauded again, not the storm of applause that followed the first song, but one filled with respect and even some admiration.

Despite calls for more, Elena shook her head and stepped down from the stage. Immediately surrounded by people, mostly men, Elena gathered her composure, hoping that her demeanor would discourage the men who thought they had their next conquest.

"Tell us about that last song, signora," a gentleman asked, as though it were not a terribly personal question.

"I wrote it ten days after my husband's death."

The group was struck silent and she hurried on to ease their discomfort. "The critics called it a theatrical tune filled with maudlin self-pity. All true music lovers, which everyone knows critics are not, loved it." She smiled to show whose opinion mattered most.

The group laughed. Then one of them suggested that "it shared true emotion with honesty."

"Like the music of Beethoven," another called out.

"Thank you for the compliment, sir, but no one equals Beethoven's genius."

Mr. Harbison announced supper and the group began to disperse, heading to the dining room. A few gentlemen offered her their arm, but Elena declined them all and stayed behind to thank her hosts and take her leave.

Lord William escorted her from the house, a choice

noted by more than one of The Gossips. She and William spoke in Italian, which gave them a measure of privacy. Not many Englishmen knew that language as well as they knew French.

"How sweet of you to see me home, dear man."

"Perhaps I will have a chance to see Mia." He stood beside her but was not still, moving up and down, from one step to another.

"That is why you are accompanying me! Do you ever do anything with one thing in mind?"

"Make love." He tried not to smile as he spoke.

"That does nothing to make me think of you as an appropriate companion for an eighteen-year-old girl. Besides, you cannot pay a call this late, William."

"You are too strict, signora." He spoke in an aggrieved tone, like a wounded lover. "You sound like an Italian mother."

"Guardian." She winced at the edge in her voice and did her best to soften it as she continued. "Now that both her father and Edward are dead, I am Mia's guardian." Most days she felt old enough to be Mia's grandmother. Was that grief or comparison with the girl's exuberant youth?

"She seems amazingly excited about spending her spring in a city where it rains more than the sun shines."

"Her enthusiasm is my great good luck. Edward and I had actually talked about the idea that an English husband would calm her." Though she had thought "balance" was a better choice of words. Mia would add life to any man's world and the right man would, yes, calm her.

"As for the weather," she added, "on a soft night like

this London seems a very kind city. The air feels like spring." She drew in a deep breath. The scent of new leaves on the trees and shrubs in the park across the road filled her senses with hope and the promise of new adventures. That reminded her of a question that William could answer. "Do you know a man whose wife died within the last year? Her name was Rowena."

"Yes, of course. Rowena was the Duchess of Meryon. Her husband is Lynford Pennistan, the duke."

"Thank you, William. Thank you." She looked off at the lighted house across the street. So he was titled. A duke, no less. Not the kind of man she wanted anything to do with.

"Why?" William asked. "Have you met him?"

"Not precisely." Elena knew she should banish the stranger from her mind. Not only because he was a duke, but because if she did not it would fuel William's unquenchable curiosity. She knew that as well as she knew her name, but that kiss made it impossible for her to resist asking. "William, what do you know of him?"

"More than I did a year ago."

When he did not add anything else, Elena nudged him. "Well?"

"I cannot share it. I promised, you see."

"Dear Mother in heaven, William, you are full of intrigue."

"I will tell you this. Meryon is a good man, very private, and his family means everything to him. No threat to his family's well-being ever goes unpunished." He nodded, as if confirming a privately held certainty. "Meryon's loyalty forever changed how I regard him, but I am not at liberty to discuss the details."

His smiled with both apology and conviction, and Elena shrugged. William could keep his secret. If it ever mattered, well, then the Duke of Meryon would tell her himself.

"Did you talk to him before I sang?" It had to have been the duke standing next to him. His seemed the right height and build. And she could not tear her eyes away from him.

"Yes, I told him he had to hear you sing. What a shame he left before you were finished. I would have liked to introduce you. He's—"

"Will you stop meddling, William!" She raised a hand to make sure he would stop talking and listen. "I have come to England to live quietly. Not to find a husband."

"I've wondered why you came back. Not only for Mia. That is altogether too selfless."

"Hardly 'came back,' William. I've never seen London before. I went straight from the house in Yorkshire to Italy, if you recall. I came here because the Italians expected me to be a living memorial to the great Verano. I want to live life on my own terms and find a husband for Mia. If I want to be introduced to Meryon I will make my own arrangements."

"Yes, I see." He stopped fidgeting with his watch fob.

"I do not need a matchmaker." He looked sheepish and she realized that it was exactly what he had in mind.

"William! Did you know he was in that room when you suggested I use it?"

He shrugged and nodded, cringing as though he thought she might hit him.

"Why did you do that?" She put a hand out to stop his endless bouncing from one step to the next.

"I hoped it would distract you from your grief. And I'm right. It worked, didn't it?" He watched her expression and grinned. "The Duke of Meryon would be quite a catch."

"You above all should know why I would marry a stonemason before I would accept a duke. They are too full of pride and their own importance, too used to power. Their most casual gesture can ruin lives."

"You should not damn all because of one, Elena. It's like saying that all women who perform have loose morals."

He had a point, but she was not going to concede it.

"Tell me this, dear aunt: Do you want to see him again?"

Why would she want to see him again? Because the very fact he bared his soul made him different from other aristocrats. Because the simple act of sitting close to him had made her feel alive, fully alive for the first time since she had returned to the social scene. He might be the same as all the others but with him *she* felt different.

"If you start this, I will do you the same favor." She raised a finger to her lips. "It seems to me that the Harbisons have one daughter who never did take and is still single." •

"I am chastened. Please spare me. She is almost six feet tall!"

"Then let me find my own match, William, and I will allow you the same."

"All right." He began swatting his leg with his hand.

He agreed too readily; she knew now to be on her guard.

"Though I do think it rude of Meryon to leave before you finished singing."

"It is just as well that he did. If he still mourns the death of his wife that last song would have been too painful, too strong a reminder of his loss."

MERYON DID NOT escape completely. Waiting on the steps for his coach, he would have had to cover his ears if he did not want to hear the song.

He sat in his carriage now, the windows open to enjoy the unusual warmth of the evening. As John Coachman made his way through the busy streets, other conveyances slowed to allow the duke's crested coach to pass.

As they passed houses, most of them dark, the memory of the last melody echoed through him. The song had been beautiful, more beautiful than the singer herself. Meryon had not thought that possible.

The anguish in her voice had ripped into him, paralyzing him with something like fear. His heart had raced, his head ached. He'd clenched his fist and taken a few steps away from the door, as if that would help. Then he'd noticed the people around him.

The coachmen stopped their chatting and turned to the window. A flower seller, apparently dozing on the servants' steps, came to stand near them. The grooms did not tease her as they usually did, but stood as quiet as the rest.

Two or three of the coachmen took off their hats and held them over their hearts. No one was spared this pain. Not king or commoner, coachman or duke.

It might have felt like she sang to him alone, but that was vanity. Signora Elena Verano sang for every man.

In their conversation, Signora Verano had proved she could awaken a man's pain with words as well as with music. If that was talent then it was a gift from the devil.

"Can you spare a ha'penny, my lord?" The words pulled him from his speculation. When the boy who had spoken saw he had heard him, he ran along beside the carriage. "My ma is hungry and so am I. My pa went north to find work." The lad stopped as the coach slowed for a corner. "Please, sir."

The duke eyed the boy for a moment. The boy watched the duke in return. Meryon wondered where the lad had mastered that unrevealing stare.

"Tell me your name."

The boy blinked and did not answer right away, but he did manage to keep up with the carriage.

Meryon knocked on the roof of the coach and the coachman slowed and then stopped. The duke reached for his purse and held up two coins. "Your name."

"Alan Wilson, sir."

Meryon tossed Mr. Wilson one of the coins. "Tell me what you know about horses."

"Enough to tell you that one of yours is close to lame."

"I was hoping to reach the stable before it gives out completely," John Coachman called down.

"Then anyone with a good eye could see that." Meryon had taken enough brandy to wonder if he or John Coachman had a guardian angel. Nonsense. God could not possibly take that much interest in every soul. "Are you looking for work like your father?"

"Not if you toss me that other coin."

So perhaps this situation did not involve divine intervention. "If you change your mind, come to Penn House near Burlington Arcade. Bring your mother. I can give you both work." Meryon tossed him the coin.

The lad caught the coin with ease and, without another word, ran off the way he had come. Meryon sat back, corked the brandy, and tucked it into the seat pocket. Alan Wilson was a younger, more lanky version of Joshua Kepless and Meryon did not need brandy to make him any more maudlin. He opened the door and climbed down.

"I will walk from here, Coachman."

"Walk, Your Grace?"

"I can see the Square from here, and God knows Mayfair is safe enough if you do not announce my title to everyone on the street."

"Yes, Your . . ." Coachman's voice trailed off. "I'll send one of the grooms to bring help"—the big man paused—"sir."

In less than ten minutes Meryon sat on the sofa in his study with Magda opposite. "The boy reminded me of Joshua Kepless, and I wonder again if I should propose my bill even if it is doomed from the start."

Magda watched, her head bent to the side as though considering every word. Now that Rowena was gone Meryon understood her love for animals, especially spaniels who were loyal, agreeable, and never talked back. Magda was the perfect companion when thoughts would not stay inside his head.

"The hungry have always been there. But I see them now because of Joshua Kepless, because he was the sole support of his mother and sister. But Magda, the poor are everywhere. This, of course, makes me wonder if I made the right decision in my vote on the Corn Laws."

Magda jumped down and climbed up next to him. Meryon smoothed her brow, oblivious to the hair the dog shed on his coat.

The Corn Laws had been his first truly important vote since taking the Meryon seat in the House of Lords, after his father's death. He had argued, debated, and even prayed. The home economy would have suffered without the tax on foreign imports.

"When I see a boy hungry or hear of a family struggling I wonder if free trade would have been a better choice." Free trade would have kept the prices down at least.

Meryon could count on one hand the number of times he'd questioned a decision after the vote. His father had insisted that once a decision was made, one must move on.

Until Kepless's murder Meryon had done that. But seeing the poverty the boy's family had endured and their bitterness over his death had made Meryon as uncomfortable as a girl at a cockfight. Money had eased his conscience, but not the sense of responsibility for all the others who streamed past on the streets.

With a final scratch of Magda's ears, Meryon stood up, walked to his desk, and looked through the items that the courier had brought from Pennford that day.

A letter from his brother, David, insisting that a decision be made on the investment possibilities that David had outlined. Ricardo's *Principles of Political Economy*, which David suggested would help clarify his thoughts. Meryon decided he would start it tonight. The book would either put him to sleep or keep him awake.

Was now the time to propose his bill to support the widows and orphans who had lost their breadwinners? Or should he invest more directly in promising manufacturing as his brother wanted him to do? Or both? There were those damn questions again. When in doubt act, he reminded himself. Action often clarified the issues more than any book ever could.

And by God's grace, London insisted on action. The streets and buildings lived and breathed on the decisions people made, good, bad, and indifferent. Indecision was like a muddy road, slowing all progress.

At least the war against Bendas moved forward. Now he had to decide what to do about Parliament, whether the children should stay here or be sent back to Pennford, and where to find a new mistress, which brought him back to the one unknown who intrigued him the most: Signora Elena Verano.

Signora Verano had managed to compel him—that was the only way to describe it—to talk about marriage, about Rowena.

Learn and move on. Nothing would remedy the mistakes

made this evening, talking so freely, answering questions so openly.

Kissing a stranger.

London was filled with intrigue, both personal and political, and Meryon was not entirely sure that the meeting had been innocent.

The uncertainty made him uncomfortable, but no amount of action could bring a plot to life before its time. If someone thought to use Signora Verano to influence or discredit the Duke of Meryon, he would know soon enough. Then take action.

6

MERYON COULD HAVE put Elena Verano out of his mind the next day if the other members of the House of Lords had not found they must discuss every detail of her beauty and her history over and over as they gathered for the Tuesday session.

"The woman is amazing!"

"Incomparable."

"Today's calendar, gentleman." Despite the exasperation in Meryon's voice, they all ignored him.

"Where will the Signora sing next?"

"How long has she been a widow?"

Meryon opened his mouth to tell them that they sounded like a bunch of old biddies when the next question made him listen instead.

"Why in the world is she spending so much time with Viscount Bendasbrook?"

Meryon looked up, counting this as another one of those taps on the shoulder by either angel or devil.

"They left together last night."

"The little runt doesn't stand a chance with her."

"He rides like a champion."

"Oh, really? And whose authority do you have that on, my lord? Your wife's?"

The conversation deteriorated into an exchange of ribald insults that Meryon ignored as he considered the information.

Leaving together could have a simple explanation. Signora Verano did not own a carriage. She did not want to go about alone at night. She was flirting with the viscount. They were lovers.

That last made no sense. Signora Verano would not need a shoulder to cry on if she and Lord William were intimate.

Unless Lord William did not wish to hear of her dead husband.

Then another thought struck him that made all too much sense. *Unless Lord William,* grandson of the Duke of Bendas, *had asked her to establish a connection with the Duke of Meryon.*

The bell sounded, calling them to the session. Meryon did his best to listen.

The lively debate on the indemnity bill amused him as much as it informed, as Meryon watched Liverpool's cronies jockey for favor, more eager to impress the prime minister than to sway the members.

He kept track of the observers as well. Their reactions gave a decent insight into what the papers would say.

Lord William's presence in the gallery interested Meryon the most. How surprising that someone as restless as the viscount could sit still for so long.

With the break called, Meryon decided he'd had enough. No third reading of the bill would happen today, much less a vote on anything more important than whose hair needed a trim.

He could use the time to better advantage at home. Besides the information on the new manufacturing ventures, Meryon knew he had to read through a report from his brother on the early plantings.

His secretary could tell him if he had made any progress on his study of Bendas and his family. Meryon most wanted to know if there was any truth to the story that Bendas had disinherited a daughter before she reached her majority.

As Meryon mulled over what he would do with such information, someone called to him. Meryon recognized Theodore Henderson, who held a Derbyshire seat in Commons.

Henderson fell into step beside him.

"Your Grace?"

"Speak your mind, Henderson." The man always asked for permission to speak as if Meryon had given him the seat in Commons as a gift for which Henderson should be forever grateful.

Meryon had told Henderson more than once that the seat was his for very practical reasons. The man had an amazing memory and his powers of observation were excellent.

"Before the session today a group of Tories expressed their complete disagreement with my suggestion that we need to protect the interests of widows and orphans."

"Go on. I want to hear the good and the bad on this issue."

"They insisted that we cannot afford the expense. That workhouses and debtors' prisons are enough burden and if we support the orphans then they will grow lazy."

"Excellent." Meryon stopped and gave Henderson his full attention. The man looked shocked.

"But, Your Grace, they are arguing *against* the idea."

"Yes." Meryon started toward his carriage again. Henderson kept up with him. "Whether they decide for or against does not matter at this point. They have not rejected it without thought. They want to know what others think."

"Thank you, Your Grace." Henderson studied his shoes for a minute. "Have you decided whether to propose it or not?"

"No. Not yet." Meryon noticed that Viscount Bendasbrook was nearby, shifting from one foot to the next, waiting for his turn. "Is that all, Henderson?"

"You may be undecided at the moment, Your Grace, but that is one of the pleasures of working with you. You decide without concern for party labels. Please let me know how I can be of further service." Henderson bowed and moved away.

Meryon pretended to ignore Lord William, who never took that hint.

"Your Grace! A moment please."

"Yes, Lord William?" Meryon continued walking and let his strained patience show. He did not care about

Elena Verano's love life. She could dally with anyone she chose, up to and including a Bendasbrook.

"Thank you, Your Grace." The viscount fell into step beside him. "Last night I wished we had had a few more minutes together. If you please, Your Grace."

"Walk with me, my lord, and I will listen."

"Last year, in my presence, you swore revenge against my grandfather for his part in organizing the abduction of your sister. I had hoped that you had forgotten that threat or had second thoughts after the death of the duchess. It is now being rumored that you challenged him to a duel."

"Yes," Meryon said as he stopped walking. "The duel is not a rumor."

"Then . . ." Lord William began.

"It was aborted due to the innocent death of a groom in my employ," Meryon said, not caring to hear Bendasbrook's opinion.

"Then the Rowlandson cartoon was not slander but the truth." Lord William could not hide the distress in his voice.

"Those are your words, my lord." Meryon folded his arms across his chest. "I did not threaten revenge. I swore that he would regret his actions. I demand justice. Justice and revenge are completely different."

The viscount looked unconvinced by the distinction between the two. "There is one more issue, Your Grace. Today as I sat in the gallery and listened to the private bills I realized that something is afoot." The young man wiped his brow with a handkerchief and went on. "My grandfather has introduced two private bills since January requesting an exchange of land that is part of the entail for newly acquired property. That is unheard of for him. I think he has done it once before in all the years of his peerage."

"You know as well as I do that Bendas has become obsessed with acquiring land."

"I suspect that he thinks that these new properties are rich in coal and are more valuable than the farmland he is selling. I can only wonder how such plums fell into his hands. Do you have any idea?"

"You can unravel the puzzle. I have no interest in it."

"I am going to do exactly that, Your Grace." Lord William stood on tiptoe. "I want you to know that despite my estrangement from my grandfather, I will allow nothing to happen that will undermine the wealth of the Bendasbrooks, which my father and then I will inherit one day. Do you understand, Your Grace?"

"Yes." The arrogant tone did not go unnoticed, but Meryon would have done the same if his entailed wealth had been co-opted. "But the question you should ask yourself is whether your grandfather is behaving in a responsible manner. No matter how these offers are being presented, I would question the brainworthiness of a man who acts before he investigates."

"Are you suggesting that he is unwell?"

"Lord William, two years ago he collapsed in the House of Lords. It was said he merely fainted, but he has never returned to take his seat again. Unusual for a man who feels so strongly about the suspension of habeas corpus and the Indemnity Act under discussion now." Meryon gestured to the groom, who jumped down to lower the steps. "I want justice, Lord William."

"We all want justice. It is only that we define it differently. But I appreciate your honesty as I hope you appreciate mine."

Meryon nodded and decided the discussion was over, but Lord William was not finished.

"I understand that you met Signora Verano last night." The viscount's tone implied something less than proper.

The words froze Meryon in place. "Why do you think that?"

"She asked me who you were."

"If we had met, then she would not have had to ask, would she?" So Lord William knew about his meeting with the Signora, and to bring it up on the heels of the previous subject must have significance.

"Are you friends with Signora Verano, my lord?"

"Yes, I am." Lord William paused, smiling slightly, choosing his words carefully. "We are well acquainted." He rose on his toes and settled again. Rose and settled.

Meryon wanted to slap the smile off the viscount's face. "How long have you known her?"

That question stopped the rising and settling and the smile disappeared. "When did I meet her?" He waved his hand in the air as if brushing away such a detail. "Who remembers when they first met someone?"

"If a woman as beautiful and talented came into my circle of friends, I would remember. How long?" Meryon prodded.

William did not take the bait but paused another long moment before he spoke.

"I play the violin, in my own rude way. As soon as the

war ended I went to Italy to hear Eduardo Verano play. We all spent a great deal of time together. I count the six months I had with Elena and Eduardo my finest experience of Italy. I expect I will see the Signora again this evening."

Lord William did not answer the question directly. Interesting.

"Why do you want to know, Your Grace?" Lord William's bland smile hinted that he had drawn the wrong conclusion.

"Signora Verano and I spoke briefly last night," Meryon said, "and if I find you using any part of my private conversation with her for your own ends, I will cease making a distinction between you and your grandfather."

Meryon made himself unclench his fist. He did not wait for a reply, but climbed into the carriage, slammed the door, and knocked for the coachman to move on.

The rest of the evening passed in a haze of annoyance—mostly at himself, for allowing this to happen. He knew better than to speak about anything that could be construed as fodder for gossips. Anything that could find its way into hands that would use it for their own gain.

He and Signora Verano had talked about Princess Charlotte's death, the Regent's deplorable lifestyle, their dead spouses. Good God, he had even told her that he talked to Rowena's dog and that the dog answered. In the wrong hands that could be twisted into malicious rumors that would undermine his credibility at the exact moment when he thought to propose a bill.

In truth, the woman could make up a story if she had

been so commissioned. He had to confront Signora Verano and make sure she would be discreet.

Meryon had his secretary root through the invitations piled on the desk. Apparently she had no singing engagement this evening. On impulse, he decided to go to her house. Never mind the hour. This situation could not wait.

7

WHAT A DELIGHTFUL DINNER, my lady."
Elena pulled her cloak more tightly around her. Rain
threatened. Where was her coach?

"Yes, it was a lovely experience, signora," Lady Margaret replied. "Thank you so much, Lord William, for accompanying her and sharing your evening with us."

Elena heard the rumble of coach wheels and pulled
on her gloves. "Please do tell Mr. DeBora that it was a
joy to see the Verano violin again. I hope he enjoys playing it."

"Oh, DeBora will not play it." Lady Margaret spoke as
though that would be akin to her riding a horse astride. "It
is much too valuable an instrument."

Lord William took Elena's arm when she tensed.
Could he feel her outrage?

The carriage came to a stop and her coachman began,

in Italian fortunately, a rant about the idiocy of Englishmen. "They move like snails!"

"Be quiet, man," William called in the man's language. "Or they will say that English servants have better manners." He patted Elena's arm, bowed to their hostess, and clambered up to soothe the coachman.

"Perhaps I should drive, Elena," Lord William suggested.

"Si! Si," the coachman called down. He went on in Italian. "The little lord has been in Italy and knows how to drive. And he speaks English, so he can tell them to move out of the way of someone who knows how to handle the reins."

Elena allowed it after making William promise he would drive as her coachman's instructor and not as a competitor.

She settled on the cushioned seat, alone at last. The dinner had been pleasant enough, the other guests all music lovers. But listening to praise of Edward and sharing amusing stories of his eccentricities reminded her too much of her widow's life in Italy.

The rain matched her mood and as she watched the raindrops track down the windows of the carriage, she welcomed the warm brick at her feet.

What a waste, that DeBora would not play Edward's violin. Mr. DeBora and his wife were completely the wrong kind of music lovers. Yes, the auction of the instrument had funded the program for young musicians, but to treat the violin like a relic. It was a crime against music! Could she have someone approach them about buying it back? Could she afford it?

They reached the lovely little house in Bloomsbury quickly. Perhaps she did need an English coachman, someone who knew the streets and did not drive like he owned them. The Roman way did not suit London at all. She would ask Tinotti.

She found him waiting in the hall.

"*Buona sera,* signora, and good evening, my lord."

"Good evening, Tinotti."

Her secretary then spent a solid minute effusively greeting Lord William. Did Tinotti think of him as a marriage prospect? Surely he knew that the two of them were only friends and not at all romantically inclined.

"What is bothering you, signora?" This from Signora Tinotti. Her housekeeper worried about everything and nothing. "You look unhappy."

"Shhh, *carissima.*" Tinotti took his wife's hand and kissed it. "It has been a long evening and it is not over yet."

With a raised eyebrow from her husband, some sort of secret communication Elena surmised, Tina Tinotti took Lord William by the arm, urging him to come to the kitchen.

Elena watched them leave, puzzled by the familiarity and the hurry. Tinotti explained it with one whispered sentence.

"Signora, you have a caller."

"A caller?" Even in Rome people did not call this late. "Why did you allow him in? What were you thinking? It's well past ten o'clock!"

"He had an air of importance and walked into the blue salon announcing he would wait for you. I thought perhaps that he..." Tinotti hesitated and cleared his throat. "Only lovers meet at this hour, signora. I thought you might want to speak with him. I did not know that you were going to bring the little lord home tonight."

Did everyone think only of her supposed need for a lover? "Did he give you his card?" She sounded as weary as she felt.

"Yes. Signora, he is a duke: Lynford Pennistan, the Duke of Meryon. He said you had not been formally introduced but that—"

She raised her hand and Tinotti stopped speaking.

"I know who he is." A brief flash of surprise was replaced by pleasure. He wanted to see her again. He could not forget the kiss either, so moved that the normal rules of etiquette did not apply. That sounded too dramatic, like one of Georges's plays, *A Heart Bewitched*. Had the duke seen it, she wondered. "Please bring some wine for my guest and some tea for me."

With a brief bow, Tinotti went off to do as she asked.

Was it a mistake to offer the duke hospitality? As Tinotti had hinted, only lovers met this late. Had the duke assumed that because she sang in public she was like a woman who sang for money, with loose morals and easy virtue?

Elena left her cloak and bonnet at the door. Sweeping into the blue salon, she wondered if her gown would blend with the wall color or if the blue-washed paint would complement it. She did not care, but it was easier to think about that than what to say to the duke.

She had spent half of last night wondering what he

thought of her singing, why he had left early, if she would see him again, if she would kiss him again.

If she would even recognize him.

Elena had the answer to that question the moment she laid eyes on him. She had never been so aware of a man in her life. She felt his presence even more vividly now than last night.

Her fatigue and sadness evaporated, replaced by an attraction that frightened as much as it thrilled. She knew nothing about the man. Nothing except his rank, his name, and that he had loved his wife.

Smiling a little, Elena curtsied without taking her eyes from him. He was so very English. That was hardly surprising. Blond hair, not too long, blue, blue eyes, and skin that would redden in the cheeks with age. High cheekbones and a strong chin with a cleft in it. And much too serious.

He had a virility that matched the very physical music of Beethoven. And yet he comported himself so much more like a Bach concerto, quiet and self-contained.

"Good evening to you, Your Grace. Lord William told me your name. Lynford Pennistan, the Duke of Meryon." She gave a deep curtsy as befitted his title.

He returned her gesture with a brief bow.

Was he angry? With her? She could not read his expression but his curt greeting betrayed him. She waited, her pleasure at seeing him edged with caution.

"I want to speak to you about our conversation last night."

"Yes." She prepared herself for something awful.

Before the duke could say anything else, there was a

scratch at the door and Signora Tinotti came in with a tray. Elena's tea was in her favorite Deruta mug and there was a very nice Italian wine. That should impress the duke.

"Some wine, Your Grace?" Elena offered the bottle for his study.

"No," he said abruptly.

Elena set the wine back on the tray, abandoning any attempt at hospitality. "All right."

Tina stepped back, glaring at Meryon. At a glance from Elena, the housekeeper left. After one more sip of tea, Elena set the cup on the tray.

"I came to clarify one issue," he said, moving so close that she could smell the scent he favored.

"Please, do tell me." She folded her arms in front of her, doing her best to ignore the scent.

"I want your assurance, your promise, an oath on the memory of your husband, that what we shared last night will remain between the two of us."

Elena heard a command, not a request. "What we talked about?" Surprised at his vehemence, she took a step back, confused. He could not mean the kiss. Of course she would tell no one about it, even if she could not dismiss it from her mind.

"You mean our sorrow?" As she thought of the other topics they had covered her irritation grew. "Or do you mean Princess Charlotte? Or our comments about the Regent? Or our very personal reflections on Edward and your Rowena?" She had to make an effort not to shout. "What do you think I would do with such information?"

"If you are friends with Lord William it is not hard to imagine how you would use it."

"What in the world does the viscount have to do with this?"

"I have it on good authority, signora, that you two are friends of long acquaintance."

"Yes, we are."

"Have you already talked to Lord William about me, signora?"

"No, of course not," she said, feeling as though her words were being twisted. "We spoke in general terms, nothing more."

"I have only your word on that."

"*Only* my word? You know nothing of the value of my word." She'd raised her voice and swept away from him, moving around the room lest she do something physical. She had never in her life wanted to hit a person, but this man begged for it.

"I saw Lord William at dinner tonight," she said, trying, with the greatest effort, to keep her tone reasonable. "The only mention he made of you was to wonder where we would be likely to see you again." It was the slightly embarrassing truth.

"Exactly." The duke smiled, a you've-fallen-into-my-trap expression that was not friendly at all. He came to her across the room. "Two things intrigue me. That you and Lord William spend so much time together and that I am so frequently a topic of conversation."

"You flatter yourself, Your Grace." She stood her ground, hoping he would not notice her blush, for she had wanted to talk to William about him far more than she had. "Lord William is doing me the kindness of helping me establish myself in London."

"I think his interests are more personal than that." The duke took a step back and though he did not look her up and down, she felt as though he was considering her as he might a new statue. Or a mistress.

"Our friendship is none of your business, Your Grace. None at all. Let me remind you that he deserves your respect. He is, after all, the heir to a dukedom."

"Even praiseworthy men can be compromised, especially in the name of family."

"What do you mean by that?" Her throat tightened and she raised a hand to rub at the pressure, reminding herself that very few people knew of her connection to the Bendasbrook family. There was no way the duke could have discovered it. No way at all.

The duke did not answer right away and she waited, her hands shaking a little. The duke glanced at her fingers, but that one flick of the eye was the only curiosity he showed.

"I mean, madame, that in order to protect a family's reputation and wealth even the honorable will abandon principle."

"That says much more about you than it does about William." Relief made her chatter on. "But then as a duke no one questions you; you are never at fault for any reason, whether it is to protect wealth or reputation, or only to show your power."

"You hardly know me well enough to make that kind of judgment."

"I only need to know that you are a duke."

She did not wait for an answer but turned her back to him, staring at the painting on the wall, a Canaletto that she adored, and prayed for calm. Finally she faced him again, more controlled but still aware of the way his presence affected her. "I will respect your privacy, as I trust you will respect mine."

"Very well." The two words were as curt as hers had been, and even though he inclined his head the duke still did not appear to be relieved. "I appreciate your cooperation."

Despite the insult and the lack of apology, Elena was sure he felt the same carnal attraction she did. He could *not* have forgotten that kiss. Surely not.

Of course, he remembered the kiss and that was why he was so irritated. The thought struck her with such force that she almost said it aloud.

He did not know what do with this attraction either. Not when he worried that she might be an enemy. Or did he think to put her off by behaving abominably? She pressed her hands to her heart.

"Good night, signora." He did not bow, but he did take two steps toward the door.

"That, Your Grace, is running away." She sat. "You are free to run, but you have yet to address the other reason you came this evening."

"Preserving my privacy was the only reason." He had his hand on the latch.

"Please sit down." It was like combing a knot out of her hair to make this man be honest about his feelings.

"No, I will not sit down. I am not one to be ordered about like a pet dog."

She rose and closed the distance between them. "At least be honest enough to admit this: that our kiss last night reminded us there is life still to be lived. You are as afraid of what you feel as you are of what I can reveal about you."

His eyes brightened. Her own heart fluttered and she smiled at the undeniable draw she felt.

"Signora, are you trying to seduce me?"

Not dismay. It was pleased surprise she heard in his voice.

"Provoking me is a unique approach."

"I am not seducing you, you arrogant fool. Is there nothing in your world between honest conversation and seduction?" She shook her head on a breath of annoyance and moved back into the room away from where he stood, away from his spell.

"Leave then." She waved a hand at him and wished he would disappear. He stayed at the door as if he had not understood that she was dismissing him.

"So, you want me to leave because you do not want a lover." The duke spoke as though he was trying to reason with a half-wit.

"Yes. I assure you that if I wanted a lover, I could have had my pick tonight."

He let her statement hang in the air for a moment, so that it embarrassed her to have been so crass.

"In fact, all you want from me now is the confession that I feel the attraction between us?"

"Yes," she said with some force. "Admit it. Be honest with yourself and admit that is the real reason you came to call so late in the evening."

He smiled, his eyes darkened, and his gaze dropped

to her lips. She stood very still as he took a step so they were closer than propriety would tolerate.

He did not touch her, but her lips tingled. He raised his eyes to hers. *Yes, I do want you. I want to undress you with more than my eyes, to hold you with more than my gaze, to touch more than your hand.*

It was the truth that she had demanded but with it came a hunger that was as exciting as it was surprising. This man, whose face rarely showed any of what he was thinking, could excite her with no more than his gaze. Attraction was too weak a word to describe what she felt. She looked away, afraid of what he could read in her eyes.

"Good night once again, Signora Verano." Taking her hand, he bowed over it, did not kiss it or even caress her palm.

Meryon was halfway to the door before he turned, bowed again, and spoke one last time. "When you are ready to take a lover, signora, do let me know."

8

MERYON THOUGHT about Elena Verano all the way back to Penn House. His imagination played with wild fantasies of taking her then and there in her salon, of claiming her before any other man realized that her singing revealed only a little of the passion awaiting a lover.

Instead of ensuring her cooperation, he'd aggravated her, nearly driven her from the room.

He could still see her standing there, her elegant body calling to him as surely as her righteous anger ordered him to leave, then saying she did not want a lover, but insisting that he acknowledge the attraction.

Shifting on the seat, he pretended his arousal made him uncomfortable. But, if he thought honestly, he would have to credit Signora Verano with another truth that made him as restless as a schoolboy called to account.

He'd behaved without examing his reasons carefully, not even considering the propriety of such a late-night call. He'd acted on impulse, damn it. He thought he'd done with that when he left his twenties.

Penn Square was dark and quiet, though most of the houses were still alive with light. The Penn House night porter came out promptly, lowered the steps, and bowed to him with a comforting familiarity. Meryon nodded, still lost in thought.

He'd gone to her house without understanding the true reason why. Yes, he did need to protect his reputation, but he could have done that far more discreetly. He could have waited for a more opportune time.

Halfway across the great hall to the staircase, the porter's cough distracted him.

"Your hat, Your Grace?"

"Oh, yes." He took off his hat and greatcoat, handing them to the porter along with his cane. The servant looked mildly concerned.

"I am preoccupied, tonight."

"But of course, Your Grace."

The man was so surprised that Meryon wondered if he had ever spoken to the night porter before. Surely he had at some point.

The porter's unquestioning acceptance reminded Meryon of Elena Verano's diatribe: "No one questions you; you are never at fault." And yes, here was his porter making excuses for him. He would have to note how often that happened.

The door to the formal salon remained open, reminding him of the days when he would invite friends back after a ball or some late-night gaming. He should tell the majordomo that there was no need to continue that tradition.

He stepped into the room. Rowena's portrait hung over the fireplace and he looked up at it, his hands behind his back.

He had not taken time to look at it since he'd come back from France.

Studying it now, he understood why. It represented how well she had suited the role of duchess. In the blue satin gown, wearing pearls and tiara, she appeared elegant, gracious, calm, and charming, but the portrait had failed to capture her essence.

The artist had not captured Rowena's naive sweetness, the natural friendliness that he thought of as her most delightful trait. That was what had endeared her to the ton.

Those qualities had balanced his sober formality perfectly. Their union had always been civil and almost always comfortable, and until tonight he would have said happy, but now he realized that one crucial element had kept them from true happiness.

Never once in eleven years had he forgotten to leave his hat at the front door. Rowena had never confused him or made him think or made him so angry he'd behaved stupidly.

There had been no passion in their marriage.

He had denied her that. Burdened with regret, he bowed to her portrait. It was time to move the painting to Derbyshire, to Pennford, where it would hang next to his. As someday he would lie beside her in the cemetery there.

Meryon wiped the wet from his eyes and hoped that heaven gave her everything that she had not had in this life.

He left the salon, walking more slowly now, not hearing the two footmen who set about closing the grand salon for the night, not noticing the new statue that had arrived and been placed that day, so lost in thought he stood at the door to his study and stared at the panels as if it took all his energy to accept the truth.

Passion held the key to a well-lived life. Not just lust, but passion in so many other areas: music, sport, poetry, food. A passion for justice. That issue had consumed his life these past months. Until tonight.

He had allowed himself to be drawn into an argument with a woman who understood better than he did the attraction that simmered between them. Now lust shouted at him, and he knew that one kiss would never be enough.

ELENA, YOU MUST admit the duke had a very clever parting line."

"He was not exiting a stage." Elena stopped pulling the pins from her hair and let the chill show in her voice as she answered her ward. "Our conversation was private, Mia, or should have been. You are eighteen, old enough to understand that."

"I could not help but hear." The girl did not look or sound the slightest bit contrite. "I was in the small room next to the salon. You know it's not possible to leave there except through the room you were in." Her voice mixed apology and petulance.

"Tell me, how did you happen to be in there?" She was almost afraid to ask. "That room is no good for anything more than storage. And I thought no one could open the window."

"To be honest," Mia said, as though making a huge concession, "I was hiding from Tinotti. He and the Signora wanted me to help them inventory the wine."

"At ten o'clock?"

"They insisted on waiting for you to come home and wanted to use the time sensibly. I told them it would burn too many candles. I did offer to teach them that game of cards we learned on the ship coming here. But they said no. They are always trying to make me do the things a servant does. They are the servants, not me."

"Mia, you know better than that. They are much more than servants. Part of the family, as you are."

"Yes," she conceded grudgingly, "but you did not *hire* me. I am your ward now that both my father and Eduardo have died."

"Yes, *cara,* and I realized quickly that you have a passion for mischief." Elena pulled out the last pin and shook her hair free. Her headache disappeared almost completely. "I suppose it is too late to try to cure you of that."

Elena could not help smiling at Mia's prideful nod.

"So," Mia said, circling back to her original question. "The duke is one of those quiet volcanoes the novels talk about. A man who is proper in public but not in private."

Mia lay on top of the bed, her knees bent under her, in a position that would have been more than painful for anyone else. Her body was supple in a way that defied description. She proved it by moving to her knees in one graceful movement. Elena prayed that it never occurred to Mia how much money she could make as a dancer or in a circus.

"Would you consider taking him as a lover?"

"What is your governess letting you read, Mia? That is a totally inappropriate question."

"Yes, I know. But would you?"

"Never." She answered with as much conviction as she could muster. "I am here so you can have your Season, not to indulge in an affair of the heart. A happy marriage is all that your father ever wanted for you." It was a convenient explanation and almost the truth.

"Or you could marry him, Elena. He is a duke. Think how many gorgeous jewels he would give you."

He is a duke. That one word stood for all the reasons she should avoid him. "I have no need or desire to marry for jewels or money."

"Yes, yes, I know." The girl sighed.

"Your disdain is unbecoming in one so young." The realization that this child did not begin to understand what was important, even after losing both her father and her much-loved guardian, pained Elena as much as the child's cynicism.

Elena undid the pearl earrings that Edward had given her on the day they had known each other for a year. "I do enjoy beauty in all its material forms but, Mia, do believe me when I say that jewels and clothes are not essential to happiness."

"I believe that is true for you, Elena, but nothing would make me happier than someone who would give me a jewel or a clock or a coach or horses, and a duke could certainly afford all those and not even notice the money was gone."

That gave Elena pause. Despite headache and fatigue this subject could not be dropped. "We have not talked about this before, but you must understand that there is a difference between taking a lover and being a kept woman."

Elena tightened the sash of her robe and came to sit next to Mia. "As a widow, then and only then, it is socially acceptable for a woman to establish a liaison with a gentleman."

She paused a moment. Yes, a lover could give her the physical fulfillment she missed, but she never thought to find the kind of understanding she and Edward had shared.

"Yes, I know that. Go on."

At least the girl was listening. "To become a man's mistress is the complete opposite. In exchange for money and gifts you allow a man to command all of your time and attention, whenever he wants. A mistress must be ready for him at his whim, have no thought but to please him, no matter what he asks for." Elena shuddered at the thought. She went back to the dressing table and began to brush out her hair. "I feel depraved for even mentioning such subjects, but let us blame it on my years in Italy."

"But of course, I meant a husband. Of course," Mia insisted. "How wicked of you to think that I meant something else."

"My apologies." Elena meant it, really she did, but she did not believe that Mia's thoughts were that pure.

"Now tell me, Elena, what instrument does he play?"

"The duke?"

"Yes, the duke."

The long-suffering patience in Mia's voice made Elena smile. "He plays no instrument that I know of. I do not think he is musical. Or that may be my pride talking. He left before I finished singing."

"He did not!" Outrage filled her face. "How could he. The man must have the feelings of a goat."

"Thank you, Mia, but not everyone hears the same way. Maybe he loves the sound of rain, the sounds of nature, and has no need for man-made music."

"Are you sure that you're not in love with him?"

"Not for a minute. Like all men of power he protects himself so that no one will take advantage of him." She was thinking out loud, explaining it to herself as much as to Mia. "He does have sensibilities he tries to conceal. I saw those when we met."

It would be entirely too much work to try to pierce that protection. And for her to have an affair of the heart, both hearts would have to be involved.

"I will ask Lord William about him, Elena. Lord William knows everyone."

"Do not discuss it with him." She almost dropped her brush and spoke with such sharpness that Mia stared at her.

"Why not?"

"For reasons I cannot begin to explain." She went back to the bedside and took her ward's hands. "Please, dearest, tell me you will be my confidante and not betray my secrets."

"Oh, yes, yes I will, Elena. You can trust me to keep all

your secrets." She was wide-eyed at the request, as though being raised to the level of confidante was a rite of passage as meaningful as a first ball.

"*Grazie, carissima.*" Elena kissed her on the cheek and released her hands, hoping she had not asked too much. "Now let me tell you about the other men."

Mia's wide eyes almost popped out of her head until Elena could no longer keep her expression solemn.

"You are not serious!" Mia threw a bolster from the bed in her general direction. "You are trying to distract me so that I will forgive you for not taking me with you to dinner. I would have loved to see Edward's violin again."

"And William."

Mia blushed prettily. Elena picked up the bolster and put it back on the bed, wondering if the girl was developing a *tendre* for him.

"Elena, I want to go to parties and enjoy myself."

"In a few weeks when the Season starts, Mia." So this was not about William at all. "I hope waiting for your first ball is the worst frustration you ever face."

Mia folded her arms across her chest and turned her head.

"Listen to me. You will need time to buy clothes. By the time your gowns are ready my place in society will be more secure. I think vouchers to Almack's is too much to hope for, but there will be more balls and fetes than you can count."

"I do not want to wait. I want it now."

"Yes, I know." This would go on until dawn if she did not put a stop to it. Fatigue made Mia's behavior more irritating than amusing this evening. "Mia, I know that cajoling, wheedling tone always worked with Edward. But I want you to think a minute, has it ever worked with me?"

"No." Mia turned to face her again, her mouth set in an unattractive pout. "You are mean, Elena."

"You are my ward. I am as responsible for you as a parent would be."

"Yes, yes, I know." The girl pulled the pins from her own hair, a ridiculous upsweep, much too old for her, that Elena had chosen to ignore.

"Mia, will you unlace my stays?" Elena slid the robe down her shoulder so the girl could reach the laces.

Mia complied and as she was unlacing the ribbons asked, "When are you going to find a maid?"

"Soon, but it is so difficult to find servants who do not mind us speaking Italian."

Mia was silent a moment. "Why not hire Tina to be your maid and find a new housekeeper?"

"Do you think she would prefer that?" Elena looked over her shoulder at Mia.

"Yes," Mia said, as the stays fell free. "Yes, Elena, I am sure of it."

Mia spoke with such conviction Elena wondered if Tina and Mia had already discussed it.

"It may not be as important a position as housekeeper but it is a much more personal connection to you."

Picking up her clothes, Elena folded them and left them on the closest chair. "All right, I'll ask Tina, but you must promise me that she will not consider it an insult."

"I am sure of it."

Mia's certainty convinced Elena that the subject had

been thoroughly discussed. And decided. "Tomorrow. I will talk with her about it tomorrow."

Elena settled herself in bed and quieted her mind. As she fell asleep an image of the duke popped into her head.

Would he call again? Probably not. Definitely not. Unless he had spoken seriously when he told her to let him know if she wanted a lover. How did one do that? Send him a letter? *Dear Duke, please come to my bed at your earliest convenience.* She smiled into the dark at her foolishness as she thought about his blue eyes. But not startlingly so. A blue that hinted at secrets that he was not ready to share.

What must his married life have been like? Had the duke and Rowena shared any of their thoughts, as she and Edward had? If they had, now that she was gone, with whom did he share his heart?

9

I THINK SHE wanted to slap me." The duke sat in the chair closest to the fire.

Magda gave a soft "woof." Meryon could not tell if that meant approval or censure. He took a sip of the wine Blix had left for him. Perfect valet that he was, Blix would show up in precisely five minutes to see if Meryon "would prefer to retire or have some more wine."

Meryon leaned his head on the back of the chair, his memory sharp with the image of Elena's golden brown eyes, the way she used her hands to emphasize her words.

She so totally embodied what he loved best about the women of Italy: their temper, yes, but also their warmth, their passion.

As she had said of her husband, she wore her heart for all to see. She needed someone to give her an outlet for all that passion. He drank the last of his wine and laughed at his self-indulgent generosity.

Magda slid off the chair and ran from the room. A sign that his valet Blix was nearby. His dog and his valet detested each other. And Meryon had no intention of dismissing either of them. Blix excelled at all a valet's most valued skills and Magda listened and never argued.

When Blix did not walk over to the table, pick up the bottle of wine, and offer him more, Meryon looked up.

"Your Grace, I beg your pardon. Your brother-in-law, Mr. Garrett, arrived an hour ago. He is in the library and asked to see you before you retired."

Meryon tried not to race out of the room like a child whose best friend has just arrived. He stopped short, confused, when he found that Garrett was not alone. A boy was with him, on the floor wrestling playfully with Magda.

Both boy and dog sprang apart when he came in. The boy stood and smoothed his hair and shirt, clean but close to a rag.

Magda raced over to Meryon, alive with energy, something he had never seen before. He opened the door and Magda ran into the hall.

"Take her," he said to one of the footmen, and closed the door before the footman answered.

"It's not her fault. I made her play with me!"

"Yes, and the footman will take her out to the park to run off her energy."

"You will not beat her for leaving hair everywhere." The boy made it a statement and Meryon recognized the worry buried under the command.

"No. Though I will see that she spends more time in the park. I never realized she had that much energy."

The boy nodded as if that was an acceptable arrangement, as if he were in charge.

Alan Wilson was about Rexton's size, but far more world-weary than his son. Wilson stood without fidgeting, caution replacing confidence. He looked from one man to the other without moving his head. Meryon saw no trust in those eyes, but no fear either.

"Now let us go back to the beginning." Meryon sat at his desk, leaning back in the chair.

"Good evening, Meryon," Garrett began. "When I arrived, this young man was at the door, trying to convince the night porter that you had invited him to call. Why would he lie, I asked myself, and have kept him company for the last hour while we waited for you."

"Are you the man I met the other night?" the boy asked.

"Yes." Meryon could not control the suspicion in his voice, surprised the boy did not recognize him.

"I would know your carriage, but all you nobs look the same to me. Well-fed and drunk."

"That is true, more often than not." Garrett laughed as he spoke. "Though tonight the duke is neither."

"And if I had been in my cups the other night, I would hardly remember you now, Mr. Wilson."

Alan Wilson shrugged and looked about. As he watched the boy's eyes move from one object to another, Meryon wondered if he was considering what he would steal.

"My coach is in the mews if you would like to visit it."

"I came to see what you wanted."

"Midnight is an odd time to call for an interview."

"You're still awake, aren't you?"

The boy did not understand the concept of impressing an employer. He acted as though he did not really want work. "I said I would offer you a position."

Alan Wilson laughed in a way that was not funny at all. "What position did you want me in? I'd have to know before I agree."

"Employment in my household," Meryon said in freezing tones. "A place where you could make more than you earn on the street, without threat to your safety. I told you to bring your mother with you. I have no ulterior motives."

For the first time the boy looked confused.

"Ulterior motive?" Garrett chuckled. "Meryon, speak in words that Mr. Wilson can understand." Garrett turned to the boy. "The duke means that his only wish is to offer work that will take you off the streets."

The boy made a sound of disbelief. "Why would you do that if you didn't want something more?"

"Because I have a son near your age and cannot imagine him on his own." Meryon had more reasons than that but he left it there.

"Aye, sir," Alan Wilson said. "He would be dead in a day."

"Do you trust no one?" Garrett asked.

"Yes, sir, my ma. Who is home waiting for me to bring something more than a story and will beat me if I don't."

"Come back tomorrow, after noon, and bring your mother this time. If you do, then I will find you a position in the stable." Meryon handed him a coin. Wilson took the coin, bit it to test its weight. After he put it in his pocket he shrugged.

"Not tomorrow. I have a job for the day."

"Then the day after," Meryon said as he wondered what kind of game they were playing.

"Yes, sir. And my mother can't come here. She has to take care of my brother and the baby."

Or she does not exist. Meryon looked at Garrett and he knew they had the same thought.

"I have time the day after tomorrow, after breakfast," Garrett said. "Shall I pay a call on Mrs. Wilson on Thursday and see if she is willing to allow her son to work here?"

"Excellent idea." Meryon wanted to know what the boy's living conditions were like. If there was a father here or away. Garrett's general observations always proved useful.

"Mr. Wilson, tell your mother that the Reverend Mr. Garrett will call on her sometime after noon on Thursday. Come here yourself to show him the way."

"Yes, sir." The boy agreed and then gave his attention to Garrett. "You're a reverend?"

"Yes."

"You don't look like one. My ma will know for sure if you're lying."

"Thank you, Mr. Wilson. I will bring proof and only tell the truth. Will that be sufficient?"

"I don't know about that, but it should be enough."

"What do I look like?" Garrett asked with interest.

"Like a soldier from the war."

"Which I am." Garrett bowed to the boy. "But as your father will tell you, the war is over. I have found another calling. What does he look like?" Garrett asked, gesturing to the duke.

"Like a really rich man who can have anything he wants."

"Almost, but not quite, true." Garrett brushed some imaginary lint from his coat.

"Almost being the significant word." An image of the woman in the darkened room came to mind. Elena Verano before he knew how difficult she could be.

With a nod from Meryon, Garrett showed Mr. Wilson to the door and came back into the room laughing. "You have an intriguing circle of friends, Lynford."

"It seems so, but after this evening I am wondering if Mr. Wilson might prefer to steal as much as he could, rather than work for me."

"I, too, saw those eyes taking in everything in the room."

"Still, the boy intrigues me. I wish I knew why."

When Garrett gave him the direct look that they all called the "vicar's challenge," he went on.

"You're right. I do know. He reminds me of Rexton and the accident of birth." He called the picture of his golden-haired son to mind. "That and young Kepless. I have a plan. Pour us some brandy and I will tell you about it."

Garrett did as asked and while they enjoyed the excellent brandy that Meryon had brought back from France, he explained his idea for a bill that would provide income for widows and orphans who had lost all means of support.

"A noble idea, Meryon—too noble, I am sorry to say."

Too noble. At their first meeting he had accused Signora Verano of being too noble, for wanting to make her world a better place. His plans were similar if on a larger scale. Intriguing. They did have something in common. "Yes, but at least it will make more people aware of the problem."

"How can they not be?"

"Because they live in such a rarified world, limited to a village or the Season and Hyde Park. God knows that was how I lived my life for too long. Hearing of my brother Gabriel's experience and your war years were my introduction to the way most people see the world."

"Then I cheer you on, for years and years and years."

"I can be patient."

Garrett's laugh became a protracted coughing spasm. With a wave of apology he pulled out his handkerchief and pressed it to his mouth. Was this something passing? Meryon did not ask but seized on a subject while Garrett composed himself again.

"I called on a lady today whose servants are involved in her life to an embarrassing degree."

"You called on a lady?"

Meryon waved that away and wished he had thought before he spoke. "I refused a glass of wine and I thought the maid would berate me then and there. Another lurked behind a door, listening."

"So you have a new friend, a new *female* friend."

"No, I do believe she is interested in someone else." And even if Lord William was not courting her, Meryon was sure that he had destroyed any hope of knowing her better. "Besides, I have no time for more people in my life."

"Oh, Lynford, you can never have too many friends. If you feel that way then you have too many of the *wrong* type of people in your life."

"Aha, the vicar speaks." Meryon poured more brandy. "Why did I ever let you marry Olivia and take up the living in Pennsford?"

"Because you knew it would make your darling sister happy and you would actually have someone you could talk to."

"I do not need a confessional."

"Stop bristling," Michael said on a laugh that became a wheeze. "No, you do not need a confessor, but you do need a confidant."

"I fear that now that you are a vicar with a secure living you have an answer for everything."

"I've always had an answer for everything, Your Grace, but this position gives me permission to speak them aloud." He tried to forestall another round of coughing and wound up almost choking instead.

"Tell me why you are come to town, Michael. To see a physician, I hope?"

"Not necessary. This is only the last of a nasty cold that everyone in Pennsford is sharing with great generosity. I knew it was a mistake to stand outside the church and shake hands, even if the weather was kind for March."

"Olivia?"

"Olivia does not catch cold. She is, however, carrying something else, which she wanted me to tell you about in person."

"She is increasing?" Meryon asked with real pleasure.

"Yes." Michael could not hold back his smile. "She was afraid the news might upset you. Apparently not."

"No, I am delighted, and shall write to her immediately and tell her so." Olivia was not frail like Rowena, and by his sister's own admission her "sturdy" body would be very good for giving birth.

By the time they said good night, they were both a little drunk. If Blix noticed he made no comment, only took Meryon's clothes after handing him the prepared list of his tomorrow's appointments.

A meeting with his man of business about the changes to his will and the required inventory of the entailed property. Good Lord, had it really been five years since the last one? An appointment with his tailor, who would give him the definitive word on whether men's clothing was becoming too staid, followed by a conversation with the draper about whatever fabric was needed for his new clothes. Tomorrow was Wednesday, so there would be no Parliamentary session, but there was dinner with the Regent.

As he swiped at his face with a cloth and cleaned his teeth, he decided he would make time to stop in at Jackson's on the chance that DeBora would be there. A rather quiet day, all in all.

Meryon went to the terrace door, opened it, and

stepped onto the small balcony, hoping a breath of fresh air would clear his head. The courtyard below was not quite empty. He could hear some feminine laughter and the low voice of a man.

Feeling an interloper in his own house, Meryon stepped back inside and went to bed, fully aware that if his days were full, his nights were not.

10

IS MIA EVER going to come down?" Elena, standing in the foyer with her bonnet in hand, asked the question of the butler, the Tinottis, and the upstairs maid, who happened to be walking by. None of them answered. Probably because they heard the testiness in her voice and thought she might snap the speaker's head off.

She raised her hands, palms out, and with a slight bob of her head made a silent apology. In a sweeter voice, she tried again. "The hackney is waiting and will charge us extra. Of all the days for the coachman to be ill. I will not be late for our first fitting or we will then be late for the draper."

"They will wait. You are the customer." Tina sounded cross too. Most likely because she was not invited on this outing.

"This is not Italy and they will expect us to be prompt. Tina, please go and see what is keeping Mia."

As Tina turned to the stairs, Mia came running down, her bonnet in hand, full of apologies.

"I could not decide what to wear and then thought it should be something easy to change in and out of."

They were out the door and into the hackney so quickly that Elena hoped they might still be able to keep to their schedule.

"I hope this woman is better than the other modiste. How did you convince Mrs. Harbison to give up her appointment so we could use it?"

Elena shrugged. "Letty had only to hear the name of the woman we planned to see, then insisted we take her appointment with her modiste and Mr. Harbison's appointment with the draper."

"This will be so much fun. How quickly can she have the gowns ready?"

Mia's excitement was contagious and fueled Elena through the entire morning. The modiste had been delighted to have "the dressing of such a vivacious young woman" and "such an elegant lady." By excessive flattery she was able to convince Mia to choose the styles that would complement her coloring and shape and, more important, were appropriate for a young woman in her first Season.

As they were leaving, the modiste asked what draper they were using. "Oh, good. They have a wonderful selection, but mind you they are not above repeating bits of gossip so have a care for what you say."

Mia giggled at the idea that anything she said would be worthy of repeating and as they walked down the street she made up three or four outrageous scenarios that had them both laughing.

They arrived at the draper's to find it filled with gentlemen, which immediately made Mia regret the old dress she had worn and made Elena wonder if they already had made a misstep and arrived at the wrong time.

The draper's wife assured her that she was at the right place and at the right time and took her into a small room. "Thursday morning is normally reserved for gentlemen but there are emergencies, and it is always our pleasure to accommodate ladies as well."

They spent an hour choosing material for the gowns they had decided on and arranged to have the fabric sent to the modiste. When she heard the name, the draper's wife smiled her approval and suggested the substitution of two different lengths of fabric. "I would not suggest this if it was anyone else, but no one handles these unique pieces better than she does."

The fabric was, of course, more expensive, but then the draper's wife offered to give them the rest of a bolt of an extravagantly colored fabric that Elena had chosen, "so that no one else will be seen in it."

Elena accepted the gift with thanks, wondering what she would do with the extra. They were exchanging details of the transaction when someone opened the door to the small salon and stepped inside with none other than the Duke of Meryon.

At the sight of her the duke stepped back, surprised, and Elena was afraid he would snub her, turn and leave without so much as a greeting. After her harsh words the night before she had no idea what to expect from him.

"Signora Verano, good morning." Meryon bowed, his eyes commanding hers not to be as rude as she had feared he would be to her. It reminded her instantly of the modiste's warning that the draper loved gossip.

"Your Grace." She curtsied deeply and then introduced Mia. Her ward was watching the duke with something less than welcome. It would be too much like a farce if Mia rose to her defense here. She hurried the introduction.

"Your Grace, may I present my ward, Signorina Mia Castellano. Mia, this is the Duke of Meryon."

Mia's considering expression softened and she dropped an appropriate curtsy. "Your Grace."

"Good morning." The duke bowed again, his smile fading a little. "Is Lord William with you?" Meryon looked around as if expecting the man to jump from some hiding place.

"No, Your Grace." It was Mia who answered. "I told him he was not invited. I hardly want him to see what I will be wearing this Season before my gowns are ready."

"How churlish of him to even suggest it." Meryon's expression went from confused to enlightened.

The girl gave him a flirtatious nod, and then turned to her guardian. "He is coming for a language lesson this afternoon, is he not?"

"Yes, he is." Elena noticed that Mia did not specify who was learning what language, as the English she was using was perfectly adequate.

Before she or Mia could say anything else, the duke spoke up. "It's delightful to see you so soon after our last meeting, signora. I regret that our conversation was cut short. There was so much left unsaid."

The draper's wife rose to the occasion. "If your ward will come with me I can give her the direction of a woman who is undoubtedly the best milliner in all of London and call a hackney for you."

Mia allowed herself to be shepherded from the room and that is how, less than twelve hours after their confrontation, the duke and Elena were alone together once again.

"Thank you for your discretion, Your Grace. That was a very elegant way to say that I was furious with you and ordered you from my house."

"If we both want to avoid gossip then neither of us has anything to worry about." His words lacked both emotion and interest.

"Thank you again." She curtsied, deciding to abandon any attempt to befriend him. He could be so prosaic that she could not even imagine him having fun.

They would do nothing but argue if last night was any example. She went to the door and waited for him to open it for her. He did not and Elena turned to see if he meant it as an insult, despite his protestation of civility. She found him staring at the carpet, lost in thought. She waited and a moment later had his attention.

"There is one more thing, signora. Am I correct in the understanding that Lord William is courting your ward?"

"Why are you asking?" There was no way a question like that could sound courteous, especially when it was based in suspicion.

"It seems I have been confused about several things lately."

That was obscure enough to be useless, she thought. "I do believe William is quite taken with Mia's sense of adventure and joie de vivre."

"That explains much," Meryon said.

And then he smiled.

She had *never* seen this smile before. It was unforgettable, utterly charming, and as powerful as his touch. It erased years from his face, even if it did accentuate the creases in the corners of his eyes. It was so fine that it made his habitual stone-faced look that much more of a crime. He should always look this happy.

He opened the door for her with a pleased nod, seemingly unaware of the effect he was having on her.

"Thank you, Your Grace." Elena laughed a little and dipped a small curtsy and went into the main room of the shop. The duke followed her.

"I will have my carriage take you home, signora. My coachman can be to Bloomsbury and back before the draper shows me what I am supposed to be buying this season."

"Thank you, Your Grace." Elena curtsied yet again. She was about to refuse if only to prove that someone would say no to a duke, but Mia did not give her a chance.

"Oh, that is so kind of you, Your Grace." Mia was all enthusiasm. "Our coachman is sick and the hackneys are so uncertain. And besides, everyone will see us come down the street in a crested carriage and be so jealous of our connections."

"It is my pleasure, Miss Castellano. If only all ladies

were as easy to please." He did not look at Elena but smiled at Mia. This time it was a social smile, not the totally irresistible one.

He spoke to the man waiting near the door. "This is my secretary, Roland. He will escort you out."

"Oh, wonderful." Mia took Roland's arm. "Now that we are acquainted, Your Grace, I will expect you to dance with me. Once I am out."

Elena watched the interplay. Only Mia would think to practice her flirtation with a duke. "Mia, dear, I think the duke has the next appointment and we are encroaching on his time."

"Oh." Mia covered her mouth with her hand and begged his pardon.

"It's quite all right. My business will not take long."

Even as he spoke a clerk staggered into the private salon they had used, his arms loaded with bolts of fabric, dark browns, blues, varying shades of gray and black.

"Miss Castellano?" the duke called as Mia made her way out of the shop. "Please give my regards to Lord William. I understand that the study of languages can be incredibly time-consuming."

"I hope so, Your Grace!" Mia called back. Then she paraded through the store, out the door, and into the duke's carriage as if she owned it. Elena followed, though she wished she could stay and make sure the duke chose one of the blues that matched his eyes.

MERYON WATCHED HER leave and spent the next twenty minutes paying only the vaguest attention to the

draper. When his coach returned he left the final choices
and details to his secretary, and instructed the coachman
to take him to Jackson's. There was nothing remotely feminine about the boxing establishment and he could do his
best to banish the pleasure he had felt on seeing Elena Verano again.

Jackson's was crowded. Several gentlemen offered
him a spot closer to the ring where Jackson himself was
spending some time with one of the newer pugilists trying
to make a name for himself. Meryon declined. He had not
come to watch; he had hoped to test his own bare knuckles.

Meryon saw Garrett deep in conversation with Lord
Kyle, discussing his immortal soul, no doubt. When the
two saw him they stopped their earnest discussion. The
three of them chatted in a desultory way for a few minutes
and then Kyle announced that he had to be off to meet his
father.

"I need a few words with you, Your Grace," Garrett
said.

Since Meryon was sure those words involved something more personal than who the next champion would
be, Meryon suggested to Garrett that they walk a few
doors down to a coffeehouse.

Out in the damp air, Garrett began to cough again,
but it did not sound as congested or last as long as it had
the night before. When he mentioned it to Garrett, his
brother-in-law shrugged.

"The irritation was almost gone but travel brought it
on again." Garrett paused and pressed his lips together.
This time he was able to suppress the cough. "Ignore it, if

you please, Your Grace. It will disappear after another good night's sleep."

They found a quiet spot near a window, well away from the crowd arguing over the upcoming budget while smoking with as much force as they were speaking. Enough to color the air with their pipe smoke.

"Now that we are alone, comfortable, and enjoying our coffee, I will listen to your lecture."

Garrett nodded. "Very well. Through bits and pieces that David has let drop and my conversation with Lord Kyle, it appears that your plan to ruin Bendas is well under way."

Meryon waited, sipping his coffee, which he had ordered laced with chocolate.

Garrett took what could only be described as a fortifying drink of his coffee before going on. "It hardly matters to me what form it takes, but I must warn you, my friend, that nothing good comes from revenge. It will harm you as much as it harms Bendas."

"I will tell you what I told Lord Kyle, as well as Lord William." Meryon leaned across the table. "I do not want revenge. I want justice."

"This version of justice looks distinctly like retribution. I have never known you to prevaricate." Garrett leaned back in his chair. Meryon recognized it as a disinclination to argue.

"Michael, Bendas must pay for his actions. After that excuse for a duel, Bendas convinced the magistrate not to prosecute him for the death of a bystander. Money eased that decision, I have no doubt." Meryon sat back, too, and pretended his calm went more than skin deep. "I will not let Bendas use his rank to absolve him of all his misdeeds. The time has come for someone to stop him. It has fallen to me and I will not turn my back on it. I owe it to Kepless, to Olivia, and to any others who have been threatened, harmed, or murdered by him."

"So you are ruining his reputation for the greater good?"

"No, you self-righteous prig." Meryon spoke the insult amiably enough; Garrett accepted it in kind.

"Lynford, I was once a spy, a cheat, and a liar. Being called a self-righteous prig is a compliment."

"You have known men like Bendas. Men who had to be stopped."

"Yes, and that is why I know that the cost is too great." Garrett shook his head. "Have you thought about the innocents who suffer in this? His son has done no wrong. His grandson was instrumental in capturing the two men whom Bendas hired to abduct Olivia."

"His family should have taken steps before this, after the events surrounding Olivia's kidnapping were taken care of." Meryon ignored the twinge of regret. He liked Lord William. "His family had months to deal with it and did nothing. I would never have challenged Bendas to the duel if they had acted during all those months I traveled in Europe."

"While you mourned Rowena," Garrett added.

"While I counted what I had lost," Meryon agreed. "The Bendasbrooks did nothing about the duke's bizarre behavior. When I heard that, it only verified what Father taught me. Never wait for someone else to do the work you should do."

"So you suggest cartoons to Rowlandson, play up his grandson's estrangement, and find some way to encourage him to buy land that will prove worthless. That one is too complicated to make sense after days of travel, too much brandy, and not enough coffee. Your brother David tells me it is legal, and he is honest to a fault, but apparently as bent on this course of action as you are."

"Before you list my sins, recall that Olivia nearly died because of Bendas, and land was at the heart of that. It seems appropriate to me that his undoing should come through his obsession with land."

"Yes, an eye for an eye. But that is not what Christ teaches."

"You know, I find that I do not care what Christ teaches in this case. I will have my version of justice. I cannot let Bendas's behavior go unpunished because he sits in the House of Lords and thinks himself above the law."

"You are not above the law either, Lynford." Garrett spoke quietly in a voice that begged for his attention.

"I do not think I am. The action I take is done because others have neglected theirs for too long.

"Here is a man who looks as if he wants to hear your lecture." Meryon raised his chin toward a man making straight for their table.

Meryon watched the man, a gentleman, work his way to their corner. He had the haunted eyes of a gambler, the long restless fingers of a man who wanted desperately to be throwing dice or playing with a pack of cards. His brother Jess came to mind. Another of the same sort.

"Do not introduce me. He must know Jessup, and with that connection it will take all of one minute for him to try to convince me to invest in some wild scheme that is little more than another kind of gamble."

"God spare me a duke's perfection, Your Grace."

This time Garrett meant the insult and Meryon leaned closer. "The fractured vision of a reformed sinner is worse, brother."

Each left the other laughing at a truth both would deny.

Meryon could swear the coach still carried the scent of Signora Verano's spicy rose perfume. Recalling the Signora was infinitely preferable to mulling over the meaning of a "duke's perfection." He reached down to pull the bottle of brandy out from beneath the seat and found both the brandy and a handkerchief tucked into the cushion. She'd left it on purpose, he was sure of it.

Meryon tried to gauge when he would see her again. When the Season started there would be dozens of opportunities. Surely at the Monksfords' musicale in two weeks or so. But Harriette's party was the same evening.

Among the women of the demimonde who would be Harriette's guests, he would be able to find someone who could fill his physical needs. He needed a mistress. One with blond hair and blue eyes, petite and thoroughly English.

But the well-placed square of cloth firmed his decision. He would hear the Signora sing again and hope for a few moments of her time in which to return her handkerchief.

YOU DID WHAT!" Elena lowered her voice. "Mia, how could you?"

"I thought if he found your handkerchief it would be more difficult for him to forget you. My governess says it is a perfectly acceptable way to remind a man of your interest."

"It is much too obvious, and the point is I do not want him to remember me."

"Of course you are saying you do not want to know him better but, even without my governess's instruction, I know that is nothing more than maidenly airs."

"I am not a maiden and do not have airs. If I wanted to know him better I would be much more direct."

Tina came in to announce that Lord William had arrived.

"This discussion is pointless. I will explain when I see the duke. You have embarrassed me beyond bearing and I will tell you the same thing that I told William. If you feel the need to interfere in my private life I will see it as permission to take a deep interest in yours. Do you understand?"

"What did William do?" Mia seemed to miss the point completely.

"Something very similar to what you did. I am sure it will not take much prompting for him to tell you."

Mia bit her lip and said nothing.

"I hope you are not biting back a laugh. This is no subject to be made light of." William came into the room. "Tell her how serious I am about this, William."

"Yes, whatever it is, Mia, she is perfectly serious. When she starts to shout like that there can be no doubt. What did you do?"

"Oh, William, the Duke of Meryon let us ride home in his carriage while he was making his choices at the draper's. Everyone on the street noticed it and is green with envy. I left Elena's handkerchief in the duke's carriage so he would not forget her."

"Clever girl." William grinned.

"William, do not encourage her. I am going up and will send your governess down as a chaperone, Mia."

"Oh, but—"

Elena closed the door on Mia's protest and thought the girl should count herself lucky that she had not sent Lord William home.

II

IT WAS RARE that Meryon was invited to dinner with the Regent. He dressed with all the care this representative of the king deserved, but without much enthusiasm. An evening with one hundred or so of the Regent's lords and ladies was almost always dull unless one liked to discuss the latest styles, who was sleeping where, and whose daughters would be making their debut.

He would find Kyle and switch the place cards so they sat near each other. That would relieve the boredom.

Blix seemed more precise than usual and Meryon had to hurry him along with a brusque, "The Regent will be much more interested in what the ladies are wearing than how I choose to do my cravat."

If luck sided with him tonight, some fascinating woman would present herself and Blix's efforts would find an appreciative audience. Of one.

Meryon leaned into the library, where he found Garrett reading, as he expected. Meryon bid him good night. "A dinner discussing Hazlitt's last essay with you would be a preferable evening."

Garrett put a marker in the book and set it aside: "Look at it this way. Perhaps the lady you called on last night will be in attendance."

"I think that highly unlikely." Though the thought had crossed his mind.

"Unlikely, eh? Then this is not one of Prinny's more licentious dinners? I was so looking forward to some scurrilous gossip."

Meryon stepped into the room and closed the door. "What did I say that leads you to believe she is of the demimonde?"

"Nothing really, only that you paid a call well after regular calling hours and that is a trifle unusual." Garrett made a steeple of his fingers and tapped the tips. "Unless custom has changed since I have retired to Derbyshire."

"Why do I always feel as though I am confessing to you? Do you not know that dukes can do no wrong?"

"Yes, but apparently you don't really believe that. I imagine from what the old vicar told me that it has something to do with your father's understanding of the true responsibilities of a duke. Rules he imparted to you."

Meryon was not going to start this discussion, not when the prince was waiting, more likely not ever. He came over to the table and picked up the book Garrett had been reading without really looking at it.

"I was angry last night. At least I thought I was, and I went to confront the lady about a situation I convinced myself was so urgent that the normal rules of courtesy did not apply."

He handed the book to Garrett, who accepted it and put it in his lap.

"How unlike you, Duke. Is she very beautiful?"

"She is the most aggravating beauty I have ever met." Meryon sighed.

"Then be prepared to offend her a dozen other times or accept the truth that you are done with grief and the wanton urges of man are alive in you once again."

"God help me, if you do not stop pontificating I will ban you from the house, you idiot." Meryon could not help laughing, which took all the threat from his words.

"That's Reverend Idiot, Your Grace."

IT'S A COMMAND PERFORMANCE, signora!"

"No, it is not, Tina. This is for the Regent and his party. Nothing as formal as a command performance for the king."

"Sit down, signora, and let me put your hair up. I want to use those jeweled clips you found."

"No, no jewels in my hair tonight." Elena shook her head even as she sat in front of the mirror. "I am not one of the dinner guests and do not want to appear to overstep myself. Just put it up. That will be enough for tonight."

Tina did as directed and both were well pleased with the results. The topaz earrings complemented the deep green dress and the long white gloves were new and felt quite elegant. Elena decided to wear her black velvet

cloak, and by the time William called for her a little thrill
of excitement had settled in her stomach.

"I am pleased to say that the prince has asked me to
be your escort to the palace." As he spoke, William
handed her a posy of violets and sweet peas.

"Thank you, my lord." She paused on the front steps
and drew in a deep breath. "I love the smell of spring.
Even here in London it is everywhere."

William handed her into the carriage and she settled
on the seat. As the coach lurched and began to roll down
the street William explained that it would take a while to
reach the palace.

"Yes, the Regent's representative explained the proce-
dure," Elena said. "There will be a withdrawing room for
my use. Signor Tinotti has gone ahead and will be waiting
for me with a palace maid, and a meal is available should
I be hungry. I will probably not be introduced before midnight."

Elena rubbed her throat. "It is a great deal of nonsense for three songs, but one does not question a prince
and, to be practical, if all goes well it is the perfect entrée
to society that I need to make Mia a success."

"Perhaps Prinny wants to impress *you*."

"I hope not. He is the exact opposite of the type of
man I would be interested in."

"Do tell." William leaned forward.

His curiosity was never-ending and amusing but she
waved a hand at him, hoping he would drop the subject.

"Let me guess. Someone who has some wealth, is comfortable with his place in life, is ambitious and responsible

enough to improve his estate rather than play all day. Oh yes, and one who lives to the fullest."

"Hmmm, that has some appeal, but you have left out the truly personal parts, which is just as well."

"He must talk and listen as well. He must love to argue and love making up even more."

"Oh, do be quiet. Are you going back for a language lesson with Mia?"

"Yes, thank you for suggesting it. She can hardly wait for the Metcalfes' ball." William slouched back on the cushions and raised his legs to the opposite seat. "Will you be nervous tonight without me there for support?"

"I'm never nervous." She lied as much to herself as to her nephew. "I've appeared before almost every European royal, including Napoleon." She raised the bouquet and enjoyed the way the scent of the flowers replaced the scent of horse.

"No nerves. Good, because there is something I have to tell you."

Before she could ask him to wait until after her performance, he blurted it out.

"The Duke of Bendas is with the party tonight."

"Bendas is there?"

"Yes. I do not know how long he will stay. This affair will last until morning and he is not one for late hours these days."

"It really does not matter. He is the least of those present that I would like to impress, and he no longer can influence what I choose to sing." She looked out the window, then down at the bouquet and picked at one of the violets that had come loose. She was not going to ask if the Duke of Meryon would be there.

"The Duke of Meryon is on the guest list too."

"Don't sound so pleased," she snapped and did not apologize. He knew as well as she did that she would have to explain that dratted handkerchief at the first opportunity. "This is not some private circus for your entertainment."

"I'm sorry. I did not know you were at odds with him."

"We barely know each other." That was God's honest truth, she thought.

"Do not find his bad side, Elena. He has a thirst for justice where Grandfather is concerned. I told you before, he is fiercely protective of his interests."

"What happened between them?"

"The duel that Rowlandson ridiculed in his cartoon. Meryon challenged him. It was Meryon's young groom who was killed, accidentally."

"Oh dear heaven, William. The poor boy." She gripped her hands together. "What were they dueling over?"

"You will have to ask Meryon. It is only now that the ton realizes that Meryon was the other party."

"Ask him? I will not. The question is, should I tell him that I am Bendas's daughter?"

"No." William spoke with conviction. "How many times must I tell you that he puts his family before everything else? If he knows, he may try to find a way to use that knowledge, and the rift between you and Bendas, to his advantage."

"All right." She drew a breath. "You are making him sound like a villain. I thought you liked him."

"I do. Very much. But on this we are at odds. Grandfather was exonerated and, for the Bendasbrooks, the incident is over. You understand that I must do all I can to protect the dukedom."

"What an awful position you are in, William."

"Father more than me. One thing I promise you is that there will not be another Bendas-Meryon duel. I will not let it come to that ever again."

"It does make the business about that handkerchief seem silly."

"Because it is, Elena." William's attitude made it clear it was not something he wanted to discuss.

"Perhaps the Duke of Meryon will leave early as well."

"Not unless he has a wish to irritate Prinny. No one, with the possible exception of those as old as Bendas, will leave before the Regent does."

She played with the flowers, trying to improve their arrangement, and did not say anything.

"Will you be able to sing with both Bendas and Meryon there?"

"Of course." She shrugged away his concern. "Singing is my great consolation, as riding is yours, William dear."

He understood that comparison and they rode on in silence.

Her father and the Duke of Meryon. And most likely a dozen other dukes, including the royal dukes. Thank goodness titles had long ago ceased to impress her. Mutual hatred was something else entirely. It would be best if she avoided both Meryon and Bendas.

FOR THE DUKE OF MERYON the trip to the palace took less than five minutes. In fact he could have reached it even more quickly on foot. The palace was brightly lit for the event, every window glowing.

Once inside Meryon knew that it would take an amazingly long time to work his way from the entrance to the banqueting room. And he knew better than to insult the Regent by arriving after he did. It was going to be a long evening.

His escort directed him down a passage. "Your Grace, the royal dukes will be in attendance as well as one hundred guests. Many of them are single women, both never married and widowed."

Prinny was playing matchmaker? Meryon wondered if he was a consolation prize for the young ladies who did not catch the royal dukes' eyes.

"I do believe there will be some dancing after dinner."

Which translated into "do not plan to leave before dawn."

Meryon estimated that approximately half the guests had arrived before he did and were lined up on either side of the red carpet that bisected the room. There were two long tables on either side of the carpet set for an elaborate meal, and a head table for the Regent and his personal guests.

Introduced to the master of ceremonies by his escort, Meryon was then announced formally to those already present. The crowd quieted at the thump of the master's staff followed by, "His Grace, the Duke of Meryon." The master of ceremonies' voice was wonderfully sonorous, reaching to the far ends of the room. His announcement was followed by bows and curtsies from the assembled and a buzz of welcome as conversation resumed.

Meryon made his way through the crowd, exchanging greetings. Most of this group was comfortable with the pomp and it would not keep them from having a good time. He saw Kyle and was halfway to his friend, who was talking with two fresh-faced women, when he spotted the Duke of Bendas.

The man was as old as dirt and tottered through the path the crowd made for him, leaning heavily on a stick. Ignoring the fact that everyone was standing, he demanded a chair be brought for him.

Meeting him in public was bound to happen, Meryon knew that, and he should have realized that Bendas would be invited this evening.

Meryon waited for Bendas to recognize him. The old man was no more than five feet away when he stopped and jerked back as though he had run into a brick wall.

"Good evening, Your Grace." Meryon stepped into his path, pleased that the conventional greeting sounded anything but cordial.

"I heard you were back from Germany." Bendas eyed him up and down as though finding fault with his attire.

Despite the fact that Bendas was misstating the obvious, the insulting perusal and the one sentence told Meryon something. Bendas was near blind. He was squinting his rheumy eyes and his neck was stuck out as though waiting for the executioner to strike.

Besides that, the old bastard kept track of where the

Duke of Meryon was, or had been, and could not remember that it was France and not Germany.

Meryon forced himself to relax his fist and nodded at the old duke's mention of Europe.

"Speak up, man." The duke raised his stick. "I cannot hear you."

"Yes, I am returned from France as I think this will be a pivotal year in Parliament."

"Humph" was all the old man said, which meant that Bendas either could not hear him or agreed but did not want to admit it.

"How is your sister?" He asked that with a sly grin that made Meryon fist his hand again.

"She is well."

"Tell me her name." The old duke raised his stick in a way that could only be construed as threatening.

Meryon reached out and casually pulled it from his weak grip. He leaned closer as he made to hand the stick back. As he wrapped Bendas's hand around the head of his cane, he squeezed a little more tightly than was necessary and whispered, "Do not tempt me."

Bendas took his stick and tried to stare Meryon down. Bendas looked away first.

"Two special acts before Parliament, Your Grace?" Meryon went on. "You must think the land is very valuable. What does your son say about the change to the entail?"

"None of your damn business." Bendas looked around for rescue but none of the crowd listening so avidly wanted the confrontation to end.

Meryon turned toward two earls who were nearby.

"You should take a look at the parcel, Sanders; it's close to your seat and you know how valuable that land has proved."

"Stop your tongue, you arrogant—"

Before Bendas could truly insult Meryon, the orchestra sounded a chord and the master of ceremonies thumped the floor four times.

Everyone stopped mid-sentence, jostled for position, and turned to the door as the master announced: "His Royal Highness, the Prince of Wales!"

Meryon knew that Olivia would want to know every tiny detail of the food service. Despite her endless attempts to educate him, he could say not more than the food would have been quite tasty if it had been served warm. He settled for the dishes that were best at room temperature and feasted well.

He had arrived too late to move the place cards around and could only thank him when the Marquis Straemore told him that his wife had done the fiddling and they would dine together.

The Marchioness Straemore sat to his right, and the lady to his left was the widow of a duke, an older woman who was nothing less than flattered to be included. "What I should like to do most of all tonight is dance the waltz. Do you think they will play one? It is everywhere now but I have no idea what the Regent thinks of it."

The marchioness made outrageous observations about the likelihood of the royals marrying any of the ladies present. Finally her husband removed her wineglass, as if that was the reason she had been so frank.

Before the marchioness could do any more than give

her husband a look of annoyance, the orchestra played the now familiar chord announcing the next part of the festivities.

"Peers of the realm and ladies and gentlemen." The master of ceremonies' commanding voice began, and in a moment the footmen stopped clearing and the master had the attention of the entire assemblage.

"Good evening once again. By His Highness's request the lady singer Signora Elena Verano will entertain us with songs before the dancing portion of the evening begins."

12

THE MASTER OF CEREMONIES' announcement that Elena Verano would sing drew a round of delighted oohs and ahhs.

When Elena Verano traded places with the master of ceremonies, she curtsied to the Regent and then to both tables. Meryon nodded as though the curtsy were aimed at him alone.

As she had the other night at the Harbisons', she waited, letting her eyes search the crowd, without lingering on any familiar face. Her glance invited them to forget trial and tribulation, lie and deception, fear and failure, and live in this moment of music. Meryon returned her smile when her gaze met his so briefly.

She looked even more beautiful tonight. The deep green of her gown set off her fresh pink cheeks. She wore her dark hair up, as she had the first time he saw her.

Signora Verano could not possibly sing as perfectly as she had the other night, even if she had lessons from the great Signor Ponto every day. Meryon tried to relax and then realized that he was nervous for her.

In a show of perfect timing, the very moment before the crowd grew restless, Signora Verano began. She sang *a capella*, a song he recognized as a traditional ballad. He had expected something Italian or operatic at least, but this was neither. She sang of love used, abused, and casually tossed away. His heart sank. This had nothing of the power he had heard before.

She sang the song with humor and the crowd was amused if not impressed.

Her expression as much as her voice invited the audience to share her disdain for anyone who did not understand that love toyed with us, especially when we tried to toy with it.

She finished. Polite applause did little to distract the audience from the abrupt departure of the Duke of Bendas. His muttering was unintelligible and the constant hushing sounds from his escort only made him louder. "Stupid song. Badly sung. Let me out before she gives me a headache."

Meryon clenched his fist and wanted to use it to pummel the useless fool.

"I want to beat up that fool duke. He should at least wait until she does another song." The marchioness rose a little and Meryon was afraid that she really was going to confront him.

"I feel exactly as you do, my lady, but surely the Signora has experienced harsher critics."

"Yes, it is the fate of all who perform," the marchioness agreed.

Signora Verano showed them all how to handle a difficult audience. She curtsied to the old man. When he had left the room she began her second song without showing the slightest upset at his caustic comments.

Meryon straightened as the first notes filled the room. Why had she started with the other when this song matched her voice so perfectly? He loved music but was embarrassingly unfamiliar with composers and such details, yet he knew enough to recognize she was singing it brilliantly.

If the song the night before had been filled with euphoria, this one promised passion. In the softest of voices that still managed to reach to the corners of the room, she whispered of a hope for love offered and shared. It did not so much touch the heart as tell them that love had touched hers.

She repeated the words, her voice no longer a whisper. The longing for love so clear, it hurt to watch her beg.

Again, she sang the same words with even greater heart, so that the offering and the wanting became a desperate need.

She finished with a soaring finale that was a passionate demand. The song ended with an abruptness that left the audience on the top of a peak with no way to climb down. Meryon wanted her more than he had ever wanted anything before.

Signora Verano accepted the cheers and shouts of "Brava!" graciously, and before the crowd was quite finished with their applause she sang her last song, an agreeable, humorous series of words that might well have meant nothing but sounded so euphonious there was no doubt they belonged together.

Singing with a speed and assurance that was staggering, she finished with a little chirrup as though one last word must escape her lips. Laughter mixed with applause as she walked the length of the tables to curtsy deeply to the Regent, who was standing and clapping wildly.

Meryon stood as the others did, feeling a totally misplaced pride in her performance. When the clapping faded the prince raised his glass of brandy. "To Signora Elena Verano. The lady who has warmed our cold English spring with a voice that calls the flowers to life."

Elena smiled and curtsied again, turning to face the rest of her audience as they chorused "Hear! Hear!" Her charming expression asked, *"What can one do in the face of such extravagant praise?"*

"Signora," the prince called out, "join us for the dancing. As a matter of fact we will count on you to demonstrate the way Italians dance the waltz. Straemore, you and your wife have been to France recently, please join the Signora on the dance floor and I must find someone to partner her."

The marchioness all but danced over to the Regent and whispered something to him.

"Of course, my lady!" The prince took her hand and kissed it with enthusiasm. "Meryon, the marchioness tells me that you are an exceptional dancer. Partner the Signora and show us how it is done." He took another long drink of brandy, which was undoubtedly the fuel for his creativity, and named four other couples to join the rest on the floor.

Meryon set his glass down and wondered what devilment was afoot that would bring the two of them together again, this time in a place as public as their first two meetings were private.

ELENA SMILED, THOUGH what she really wanted was to run from the room. Her father's reaction had unnerved her and though she had known that seeing Meryon again was inevitable, it only added to her uncertainty, especially when she was sure that the duke wanted to dance the waltz with her as much as he wanted marzipan for breakfast. With William's warning racing through her head, she would now think twice about every gesture he made. And the handkerchief. What must he think of that?

Meryon came to her without demur. If she ever needed proof that he was a gentleman then this was the incident she would cite. He bowed and offered his hand with as much civility as he had promised, as if they had never met, kissed, argued. It helped steady her some.

"While I was in France last year," he said, sounding like a tutor preparing a student for a lesson, "I observed that the French dance the waltz with more intimacy than the English. I imagine the Italians do as well."

Elena curtsied and rose. "Yes, but I have only danced it once or twice, and only with my husband."

"It will remind you of him." He spoke with some

certainty and before she could answer he added, "I apologize for the prince's thoughtlessness."

"Oh no, not at all, Your Grace." Dancing was the least of the memories she treasured. "It is only that I am not very experienced."

He smiled a little and Elena wished she had chosen a different word.

"The prince is busy with his matchmaking." The duke glanced toward the head table. "I think it will be a few minutes before we begin."

She followed his gaze and saw one of the royals arguing with his brother over whom he should partner.

"Your Grace," she began and then the words came tumbling out, "my ward, Mia Castellano, the girl who was with me today—she borrowed my handkerchief and then left it in your coach. Her governess has been filling her head with all sorts of nonsense about how to attract a gentleman. I apologize for her behavior. She is young and inclined to romantic fancies." *Stop, Elena,* she commanded herself. *Stop babbling.*

"Your handkerchief." Meryon looked intrigued but sounded as though he knew nothing about the item. "In my coach. If I find it I'll be sure to send it back."

"You did not find it?" Elena closed her eyes, mortified. Now he would think she was a fool.

"No, not that I know of," he said slowly, "but I will have the groom look for it."

"Thank you." And then the words tumbled out again. "As embarrassing as it is to explain something like that, I am relieved that you did not find it. I would never want you to think I would resort to such trickery to claim your attention." *There,* she thought, *please let that be the end of it.*

"No such trickery is necessary." He stopped her heart with his smile. "Some generous angel has given me a second chance, Signora Verano." He bowed to her a little. "I would very much like to know how you *would* signal interest in a gentleman's attentions."

"I want no one's attentions, Your Grace." *Especially yours.*

"Now, you see, I cannot tell if that is an honest protestation or flirting."

"I hate flirting." She did not raise her voice, but the effort to keep her voice down made her words sound more fervent than she intended. At least no one was paying any attention to them. They were all watching the bickering at the prince's table.

"I rather like flirting," he countered. "I think of it as an invitation designed to protect one's own interests."

"I hate it," she insisted, sounding to her own ears like a child refusing a treat. She wanted more than anything to leave the room. Which *would* attract attention.

"As long as you do not hate me, signora."

Oh, she thought, *this is awful.* He did not realize that he was flirting with his worst enemy's daughter. "You are being quite unfair, Your Grace. I find this an unpleasant conversation but I cannot leave the floor without causing gossip."

"My apologies, Signora Verano." Surprise replaced his teasing tone. Surprise and a small glint of bafflement at her distress.

And I still have to dance with him.

"I only wanted to—" The duke stopped, regained his usual air of command, and went on. "I will change the subject and tell you how impressed I was with the way you responded to the Duke of Bendas's rudeness, over something as simple as your choice of song."

"Oh please, don't," she whispered. That awful moment. She should never have chosen that song. It was an arrogant gesture and Bendas had paid her back. She could feel tears well.

"Signora?" He spoke as though she was about to faint. "I am sorry."

Elena heard the shock in his voice even though he whispered the apology. "I never meant to upset you. Please, I can tolerate tears but not when I cause them. You handled him so well I thought his behavior did not matter to you. Here, take this."

He handed her a handkerchief, her handkerchief.

"You did find it." She grabbed it from him, her need to cry evaporating.

"Yes." His embarrassment was rueful. "I thought I would keep it as a souvenir of a beautiful woman whom I wished to know better, but I think you need the distraction more than I need the memento."

"Thank you, Your Grace." She tucked the handkerchief away, wondering if he was telling the truth. He wanted to keep her handkerchief. It had the ring of one of Mia's novels, but charmed her nonetheless.

The silence between them lengthened until the duke whispered, "I will say nothing else. It is as my brother-in-law warned me earlier. When dealing with a beautiful woman I will have to apologize more often than is good for my pride."

She smiled at the absurdity of a duke with wounded pride.

"But Garrett assures me that every apology is worth the effort, for my interest in you is a sign that I am done with grief and a man fully alive once again."

He waited. Yes, he was fully alive and seemed to have the same effect on every inch of her body even if her mind insisted it was a mistake. "It is not wise for me to be interested in you." She took a small step back to add action to her words.

He laughed loud enough to attract the interest of the people closest to them. "Of course it is unwise. Surely, Lord William has warned you against me. There is no love lost between me and his grandfather."

Aware that a few of the party watched them she tried to smile when she answered. "If I say he has mentioned your, uhm, 'thirst for justice' was how Lord William phrased it, then you will think that all we do is gossip about you." Her smile grew more genuine at his pleased expression though she had no idea why he should be happy about that comment. "If I say, 'No, we have not talked about the issue,' I would be telling a lie."

"I am relieved to know that the viscount sees it as a fight for justice. I will leave it at that. But it verifies that the respect I have for Lord William is well placed."

In spite of his name being Bendasbrook, Elena thought.

The duke went on without a breath. "Miss Castellano's English has certainly benefited from her language lessons with Lord William."

Was he suggesting that they were practicing something other than language? She worried about that every
time the two of them were together.

"His Italian has as well."

"They are two very passionate people." He spoke as
though he knew what he was talking about. "And you
know as well as I do that passion can overwhelm wisdom
in a heartbeat."

"Then passion is a kind of insanity we should both
avoid."

"Oh, but my dear lady, it is not always a choice."

His grin beguiled her and as the orchestra finally
struck a chord she closed her eyes, reminding herself that
she did have a choice.

"I am dancing with you because the Regent suggested
it," Elena said as she put her left hand on Meryon's shoulder, as his left hand lightly touched her waist. He wore
gloves so she could feel strength, but not anything more
personal. It was quite enough.

"And I thought that you never told a lie," he said as
she put her right hand in his left.

They stood as far apart as their arms would allow and
looked each other in the eyes as the music began. His
smile made up for the distance that separated them.

The violins played an introduction and when the orchestra joined in Meryon led her into the first steps. He
was so assured, so at ease on the dance floor that she relaxed, felt as one with him dancing as she would in an embrace. In less than a minute she surrendered her worries,
closed her eyes, and let the moment be the sum of her
world. It was a little bit of paradise.

"You truly can dance well." She forced herself to speak when the main theme repeated, reminding herself that they were not alone. She could easily imagine what The Gossips would make of it if they saw her with her eyes closed and a smile of such pleasure. It hardly mattered that it would be the truth. "Not that I am surprised."

"Thank you, but it is easy with a partner as graceful as you are."

"Oh, that is a lovely compliment, Your Grace. I can keep time to the music, naturally, but you are the master here. It's as though the music is part of you."

He opened his mouth to deny it, and then his expression changed to agreement. "I suppose it does. I guess everyone does not feel the music echo in them this way." He spoke as though he only that moment realized it. "I always thought I liked the waltz because it reminds me of the footwork one uses in fencing, but dozens of men fence and most hate the waltz."

They did not talk for a moment. She let the music surround her again, surround them, and wished they had no past to cloud the moment.

He guided her away from one of the other couples with the slightest pressure on her shoulder. "It is amazing how much we know about each other and we still have not been formally introduced."

"I suspect there is a reason that people do not begin their acquaintances in dark rooms." When he smiled at her, she almost stumbled.

"There are more reasons than one not to meet in a darkened room, signora. But I know what you mean. We knew too much of each other before trust was a part of the friendship."

She did not answer him, and shifted her gaze from his eyes, trying to decide if she trusted him now.

"I trust you, signora. I apologize for the other night. I did not understand what you understood from the first. That I came to call for more than one reason." As the duke spoke his gaze dropped to her lips. She would have stopped dancing and stood still but he had more presence of mind and kept them moving around the floor. Meryon did not press her closer, he did not do anything more than raise his eyes to hers. *I want you.*

He did not speak the words and it could have been that she saw it because it was the truth she'd asked for last time.

He smiled, that utterly captivating smile that was as intimate as the dance they shared, and she knew she was not wrong. He wanted more than to dance with her.

"We are adults. That means we should be able to speak of such things as passion without embarrassment. Is that what you wish, Your Grace? To speak of passion."

"Elena," he said in a voice that burned with ardor. "Passion does not require words."

When she had no ready answer for that truth, he went on.

"If we were anywhere but here I swear I would kiss you."

Her lips tingled and a thrill raced through her, a shiver of heat that settled in her breasts and belly, and lower where she could feel her body dampen with longing. As quickly she was afraid and she stiffened a little in an effort to subdue the yearning.

"I will wait for you to trust me, Elena." Meryon loosened his hold as he spoke. "But I warn you, my brother-in-law laughed at me when I told him I could be patient."

He let go of her waist and, still holding on to her hand, stepped back and bowed to her. Oh, the dance was over. She was completely distracted, had not even heard the music end. How could he be so in control when he had quite shamelessly seduced her on the dance floor?

The group observing applauded all the dancers and Meryon escorted her to the prince, who was waving at them to come closer.

As they reached him, Meryon bowed again and whispered, "That was my pleasure, and the word was never more truly meant." He smiled at her, that true from-the-heart smile, and she blushed.

The prince called out, "You must teach me how to dance like that."

13

MERYON FOUND MAGDA asleep under his bed. At five in the morning, she had the right idea. He needed no more than Magda's welcoming "woof," but she crept out, stretched, then leaned against his leg. She looked up at him with eyes that begged him to tell her about his evening.

"You would not think teaching a prince to waltz in the French manner could be so exhausting. I can only imagine how well he will sleep tonight."

Meryon sat on the settee and Magda jumped onto the chair across from him, her head on her paws her only concession to her wish for sleep.

"If you know the answer to this I will personally escort you back under the bed." He downed the wine left on the table. "I must find out how to have a discreet affair."

Since Blix had not read his mind and come to pour more wine, Meryon stood up and helped himself.

"It's damned embarrassing to admit that I have been among society for more than twenty years and have no idea how to keep that kind of secret." He sipped the wine, decided he'd had too much too fast, and set the glass on the table at hand. "It would only be a matter of time before someone found us out. It is so common an occurrence I cannot see what that would matter." Of course, Signora Verano might think differently.

Before Magda could offer any sniffs of approval, or disapproval, Blix came into the room. He looked well rested and ready for the day when Meryon's evening was ending. Magda slipped under the bed and Blix made short work of helping the duke into his nightclothes.

As Meryon fell asleep it occurred to him that while he might not have the slightest idea how to conduct a clandestine affair, he did know how to care for a mistress. The house on nearby St. German Street had served him well in the past. It had an ambience he had always enjoyed. Small and snug, rather like a hiding place to which only he had the key.

If Elena came to him as his mistress he would know exactly how to behave, how to make her happy, and he would be able to see her as often as he wished.

Meryon dreamed of her, not at this house, or the one on St. German, but at the house in Richmond.

As he escorted her up the steps he told her a secret. How unlike him. He loved this house most of all the twelve that were part of his estate.

In Richmond, he could keep the demands of London

at a distance and remind himself of England, the island of lush green fields, rolling hills. The land sustained him body and soul.

His dream Elena smiled and raised a hand to cup his cheek. She kissed the corner of his mouth as though the taste of him could sustain her.

As they proceeded from one bedchamber to another, he insisted that she look out the window of each. From one she could see the way the lawn swept down to the river. From another the way his father had planted trees and gardens to tease the eye. From yet another, the fountain that he claimed as his favorite.

Even though he thought he would go mad if he did not kiss her, he kept on talking about the place, how it made him happy, that more than one difficult political problem had been resolved here at the table after a day on the river and a sumptuous dinner.

Elena pushed open the window and the melody of a country afternoon filled the silence. Birdsong, leaves rustling in the breeze, the sound of gardeners some long way off, insects buzzing, and her light laughter as she leaned back against him.

He pressed a kiss to the spot behind her ear, the skin smooth and pale and smelling of roses.

She turned in his arms, took his face in her hands, and kissed him. Her mouth. His thinking ended there as lust overwhelmed him.

Her lips and tongue enslaved him, filled him with such a hunger that if she stopped he was ready to beg at her feet for more. Stripped of power, he wanted nothing but what she wanted.

Elena ended the kiss as he struggled to gain some control, to show her that he was the answer. Magda's barking woke him up before he could convince her that he was all the lover she would ever need.

Meryon did not move, could not, still trapped in the mindlessness of that kiss. He realized that a new maid had come to start the fire, not the one who understood that she must coax Magda out from under the bed before she began her usual chores.

Even though he had left orders for the fire to be started at noon, Meryon pretended to sleep through her bothered whispers. When she left with the dog and the chamber pot he dozed into a much more satisfying reverie, one that he could orchestrate from that part of his mind that knew this was a dream.

He kissed Elena and left her whimpering with frustration. She agreed to be his mistress with an eagerness that was another valued quality of the Italian.

After that, they shared as erotic a coupling as his mind could conjure. He found it far more satisfying than the custom of drinking a toast to the arrangement, and more of a commitment. Once they were bound by sex, they were bound together in the way that mattered most.

MERYON STAYED ABED until he heard Blix in the dressing room. The butler handed him the list of appointments, which he did not need, not today.

He would give Parliament a miss, an impulse grown

from a brilliant idea that popped into his head upon waking the second time. He sat at his desk, before his breakfast, and wrote an invitation. He had a boy run it to Bloomsbury, asking if Signora Verano would ride with him in the park at five o'clock.

He tried to read Ricardo's *Principles of Political Economy* but his mind kept drifting back to the invitation. When he began to worry that Signora Verano had accepted an invitation ahead of his, Meryon decided that he must find a distraction unless he *wanted* to act like a lovesick fool.

Garrett was off at his meeting with Mrs. Wilson and would surely have a tale to tell, but in the meantime Meryon would spend some time with the children. They always distracted him quite delightfully.

Rexton was flattering in his welcome.

"Papa! Papa!" He jumped up from his seat at the study table and ran to grab his father around the waist in a ten-year-old's version of a hug.

Meryon bent over to lift him up and return the hug. Rexton's tutor leaped to his feet, much abashed at the boy's informality. The duke shook his head and held the boy a moment longer.

"My lord," the tutor used his teacher's voice to address Rexton, "since we are working with globes today why not ask the duke, your father, to show you where he has traveled?"

The boy wriggled out of his father's hold and took his hand, leading him to a chair. The globe was on the table between them.

Rexton loved every minute of it, and the duke had to

admit that his son might look like his mother but had his own way of expressing interest that was all boy. When they had exhausted every possible avenue of questioning from "What do Spaniards eat?" to "How big was the ship that took you to Greece?" Rexton insisted that his father watch Alicia walk.

They found the little girl in the day nursery with the nurse. Both were delighted to exhibit Alicia's walking skills. It was hardly a relaxing interlude, unnerved as Meryon was by the uncertain steps that still outnumbered the confident ones. She had mastered falling on her bottom without harm and waved her hands with delight when everyone laughed as she plopped onto the carpet. By the time he left them he felt as old as the stone of Pennford Castle.

Rexton must have been coached by his tutor. As he said good-bye, he bowed to his father and thanked him for coming. Then he illustrated that he was still a child when he made the duke promise "to show me all the treasures you brought back from your trips when we go to Pennford."

Meryon worked his way down the stairs and along the halls back to his study, mentally listing what those treasures would include. There were one or two books of erotic drawings that no child should see. It was all Elena Verano's fault that those were the first items to pop into his mind.

When he reached his study, he hoped to find an answer to his invitation. No envelope sat on his desk, but Garrett had returned from his mission.

"Tell me what you found." Meryon sat on the sofa and invited Garrett to sit across from him.

"First, Your Grace, the visit to young Wilson's mother reminded me rather uncomfortably of the scouting missions I undertook when I lived in France."

Magda came out from under his desk and sat near Garrett, who reached down to play with her ears.

"That possibility never occurred to me." The reverend did not care for the reminder, Meryon realized, as Magda cuddled closer to Garrett. "I will not ask you to do something like that again."

"Thank you, Your Grace."

He bowed from the neck and Meryon recognized that this man carried old wounds that might never heal. Magda jumped onto the sofa and settled beside Garrett. Rowena's dog knew how to comfort better than he ever could, Meryon thought.

"Mrs. Wilson is managing well enough without Mr. Wilson. She has a new baby girl, who appears sickly, and a boy of about two. Alan is actually fourteen years old."

"Small for his age."

"Yes." Garrett looked off for a moment. "His mother appears well fed and very healthy. The two-year-old has the round eyes of a child who does not have enough to eat. The babe is too young to do more than cry, which she did most of the time. Alan would try to shush her, all the while glancing at his mother. I do believe that young Alan is a great help with the other two and is severely disciplined when he is not."

Garrett shook his head and Meryon could see his upset, but did not comment.

"I told the boy and his mother, as you instructed, that when he comes tomorrow there will be work for him in the stable. He seemed pleased, so pleased that he came back with me to talk to the head groom. He rode on the top with the coachman, but John Coachman reports the boy did not say a word."

"Afraid of a cuff on the cheek, I expect."

"Yes, I think his mother is a bully."

"And that bothers you most of all."

"Meryon, I can think of few things worse than being under the control of someone who takes pleasure in showing their power." Garrett ran his hand through his hair and let out a huff of breath. "I think Mrs. Wilson's husband ran away. He may be looking for work up north, but I do not think she will ever see him again."

"I hope that what the boy earns here keeps him honest." Meryon stood up. What Garrett told him confirmed his decision. "I want him to be my tiger. I will take the cabriolet out today and use one of the other grooms as tiger, but as soon as he is vetted by the head groom and the coachman I want him to serve me there. I'll speak with the head groom myself."

"I would not swear him honest, Meryon. If his mother tells him to steal he will, though I think it's Magda the boy covets most of all."

"He is welcome to take her to the park when his work schedule permits. Rexton often takes Magda with him when he and his tutor go out, but I cannot imagine the dog complaining about too much rolling about on the grass."

Garrett agreed and excused himself as he had several

errands to perform if he wished to remain in his wife's good graces.

Meryon sat at the desk and rearranged every piece of paper on it, wondering if the maid who cleaned might have misplaced the response he waited for. When every piece of paper had been scrutinized, organized, and carefully stacked, and still no reply appeared, Meryon decided that he would call on her personally. He sent for the coach and found Alan Wilson riding in the box with the coachman.

John Coachman insisted that the boy needed to learn the city from his vantage point. It was such a weak explanation that Meryon had no doubt that Wilson had somehow nagged John Coachman into letting him come along.

The coach wound its way to Bloomsbury without mishap, though it seemed to take longer than usual.

"Somebody is talking up the crowds, Your Grace," John Coachman explained. The old man did not have to add, *And no good will come of that.*

Meryon put down the papers he had been reading and watched the groups spill by. Men and women, a surprising number of young men and boys. He wished he knew someone who would fit in, who could listen and report back whatever it was that would attract such a sizeable number of people in the middle of the day. The ragtag end of the group passed by, laughing and taunting one another, ready to break into a fight at the first temptation.

They kept to the side of the road, more interested in themselves than in the conveyances passing them, but no sooner had they gone by when some way behind Meryon a firecracker exploded, then another, closer. The carriage rocked and a third exploded, closer still.

Too close for comfort, he thought, just as the carriage lurched forward. He braced himself with a hand on the wall, annoyed he did not have the reins, but the carriage steadied quickly. Thank God Signora Verano was not with him. The first good thing to come from her refusal.

The boy, John Coachman, the horses. Any one of them could be injured. The idiot troublemakers would pay for their prank if there was so much as a splinter. Meryon kicked open the door and jumped out before the two grooms who rode at the back reached the front of the carriage.

The footmen calmed the horses while John Coachman held the reins. Alan Wilson stood in the well with the coachman, looking nonplussed at all the commotion.

"You could have lost a hand," Coachman shouted. "Then you'd be no good to the duke."

"Better to lose a hand than have the horses bolt and break a leg," the boy answered, with such calm one would have thought he tossed firecrackers every day.

When Coachman saw the duke he bowed. "Someone threw a firecracker and the wind blew it up here. Wilson caught it and tossed it up into the air." Coachman shuddered at the near disaster.

"Heroic, Mr. Wilson." Meryon climbed up so he was eye level with the two on the seat, though he did not climb into the box. So Wilson was his guardian angel after all. "Did you see who threw it?"

"No, sir, Your Grace. I smelled it and knew it for trouble." The boy's calm disappeared as he realized he was the center of attention. "It was easy enough to catch and toss it up so it wouldn't bedevil the horses."

"The horses." Meryon bit back a smile. "I think you like animals more than people, Wilson."

"Most times I do," he admitted without apology.

"Which is why you started work a day early. Coachman, be sure he has some supper before he goes home." Meryon jumped down easily and went forward to see to the horses. The grooms were well trained and he stood to the side, arms folded, and let them do their work.

It took another few minutes before the horses were calm enough to move on. The other conveyances moved around them, their horses not at all upset, but then as Wilson pointed out, they were so old they were all probably deaf.

So much the better, Meryon thought, or someone would surely have been killed in the melee.

Meryon sat deep inside the carriage where he could not be seen as he considered the ramifications of what had occurred. Disaster avoided, yes, but it appeared that the crowds grew bolder or attracted toublemakers.

Their presence reminded him of the prizefights he'd attended with David. You could always find a group of scalawags mixed in with the gentlemen and country gentry. Those good-for-nothings only cared about fighting with each other or, at worst, picking pockets. If the city crowd attracted the same sort, worry was misplaced. But if they were the extreme of the political sort, then he would have to report it. He needed to know.

A few houses down from the Signora's he knocked on the roof and called for Alan Wilson. "In the coach."

Wilson climbed up and in with some hesitation and Meryon wondered how long it would take the boy to trust him. He did not seem any more impressed with his ducal rank than Signora Verano, and as it was with her, he would have to earn the trust. How odd that the two, so different, should see him the same way. Well, almost the same way.

"That crowd that went by before."

"Close to a mob, they were," the boy corrected.

"I want you to follow that mob and tell me what they are talking about. Mix in the front, the middle, and the last stragglers."

"Why?" Narrow-eyed suspicion demanded the truth. It would take this one a while to learn not to question orders.

"I need to know if those firecrackers were a lark or something one step up from a riot."

The boy nodded as if that explanation made sense.

"Taking me from the horses will cost you, Your Grace. I'm in training and time away will earn me a beating."

"Not from anyone in my stable. We had a problem with that last year and I dismissed them all. This head groom knows how to treat the lads."

"Not from him." Wilson spoke as though the duke was no more than a stupid girl. "From my mum."

"Do not tell her, Wilson," Meryon said, stating the obvious.

"I told you, she can smell a lie."

"Yes, you did." His words were thoughtful. "In that case I think you should live in for this first week. You will learn the details of life in the mews and how I want work done. Tell your mother it is one less mouth to feed."

"Yes, sir, Your Grace." The boy's smile welcomed him to the world of subterfuge.

Meryon pulled out a coin. "Report to me after the session tomorrow, and take this to your mother tonight. Tell her that I gave it to you for preventing an accident. That's the God's honest truth."

"Yes, sir, Your Grace."

The boy popped open the door, climbed up to speak to John Coachman, and leapt back to the ground, moving off at a slow run, heading toward Russell Square.

Meryon watched him go, confident that Alan Wilson could handle the situation better than anyone else he knew, except perhaps his brother-in-law. Now if only he was as sure that the boy would bring back the truth.

14

THE KNOCKER WAS OUT on Signora Verano's door. With a word to his coachman, Meryon climbed out of his carriage and raised the brass harp and let it fall with a satisfying thunk.

As the servant showed him into the blue salon Meryon realized that the last time he had come here he had been in a significantly different frame of mind. If he recalled the event, certainly Elena did too.

If he had any understanding of female sensibilities, an apology would have to come before anything else. He would think that the waltz had resolved any such disagreement, but she already thought his rank equaled arrogance and an apology could not possibly make things worse.

Signora Verano wore a round gown, its leaf green color accentuated by the leaves embroidered around the neckline. Even though her attire was informal she still

looked every bit as appealing as she had when dressed for
the Regent. Meryon most definitely wanted her company,
and not only in the park.

He bowed to her with dignity and then took one step
closer. "This morning I sent a note inviting you to ride
with me in the park today. Shortly after I had it delivered,
however, I realized that it was presumptuous of me to
think that our chance meeting at the draper's and our
brief time together last night, dancing the waltz, provided
sufficient apology for my churlish ill manners the last time
we were in this room."

Her long silence made him feel like a fool. He thought
that a well-crafted apology, despite the fact he had made it
up on the spot.

Finally she pursed her lips and then spoke. "Thank
you for the invitation, Your Grace. I am sorry that I am
not free for a ride in the park until next Wednesday, but
I would be delighted to accept for that date if you are
free?"

"Next Wednesday. Yes, that would suit me, except
that it is almost a week and too long to be without your
company." He waited to see if she would explain why her
acceptance sounded so reluctant. Why she showed no
pleasure at the invitation.

She walked over to the same painting by Canaletto
that had bemused her before.

"I should have brought flowers." He announced it deliberately to distract her from the painting. "Flowers are an
essential part of any expression of regret."

"Do you think so?" Elena abandoned the painting

and her indecision had disappeared. "I think sincerity is the most important part of an apology, which I might add I have not heard from you yet. You acknowledged the need for one but have yet to say the words."

He stilled, then inclined his head, more irritated than contrite. Schooling his voice, he tried for the tone he used when he had had to apologize to his tutor, a tone he had not used for twenty years. "Please accept my apologies for the disgraceful way I spoke to you at our meeting in this room. I do regret it most sincerely." He paused. "Are you satisfied with that?"

"No," she said, laughing as if she enjoyed his discomfiture. "If you were truly sorry, Your Grace, you would have sent me a letter of apology, waited a day or so, and then invited me to go for a drive with you. This apology seems to be born of necessity and nothing more."

"You look for insults where none are intended, signora." Now he recalled that he had also been very annoyed the other night. He had forgotten. "Listen to me."

Meryon crossed the room so that she could feel as much as hear what he had to say. "Last night, after we danced together, I admitted to myself that I wanted to see you again as soon as possible."

The laughter in Elena's eyes disappeared, but the softness was even more endearing.

"Signora, attraction is too tame a word for what I feel when I am near you."

"Oh, thank you." She put her hands together, her smile one of pure joy. "For a moment I regretted accepting your invitation, but when I catch a glimpse of your heart

I know there is nothing I want more than to know you better."

Instead of coming even closer to him, of inviting his kiss, a look of regret replaced the smile and she stepped back, as though two steps would make her less a temptation.

"I look forward to seeing you next week, Your Grace, but I am to have a music lesson and do not wish to keep Signor Ponto waiting any longer. If you will excuse me."

"Of course." He bowed once again.

She escorted him to the door and waved to him as his carriage drew away. Halfway to Penn House Meryon recalled one of Garrett's oft-repeated beliefs. "The brain and the body are too often in conflict. It is man's greatest burden." How could he have been married to someone as accommodating as Rowena and find this mercurial woman so attractive?

Elena Verano liked to argue. What he could not decide was whether that added to her appeal or not.

MERYON FOUND HIMSELF too easily distracted by even the most inane reminder of Elena Verano. The odd accent of one of Garrett's callers, the tune that one of the maids hummed as she wiped down the marble in the hall. By the time he arrived at the House of Lords he longed for a spirited debate even on the same tired subjects. He hoped today would be the final discussion and reading on the indemnity bill. Once passed, the bill would put to rest any liability for arrests made during the suspension of habeas corpus.

Lord Gilbert stood to speak for the Tories. His usually rambling style was noticeably absent, though he repeated various aspects of his point at least seven times. Meryon listened the first time and the second time watched the response of his peers.

"England's greatness is built on the yeoman stock, on the families that nurture our youth, from the downs of Sussex to the heights of Northumberland. It will be so forever. The land provides what the family needs and the city destroys it. Our wealth is in the land and what it nurtures. It is like a mother whose milk nurses her child."

Children. Elena Verano never mentioned any—though miscarriage or childhood death were hardly the subject of social conversation.

A group of Tories cheered something the man said and he made himself pay attention again.

"It is the country we must protect in order to protect the family."

More approval. Meryon counted heads. Not a one was in favor of change. They did not seem to appreciate what he had learned from David and Garrett, that change was coming whether they were in favor of it or not. Did it mean something that not a one of Gilbert's supporters was under fifty?

"The city is a lair of hatred and discord and temptation. Without the calming mien of their wives and families, men are given to drink, debauchery, and conduct that threatens all, even the law-abiding, the innocent."

He would wager that London did not compare to the drink and debauchery in Rome or Milan or, God help them, Venice. He'd always assumed that the Veranos had lived in Rome. Or had she told him? Rome, he was sure of it.

"Family is the foundation of our greatness."

When Meryon looked up to measure Kyle's reaction, he found his passionate Whig friend with his arms crossed and disgust written all over his face.

He had counted Kyle a friend since Oxford. You would think he would understand an impassioned personality, but he could hardly challenge Signora Verano to a fencing match or a round at Jackson's, which always seemed the most practical way to even out Kyle's temper.

He endured the rest of the speech by thinking of a way to "even out" Signora Verano's, most of which involved a bed. He dearly hoped he would be lucky enough to see her at some social event in between now and next week. He could have Roland check the invitations and see which she would most likely attend.

He found Kyle waiting outside the building. The rain had let up some but Kyle ignored it and the umbrella that Meryon's groom met him with.

"What are you going to do?" Kyle demanded as though he himself were the duke.

Meryon remembered how frustrated he had been when he was confined to the gallery and his father had not spoken forcefully enough on an issue or had allowed himself to be swayed from a chosen position.

"Damn it, Meryon, you see what they're trying to do, don't you?"

"Yes," he said calmly. "It suits me perfectly." Kyle always rose to the bait.

"It suits you!" Kyle's temper was closer to bursting.

"Yes, the idea that family is the heart and soul of England runs parallel to the idea that we must take care of those families who have lost their wage earner. Just as we take care of our mad king and his unmarried daughters."

"Yes, yes, but what are you going to do?"

"I think I will make up a party to attend Georges's play. Garrett met him and I should like to see what all the fuss is about."

Kyle punched him in the arm.

"Kyle." Meryon stepped out of the range of his fist, brushing his arm as though Kyle's swipe had left dirt. "I will meet you at Angelo's at noon tomorrow so you can vent your anger with a sword. As for Parliament, I will bide my time, and speak when I think it will do the most good."

"My apologies for assaulting you, Meryon." Kyle put his hands on his waist and blew out a breath that was filled with frustration. "I plan to find a hell and lose as much money as possible."

Meryon waited for the coachman to lower the steps. "Tomorrow at noon at Angelo's."

Kyle raised a hand in agreement.

"And remember, Kyle," Meryon called to him, "a night of debauchery is no excuse to absent yourself!"

Alan Wilson waited for him by the carriage, opened the door, and at Meryon's invitation climbed in, bringing a dose of wet with him.

"My mother thanks you for taking such good care of me."

"Does she. I think you lie, Mr. Wilson. I think she ranted and raged over who would take care of her while you waited on the quality. But she let you come because you gave her the coin and promised there would be more."

The boy straightened, looking more afraid than impressed.

"Your mother is not the only one who can tell lie from truth," Meryon explained. In fact he knew more than one petty tyrant and their methods were always the same. "Tell me what you learned among the crowd."

"Nothing much." Wilson cleared his throat and wiped his nose with his sleeve. "At the front they talked about how we need change. They could not agree on what kind. Finally one shouted that the way they were talking nothing would ever be done."

Not unlike Parliament, Meryon thought, but with a different kind of power, the power to riot at the least, to lead rebellion at the worst.

"The middle crowd was all spread out. Men and women, some with children. I guess they were out of work and looking for some fun."

"A good observation, Mr. Wilson."

"The last of them, like the ones that threw the firecracker, they were looking for trouble or a quick bit of cash, pickpockets and the like."

"I imagine there were some familiar faces there." Meryon tried for a conversational tone.

"One or two. They wanted me to come along but I told them that I have a regular job working with horses.

I didn't tell them who I worked for, sir, Your Grace. I never will."

Time would tell on that score, Meryon thought. He could not doubt the boy's sincerity at the moment. He hoped that well-fed and warm would make up for the long days Wilson spent at someone else's beck and call.

It could be the crowd—hardly a mob, despite Wilson's expertise—had moved into the Bloomsbury neighborhood or lived in service there.

As for what Wilson had reported, it sounded innocent enough. No threat to Elena Verano or her household for now.

Next time, for surely there would be a next time, he would find out what interests led the group. Talking to them personally might make a difference, though there was the distinct possibility that the difference would make things worse instead of better.

He could send the Signora a note suggesting caution but thought a word to Lord William might be more wise. He called often enough and, as much as Meryon hated to admit it, Elena would listen to Lord William and only argue with a duke. Her safety mattered more to him than his vanity.

WITH THE PROMISE of the owner's box at the theater, Meryon ate a hurried dinner while reading through letters from his man of business and his brother detailing the efforts to unearth information on some of the more scurrilous stories involving the Duke of Bendas. There proved to be no truth to the rumor that he had attempted to trade his grandson for a healthier child. Lord William's parents had been fiercely protective of their son.

Yes, he had dismissed a housemaid when she had made too much noise coming into his room one morning, but there must be a dozen other members of the ton who would sympathize with that. There was no truth to the story that he had beaten a stable boy to death when he had taken too long bringing his horse around, but it was true that he had ordered his carriage to go on when it had struck a man who had stepped into its path.

The most damning of all was Bendas's general lack of concern for anyone beneath him. The idea that the world lived to satisfy his wants and needs. Another cartoon would tarnish his image a little more, but Meryon knew he had to find something that would set the seal on Bendas so justice would be served.

Meryon found Blix in the dressing room fussing over a waistcoat. Waving approval at the dark green, Meryon thought about his week thus far. There was the usual: time in the House of Lords, reading the mail. And the unusual: hiring a servant himself, spying on a crowd.

Signora Verano fell into a class all by herself. As a matter of fact she had made herself very comfortable in a sizeable portion of his mind, so that she would pop into his head in regard to almost any subject he considered.

She was unique in her aggravating conversation today and every other day, so that it seemed as though she was the one in charge.

Except on the dance floor. He would have to meet her

there more often. He had walked out of her house feeling mightily uncomfortable at her insistence that everything run her way. His imagination played with who would have control in bed. He did not know the answer, but Meryon did know that it would be a pleasure to find out.

15

EVERY BOX WAS FILLED to capacity and the pit was as crowded. Meryon made his way to the owner's box and wondered how Garrett had managed such a coup. They arrived only a few moments before the curtain and Meryon scanned the boxes for familiar faces. He found, to his pleased surprise, Signora Verano with her ward and Lord William. He bowed his head when Lord William saw him and Elena nodded back, with a quiet smile.

"Good evening, ladies and gentlemen."

Georges was a good-looking man despite the way life had marked him. Not with scars, but with lines of worry that were carved in deep creases on his face. He was not worried now. He bowed to the owner's box, his eyes on his ducal guest, before he continued his introduction.

"This evening I will present to you, as usual, three vignettes on one theme. Tonight's theme is greed and pride.

All of these vignettes are fiction and every one of them is the truth."

The crowd settled, unusually quiet. The first piece took the audience to France during the Revolution. A duplicitous maid was eager to condemn her mistress, a comtesse, so that she could claim her employer's clothes and jewels. The former maid suffers the guillotine when her pride kept her from admitting her humble origins until it was too late.

The audience applauded with gusto, sure that her downfall was her greed as well as her pride.

Meryon watched Elena watch the play. She seemed to lose herself completely in the story, going so far as to cover her eyes when the blade of the guillotine dropped. He wished he were next to her to give her comfort, instead of teasing her as Lord William appeared to be.

The second vignette concerned a prideful man with a beautiful wife. At first the woman was pleased as could be to make such a fine match and flounced out of her house when her widowed mother protested the match.

The man was enchanted with his bride and showed her to all his friends, who were jealous and lustful by turns.

In time he enslaved his wife with his kisses. More often than not, there was a look of desperation in her eyes, beneath a false smile.

Elena watched this piece with her hands over her mouth.

Trapped in a nightmare marriage, the heroine of the piece decided to run away, going back home to find that her mother had died. Her husband found her there and she pleaded with him to take her back. He did, but the final scene left little doubt that her life would be even worse now.

The intermission was called and the audience buzzed with excitement. The sexual overtones of the second piece were shocking. And exciting. Meryon had no doubt there were any number of women of the ton who would trade pride for pleasure.

Like the rest of the ton, Meryon and Garrett left their box and mixed with their acquaintances in the passage. They came upon Lord William's group as Miss Castellano was asking if anyone knew Georges.

Garrett launched into a story of his connection with the new playwright. Within a minute it was clear that his story was as much a piece of comic fiction as anything on the stage.

Meryon offered Elena his arm. She accepted his escort with alacrity and they proceeded from group to group of acquaintances exchanging comments about the show. He did not think they had ever been so comfortable with each other before. Her hand lay in the crook of his arm and he could not feel one bit of tension but rather a connection.

When one of the women began to speculate on which actress was Georges's current mistress, Elena did not have to say a word for him to know that she would prefer to move on, until they found a spot that was relatively private.

"Thank you," she whispered, her breath teasing his ear. "There is so much worth talking about, and they can only discuss which actress is the prettiest."

He patted her hand. "When the truth is that not one of them can hold a candle to you."

"Nonsense. They all have youth on their side."

This time he kissed her gloved wrist and felt her fingers curl around his for a moment. "You make youth sound desirable, signora. Tell me you would prefer to be eighteen again and I will not believe it."

"Would you?"

"Never," he said fervently. "I was in constant fear that I would put a foot wrong, make some girl think I was interested when marriage did not appeal to me at all. My father cancelled my Grand Tour because of the unrest in Europe and I did not think I would ever be able to discuss art or music with confidence." He shuddered. "Not eighteen. No."

"I would. It was the year I sang in public for the first time. I knew I would never be good enough to sing on stage, nor would it have been proper, but I found an audience among society in Italy and I was as happy as I had been since—" She stopped and didn't finish the sentence.

"Since . . . ," he encouraged.

She looked down so he could not see her face and shook her head. "I had not been that happy in a very long time."

He kissed her cheek and spoke softly. " 'A complete fool' is the only way to describe someone who would hurt you like that."

She smiled and touched the spot with her hand.

The thought came to him that between one sentence and the next they had moved beyond flirting to the kind of conversation they'd had the first night they met.

"Pride. It was pride that caused it. If that is the theme of these short pieces then my story could be staged as easily as the others." The first bell sounded and they automatically turned around. "That horrible man in the second play was as prideful as the woman," Elena insisted. "Why did he not suffer?"

"In our world men are rarely made to pay for their pride. I do not need to know your experience to know that pride is more often seen as a man's right, and not as arrogance."

The answer might have been honest but it did not please Elena.

"I have heard that some of these stories are ongoing," he went on. "That Georges will do another where the man will face the consequences of his actions."

"I hope so. A man can ruin a woman's life and there is no penalty for it. I wish Georges would allow a woman to write one of his plays."

Meryon laughed. "He is the man of rank in this theater and I do not think his pride will allow it." *Change the subject, Meryon.* "The first piece had a more just resolution and could have featured either a man or a woman."

"Yes," Elena agreed, somewhat mollified. "Lord William saw a version last week in which the servant was a man and the comte insisted he wear his clothes. The servant died despite his protestations of innocence."

"You see that is another lesson we can draw from the first piece tonight. It makes me wonder what would happen if my son traded clothes with my groom."

"Do not say that out loud, Your Grace." Elena raised a

hand to his mouth to stop him from speaking. Her finger-tips barely brushed his lips but his whole body envied the touch. Elena dropped her hand as fast as she had raised it. She let go of his arm, but stayed beside him.

"Mia did it once with her maid and I still have not for-given her. She is as precocious as Lord William. In that I do not think they are well matched, if only because they are so much alike. I suppose they will work that out for themselves. Neither one of them will listen to me."

He recognized the rush of words as a way of covering her embarrassment. Elena had felt the same shock that he had at her touch.

As the final gong sounded they made their way back to her box. He bowed over her hand and strolled back to the owner's box with Garrett, only half listening to what his brother-in-law said. "I wish my sermons would gener-ate half this discussion."

"Hmmm. Yes, I'm sure," Meryon muttered.

"If they did, I could tell them that the days of the dukedom are numbered and I should be their leader."

"Yes." Meryon stopped and tried to replay what Gar-rett had said. "That is total nonsense, Garrett."

"I said that to prove that you can still hear in spite of those lovebirds singing."

Meryon ignored the comment and moved his chair so he could see Elena as well as the stage.

The last piece was a comedy as Meryon expected it would be. But one with a lesson as powerful as that of the other two.

The mayor of a small town in France had a daughter who was her most beautiful when she played the piano.

The mayor was anxious to marry her off to a wealthy man and invited a candidate to dinner even though his daughter did not like him. In retaliation, the daughter deliberately played badly in the wrong key and the would-be suitor, who had very sensitive ears, left shortly thereafter without so much as hinting at interest in the daughter.

Her father was so angry that he moved the pianoforte to the city square and insisted that she play to earn her keep. She was too full of pride to ask for forgiveness and did as he commanded. As the curtain fell, it had begun to rain onstage and a gentleman stopped his carriage to offer her a ride. The girl's father ran after the carriage, realizing that it was not only her pride that had led to her downfall, but his own as well. He was run over by the piano, which had suddenly developed feet and come after him.

As the story unfolded, Meryon saw Elena grow more and more stricken.

She did not laugh at the machinations between the father and daughter, who were too much alike and thus doomed to dissension.

She did not laugh as the daughter played the wrong notes and winced at her own poor performance. He stopped watching the action onstage and kept his eyes on Elena, willing her to look at him, to ignore whatever caused her pain.

When the short play ended with the girl's obvious fall from grace, Elena stood up and left the box precipitously. Lord William and Miss Castellano followed in some confusion.

On impulse, Meryon made to follow her. At that moment, with the last of the applause fading, Georges himself came into their box, and whatever Meryon had hoped to do for Elena was squelched by the requirement of good manners.

Garrett and Georges greeted each other as old friends, which answered one question. Even if his story to William and Miss Castellano of his friendship with Georges had been preposterous, the two knew each other. From the war years; Meryon had no doubt of it.

Georges accepted Meryon's praise with modesty, insisting that storytelling had always appealed to him, and "Is it not fortunate that I have so many stories to tell."

They talked about how he would accommodate the crowds once the Season started, and about the unlikelihood of a visit from the Regent, since too many of the stories would seem to be critical of him. Finally, Georges declined to join them for supper as he had "a lady awaiting my attention."

Garrett was unusually quiet all the way back to Penn House. Meryon welcomed the chance to think through Elena's reaction to the last story. And his as well. He would have done anything to ease her hurt. That she had not once looked at him or sought him out told him that the trust he longed for was still not complete.

TINA! LEAVE ME SOMETHING to wear to the Straemores' this evening," Elena begged. "They did not promise the gowns for today. They were only hopeful."

"Si, signora." Tina spoke with an absentminded air, intent on emptying the clothes press. There was an impressive stack of apparel of all kinds on the nearest chair.

"Wait, wait." Elena walked back into the dressing room. The small space was a complete shambles. Despite the neat piles, it looked like the press had exploded, with bunches of fabric landing everywhere. She pointed to the stack that was almost as tall as Tina. "These are the dresses we are keeping, yes?"

Tina shook her head. "No, signora. They are sadly out-of-date and should be given away. Or perhaps some of the better material can be remade."

"I cannot replace my entire wardrobe. It would cost a fortune and six more trips to the modiste."

"*Cara* signora, you have a fortune. Why not enjoy it?"

One of the more timid housemaids appeared in the door. Tina waved her into the room and ordered her to collect the gowns that were no longer useful.

"Do not take everything. I ordered nothing for a ride in the park."

"What ride? With who?" Tina sounded more like a governess than a maid.

Elena cleared her throat. "On Wednesday, with the duke."

"The duke is taking you up in his carriage!" Tina dropped the clothes and all but leapt for joy. "It will be the perfect way for you to meet more of society."

"Tina! You speak as if that is all the Duke of Meryon is good for. I happen to like him."

"What do you see in him, signora? Or is it that you are trying to prove to yourself that you will never find love so you will not make the effort? For it is clear to me that this duke is not at all worthy of you." She made his title sound like the name of some mangy cur found in the mews.

Tina did not wait for her mistress to try to make sense of her theory.

"I know the perfect dress, signora. The deep violet, the one that has the matching velvet cloak with the fur trim. That wonderful bonnet you found in Paris will be perfect with it. How fortunate it is still cool enough for it. I thought that it would be much too out of style before you had an opportunity to wear it again. Let me find it and make sure it does not need pressing. There may even be time to add another row of ruffles; they are so in fashion now and with your height it would not look as stupid as it does on most women. Now you will need. . . "

Tina hurried back into the dressing room, her monologue continuing no matter that Elena could not hear her. She did not need to. Both of them knew that since her appearance at the Regent's dinner party, Elena's social life had increased significantly, and even with the new gowns she would be hard-pressed to have enough for the entire Season, especially once Mia made her bow and they were out every night.

Elena sat down and began going through the gloves that Tina had directed her to sort. Mia would look wonderful in white but even better in white washed with pink or a pale blue, perhaps with a pattern embroidered around the décolletage since the girl could not yet wear more than a string of pearls or a simple locket. It was easier to think about what colors would suit Mia than to think about her own upcoming ride in the park with the duke.

To be seen driving together was a gesture whose importance had not escaped her. This time no prince had ordered them to dance, nor had they met by accident at the theater.

He had invited her and she had accepted. She knew what would come next. His kiss on her cheek had been such loving consolation. That, coupled with the bolt of desire that had swept through her when she brushed his lips with her fingers, told her that they would be together when the time was right.

The combination of nerves and excitement told her the time was not quite right. Not yet. But every time she saw him, the moment drew closer.

Elena concentrated on the gloves, wondering why she had ever thought yellow was an attractive color to wear on one's hands.

16

THE MARCHIONESS of Straemore tucked her arm
through Meryon's as she escorted him and Garrett into
the large salon on the ground floor. "We see you twice in
one week, Your Grace. What a pleasure. I am sorry to say
we will be much more formal than usual this evening, at
least for a while."

The marchioness took Garrett's arm so that she
walked between them and whispered, "The Duke of Bendas is here."

"He is becoming a veritable socialite," Meryon observed.

"The Gossips say that he is not well." The marchioness looked at Meryon and then Garrett to see if they
had heard the same rumor. "Perhaps he is trying to put the
lie to the reports of his ill health."

As they entered the salon Meryon saw Bendas sitting

in a corner with both his personal servant and the marquis's brother dancing attendance on him. "That has the
makings of another cartoon." Meryon could visualize it.
An old man being waited on as though he were a sickly
old lady.

"Be polite, Duke," the marchioness insisted, and
turned to Garret. "Be sure he is, Mr. Garrett. You have always been the soul of discretion and I rely on you in this."

Garrett bowed to her, and with a decisive nod of
thanks she turned back to Meryon.

"I know how difficult old men can be, for my father-
in-law was quite insane, but Bendas is so old that he will
die soon and life will be easy again."

Meryon chuckled at her irreverence and bowed as she
left to greet another guest.

"The marchioness is French, you know." Garrett
handed the duke a glass of wine.

"As if that is an adequate explanation for her unconventional view of life."

"It is for me. You forget I lived as a Frenchman."

Meryon laughed again, as Garrett seemed to expect it.

"Come greet Bendas with me." Meryon did not wait
for Garrett, but crossed the room.

"Bendas! Twice in one week. You are becoming a gad-
fly."

Bendas glared at Meryon.

"Or is it that you feel the need to reassure the ton that
you are well. You do not present a very convincing picture.
Sitting while everyone else stands, and leaning on your
cane all the while."

"What do you want, Meryon?"

He leaned closer and spoke more softly. "I want you to pay for your crimes."

"What, man? Speak up."

"I said that I want you to pay for your crimes." He spoke in a stronger voice, stronger than necessary. Those closest stopped what they were doing to see what Bendas would say.

"It is called justice, Bendas. I doubt you even know the meaning of the word." Meryon eyed the old man's attendant. "Rogers, be sure he does not stay up too late."

Meryon turned to his small audience, disappointed that none of The Gossips appeared to be in attendance. "I have it on good authority that Bendas will be on the front page of the papers tomorrow."

With a nod to the group, who curtsied and bowed in return, Meryon crossed the room again, as far from Bendas as was practical, where Garrett stood looking only mildly interested in what had transpired. "The marchioness is liable to come over and box my ears for not keeping you under control."

"That could be the beginning of something interesting." Meryon smiled as he sipped his wine.

"Not with her husband in the same room. As God is my witness, Lyn, this will come to no good."

"Oh, stop being such a doomsayer." Meryon surveyed the room, noting familiar faces. "I enjoy this sort of gathering more than any other."

"Yes, you have a chance to ruin a man's reputation and then entertain yourself with conversation and cards."

"Conversation will flow as freely as the wine." Meryon sipped his again. "I will find a sympathetic audience and begin a discussion of my ideas on the care of widows and their children."

"Meryon, people are here to relax. You yourself insist that politics descends to gossip at parties." Garrett nodded to someone and raised his glass in greeting. "Though your interest in widows and orphans would be the perfect entrée into discussion with the right lady."

"You are newly married, Garrett. To my sister."

"Yes, and very happily married, but I am not struck blind. There are some lovely women here. And you, need I remind, are not married."

"If I find the opportunity I will bring up my ideas for a bill with whoever will listen, even if she has a mustache and he wears a puce waistcoat."

"God spare me." Garrett winced, closing one eye as if in pain.

"He may but I won't." As he spoke Meryon scanned the room and found more than one person who he thought would be receptive to his ideas. "Or I could ask one of the artists to recommend someone to do a painting of the children. Hardly a portrait, not at their ages, but something to have of them when I am away from them. A miniature perhaps."

"That is an excellent idea," Garrett said.

"I live for your approval, brother."

It was so obviously not the case that Garrett laughed as he grabbed another glass of wine. The laughter drew Straemore's attention and he turned to welcome them both.

The marchioness called to Garrett to come answer a

question about divorce and annulment and with a glance filled with alarm, Garrett left Meryon with Straemore.

They talked in a random way of Parliament and horses. All the while Straemore kept his eye on Bendas, who looked unhappy and irritated as though he would order torture for anyone who approached him. Straemore shook his head. "I have you to thank for his ill humor. He does not belong here at all."

"You must have known that when you invited him," Meryon said, offering no sympathy.

"You try telling my wife 'No,' about something important to her. Marguerite thinks being estranged from one's family is the greatest sin in the world. I told her she could invite both Bendas and Lord William but that she could do nothing, absolutely nothing, to bring them together."

Meryon patted his school friend on his arm. "Good conversation is not enough for your wife. She hopes for a little drama too."

Straemore rolled his eyes. "She wants everyone to be happy." He imitated her French-accented English. "To which I add, 'whether they want to be or not.' And here are Lord William and Signora Verano now."

The marquis excused himself to greet his newest guests.

Huzzah, Meryon thought, feeling like a man who had won the lottery. He'd hoped she would be invited to this mix of art, science, and the ton. He joined the group Garrett was entertaining and watched Elena Verano as his brother-in-law told a story Meryon had heard at least three times before.

LORD WILLIAM AND the Signora glanced at Bendas and
then put their heads close together. With a firm nod from
the Signora, the viscount went down the hall, apparently
to the card room.

Elena Verano stepped into the salon and inclined her
head when she saw Meryon. He smiled and she smiled
back. If he had been a virtuous man he would have said
the smile made his evening complete. But he wanted
more.

He wanted to hold her, touch her, undress her, and be
with her in every intimate way possible. He forced himself
to look away and laugh as Garrett finished his story.

Within a few minutes the Signora joined their group
and listened to the discussion of a regency versus the ab-
dication of a monarch. Her real interest in the subject impressed him as much as the way the gown she wore
emphasized her statuesque body and the upsweep of hair
accentuated her lovely neck.

After a few minutes she posed a question. "Is it not
like any family, where there is always hope that the patri-
arch will recover, will be able to resume his position as the
head of the family? Or am I being too simpleminded?"

With the one question she sparked an animated debate on the similarities that all families shared. He
watched her expression change as she followed the discussion. Agreement, skepticism, amusement. He could
see her mind work as her expressions changed.

"Do you not agree that there are times when the head

of the family must be relieved of decision-making responsibilities lest he endanger the family well-being?" Meryon
thought of Bendas as he spoke. "Essentially, that is what
happened when the king became too ill to govern."

"But, Your Grace, is it not true that a man can be relieved of decision-making not only when the family is en-
dangered but to further the family's well-being?"

Meryon did not recognize the speaker. A man of science, he decided. He had the distracted air of a man who
spent most of his time thinking and was not quite sure
how he had wound up in this salon, much less this discussion.

The statement silenced them all for a moment as they
considered his idea.

"When men joined the army to fight Bonaparte,"
Elena suggested suddenly, looking pleased with her idea.

"Or to look for work after the war," Meryon added,
thinking of Alan Wilson's father.

"Exactly. In both cases the family is better off without
the head of the household, even though he is not a threat
to their well-being," the gentleman persisted.

"How can that be? The children and the mother are
left behind with no one to see to their safety."

Meryon tried to find the speaker, since this statement
played right into his interests, and waited to see what the
philosopher would say.

"They will manage with the help of family and friends.
Ask any woman who was alone throughout the war. The
difficulty is that the head of the household will return to
different circumstances than when he left. When a family

member is detached from the family, the family is never the same."

Several people turned away from the discussion. Meryon stepped closer, as did Elena.

"The Regent would be a completely different man if his father had remained healthy. Anyone who has suffered a loss of child or spouse knows this, but death is not the only way to lose someone."

There were nods of agreement and some uncertainty, but no one appeared willing to take on a debate that would show them as insensitive.

Meryon thought of Rowena first, then Elena's Edward, and looked to her again, surprised to find her eyes narrowed and her lips pressed together, angry rather than melancholy at the reminder of her loss.

Someone approached Elena and she stepped away from the group. She listened to the woman with sincere interest and then answered. Both of the women laughed and walked toward the drinks table as their discussion continued.

The few others left, leaving Meryon alone with the man of science. "I beg your pardon, I do prose on, Your Grace, but the way man behaves fascinates me. It will be a study all its own one day."

"I should like to talk to you about your studies in regard to a bill I am considering."

The man bowed, clearly flattered.

"Contact my secretary and he will set an appointment at your convenience."

"Thank you, Your Grace."

Meryon moved away, perfectly content to watch Signora Verano talking with a group of women. The way she enlivened any group she joined fascinated him.

"May I know what you are smiling at, Your Grace?" The artist who had painted his portrait was at his side. "It must be prodigiously amusing to make you look like that. Or have you won the support you need for a bill in Parliament?"

"Good evening, Lawrence. My daughter called me Papa for the first time today. Thinking of her makes me smile," he lied, hoping the homely little tale would also explain his discomfiture at being caught grinning. "Do you honestly think that success in Parliament is all that makes me happy?"

"Your Grace, I'm not sure I have ever seen you look quite that pleased. Could I convince you to pose for me again?"

Meryon shook his head but did ask him if he could suggest an artist for the miniature of his children.

Lawrence had several friends who would like the work, and they talked about the way the current economic and political difficulties were influencing the artist.

The next time Meryon searched her out, the Signora stood alone. Bendas's man, Rogers, approached her before Meryon could join her to offer a glass of wine he had collected from a waiter. "Signora, excuse me, but the Duke of Bendas would like a word with you. He is old and infirm and would be honored if you would come to him."

She looked surprised. As she accepted Rogers's arm Meryon realized he had never before seen Signora Verano look ill at ease.

ELENA FORCED HERSELF to smile. For the first time in sixteen years her father had sought her out.

She felt nervous in the way she had in her first years of singing before an audience and that reminded her that this was just another kind of performance, even if Bendas had set the stage to his advantage.

Several of the party watched with curiosity, which was several too many. Bendas stood when she came up to him, making it look as though it were the most difficult thing he'd done all day. Rogers came closer to him in case he should need assistance. He was old, yes, she would admit that, but no more infirm than most men who had lived too long.

Elena curtsied deeply to Bendas, as one should to a duke. He wore a black coat and a garish green waistcoat. It was easier to deplore the green vest than acknowledge the fact that he was wearing a scent she recognized. As a child the trace of it in a room could make her feel like a failure.

You are a grown woman. His scent was no more than the pointless vanity of an old man.

"I see you have been well trained, madame."

Several thoughts passed through Elena's mind. In how to curtsy? Or was he referring to her singing?

"*Grazie,* Your Grace," she said, after a pause that made it clear she did not consider his words a compliment.

"Speak English, woman."

So this was a test.

Elena inclined her head with a polite smile on her

face. For the first time she realized those fourteen years under his roof had prepared her for the life of an artist, subjected to criticism of her heart's work. She should thank him someday, but not tonight.

"I heard you sing at the Regent's and will hire you to perform at my house in town. Next week."

It was the last thing she expected him to say. Unsure of whether this was a peace offering or an insult, she gave him the same response she would give to any stranger.

She held up her hand before he could go any further. "Thank you for the honor, Your Grace. It is not a matter of hiring me, as I do not accept payment for singing. If you would like to invite me to sing for you, I will have the gentleman who handles my performance calendar call on you."

"So you are angling for an invitation," he said, as though he had not this moment suggested it to her. "Do have your *gentleman* call on mine," he added derisively. "Rogers will make the arrangements." He did not even look at the man.

"Yes, Your Grace." Rogers bowed to her and Elena nodded.

"If no one pays you to sing, madame, then why do you do it?"

"It is a gift that is best shared. My only wish is to make people happy."

"What a noble sentiment. But I don't believe it for a moment. If that were true you would never have sung that ballad last night."

He had recognized the song. And he was right; she had sung it for the meanest of reasons.

"Besides," Bendas went on, "what you give for free, no one properly appreciates."

"Price is irrelevant. I am not in trade." This conversation was becoming dangerous.

"You're not? So you would have the ton accept you as a lady."

"I *am* a lady, Your Grace."

It was now beyond dangerous. She was going to lose her temper, which was most likely what the duke was hoping for. If he could not convince the ton that she was common, then he would show her as a shrew. And simply walking away was not the way a lady would behave. Elena prayed for rescue.

17

I BEG YOUR PARDON, Bendas." The Duke of Meryon stepped between Bendas and Elena. He forced himself to relax his fist. "The marquis has promised to show Signora Verano the Canaletto he brought from Italy."

Meryon took Elena's arm. He had not heard what they discussed but the tension between them was obvious. Bendas had been goading her, pushing her to lose her composure, and he had almost succeeded. His reason for such ungentlemanly behavior remained the larger question.

No matter why, she needed help and while she had not cast him as the hero of this piece, he knew she had a good imagination.

"If you will excuse us." Meryon bowed from the neck.

Elena held onto his arm as though it would keep her from sinking beneath the floorboards.

"Were The Gossips watching?"

"The Gossips are not on the guest list. The only one who could not look away was the philosopher we spoke with before. And me."

He felt the tension in her body ease.

"Why did you interrupt us?" she asked with all the gratitude of a mouse denied the cheese in a trap.

"Are you angry at me for helping you?" Really, he could never tell what mood would win out. "You looked upset by the conversation."

"I was not."

"Signora, stop trying to irritate me."

Elena nodded stiffly and he could feel her concentrate on quelling her temper.

"As to why I came to your aid, I have suffered from your mercurial temperament often enough these last few days that I feared Bendas would not survive your wrath."

His words had the desired effect. She smiled. Perhaps he did know her a little. Elena allowed him to lead her down the hall, following a servant and the marquis.

When they reached the front of the house, a footman opened a door and Straemore bowed them into the room. "Signora, I am sorry that you were embarrassed by a guest in my house. Bendas is leaving. Please excuse me. I will return in ten minutes."

"Thank you, my lord."

Voluntary or not, Meryon did not doubt that Straemore would see to it that Bendas left immediately.

The marquis left them and closed the door.

Elena did not go to the painting, but faced Meryon,

her eyes filled with suspicion. "How do you know that I love Canaletto?"

"I noticed how you stared at the one in your blue salon. It seemed to calm you." At the risk of offending her he went on. "I think it may be what you need right now."

"Yes, thank you." She dropped her gaze and smoothed her skirts. "I want to be offended that you would presume to know me after so brief an acquaintance, but it happens that you are exactly right. Canaletto is just what I need." She turned from him then and glanced at the other paintings before walking to the one that was unmistakably by the Italian master.

It was an oil, depicting a view of a harbor with boats docked at the quay and a series of villas overlooking the water. She moved to an angle that caught the candlelight perfectly, and Meryon could almost see her relax.

He tried to judge for himself why Canaletto's work calmed her. This scene had an urban feel, whereas the one at her home depicted a lake in a rural setting. They both featured water. If she liked rivers, he should invite her to the house at Richmond. The effect of the sky meeting the water always made him pause to appreciate nature's art.

"Tell me what you see, signora." He stood next to her, almost touching her shoulder with his, and tried to see through her eyes.

"The way he paints the sky. It's so familiar. I can lose myself in his clouds or in the small slice of the world he portrays."

He dutifully looked at the white clouds scattered across the sky and noticed how many different colors of blue the artist had used to great effect.

"Do you see how his paintings are always filled with people? At first you look and you see that this scene is of the river and boats. But if you look closely you will see people everywhere. They are in the riggings, on the shore, even a woman on that balcony in the background."

She pointed to the tiny figure that seemed to be waving at someone. "I can lose myself in this little world and let it soothe away whatever has upset me. Or it reminds me that each one of these people represents pain and grief that I know nothing about. It cures me of selfishness."

Meryon attempted to find some solace in the work but it was impossible for a painting to be soothing when Elena was so close.

"That is not all." As she spoke, Elena moved away from him and began to circle the room, stopping at each painting but giving them no real attention. "With my sensibilities calmed, I can think more clearly about what has upset me."

"How magical."

"I think not," she said, looking over her shoulder at him.

He saw an intimacy in the gesture, the way she turned to make sure he was listening, to make sure he knew this was important. He left Canaletto's painting and watched her even as she turned back to the wall.

"Everyone has some way to ease upset so they can think more clearly."

"Yes, you win the point, signora. My brother David loves his boxing ring, and some days I need it too. Or fencing."

She finished her circuit of the room and put her

hands on the back of the chair in front of her, the full glory of her eyes on him.

"Bendas is right about one thing." His grudging admission made her smile. "We rarely act for the purest of reasons."

"Do you mean to say that the action is right and true but the reason can be selfish?"

"I mean one can perform a kindly act for *more* than one reason."

Understanding lit her eyes. "You rescued me from an upsetting interview and a selfish reason was one of them."

She did not wait for his answer, but coaxed him with her words and with her smile. "Was it so I would think well of you?"

"Perhaps," Meryon conceded, using the same teasing tone she had. "And that invites a reason even more selfish, for it would mean that if I stepped closer"—he matched action to words—"there would be no objection."

He stopped directly in front of her. "I think I could learn to enjoy our, hm"—he paused—"spirited discussions, but I like it even better when we are in agreement."

ELENA RAISED HER FACE to look into his eyes and felt a blush, something she thought was the province of the untried. But his expression left no doubt of his intention.

"I have wanted to do this for longer than I even realized, but since last night it has become an obsession." He bent to her, very sweetly giving her a moment to step away, to say no, and whispered his own caution. "Though one could argue that this is the wrong thing for all the wrong reasons."

Elena stepped closer so that she was enveloped in his aura, the sandalwood and lemon surrounding her as fully as his arms. His face was all she saw before she closed her eyes and his mouth touched hers.

Even his lips felt British, cool and confident with passion hidden somewhere, begging to be freed. Small kisses, more sampling than greedy, each one a little deeper until she was lost in a desire that arrowed to her belly and lower. She pressed her mouth and her body fully to his, not so much desperate as wanting more than a kiss could give. He must have felt the same because he pulled her closer.

The kiss ended but the embrace did not. Meryon pressed his lips against her cheek, her ear, her neck, before holding her head to his shoulder.

It was, or rather he was, the most confusing combination of protective and provocative. Even in this almost innocent embrace she felt him claim her, his hold marking his mastery. It amazed her that she welcomed it. That she wanted him to demand all she had to give.

IF THE KISS had sealed their future, the feel of her nestled close roused every protective instinct he had. He needed to know why Bendas had so provoked her.

"Elena, I must ask you something." He eased back a bit, still holding her lightly. "Bendas. He deliberately baited you."

The tension returned. Her eyes grew troubled; she stepped back. Meryon persisted.

"Bendas becomes more and more difficult of late, but I have never seen him be so rude to a lady before. Tell me why he chose to confront you."

"I wish I understood what he wanted." Elena did not look at him as she spoke and Meryon recognized that she had not answered his question. "What I would like to know is why you rescued me." She tried to mask her question with the teasing tone he knew, but the strain in her voice showed through.

He took her hand and kissed it.

"Which I will tell you once you have answered my question. You must have some idea why Bendas would single you out like that."

She pulled her hand from his as he watched her debate her answer. Meryon hoped that she had decided in favor of the truth.

"We, the duke and I," she said finally, "have a connection that I do not choose to recognize." She waited a moment. "That is all I will say."

She is his illegitimate daughter. A stream of thoughts flitted through Meryon's head as embarrassment robbed him of speech. When had Bendas gone to Italy? His wife had been Italian and they had gone more than once before the war. Signora Verano was thirty, if not a little older.

Given the years Bendas would have traveled there, Elena could never have been his mistress. That idea disgusted him. Bendas's illegitimate daughter, he decided. Great God in heaven. He schooled his expression, deciding he would work it out later. "Thank you for your honesty, signora." He bowed to her.

"You're welcome." She inclined her head. "Now tell me why you rescued me."

"I told you already."

"No, Your Grace, you told me that you thought I needed rescue, but not why you were the one to offer it." There was no annoyance in her voice, just that unrelenting curiosity.

"Oh, I see." Yes, there was a difference. "It must mean something that I grow used to the way you make me think about what I do. No one has ever done it before. Well, my brother-in-law, Michael Garrett, will often give insight, but he rarely questions me." He had the other night about Meryon's desire to see Bendas brought to justice.

"Your title intimidates almost everyone, Your Grace. Sometimes, even family."

"But not you. Apparently deference is a word with which you are not familiar."

"I learned before I was an adult that there are times when people do things that make no sense, but because of their rank they need make no explanation. A duke like Bendas is no more than a man with responsibilities that often outweigh his ability."

"What a generous way to speak of Bendas's failings." He hated the man for a dozen reasons. Now he had one more.

"I rescued you so that I could claim a reward." He pulled her into his arms again; this time he did not give her a chance to say no.

He saw surprise before their lips met. He felt surrender the moment he deepened the kiss and he let go of every complication for the simple truth that they wanted each other.

They both heard the marquis call out to someone as he came for them. They separated quickly and he hoped Straemore did not notice how well kissed she looked.

As the marquis reached the door, Meryon reminded her. "Wednesday. I will see you on Wednesday at five o'clock."

They spent the rest of the evening in the same room and barely looked at each other but Meryon observed when she moved from one group to the next, when she refused another glass of wine, her delight in the food. The very air currents shifted as she did and he wondered if she felt the same.

Garrett announced that he was leaving with a friend who had offered a ride. "I am too used to country hours to stay up past midnight."

Meryon walked with him to the door and came back to find that Elena had joined a cluster of guests around a piano that someone played with more spirit than skill.

She held up her hands, refusing to sing without practice. Her appeal had not diminished one iota, but their story had become more complicated. Even as he stood listening to the conversations around him, Meyron's mind was consumed with one fact: She was of Bendasbrook blood. And one question: What difference would it make?

By design—his—they left at the same moment and stood on the steps waiting for the coaches to come.

"I won at cards and did not have to see my grandfather," Lord William declared. "All in all, a fine evening."

If the viscount knew that Elena Verano was related to

him by blood, he gave no sign of it. It could well be that the Signora had come back to England to confront her father, though Meryon could think of no way such an incident would serve her obvious interest in establishing herself in society. The widow of a famous musician, perhaps, but the by-blow of a duke, never.

Lord William was recounting a particularly challenging hand when a horrendous sound ended the story. Down the street, not more than twenty feet away, a carriage lost its wheel. The coachman fell from his seat but the boy riding next to him was able to leap from the height and land on both feet, even as the wheel fell off completely and the street-side corner of the carriage crumpled, crushed into splinters by its own weight. The horses tried to race away, still attached to the traces. The boy was doing his best to control them, grabbing the reins that trailed on the street. Meryon took off, calling out as he ran, "Pull the coachman out of the street! I'll help Wilson with the horses!"

The chaos of the accident lasted less than a minute. Like everyone else, Elena watched the drama unfold. Everyone but the duke, who reacted with such speed that he was at the carriage before the dust settled. He helped the groom by holding the lead horse's bridle, unmindful of his clothes or anything but the well-being of his cattle and the boy.

"That's Meryon's carriage!" William announced as he began to move down the street to lend a hand.

"Come back inside, signora," Straemore urged. "It will be a while before the carriages can move past."

"No, no, I want to help." But she stayed on the steps,

uncertain as to how she *could* help. Meryon turned the horses over to the grooms who rode at the back of the conveyance, neither of them hurt any more than the boy who stopped the horses.

The duke pulled the boy by the arm over to the spot where the coachman lay, unmoving. A man came out of the house and hurried to them, calling, "I'm a physician."

The boy knelt beside the coachman and Meryon stood with his hand on the boy's head as they both watched the physician examine his patient.

The boy's eyes were wide with shock and Elena turned to Straemore. "Can you have someone bring them brandy? I think the boy is too upset to stand. He looks on the verge of passing out." Elena pulled a vinaigrette from her reticule and hurried to the small circle.

"Here." She handed it to the boy. "Sniff this."

The boy did as he was told, drawing too deep a breath. It gave him an excuse for watery eyes, and his efforts to control the cough that followed were as good a distraction as any.

John Coachman groaned, and it was the happiest sound she had ever heard. Meryon relaxed visibly. The boy turned, ran, and retched in someone's garden.

One of Straemore's servants appeared with a tray holding brandy and glasses, another with a blanket to cover the coachman until he was able to move. Far better than using it as death shroud.

Elena poured a sizeable tot for Meryon, who accepted it with a grateful nod, his eyes on the coachman and the physician treating him. He drank it in one swallow and handed the glass back to the servant, who held the tray as though serving drinks in the street were part of his normal duties.

Meryon took both her hands. "Thank you for the brandy and the vinaigrette. I must talk to Wilson and see if he can give me some clue about how this happened."

"Yes, yes, of course. I am more hindrance than help now."

"And if you do not leave now, when John Coachman opens his eyes he will think he is in heaven with an angel tending him." He squeezed her hands and kissed her with his eyes.

Elena withdrew her hands slowly and walked back to the steps as John Coachman began to move. She paused and watched as he pushed the blanket off and rose, none too steadily, to his feet. Meryon grabbed him and led him to a chair that someone had brought out.

Guests were streaming out of the Straemores' to see what had happened. The crowd around the carriage grew. Meryon had his hands full answering questions when she was sure he had more important things to do.

William managed to have her carriage brought around the block so that they could leave, which, at this point, seemed to be the way she could help the most. She wanted to stay, but she had no right.

As she climbed the steps into her carriage she looked back at the crowd and saw Meryon watching her even as he spoke to someone. He stopped what he was saying when he saw her and raised a hand. It was thank you, good-bye, until tomorrow, and was all the gesture she needed.

He called to the boy, putting his hand on his shoulder, and as they walked away from the crowd, Elena knew that Meryon's heart was greater than his rank. He cared. He might hold the title of duke like her father, but it was all they had in common.

18

THE MARCHIONESS INSISTED that they all come back into the house lest they be accused of a "seditious meeting." Her guests laughed at the suggestion that they would do anything illegal, but followed her nonetheless.

Straemore's head groom had come out, and when Meryon asked he readily agreed to oversee John Coachman's transport home and the other details.

Meryon did not care if the groom burned the coach in place. At this point he wanted to talk to Wilson while the incident was still fresh in his mind. Such an accident merited investigation.

He put his hand on Wilson's shoulder. "Boy, come tell me what happened. Everything is taken care of here, and watching John Coachman will not make him steady on his feet any more quickly."

Wilson stood up but could not take his eyes from the coachman. Finally he looked at Meryon. "I didn't do anything wrong. Really, I didn't." The boy's hard eyes were filled with tears.

"No one thinks you did. If you tell me what happened we can figure out who was responsible, but you are the newest groom and the least likely to be at fault."

The boy gave a jerk of his head.

It was a mild evening and Meryon led him over to the steps of a nearby, darkened townhouse.

"We were going round and round the block so I could see how a coach and four feels. The coachman let me hold the reins on the straight part."

"Wait." Meryon felt the boy shaking. "We will walk back to Penn Square, Wilson. It is better for you to keep moving than to sit still."

The boy stood up, straightening his now filthy livery. As they moved down the street, Meryon kept a firm grip on his cane. Walking home was becoming a habit. The streets were empty, except for a man running up the stairs to a house, and a serving girl, still wearing her apron, shooing a caterwauling cat away from another gray stone residence.

"Alan, start at the *beginning* of the evening."

"I had supper and the head groom said that I should go to bed."

Meryon had not meant quite that early in the evening but he listened without correction.

"It was eight o'clock, sir, Your Grace. I had work to do. That's what I told the head groom. I watched the groom real close and helped him cinch here and there. Then we walked around the carriage and checked to make sure that nothing was amiss." The boy stopped dead in his tracks. "I swear, sir, Your Grace, that all was as it should be."

"Go on." Not all the mud holes had been filled yet this spring and the winter had been one of freeze and thaw. Easy enough to lose a wheel if you drove over the same bad spot as many times as they had while giving the boy the feel of a coach and four.

"There are still mud holes. Could that be it?"

"For now, Wilson, tell me what happened. We will speculate on the cause later."

"Yes, sir, Your Grace." He thought a moment. "When we reached the party house, one of the maids come out and invited us in for cake. The coachman made the second groom stay with the carriage and the rest of us went. It was a cozy kitchen and there was a fire and maybe we stayed longer than we shoulda. But I took some cake out to the second groom like John Coachman told me, and he was asleep inside the carriage." Wilson did not raise his head but did move his eyes so that he could watch for the duke's reaction. "I ate his cake, sir, Your Grace."

"I would have too."

"Really?"

"Yes, then I would have rocked the carriage to wake him up and run and hid as fast as I could."

The boy did not even try to deny this summary. "Do you think that's how the wheel broke?"

"No, I do not. I think that the dark made it hard to

see the wheels in the stable in the mews. And since no one suspected trouble no one looked too carefully. They did as they were told, in a hurry to be on their way so I would not be kept waiting."

"I suppose."

Having established that his employer was not about to dismiss him or hit him for simply telling the truth, the boy walked with more confidence. His too-big shoes still slapped the street, but he had straightened and held his head high.

"Tell me what you think happened to loosen the wheel."

"I think someone broke it on purpose so it would come off when you were in it, and the reason it came off sooner was because John Coachman was training me." The boy's voice shook with anger and then he watched the duke with uncertain eyes. That wild opinion had drained Alan Wilson of his newfound assurance.

"An interesting opinion, Mr. Wilson. I will investigate it."

"What do you think happened, sir, Your Grace?"

"I think the wheel came loose for some reason we will never know and we need to inspect all the carriages more carefully in the future."

"Yes, sir, Your Grace," the boy agreed. "But I still think the coachman should carry a pistol from now on."

They walked the last block in silence.

GOD HELP US. What an evening." Meryon handed Garrett a glass of port and invited Magda to sit next to him.

"Everyone is all right," Garrett said. Olivia's endless optimism seemed to be contagious. "The carriage can be repaired."

"Replaced. Its alignment is ruined."

"Replaced. And you can afford it, Lynford. Did the grooms or John Coachman have any idea how it happened?"

"No. The coachman and Wilson insist that when they inspected it before leaving everything was as it should be. That kind of flaw is hard to miss, so I expect they are right."

"So something must have happened on the way to the party or while the coachman was training Wilson. Or when the carriage was unattended. Lyn, it could have been sabotage."

"Wilson agrees with you, but there was someone with it all the time. No, it was an accident."

"Humor a suspicious old soldier and have your coachman carry a pistol."

"Again Wilson is one step ahead of you with that suggestion. I thought him bloodthirsty. I'll keep one in the carriage as well."

"Thank you." They sat in silence for a while. "Do you fancy a chess game?"

"You left the Straemores' because you were tired and now you want to play chess. Men of God are not supposed to lie."

"I was tired. Tired of making conversation with people I do not know well enough to be completely honest with them. Diplomacy does not suit me at all."

They settled at the game table and Garrett made the first move.

They played in silence for twenty minutes. All the while Meryon debated telling Garrett what he had learned about Elena Verano. When Meryon lost his queen to a bishop, he sat back in his chair and held up his hands.

Garrett's shock was sincere. "You never lose. You never concede. Are you sure you were not knocked on the head tonight?"

"In a way I was, and I've debated for an hour whether to tell you or not." He returned the pieces to the starting point as he told Garrett of his conversation with Elena Verano and his supposition that she was Bendas's bastard daughter.

"Lynford, you have spent too much time among The Gossips. There could be a dozen reasons why the Signora and Bendas do not speak." As he numbered them he tipped over the pieces that were still standing. "Bendas insulted her husband. His wife insulted Signora Verano. She had an argument with him over Lord William. Bendas criticized her singing ability. He embarrassed her in some other way. I could go on and on but I've run out of pieces to topple."

"She said that they have a 'connection.' That means something more than an insult."

"So now we are going to debate the definition of the word? Where do you keep Mr. Johnson's dictionary?" Garrett did not move from his seat. "If the connection is one of blood, what we should be discussing is whether you will continue to woo her."

"I do not need to discuss that. It does not matter to me who she is."

"For God's sake, Meryon, you *hate* the man you now believe is her father. And you can honestly tell me that it makes no difference to you. I do not believe it."

"Believe what you will. I want her and I do believe that she wants me."

"Then this is about no more than lust? There is nothing noble in that, Meryon."

"I am not pretending there is."

Garrett steepled his fingers and waited, but he did not have to speak for Meryon to see the disapproval that had taken root. "So, when you are done with her, it will be no more than another element of revenge against her father."

"No!" Garrett made him sound like some cad from one of Georges's plays. "If her relationship to Bendas mattered to her she would have told me about it. Our friendship is completely separate from that."

"As long as when it is over, she believes that as well. And Lord William. The two of them are very close. Hurt her and you hurt him. And the other way around."

"Stop the sermon, Garrett. I know what I am doing."

"Yes, I'm sure you think you do."

ON WEDNESDAY, BY the time the clock chimed five-fifteen Elena had completely shredded her handkerchief. As she tossed the useless bit of cotton onto the sideboard near the front door, she realized that despite her nerves she was more angry than relieved that he had decided not to come.

It was clear to her that she had no straightforward sensibility where the Duke of Meryon was concerned. Except for the attraction that was a genteel word for lust.

She peeled off her gloves and was untying her bonnet when there was a knock at the door. The butler opened it and Meryon hurried to her. He held himself still for a moment then bowed to her.

"My deepest apologies, signora." The words held a wealth of embarrassment. "I would prefer to blame the number of conveyances and people on the road, but honesty compels me to admit that I did not leave enough time. I hope you consider me merely fashionably late by Roman standards."

His red face, his obvious sincerity, made her smile.

"I understand, Your Grace." She spoke with all the sympathy she could muster. "Bloomsbury is not that far from Mayfair, but Tinotti was telling me the streets are full of people today."

As she retied her bonnet and pulled her gloves on, she lectured herself. *This is much easier than singing to a room full of strangers.* It was a perfectly ordinary ride in the park with a duke. It was not his rank that made her nervous.

The touch of his hand at her back ended her self-lecture.

He did not seem to feel her tremble. Or was that why he spoke as if it were the chill that made her shiver?

"I brought the cabriolet in case it should rain, but have left the cover down as it does appear that the sky will lighten."

"You have a cabriolet?" So there was a little bit of

adventure in the man. "No wonder it took longer than you expected. I imagine everyone wanted a look at it."

As they approached the carriage, she stopped to examine it herself. It was not as big as a curricle, and was less elegant, with a small boy called a "tiger" instead of a groom and, more notably, a single very beautiful horse instead of the usual pair.

"I've heard of them but this is the first one I've seen, much less been invited to ride in."

While the duke did not smile, he did seem gratified by her appreciation.

"We will raise the top in case the weather turns on us." He gestured to the tiger, who jumped to attention even before the duke turned to him and proceeded to do as bid.

"And I want to assure you that every wheel has been thoroughly inspected."

"I never doubted it."

Meryon used the one high-placed step into the carriage and then turned to help her up. The tiger scurried around from the back with a neat little set of steps that made it easier for a lady to climb into the seat.

Meryon held out his hand, offering completely necessary support, which she accepted. Gathering her skirts with her other hand, she climbed up and into the box, where they stood face-to-face.

He raised her hand to his lips and pressed a kiss to the back of her wrist. Even with the leather of her glove between her skin and his lips, she could swear she felt the warmth of his breath on her hand.

She smiled and looked at him from beneath her lashes as she took the seat he offered.

The duke drove carefully, the cabriolet just the right size for the narrower streets of Bloomsbury. Elena let him concentrate on the road and let herself concentrate on the feel of him beside her. It was distraction enough. He did not need conversation any more than she did.

The weather cleared as if on order from the duke. Hyde Park was crowded with carriages, horsemen, and ladies in groups, some with servants following discreetly behind.

Elena had never been on Rotten Row before and was hard-pressed to see it all. Without taking her eyes from a peacock of a man carrying a monkey on a lead, she laughed. "It is a kaleidoscope of color and sound. The first place I have seen here that reminds me of Rome."

"Seeing it through your eyes makes it all new to me."

She gave him her attention and found that he was barely watching the road, his eyes intent on her mouth.

"I have done this too many times to count and have never found it as entertaining as I do watching you enjoy it."

They smiled. She was sure it was the kind of smile that some poet had called "the smile of two hearts yearning." Who knew how long they would have done so if a voice had not hailed them?

"Signora Verano! Meryon! Well met!" Lord William pulled his horse up beside them and bowed from his saddle.

"Good day to you, my lord," Elena called out. "This is marvelous! Did you see the man with the monkey?"

"Lord Vilforth? Yes, we all avoid him for he insists that we shake hands with his pet and the monkey's manners leave much to be desired. But if you would like to meet him or Lord Vilforth I'm sure that the duke would introduce you. Is that not so, Your Grace?"

"No, it is not. Vilforth will want to discuss his animal's last meal, and next one, and where they are going for the evening." The duke turned from William to face her as he added, "That is not how I would choose to spend my time with Signora Verano."

Elena could not look away from the warmth of the duke's eyes. He did not look away either, even as he addressed Lord William. "Do feel free to give Vilforth's monkey our regards."

If it was a hint for William to leave he did not take it. He stayed and then another gentleman rode up to join them. He seemed on very familiar terms with Meryon and Elena enjoyed the camaraderie between them. Meryon introduced him as Lord Kyle. Three more much younger men came along and were also introduced.

They all greeted her with enthusiasm, but the cabriolet was what they were really interested in. As they discussed its general design and merits, William urged his mount around the carriage, admiring it as he made the circuit. He stilled his horse right next to Elena, where he could speak to her while Meryon's friends held his attention on the other side of the carriage.

"Elena." William spoke quietly but with determination. "Save those gazes for the bedroom. Both of you are too experienced to succumb to . . . " He waved his hand as if afraid to voice the word he was thinking.

"Desire." She finished for him.

Meryon had his back to them and William lowered his voice even more. "Be careful, *cara*. He is a duke."

"Are you warning me? You, who do not know the meaning of the word caution?" She let the disapproval show in her voice but kept it at little more than a whisper. "Attend to your own business, William."

Before William could respond, the duke, and perforce his friends, turned to include her in their conversation.

"When will Miss Castellano be in society, signora?"

William's horse sidled and Elena knew that her nephew did not like that question at all.

"She will play the pianoforte at the Monksfords' musicale the Thursday after Easter, and the Metcalfes' ball will be her first opportunity to dance."

"There, gentlemen," Meryon said. "She is a lovely lady, and she loves to dance. Or so she tells me." Meryon gave Lord William a smile that was not overly friendly. While the others laughed among themselves, the duke turned fully to Lord William. "You interfere in my personal life and I will interfere in yours, my lord."

They nodded at each other and Elena remembered that William had promised there would never be another duel between a Pennistan and a Bendasbrook. Apparently he was referring to the kind with pistols.

"Lord William, join us," Lord Kyle called. "We are going to a balloon ascension in Green Park."

"Indeed, it sounds an adventure," William said. To Elena he added, "What a shame that Mia is not able to join us."

"We both know she would find a way to be included in the ascent. Go and have fun."

"Good day to you both." Lord William called out to the others and rode hard so he could catch up with them. Elena wanted to pull the carriage robe up over her face, for it was obvious that Meryon had heard William's warning.

19

PERHAPS WE SHOULD GIVE William a seat among The Gossips." Elena tried to sound amused, rather than annoyed.

The duke laughed. "We both put him in his place. I think that should count as punishment enough."

"You are more generous than I would be."

He began driving again. "Your friendship with Lord William seems odd to me when you consider that his grandfather caused you such pain."

"I would think it makes perfect sense since they are so rarely in accord."

The duke nodded in reluctant agreement and Elena decided it was her turn to ask a difficult question, if only to distract him from pursuing the subject of her relationship with Bendas. "The Gossips say that there is no love lost between you and Bendas either."

"I hate him. I have called him incompetent, dangerous, and a disgrace to his rank. To his face."

"Oh dear, and I was afraid you did not know how to speak honestly."

The duke laughed as she hoped he would, then asked, "Has Lord William told you nothing of the cause of this antipathy?"

"He told me that he knew you better after something that happened last year, but had promised you that he would not discuss it."

They rode on in silence for a while. "If you will promise me discretion, I will tell you the story. I value your word, since it involves more than my own reputation."

"Of course, and I am honored." This offer of trust did as much to seduce her as a kiss.

"Bendas wanted Lord William to marry my sister, Lady Olivia. She is short, which had obvious merit in Bendas's eyes, and altogether delightful. During her Seasons they seemed well suited, so I asked her how she felt about him.

"When she was obviously *not* interested in his courtship I sent a letter informing Bendas. He was not pleased, and arranged for her to be abducted—"

"Stop, Meryon." She could not see his eyes, but he must be teasing her. "You are making this up."

"I am not, though I know it sounds preposterous."

He was so offended that she had to believe him.

"I can count on two hands the number of people who know the whole truth," Meryon added.

"Bendas must be insane."

"I've concluded the same. He aimed to ruin Olivia's

reputation so that no one but Lord William would marry her. As soon as William found out he came straight to Pennford. But by that time Olivia had been rescued and found her way back to us."

"The poor girl." Elena could still remember how frightened she had been when she had been sent away, even though she had a home to go to. To be taken away by force would be a hundred times worse.

"It does have a happy ending, no thanks to Bendas. She married her rescuer."

"Mr. Garrett?" He seemed such a quiet, gentle man. How very interesting. "Before he arrived on the scene it must have been a hideous experience for her."

"Yes, and for us who had no idea where they took her or how to find her. Not long after that my wife died and I hoped that by the time I came back to the social scene Bendas's son would have taken control of the estate. He had not, so I took matters into my own hands."

He told her about the duel and the death of his groom.

This was even worse than the way Bendas had treated her, Elena thought. How could her brother not have taken steps to remove him?

"Thank you for telling me, Meryon. I promise your secret is safe with me. Based on my experience with Bendas I agree that your actions are warranted. I will say nothing to William. I promise."

"Lord William already knows everything I have told you, one of the few so informed," Meryon said as he turned his attention to directing the horse around a cluster of men and women on horseback.

Oh dear God in Heaven. He has told me everything and I still have my secrets. "You know that I am in accord with you on this. I consider the duke no more reputable than a pickpocket," she began, even though she did not think Hyde Park was the best place to tell him of their kinship.

Meryon gave his attention to directing his horse between other conveyances and men and women on horseback, then he spoke again, very quietly, for her ears alone. "I understand your feeling, Elena, and that is all I need to know."

Someone called to him and he turned to wave. Blessed with his permission, Elena tried to put the confusion out of her mind, but the deep, dark blue of his coat was not compelling enough to make her forget that as they grew closer, more intimate, the secret she kept would become bigger and bigger.

Both of them exchanged greetings with those they recognized or who recognized them, and Elena noticed more than one of The Gossips make note of this new couple.

She felt his arm brush hers as he reined in the horse, with the still-amazing song of attraction that came with it. Whether to become involved with him or not no longer seemed an option.

What was too much to give and what was too little? Did she even have a choice but to give all of herself?

Elena noticed they were a good distance from other carriages. The raised cover of the cabriolet blocked them from sight and while it looked quite proper it was almost as private as a room with the door closed.

Was he thinking the same thing she was? When he

smiled there was little doubt of it. His eyes danced, the lines near his eyes emphasizing the goodwill that radiated from him.

"Just a moment." He was still smiling as he turned his head. "Wilson!" he called, and the tiger jumped down from his perch behind them.

"Yes, sir, Your Grace."

The boy stood before them with such pride that Elena thought he might pop the buttons on his livery.

"I dropped my walking stick. Retrace our route and find it, then wait for us at the Park Road gate."

"Yes, sir, Your Grace." He turned and walked slowly along the route they had followed, studying the road so intently that he was almost hit by a phaeton.

"Your cane is right here, Your Grace."

"Yes, I know." He shrugged. "I wished some privacy."

The smile was back, still so tempting. She forced her eyes away and stared at the green of the grass and the buds on the trees. "Will he not be afraid when he is not able to find it?"

"What does the boy have to be afraid of?" He touched her hand with his fingertips, drawing her attention away from the trees. In response, as natural as Adam and Eve in Eden, Elena put her hand in his, watching the way his black gloved fingers covered the dark lavender that she wore.

She cleared her throat. "Will he not worry about being dismissed if he is unable to find it?"

"Oh, yes, I see what you mean." He glanced over his shoulder, but even she could see that the tiger was now out of sight. He turned back to her. "Elena?"

"Yes." She raised her eyes to his, smiling at the way he used her given name, breathed it out with an air of fond exasperation.

"You care too much."

"That is impossible, Your Grace."

His smile mellowed and he sat back, still holding her hand. "Then I will explain why he has nothing to fear."

"What a gesture, Your Grace." She would have curtsied if she had been standing. "Thank you."

"Nonsense." He let go of her hand. "I am sure the coachman explained to him the way of the quality when he explained all his duties. Wilson will not find my walking stick. He will wait as I ordered. I will tell him I had not lost it after all and he will learn there are times when I wish him to disappear."

"Then the next time you are in the park with another lady," Elena said, still grinning, "your tiger will be the one to announce your walking stick is missing."

"There is no other lady I want to be seen with in the park." The intensity was back, banishing her smile and his, drawing them together, intent on one thing.

He took her hand again and kissed it. "Elena, I want to talk to you about something."

"Meryon!" She could not stand it any longer. "How can you think of anything but this?" She laid her hands flat against his coat, feeling his breath quicken, and ran them up until they reached his shoulders. Then leaned toward him, all but demanding a kiss.

With the ghost of a smile he gave her one. His lips warmed quickly with an ardor that was neither innocent nor practiced, but filled with honest desire.

Oh yes, she thought as she gave herself to him. He pushed her cloak aside, crushing her to him, surprising her with the strength of his arms. His embrace made her feel as though she were a treasure that he was afraid would escape.

The smallest frisson of fear aroused her even more and she opened her mouth to him with an abandon that she had thought lost forever. The sweep of his tongue, the smell of sandalwood, the beat of his heart, all her senses but sight were filled with him. Even with her eyes closed she could see an invitation that had been offered, and she eagerly accepted.

He ended the kiss too soon, but touched his lips to the corner of her mouth and to her cheek as he moved away, promising that this was only the beginning.

Drawing her close again, he did not kiss her, but pressed his lips into her hair.

"Elena."

He was the duke now. It was amazing how quickly he gathered his self-control.

"Elena," he said again, "I have a house in Mayfair."

"Oh?" Yes, of course he did. Her brain was fuzzy, still feeling his lips, still tasting him. With effort, she took command of her senses and listened.

"The house has a cozy feel," he went on, "but I think it quite perfect in every detail."

She eased away from him to see if he was teasing her. "The Duke of Meryon's house is small? That cannot be."

"Oh no." He smiled a little, a social smile, the briefest apology for the confusion. "The ducal residence is a huge place off Berkeley Square, guaranteed to impress anyone.

My grandfather saw to that. No, the house I am speaking of I own personally, for my own use."

Was he going to suggest that they go there?

"I want to go there more than I want to sing, Meryon, but it's too soon. We hardly know each other."

He kissed her with such intensity it was more of a branding than a gifting. "Come and dine with me. Garrett will act as our chaperone and we can become better acquainted."

"This evening?"

"Yes, tonight."

Did he mean it to sound like an ultimatum, or was that a command? It could be no more, or less, than ducal habit. It didn't matter. He had not tried to seduce her with promises or more kisses but had accepted her hesitation.

"Tonight." She echoed and kissed him, intending a sweet touch of the lips. It became more and deeper. They broke apart, laughing.

"Dinner first," he said, as if he could read her mind.

Meryon gathered up the reins, concentrating on turning the horse and not letting his sensibility communicate itself to the animal. *Soon, soon. They would be together soon.*

It said something for their acting skills that they traveled the length of Rotten Row and to the gate at Park Lane appearing before the ton as though all they had in mind was seeing friends, enjoying the weak sunshine.

Wilson stood on watch for them, at the gate as he had been told. The boy hurried to him almost in tears for his failure to locate the supposedly missing stick. The duke held up the cane and gestured for the boy to hop on the back.

"My father lived in France during the Revolution." He glanced at Elena to be sure he had her attention. "He taught all of us to value the servants, pay them well, be sure that the house steward listened to their needs and complaints."

"Yes, Your Grace."

He could tell by her expression that Elena had no idea why he had brought up this subject.

"Now you have taken it a step further. You have made me care about Wilson's sensibilities. I do not thank you for that. Now I will have to work not to see each one as an individual and wonder what they need."

"Yes, Your Grace."

"And that means you expect me to?"

"No, of course not. Only to think about it."

"Oh, I have a great deal to think about. I think you try to distract me from what I want to think about most."

"Dinner?" she asked with a sweet innocence that she compromised with a devilish smile.

"Most assuredly not." He emphasized the last word. "But I suppose I should think about what Cook, whose name I do not know, will say when I send word that we are a party now and not just a meal for Garrett and me."

20

DINNER BECAME MORE of an event than Meryon anticipated. His brother Gabriel and Gabriel's wife, Lynette, along with two of their children, had arrived with no advance notice. Gabriel insisted that he had written two weeks before, advising the household of their visit.

Lynette, mortified, admitted that they would probably find the letter buried under some pile or other once they returned to Sussex.

"It hardly matters," Meryon said. "The nursery will hold a dozen and to have two older boys to play with will make Rexton deliriously happy."

"And his nurse will hate us forever." Lynette spoke the words with no laughter in her voice.

"Nonsense. Yesterday she hired a new nursery maid and a schoolroom maid. And my tiger, Wilson, helps with Magda in the evening. The nurse has too much staff."

Gabriel let himself be convinced, and with assurances that their rooms were always kept ready, the housekeeper escorted them up the stairs.

"Are their rooms really kept ready?" Michael asked Meryon once Gabriel and Lynette had left the room.

"Yes, because those mysterious letters Gabriel insists he sends never actually arrive."

As he dressed, Meryon wondered what his family would make of another unexpected guest. Of course it was hardly a faux pas in this unconventional gathering of Pennistan relations.

He laughed, causing Blix to nearly cut him as he trimmed his hair. Garrett had been a spy, less than a gentleman, for years. Now a vicar, Garrett understood discretion and human weaknesses better than most, and Gabriel and Lynette were such an eccentric couple that he suspected they would approve of his behavior before they would be shocked by it.

So the five of them sat down to dinner. They all welcomed Elena warmly, pretending there was nothing unusual about an unrelated female guest at their table, seated on the duke's right.

Meryon could not recall a more delightful dinner. He let the talk flow around him. He certainly did not need to direct it. He could barely fit a word into the conversation. Elena would include him, often directing her comments to him, but the others acted as though they wanted to impress Elena and did not know, or care, the name of the man next to her.

In no time, the group made unexpected connections.

Before the footmen removed the first course, Lynette remembered that she had heard Eduardo Verano play more than once during her years in Europe.

"Verano had a way of reaching both the heart and the brain," Lynette explained to the others. "He shared his very self when he played."

When Elena's eyes grew teary, Lynette hurried to apologize for mentioning her husband.

"Oh no," Elena said hastily. "I am touched that you remember Edward's talent. He and I consider a memory like yours the finest tribute in the world."

Her loyalty impressed him. Well, everything about her impressed him.

By the time the last course arrived, Elena asked that Lynette and Gabriel explain more about their project.

She leaned across the empty table and insisted when they demurred. She turned to Meryon. "Command them to tell me, Your Grace." He picked up her hand and kissed it lightly.

"Her wish is my command, brother. Tell her about the project."

Complete silence reigned for the first time since they had sat down to dinner. Lynette and Gabriel looked at Garrett, who gave a slight nod and reached for his wineglass.

"I've never known you to be so humble, Gabriel. I warn you if you do not tell the Signora I will, and you know I will make a hash of it."

"Very well." Gabriel acquiesced with a slight distracted air. "If you insist."

Meryon knew the work involved an attempt to prepare a modern version of the knowledge of the human body shown through the use of cut-paper silhouettes, layering the musculature, the heart and respiratory system, and other body parts over the human skeleton.

Elena, however, struck to the heart of the matter. "So your project represents both art and science? Is it what brought you together?"

"Not really," Gabriel said and shared a secret look with his wife. "But it is what keeps us together."

Lynette laughed at the absurdity, raising her serviette so she did not spray the table with wine.

Michael took up the issue. "You know, he could be right, Lynette. All those days when you will not talk to each other because your art and his science do not agree?"

Lynette nodded.

"Olivia insists it is arguing that keeps a marriage strong." Garrett looked around the table.

"Oh, yes," Elena concurred. "I agree completely."

Meryon sat back a moment. He had never in his life experienced any estrangement from his wife.

"The duke and I have spoken of this." Elena gave him a smile that made his stomach flip. "I think that trust between a husband and wife adds passion to all dimensions of a marriage."

There was complete silence at the table and Elena blushed. "I am sorry if that was inappropriate."

"Not at all, signora," Gabriel said. "How long have you known Lyn? He is not usually so forthcoming, even with us. Tell us your secret."

"She likes to make me think." Meryon answered the potentially embarrassing question for her. "You see, signora," Meryon added, "you have reminded them of what they have in each other. Stop blushing. We are all married, or have been."

They all agreed and began to discuss the travesty that was the Prince Regent's marriage to Caroline of Brunswick.

Eventually Lynette suggested that she and Elena retire to the salon while the gentlemen smoked or drank port. Though Michael and Gabriel agreed, Meryon had no intention of subjecting himself to their questions. It might also have had a little to do with a desire to be alone with his lady.

"We will dispense with that this evening, Lynette, and join you for tea immediately. The Signora and I are expected elsewhere."

He made sure not to look at her, in case she was blushing or would blush. The others accepted the announcement with aplomb and abandoned the dining room together.

They were in the salon, sipping tea, with Meryon wondering exactly how quickly he and Elena could say good night to the others when the sound of running feet, the four-legged kind, distracted them all.

Meryon heard more running sounds and yelling of the boyish variety before he had the door completely open. He stepped into the hall; Magda saw him and leaped into his arms.

Rexton, Wilson, and one of Gabe's boys raced down

the stairs, yelling at Magda and one another, apparently unaware that the duke, who was, respectively, their father, employer, and uncle, could hear every word they said.

"If she bothers the duke and his company it will be my head!" Wilson insisted.

"If she dies I will beat you up," Rexton shouted.

"If my mother catches us she will beat me up!" Peter did not so much shout as moan.

The three skidded to a halt when they saw Meryon holding a shaking Magda.

"She is perfectly safe. Rexton, tell me what made her run away from you." Meryon could hear the other adults behind him, but the boys had eyes only for him.

Wilson stepped back and let Rexton speak. "The maid wanted to brush Magda's hair and you know how much she hates that. So she was running around the room and we were chasing her." He paused a moment and Wilson whispered something to him. "Someone left the door open and Magda ran out and we wanted to catch her before she interrupted your dinner party."

Meryon turned to Wilson. "Take Magda out, on a lead, for her nighttime walk. The rest of you go back to the nursery."

Wilson's relief was obvious. He took Magda and made soothing noises as they moved to the back of the house.

"Sir, may I go with him? He might need help if Magda runs away." Rexton did his best to look responsible, but no father in his right mind would let a boy his age out alone at night.

"No, son. Later this summer when the sun sets so late, you may go, but it is up to bed now."

Rexton nodded, his eyes swimming with disappointment. When he could see that tears would not work with his father, the boy turned, touched his cousin on the arm, and yelled, "Race you!"

They were out of sight before Peter's parents could say anything.

"You do not believe that story, do you, Lyn?" Gabriel's incredulity illustrated he had learned a lot about children in the last few years.

"Of course I don't believe him. But it would have been unfair to ask either Peter or Wilson for the truth. Wilson thinks that I can tell lie from truth and knows a lie would ruin the trust I have in him. But if he told the truth then Rexton would hate him and Peter forever."

"Forever being about a week," Garrett explained and then went on. "How long do you worry about every noise and cough?"

"If you believe my mother," Gabriel's wife offered, "parents never stop worrying about their children."

"That's enough to make me look for the brandy," Garrett said, and they all laughed at the man who was on the verge of fatherhood.

Meryon caught Elena's eye and she gave him one of her sad smiles. They were so rare that they always tugged at his sensibilities. In this case he thought it might be because this was a conversation to which she could not contribute, having no children of her own.

"The Signora will tell you that young people in their teens are even more of a challenge."

Elena's sad smile disappeared. "My ward is eighteen, and to her the thought of waiting for anything is torture."

"And she could find work as a matchmaker. She left Signora Verano's handkerchief in the coach so that I would have an excuse to call on the Signora again."

"Clever girl," Gabriel said.

"That supposes that I had not devised my own plan for calling on Bloomsbury again."

They teased him about his plans as they drank their tea. Meryon finished his with an indecent gulp and announced that he and the Signora must leave. A flurry of good wishes followed. Lynette gave Elena a warm hug; Gabriel and Garrett's farewells were less intimate but not less friendly. As they left the salon, Meryon heard Gabriel offer Garrett another brandy and Lynette announce that she was going to the nursery to make sure Rexton and Peter had found their way back. Meryon knew he and Elena would not be missed.

After he called for her carriage, they waited in the reception room.

"I suspect, Your Grace, that the truth is Magda wanted to make her feelings known when you told her that she was not welcome in the dining room tonight."

"Either you recall our first conversation when I told you that Magda is my confidante"—that seemed a hundred years ago—"or you heard Lynette ask me why Magda was not invited."

Elena answered with her eyes. *I remember every detail of that night.*

He reached for her hand but she ignored the gesture

and stepped away and circled the room, pausing to admire the Canaletto he had moved down from the library just this afternoon. She did not comment on it but finished the circuit.

"Why did we not introduce ourselves the night we met?" she asked as she sat down.

"I have no idea."

"I do."

She almost always did have an idea, which she almost always wanted to share. He loved that about her most of the time, but right now words were not what he wanted to exchange with her.

"I think..." She remained seated and looked up at him. "Exchanging names would have made our first meeting more proper than the intimate exchange that we both seemed to need. Look how long it has taken for us to know each other, to become comfortable together again."

She patted the seat beside her, but he chose the settee parallel to the one on which she sat so he could watch those glorious eyes as she talked. "I cannot imagine you know me much better now than you did before dinner." His words sounded like a challenge or a game. Not intentionally.

"I do know you much better, Your Grace."

"Then you can read minds, signora. You four had such a lively discussion that you found a new subject before I could comment on the previous one."

He had maintained his usual demeanor, not anxious to call attention to his singular guest by behaving differently. As if she did not shine from her place next to him, her beauty all but announcing his intention. "Tell me what you learned."

She gave him a coquettish shrug, moved to sit next to him, and then kissed him on the cheek. It was so unexpected that he knew he must have looked shocked.

"I love that expression, as though I have done something that you are totally unprepared for. It was the littlest kiss, Meryon." She smoothed her skirts.

It had caught him unawares—no, that was not it, it had caught him *unprepared*.

"I know that your family loves you." She folded her hands in her lap and looked as decorous as the thirty-something lady she was. "They love you and you love them as surely as you love your children. And I learned that you are lonely."

"I would be more comfortable if you said you know that I prefer turbot to flounder, signora." Meryon did his best to relax but could not smile. She knew he was lonely, and what did he know about her? That she must walk out her restlessness before she sat down.

"Then I will apologize, a very small apology. I did take advantage of Gabriel and Lynette's openness, because it is important for me to know you better."

He was beginning to feel a trifle annoyed at her pleasure in his discomfiture. "There are very few people who have seen me with my family in such informal circumstances."

"Your Grace, if you consider it such a threat then why did you invite me?"

He heard no anger, only curiosity. He could never predict what she would take offense at.

"No one expected Gabe and Lynette. And Garrett is excellent at drawing out information."

She reached over and put one of her hands on his, waiting until he looked up at her. "Meryon, there is nothing I would not tell you. Ask. What would you like to know?"

21

ELENA'S QUESTION HAD a dozen different answers. Meryon wanted to know the truth about her parentage, what her youth had been like, when she first understood what a gift her voice was, how she met Verano, why they had no children, if she wanted him half as much as he wanted her. But in the deepest corner of his heart he did not want to know her any better than he did now, wanted nothing to threaten their friendship.

"No questions," she surmised, misunderstanding his hesitation. "Well, that is disappointing. One would think that you do not wish to know me at all. In that case I will tell you the rest of what I learned."

"Elena." He freed his hand and cupped her neck. "I can think of another way I would much prefer to use our time together. I do believe that you know me even better than I know you. Let me send your coach home and call for my own so we can visit my house on St. German Street."

Elena kissed him, closing the last inches between them by wrapping her arms around him.

Meryon knew one thing beyond doubt. That this woman in his arms, her mouth on his, gave herself completely. He felt unworthy of such generosity, but he was a man and not a saint. Some sound, barely heard, made them part and a moment later the footman scratched at the door to tell them that the carriage was waiting.

Meryon told the footman of the change of plans, and neither he nor Elena complained about the minutes it gave them to become better acquainted.

Finally Meryon was helping her with her cloak. In the hall the porter had his greatcoat, hat, and walking stick. They waited for the porter to go outside and open the coach. Elena leaned against the wall near the door and whispered, "I think this part is called anticipation."

He kissed her quickly, lest someone should walk by. "I have always thought anticipation vastly overrated."

Meryon helped Elena into the carriage. They sat on the bench seat facing the front. The down blanket on top of the warmed seats made the three-block trip to St. German as comfortable as a seat in a well-warmed salon. They sat, her head on his chest, his arm pulling her close, not kissing.

He knew that once his mouth touched hers he wanted no interruption, no distraction, and as many hours as they could spare from a world filled with other people.

The moon was in its spring prime, one of those nights

when you could read by its light. As they drove through the gates that set the house back from the street the moonlight cast cold shadows on the façade, making it less welcoming than it appeared in daylight. Candles lit the arched windows on either side of the matching arched doorway, and the warmth they hinted at made him want to hurry inside.

He loved this place, if one could love a thing of stone and plaster. When he walked through the door, he left all his cares outside and enjoyed the purely selfish, sensual hours, always leaving rejuvenated in body and spirit.

"Oh, Meryon, it is not at all what I expected, but nearly perfect. I love the way it is set back, separating itself from the rest of the houses." She let him hand her down the steps and hurried through the cold to the arched front door.

A maid, an older woman, met them, took their hats and coats, and disappeared.

"Is there a garden out there?" she asked, gesturing toward the back of the hall that ran straight through the house to a set of glass doors at the back. "There must be. Flowering trees and a little fountain perhaps."

"Yes, there are trees and I will have a fountain installed tomorrow." Like Hyde Park, he loved seeing this place through her eyes, as if for the first time.

With a hand on her back, he urged her into the salon to the right of the entry. There was champagne on the table. He should have told the maid to put it in the bedroom and saved both of them any more waiting.

He opened the champagne with a decorous pop, even though he rarely performed this chore himself.

STRANGER'S KISS 237

"Were you that sure of me?" she asked as he handed her the glass.

"No, my dear, if I had been sure of you I would have had the bottle open already."

She raised her glass and touched it to his, walking over to one of the windows. Facing him so that the arched window framed her whole body, she sipped her champagne.

"Tell me how you found this place. Please," she added and set her glass down on a table.

Her composure tried his patience. He did not want conversation. He would be happy to tell her anything after they had used the bed upstairs. Feeling crass for thinking like a randy schoolboy, Meryon reminded himself of his age and maturity and sipped the champagne for strength.

"The house is modeled after Le Pavillon Colombe outside Paris. I think I told you that my father spent several years in France before and during the Revolution. He hired a French architect to design a cottage with the same exterior as Le Pavillon Colombe but with an interior of his own design. The duke, my father, gave it to me when I reached my majority."

"It seems an extravagance, a *wonderful* extravagance," she added quickly, "to build a house of two stories in the middle of the city. Do you not feel overwhelmed by the taller houses?"

"When you see it in the daylight you will have to tell me if you still think it perfect." He set his glass down and could not decide whether to thank or bludgeon his tutor for teaching him how to control himself. "Let me show you the rest of the house."

THE BEDROOM. I ESPECIALLY *want to see the bedroom,*
Elena thought. But something had changed. He did not
seem as enthusiastic now. Who needed champagne when
her mind, body, and heart were as ready as they could be?

"It's so comfortable. It makes me wonder why we all
want such grand houses." Elena made the comment as
they started up the stairs, having seen three salons on the
ground floor, a parlor with a library behind it, and a dining
room across the hall.

As she played the gracious guest to his gracious host,
it occurred to her what this house was intended for. It was
where his mistress would live, and how wonderful that
there was none in residence.

"It requires only a small staff as well." Elena stopped
on the first step and turned to him. They were eye-to-eye
and Elena leaned into him, hoping to find the man she
could not resist. She kissed his cheek and then buried her
face in his neck, breathing in the smell of his skin, hair,
clothes. She whispered into his ear, "I said that so you
know that I can be practical."

He laughed and she relaxed. She loved to hear him
laugh and vowed to make him laugh at least once an hour.
It made her happy, not to mention that when she was
pressed this close to the man, his laughter was very arousing as it traveled the length of her body, all the way to her
toes.

"If you would like we could go to the library and talk
awhile."

Elena could not tell if he was joking or not. Could he

be nervous? He did not seem nervous, but there was some reason he was keeping himself at a distance. She so liked to be seduced but perhaps now it was her turn. Elena took his hand and pulled him behind her up the stairs. "Is there more than one bedroom?"

This time *he* did not answer but took the lead, pulling her into the largest of the rooms, and her spirits rose.

There appeared to be small dressing rooms on either side of the bedchamber, which was square with a huge bed along the outer wall. Quietly glowing fireplaces at each end made it warm enough to move about naked if one so chose.

"The maid will help you undress." He gestured to the door near the fireplace at the end of the room.

Her heart fell and this time it was bruised a little. *A maid would help her undress.* That was no more passionate than a tour of the house.

"No, Your Grace, I do not need a maid's help." She whirled around and stepped into the passage. "If you are trying to make this as unromantic as possible then you have succeeded. There is no urgency, no passion." She wanted to cry but kept her voice even. "If you will not share yourself completely here and now, I do not think—"

Before she finished the thought, the duke scooped her up in his arms. She gave an inelegant squeak as he swept her into the bedroom, kicked the door shut, carried her to the bed and dropped her on it as though a punishment was about to begin.

He came down with her, both of them still fully dressed, his eyes alight with passion and a little anger. He framed her face with his hands and then ravished her mouth.

He trailed kisses down her neck to the crest of her bosom, he pressed his hand below her belly. The feel of him so close to her arousal made Elena gasp.

"Please," she begged, and while that could have meant any number of things, he understood.

Meryon stripped her with an efficiency of desperation and then undressed himself almost as quickly.

"You are all that I want, all that I can think about." He pressed his body to hers so that skin touched skin. She was so anxious to feel him inside her, preparing for pleasure was not a conscious thought. But he held back. She twisted beneath him, her hands on his back pulling him closer. There was no need to tease and tempt when her body was all but screaming for him.

She gave a tiny cry of frustration and he came into her with such power that within seconds an orgasm exploded through her.

He stroked, deeper and deeper, and his own release came so soon after hers that it added a coda of pleasure that was almost unbearable. Her body arched under his, her hands gripped the bed linen as she urged him closer, not wanting the feeling and the union to end. He stayed with her until the red-hot connection melted into something more comfortable.

Meryon kissed her and then lifted himself from her and rolled, pulling her on top of him with one hand, grabbing the sheet from the floor, even though they were both so warm that the covering seemed unnecessary.

Elena laid her head on his chest and slid a little to the side so all her weight was not on him, but they were still touching from head to toe. He pressed another kiss to the top of her head. As she moved to kiss him back, tears started. They came from nowhere, a confusing welter of emotions rising with them, happiness, heartache, relief. They poured from her, followed by gulps for air that were as necessary as they were unattractive.

"I never," she started, and then buried her face in his shoulder when she could not quite finish the sentence. He smoothed her hair and comforted her, an action so unlike a man that she fell in love with him right there. The tears ended almost as quickly as they began. "I never thought I would ever feel like that again." She looked up at him and added, "In fact, I don't think I have ever felt like that before." She shook her head, still bemused. "I have never had quite that mindless an experience of sex. It was all feeling, like a torrent of it."

He smiled, that heart-winning smile that was completely unnecessary since her heart was already won. "I am relieved. I hoped that we shared mutually, but now I am worried that I was cheated, as I do not feel at all like crying."

She laughed and then winced. She reached for the hairpin that had come loose and pressed into her neck and not her hair. Elena pulled it out and tossed it on the floor.

"Sit up and let me take the pins out," he said. "I have only been able to imagine how long your hair is."

"I had Tina put it up with my favorite pins so that I would look elegant at dinner." Elena sat up as she spoke, drawing the sheet up to cover her breasts even though he was behind her.

"I think you would look elegant with your hair in braids. Your elegance comes from somewhere inside you, and I am so happy it disappears when you make love."

She could feel him draw out each pin as he spoke. He worked with care. He placed each pin, jeweled or not, into a glass bowl set in a bronze shell at the feet of a mermaid whose long hair did not cover her breasts. There was a comb on the table as well as a candle and flint. Meryon reached for the comb and began to pull it gently through her hair.

"I think that wearing your hair up in such an elaborate style was your last bit of feminine indecision."

"Perhaps." Her arousal had faded, replaced by a tinge of anxiety. She was no longer a young girl, but a woman who was feeling the first signs of age. A wrinkle here and there. She pulled the linen up around her, sure that her breasts were not as uplifted as they used to be.

Her hair seemed to lack the luster of her youth. Would he notice? Men always aged better than women, if they did not run to fat—and there was not an ounce of fat on the duke. Meryon had the body of a god and she was no goddess.

He pressed a kiss to her neck. Elena could feel his breath on her shoulders, and the soft caress made her forget fretfulness and shudder with pleasure.

"Your hair is down to your waist," he announced as he pulled her back against him, and she could feel his arousal press into her thigh so she said what she knew he wanted to hear.

"I am a greedy, selfish witch to have visited an erotic Eden and still want more."

This time they moved more slowly, exploring each other's bodies. He had a scar on his back. When she kissed it, he mumbled, "Stupid fencing misstep."

He declared that the line of her neck was exquisite, exceeded by the path from her shoulder to her hip, over the swell of her lovely breasts to the sweet roundness of her stomach.

She loved the feel of his legs wrapped around her, all muscle, with nothing tender about them.

When they had tortured each other long enough, he pressed her back on the pillows, imprisoning her hands with his. For a delightful minute she felt like a concubine awaiting her master's pleasure. She almost wished that Meryon would take the next hour entirely out of her hands and use her with all the mastery he must have at his command.

"You look as though you are waiting to be ravished." His expression was both wicked and willfull and she could only nod.

"I want you whether you want me or not," he said, not smiling. "I will tie you to the bed if I must. I do not have to, do I?"

"No," she gasped as he pressed into her and then held perfectly still. She wrestled under him, begging for more with her thrusting hips. When she arched her body he still bracketed her hands, forcing her submission.

"Do not move, Elena."

Her body tensed with the effort to obey him.

He moved in and out, but as soon as she moved her hips he stopped.

"Hold still." He spoke with a sharp edge to his voice.

"I can't. I can't," she told him and he smiled as though those words were exactly what he wanted to hear. They moved together but he held her pleasure just beyond completion until she thought the frustration would kill her.

"Do not close your eyes."

Elena obeyed him, almost afraid of the consequences should she disobey. If he left her like this it would be an insult beyond bearing.

Meryon plunged into her again, finding the exact spot of release by either chance or genius, she was beyond caring. Even with her eyes open she lost sight of him as an orgasm swept her into a world of pure sensation.

Meryon followed her, releasing her hands, cradling her to him. They clung to each other as if lost at sea with the other their one hope of rescue.

Finally, with a long breath, he moved away from her. Elena curled up with her back against his chest. His deep even breaths told her he had fallen asleep. Elena lay with her eyes open, wondering if there was anything she would deny this man.

22

MERYON DIDN'T SLEEP, at least not for long. Eventually, he pulled away from her, despite her soft protest, and sat on the edge of the bed. The room was colder now, but he stayed uncovered, his body still restless if not too warm.

What had he done? How could he have behaved like that? Even his mistress had never aroused that kind of behavior in him. With her, sex had been a way for him to relax, to be selfish, to take what he needed. With Elena he had given as much as he had taken, but with a frenzy and dominance that were as foreign to him as tears were.

She had not complained, not at all. If she had asked he would have stopped. Could he have stopped?

He felt her hand trace his backbone with a lover's touch. It made him want her again, right now. How long would he have to wait?

"I do have to go home tonight, Meryon. Tina is not expecting me until late, but if I do not come at all she will tell her husband and they will worry."

Meryon did not comment on the way her servants ruled her life. It was the wrong way to tell her that he did not want to let her go. Not now. Not ever. "I will see you tomorrow."

She did not answer him at first. He looked over his shoulder. "I may enjoy a little dominance in bed, Meryon, but that is the only place."

He turned to face her. "You were not afraid?"

Now she laughed, her frisson of annoyance disappearing. "No, not really, rather deliciously frightened."

Elena slipped from the bed, her delightful backside as full and round as her back was straight. She began to pick up her clothes. She came back to stand at the edge of the bed, her clothes pressed against her bosom. "Please believe me when I say that I am so afraid of you I can hardly wait until we can lie together again."

He came from his side of the bed, toward her, shrugging into the banyan that lay on the chair nearby. It was not what he wanted to do at all. "I am not going to let you go." He took her into his arms, kissed her, and hoped she could feel the combination of happiness and dread he felt. "I want to keep you here, in this bed, forever."

"And I would stay even without being tied to the bedpost, but not tonight." She kissed him and he could feel nothing but her satisfaction.

Elena disappeared into the dressing room. He heard the distant ring of the bell as she called for the maid to help her dress.

If they had been completely alone in the house, he might have shown her that he was not entirely joking about keeping her in this bed forever. He wanted her here whenever he needed her, which could well be every minute of the day. He pulled the banyan around his nakedness and felt like he was covering the base part of him with a gentleman's veneer.

Meryon gathered his clothes and went to his dressing room. With each layer of clothing he felt more himself, rather than a man whose animal urges ruled him. As he tied his cravat and struggled into his very well cut coat he realized why he had used her so. He wanted to prove to her and to himself that he was in control.

Elena was every bit a lady when they met again in the salon. "We are so proper, after having been not proper at all. What are we afraid of, do you think?"

He put down his glass and picked up her cloak, holding it out for her. "I am not going to even pretend I know why we are circumspect. I am going to take you home, count the hours until we can be together again, and sleep so the time passes more quickly." He kissed her, as though it was a seal on every sweet memory of the last few hours. "My dear, I do not think we have to have all the answers as long as we are happy."

Acting as groom tonight, young Wilson lowered the stairs and pushed the door shut with growing confidence. The carriage was their warm cocoon once again, but they used the cold outside as an excuse to sit as close together as possible. Until Elena announced temptation too great and moved to sit across from him.

Meryon was sure from her expression that her mind was filled with thoughts as lascivious as his.

"Tomorrow," Meryon said, as he took Elena's hand and kissed it. "I will send my carriage for you and meet you at the St. German Street house. At four o'clock."

"Yes, all right."

Elena smiled at him, but her agreement was more guarded than he liked. She had said yes and he would be an ass to press her for more enthusiasm.

They rode in silence until he heard a sound, suspiciously like a yelp. From a dog. He ignored the first one, but the second and then the third had him rapping on the roof for the carriage to stop.

Wilson came to the door promptly.

"Either Magda is up there with you or you have been spending so much time with her that you are beginning to bark like she does."

"Yes, sir, Your Grace. I'm sorry, but Magda followed me here. We din't have no choice but to keep her with us since we din't know how long you would be."

"You make it sound so reasonable, Wilson. How unusual that it has never happened before."

"I have a way with animals, sir, Your Grace. I like them and they like me."

That was true, but Meryon suspected that Wilson had deliberately brought Magda. While he mulled over an answer, Wilson decided they had finished conversing and without waiting to be dismissed he gave a brisk nod, closed the door, and climbed back up onto the driver's seat.

Elena tried to hold back her laughter but a little giggle escaped. "You must like that groom very much or else you would have fired him on the spot."

"His family needs the money. His father is north looking for work." When she merely raised her brows he went on. "Yes, I like the boy. He has an answer for everything, a natural intelligence that I would hate to see wasted." Meryon wondered if the boy could read and write. "Alan Wilson reminds me of Rexton and the accident of birth." Meryon called the picture of his golden-haired son to mind. "Wilson's father has been gone for months, if not a year, and the boy had been earning money doing God knows what until I hired him. I don't think Rexton could find his way from here to Penn Square. My son's current talent is asking questions to which no one knows the answer."

"I think we do what we have to do, Meryon. It could be that your son would surprise you."

Elena shifted back to his side of the carriage, but did not close the space between them. "I was on my own at fourteen."

"Good God. You were still a child." He could easily believe that Bendas had allowed that, but had no idea why. He kissed her and drew away quickly before it could become something more. He did want to hear her story.

"I began singing before I said my first words. My mother wanted to give me singing lessons. Her husband insisted it was a waste of money. It was a constant source of conflict between them." Elena was quiet a moment, then drew a deep breath as if it would give her strength.

Meryon clenched his fist at his side and waited. This

was her story to tell. "When I was fourteen my mother died. A few weeks later her husband asked me to sing for a friend and he did not like the song I chose. The next day he told me to leave the house, to sell my talents on the street."

"With no reason given." That explained the upset at Georges's story about the girl who played the piano.

"He did not need to give me one. His word was law."

Now Meryon did reach out. He gathered her into his arms, sitting her on his lap, rocking her as one would the child she had been.

"I am so sorry for the little Elena, but I also know that struggle was part of making the glorious woman you are. Believe me when I say that the woman before me is as lovely and as honest as the sun is hot."

"I had an ally. My godmother. She gave me a home without hesitation and we eventually settled in Rome. And the rest is much happier than the beginning."

She kissed his cheek, and as the carriage rounded a corner she slid from his lap to sit beside him. He relaxed his fist and took her hand and held it.

"That rather dour story is by way of telling you that children will call on resources that we do not even suspect they have. Lord Rexton is your son, Meryon, and that tells me he is thoughtful, observant, and kind. Even kindness stands one in good stead in dark times."

"I would argue that but I have seen it too, when Garrett took care of Olivia. His kindness saved her life at some cost to himself."

ELENA WANTED TO tell him how sweet and dear he was, but was sure he would consider it an insult. Instead she cupped his chin in one hand and framed his mouth with her lips.

There was nothing but the two of them, no past, only this all-consuming present and the hint of a future. A little moan escaped her as she gave in to the delicious feeling that reminded her of their lovemaking.

He ended the kiss with his own sound of regret, holding her a moment longer. She saw something in his eyes that was more than passion, less than commitment, but filled with love.

"I suspect that you know more of the mean part of the world than I do, Elena, and I would have taken it all on myself to spare you that. But Gabriel has yet to invent a way to travel into the past."

Elena leaned her head on his shoulder. Did he know that it was not possible to rescue everyone? "Beggars must approach you every day."

"Yes, and giving them a coin now and again is not a long-term solution."

"Your goal being to save England's future one boy at a time."

He laughed, which surprised her.

"Oh my, you are learning not to take every word I say as an affront."

"I have been taught by a master. You. Besides we now have a better use for our passion than arguing, do we not?" They spent a long moment proving it to each other.

This time Meryon moved to take the seat opposite

her. "I am going to propose a bill to give monetary and educational assistance to widows and orphans."

"That sounds very ambitious. Admirable, make no mistake about that, but much too expensive to gain support in these times."

"Yes, I know." He did not seem at all daunted by her criticism. "It's both the best and worst time to make such a proposal. I accept that it will not succeed this year or even next year. I plan to send a letter to William Wilberforce."

"Will his support help you?" The name sounded familiar but she could not place who he was.

"He may lend his support. His ideas are very progressive. But what he can teach me is how to persevere. His efforts to outlaw the slave trade took more than fifteen years."

And who will teach you patience? She did not ask him that. Nor did she ask him if he had any idea what a cause like this would cost him in heartache and despair. He had been part of Parliament for years now. He knew what it would take.

They rode the rest of the way in silence. As soon as the carriage slowed at the house on Bedford Place Elena's maid opened the door.

"What in the world?" Elena could make no sense of it. Tina had wrapped herself in a knitted shawl, totally inadequate against the cold night air and not at all like her usually careful appearance.

"I'll come in with you. Signora Tinotti looks upset."

"No, no. It is most likely some domestic upset that

would have you rolling your eyes." Tina would be truly hysterical if something terrible had happened.

Meryon hesitated, then took her hand and kissed it quickly. "Send word if you need help and if not I will see you tomorrow, soon after four o'clock."

The boy lowered the stairs for her, the dog over his other arm.

"I will take Magda now, Wilson," was the last thing she heard Meryon say.

23

WHAT HAPPENED, TINA?" Elena asked as soon as she closed the door behind her.

"Where were you, signora?"

Tina sounded like the disgruntled mistress, rather than the servant. It appeared to be a rhetorical question as Tina did not wait for an answer.

"Mia has disappeared. She was with Lord William in the salon with the governess as chaperone. That stupid woman tells me that Mia excused herself and went upstairs and then Lord William announced he was going to leave and would the governess explain that he remembered a promise he must act on. When the governess went upstairs to tell Mia, the girl was gone!"

"William and Mia left together?" Elena was not sure if the two of them together made it better or worse. Better, much better, she decided. Mia alone in town at night was a horrifying thought.

"The stupid butler had gone off to have his supper, not at his post, and did not see either one of them leave." Tina spoke as though supper were an indulgence the butler was not worthy of.

"If I know Mia," Elena paused, and after a moment's thought went on, "and William, they timed their departure so that no one would stop them. What time was the butler off for supper?"

A rap at the door, followed by its opening, ended their discussion. Mia and William came stumbling in. Mia was giggling and William was trying to shush her with whispers that were loud enough to be heard across the street.

"Are you two drunk?" Elena asked, shocked not so much at their behavior as at William's hand in it.

Mia stopped so fast that William ran into her back and the cloak she wore enveloped them both. The girl turned and threw her arms around his neck. "Thank you, my lord. That was such a grand adventure. It is worth whatever punishment Elena contrives."

At least, at the *very* least Elena would be grateful that Meryon was not here to witness this disaster. She had no idea what he would think but her mortification would have been unbearable. "Mia, you make it sound like I spend my days and nights thinking of ways to punish you. As I recall you promised that with your come-out so close you would be on your best behavior."

"I said I would *try,* and, truly, I did try." Mia bit her lip and tried to look penitent.

"Go to your room, go to bed, and I will talk to you in

the morning when I have had time to devise an appropriate discipline."

A rebellious expression replaced Mia's remorse, but Elena saw William's slight nod and Mia was solemn again and halfway up the stairs.

"Elena, I can explain," William began.

"Not here." Elena held up her hand to stop his babbling. "Come into the salon. Now."

He followed her with a cheerfulness that seemed to belittle the seriousness of the situation.

"Shall I bring some refreshment, signora?"

"No, Tina. His lordship will not be staying long." Elena pulled the door closed.

"What were you thinking?" She tried to keep her voice level but when she did that hysteria crept in and hysteria was not what she was feeling. So she yelled at him. "I am furious with you, do you hear me?" There was no doubt he could hear but he was smart enough not to say that.

"Elena, I know how it looks but you have to let me explain."

"I don't *have* to do anything. With one sentence I can forbid you this house." Elena walked over to her Canaletto but even his blue sky could not calm her.

"Yes, I know. But if you do that, things will grow worse."

"Is that a threat?" She faced him, all but seeing red.

"Oh, God, no. It's only that—" William stopped, and when he began again, he was pleading. "Let me explain and you will, I hope, understand why I went with her."

"All right." She sat down and smoothed her skirts, and

when he would have sat beside her, she raised her hand to stop him. "Do not sit. You have behaved like an unconscionable schoolboy and you will stay standing while you explain."

Was that barely restrained annoyance she saw on his face? If it was, he did not give voice to it and stayed where he was, in front of her, slapping his gloves against his leg. Finally, he tossed his gloves on the table and began.

"I came to see Mia yesterday evening for our regular English lesson. Tina's governess was with us as chaperone which, mind you, is as good as having a statue on guard. She sat on the other side of the room, reading, and as long as Mia spoke quietly, the woman showed no interest in what we were talking about. We could have been planning to visit Napoleon on St. Helena and she would not have known."

"So this began last night?" *Visit Napoleon? Do not put ideas into Mia's head.*

"Oh," William said with resigned insight. "I think it's been brewing in Mia's head for longer than that, but she first told me about her plan last night."

"Go on." *Was he going to try to shift the blame onto Mia? How very ungentlemanly. On the other hand, the girl most likely had instigated whatever it was that had her out and about town so late in the evening.*

"She told me she was planning to sneak out, dressed as a boy, to see what London was like at night."

"Dear Mother of God."

"Yes, well." He paused and seemed lost in thought. "Now that I say it aloud, I must admit that I think she was trying to shock me into doing exactly what I offered to do."

Elena waited, beginning to feel that William might have been more dupe than accomplice or, worse, instigator.

"We discussed it awhile. I did try to talk her out of it, but there is a look she will give you that says there are no words that will change her mind."

Elena had seen that expression, a kind of disinterest with a distinct sparkle in her eye.

"Finally, I told her that I would come back tonight with a coach and take her, dressed as a boy, to see some of the buildings and great city houses that were hosting parties."

"You idiot."

"Yes, well . . ."

Elena half listened as William went on, noting that he did not try to defend himself, which, Elena decided, was to his credit.

"I came back this evening; her governess sat in the corner again, so we were sure she suspected nothing. About fifteen minutes before the butler went for his supper, Mia went upstairs and with the help of one of the housemaids she changed into boy's clothes. Then she threw her cloak over all and came running downstairs and out to the coach not one minute after the butler left his post."

There was a tap at the door and this time it was Tinotti, who came in with a bottle of wine and two glasses.

"Thank you, Tinotti." Elena stood up as he uncorked the bottle. "You have read my mind. I may not feel very hospitable toward Lord William, but I do believe we both could use something to ease our nerves."

"Jealousy can make it difficult to see things clearly, signora." Tinotti handed her a glass as he spoke.

"Mia is jealous?"

Tinotti looked from her to William. Elena followed his gaze in time to see William frantically shaking his head.

"You think *I* am jealous?" Elena slapped the glass down on the table next to her. "Jealous of William's attention to Mia?"

It was all she could do *not* to blurt out what she had been doing tonight. That would disabuse them of their ludicrous notion. "Believe me, Tinotti, when I tell you that I am not, and never will be, jealous of anyone who captures Lord William's attention. Never. He is like a brother to me."

"Or a nephew," Lord William suggested. "We are friends, no more."

Tinotti backed up to the door. "I am sorry I misunderstood, signora. I will leave you to your discussion. Will you want to see Mia?"

"No. I told her to go to bed. I will speak with her in the morning." *I hope she does not sleep a wink,* Elena thought. *I am not sure I will.*

Tinotti hurried out the door, closing it again.

"Where were we?" Elena asked sweetly as she turned back to William.

William was swirling the wine in his glass, staring at it as though he could read the future in the red circles. Setting the glass down, he put his hands behind his back.

"Mia and I left here and I had the coachman drive us

all around Mayfair. There was a ball this evening, and some sort of bacchanal at one of the bachelor establishments, and the theater was busy, as you know. I made her sit back in her seat, not hang out the window, and explained to her what she could expect at each of the events."

"Including the bacchanal?"

"It did not look at all lascivious from the outside, more a house lit up like a tree on fire. I know who lives there and the sort of parties he favors. I told her that it was a political dinner party that would be unutterably boring."

He took a healthy drink of his wine. "Please believe me when I tell you, Elena, that being with me was far safer than what Mia proposed."

"If you had thought for a moment, William, you would have realized two things. First, you would have known right away that Mia's plan was a way to trap you into taking her. She is wild but not stupid, and going out alone at night, even dressed as a boy, is unsafe *and* stupid. Second, if you had told me I could have come up with a solution that would not have compromised you or Mia."

"Yes, I see that and I'm sorry."

"I do not believe you, my boy. Admit it, you thought it a capital idea and could not wait to show her around London, after dark." Elena could tell by his rueful expression that she was right.

Finally he shook his head on a sigh. "I can see I was too easily convinced. It was her eyes," he admitted. "She has that way of regarding a man as though he had it in his power to make her dearest wish come true. Even if it is no more than picking up her handkerchief."

"You two are alike, you know."

"Do I look like that? If only I had known."

"No, your eyes do not make me want to obey your every command." Though she could think of someone whose eyes did and had. She cleared her throat and her mind. "Both of you want to live life to the fullest, and for the two of you that does not mean anything as tame as playing the violin to perfection or learning to sing well."

"Yes, you are right," he said, sobering. "Perhaps it is because we do not have artistic talents to distract us."

It was nothing so simple, Elena knew that. William had something to prove to himself and to the world. And Mia, well—Mia wanted all she could have, wear, hold, or own. No one but God knew why.

"It is a shame she is not a man, Elena. We could have great fun together." He took a sip of his wine and it was as though the liquid inspired him. He looked up, back down at his glass, took another sip, then set the glass down. "I could marry her."

He spoke quietly, as if afraid to say it too loud, not yet sure whether it was an actual idea or brain fever.

"I would not deal you a life sentence, William. I was hoping for a match that would tame her, not set her off like a fireworks display."

"You mean that you're not opposed to a match because I'm—" He stopped and changed his wording. "For any reason in particular? I mean, other than your worry that I would not be a good influence on her?" He tried to control his devilish smile, which made him look all the more wicked. "There's no other reason?"

Because you are short? Because you are a Bendasbrook? A

little voice she did her best to ignore reminded her that once Mia was married, the girl's behavior would no longer give her headaches.

"William, dearest, you are free to marry her if your heart is involved. But you must wait until June to speak to her of marriage. It will give you time to see how you can influence her, for the better, I hope, and it will give her a chance to experience her Season without any thought of commitment."

When he would have protested, she held up her hand. "If anyone else comes to me, I will give you fair warning."

"It would be like her to elope," he mumbled, but Elena heard it anyway.

"Do not even put that idea in her head." She went to him, bent down, and kissed him on the cheek. Then she picked up his gloves and handed them to him. "Go home, William. I will talk to Mia and see if I can make her understand how lucky she is to have you on her side."

Elena rubbed her forehead and the all-too-familiar headache that was starting. "I will have to do it without making it sound like your behavior tonight was anything but reprehensible. It sounds impossible but since that is the word I would use to describe Mia, it may work."

"Thank you, Elena. Thank you." He took her hands and kissed both and hurried out the door.

But do you love her? That was what Elena really wanted to know. Or do you see her as someone who would accept you because you can offer her jewels, clothes and, oh yes, a wild adventure or two?

If they married, someday Mia would be the Duchess

of Bendas. Too far down the road. Much too far. First Elena had to decide how to handle her ward and whether she should hire a new governess after she dismissed this one. No, that was an easy enough decision. She and Tina would do their best between them. No stranger coming into their lives at this late date could begin to understand or change the girl. She was almost eighteen, held back from her time in society by the deaths of her father and her guardian. Any girl would be restless.

Mia was not "any girl," but a unique combination of charm, stubbornness, and petulance. Nothing would change that. A decent night's sleep might help Elena come up with a compromise that would make Mia happy and keep the rest of them sane.

She sipped the rest of her wine and stared at the Canaletto painting, but her mind was on neither. Instead she relived her afternoon and decided that the chaos of the evening was a fair price to pay for the hours before it. Later, she dreamed of the hours to come in the perfect house on St. German Street, in the pale blue bedroom, in the great lake of a bed with an amazing man beside her.

24

MERYON WENT DOWN to breakfast late. He'd slept well and was feeling better than he had for months. He hoped Elena had slept well too. Now that he had seen her with her hair down, it was a challenge to think of her anywhere but in bed, with her hair falling around her shoulders, not quite covering her breasts.

If he hoped to avoid his family he chose the wrong time for his meal, though it appeared that the three of them had been at breakfast for some time.

Michael and Gabriel read the paper. Lynette was still eating, but nearly done.

They all greeted him with varying degrees of good humor. Gabriel wasted no time in complaining about the paper's account of the Parliamentary debate of the last three days running.

"Spare me the details, Gabe. I heard it in person,"

the duke begged, taking a long drink of the coffee the footman poured, imagining Elena drinking from her mug and wishing they were sharing breakfast.

"Why do you not speak against the continuation of the Seditious Meetings Act? It is ridiculous that you must have a permit for more than fifty people to gather. What about organized fistfights and horse races?"

If this were Elena arguing with him over the breakfast table he knew exactly how he would end the discussion.

"What is so funny, Meryon?"

Gabriel's narrowed eyes reminded Meryon that his brother had a temper, and he pushed Elena to a cozy corner of his mind and spoke in a calm, rational way, momentarily horrified that he would have to spend the rest of his life setting a good example for his siblings. "Gabe, I choose not to speak now because I agree with the prevailing view that the Seditious Meetings Act be allowed to expire. There are other issues that concern me more than what is currently being debated and I want the lords' attention when I do speak. One way to ensure that is to keep quiet until I have words I want them to listen to."

The footman brought him a plate filled with eggs, some beef, and mushrooms. Meryon ate through Gabriel's continued argument, mostly with himself, regarding the consequences of endless discussion on a pointless issue, when more pressing subjects like the budget were awaiting their attention. "There are people everywhere out of work, hungry, looking for a way to buy food for their families."

"I am well aware of that." Now was not the time to tell Gabe about his plans for a program to support orphans and widows. Meryon knew this mood and only one thing would help dispel it. "Tell me, Gabriel, are you angling for a round at Jackson's today?"

At that invitation Garrett lowered the paper, eyeing the two men with interest. Lynette abandoned the last of her toast and looked from one to the other. Her gaze settled on her husband. The staring contest ended when Gabriel gave his wife a rueful shrug and she went back to her breakfast.

"I'm sorry. I know you give fearsome thought to your votes and I suppose some debate is essential." Gabriel gathered his thoughts for a moment. "I am tired of the way we complicate simple things with pointless debate or antiquated assumptions."

Antiquated assumptions. That is at the heart of his anger, Meryon realized. Someone had insulted him. Or Lynette. Yes, someone had insulted Lynette. She watched her husband with an expression of love and a little heartache.

Gabriel pretended to return to his paper. Meryon watched Lynette stare at the raised page for a moment. Then she took a sip of her tea and spoke. "He is upset because we were not invited to present our work at the Royal Academy of Science. The letter of rejection was in the post this morning." Leaning a little closer to her brother-in-law, she went on. "There is also the possibility that they consider the work more art than science."

"Which is entirely reasonable," Meryon agreed, "but it should at least be considered by a larger audience. The fact is that the artists will always suffer setbacks." He sat back in his chair. "You should talk to the Signora about this. Yes, her field is music but there must be similarities. She has nothing kind to say about critics."

Gabriel gave his brother a look that would have melted ice. "Thank you for your unsolicited advice, brother, and do tell us," he paused until he was sure he had everyone's attention, "how was your evening?"

Garrett began coughing and Lynette made a sound of disgust but all three watched Meryon for his answer.

He gave his brother no more than a smile. He would have restrained that if he could. His evening had been wonderful, so perfect that he could not imagine today would be better, but he was going to try.

Meryon applied himself to his eggs before he spoke again. "When shall we meet at Jackson's? Sometime before four o'clock. I have an engagement then. Garrett, are you with us?"

THE HOUSE ON St. German Street was exactly what Elena needed, quiet, blessedly quiet, with no young woman alternately crying and threatening, no servants fretting, no Lord William to refuse at the door.

Seating herself in a chair with a view out the front window Elena accepted the tea that the maid offered and waited, not at all disappointed to have a few minutes to compose herself before Meryon arrived.

The duke drove his cabriolet down the short drive not five minutes later.

Meryon jumped down from the carriage without waiting for the steps to be lowered. He gave his attention to the tiger, and in the golden light of the time after noon, the duke was cast in a light that made Elena as hungry for his touch as she was for tea after a difficult day. This hunger was arousing, not comforting, responding to nothing more than the sight of him.

Elena was flustered for a minute, not sure whether to greet Meryon with the decorum of a guest or run to the door and throw herself into his arms. Laughing a little, she waited until the duke came into the room before greeting him with a curtsy and then a kiss.

The lovers acted as though they had been separated for months instead of hours. The kiss fueled the hunger. Elena could feel Meryon's arousal and surely he could feel her eagerness.

Elena grabbed Meryon's hand and they ran up the stairs together. At the top she turned and kissed him again. "I have not felt this abandoned ever, never. We haven't even said hello."

"I will tell you about my day and you can tell me about yours." Meryon pushed open the door to the bedchamber. "Later."

In less than a minute, the dress, so carefully chosen earlier, fell to the floor along with the petticoats and stays until Elena wore nothing but a shift. With a haste equaling Meryon's, Elena yanked his coat off, not caring if a seam ripped.

Meryon pulled off his boots. Elena unbuttoned his pants and raised her shift so that she could mount him where he sat on the edge of the bed. She controlled the movement, and the first time Elena raised her hips and felt him inside her she forgot the awkwardness of their position.

Neither one of them had more than two minutes to enjoy the tension. When Meryon's seed spilled into her, Elena arched her back, holding onto his shoulders with both hands, and felt him as deep in her as it was possible to be. They collapsed beside each other on the bed.

"Who ever thought watching you climb from the coach would be all the seduction I needed?"

Meryon kissed her temple. "Or that your eager kiss would erase any doubts I had."

"Doubts?"

"Yes, I'm sure I had some but, as I said, they were all erased by that perfect, welcoming kiss."

"If it was perfect, Meryon, then we never have to kiss again, do we?"

"Nonsense. We must try and try and try to capture the same magic again."

"Oh, I see." Elena gave him a quick kiss that was not close to perfection but quite delicious, tasting of him as it did. Elena fell onto her back. Their legs were hanging off the bed but neither made an effort to use the mattress more conventionally, as though movement would break the spell.

"Do you think it will always be like this?"

"God, I hope not, what will I tell my tailor?"

"That you are supporting the economy in your own selfish way."

"If I told him that, then there is no doubt we would both be in a Rowlandson cartoon."

Elena scrambled up, still wearing her very wrinkled shift. "You will become chilled if we do not cover our- selves."

Meryon shucked off the rest of his clothes as Elena pulled the shift over her head. Then they both slid under the covers.

The shadows were deep in the bedroom even though the sun would not set for several more hours. Meryon and Elena settled themselves, her head on his chest, Meryon's arm around her.

"We are in some netherworld, between life and heaven." Elena drew a deep breath and was sure she could smell spring. "Tell me about your day, Meryon."

"Ooof," Meryon said. "I am very much back down to earth."

"Yes, my day was like that too, but now the worries seem a hundred miles away instead of just a few." Elena watched his chest rise and fall and tried to match her breathing to his.

ELENA COULD TELL the moment Meryon fell asleep, and her eyes drifted closed too. The time that passed could have been five minutes or an hour.

Shifting in the bed to ease a pleasurable stiffness, Elena stilled instantly when Meryon made a sound that was almost a moan. "Have I hurt you?"

"No, no, sweet." Meryon kissed her hand. "There is too much shadow in here to see the bruises, but my brother, Gabriel, fair marked me all over at Jackson's today. He was in a foul mood at breakfast and some time in the ring seemed the best way to erase the ill humor."

"So you are starting at the end of your less than perfect day?"

"Yes, I suppose I am. Mind you, I did not intend to be the loser. The man's in fine form; keeping up with all those children must be the key."

She loved listening to him talk like this. It reminded her of their first meeting and wished it would always be so.

"Gabriel is so impatient. He wants me to solve all the problems of hunger and unemployment right now and in my spare time find out why he and Lynette are not allowed to show their work at the Academy of Science."

Meryon might be more patient but he was not any less caring because of that. She raised her head and pressed a kiss on his chin. "Hunger and the need for more work have been with us as long as we have had cities, and even before that when crops failed."

"Precisely, and will take almost as long to cure. As for the Academy of Science, I have no cachet there. None at all. The academy is a group of men who are not anxious to see change despite their interest in science. A new bug or a fancy clock is all the group wants to read about."

"Perhaps Lord and Lady Gabriel should start another society to which the Duke of Meryon could lend his name and support. One that welcomes papers by anyone no matter what their gender or even their religion."

"That's a wonderfully egalitarian idea, Elena, but not likely to be taken seriously."

"Don't be patronizing, Meryon." She tried to look him in the eye, but could see no more than his chin. "In France, men regard women as having a value beyond the bedroom. Why can't the English be so bold?"

"I have no idea, but something the French do will not

win you support among the men of science. They are still annoyed by all the work Napoleon's men did during the war."

"Which makes my point, as I am sure some of those men were women." That reminded her of her evening. "Which brings me handily to my day, which began last night the moment I walked in the door."

Meryon listened to her account of Mia and William's misadventure with satisfying interest.

"That led to an absolutely awful morning. When I told Mia that her behavior meant a postponement of her first ton event, the girl had a tantrum that makes my temper look controlled. By the time Mia was done crying and screaming she had thrown a vase at the window and broken both."

Meryon's amazed "Good heavens" was all the sympathy Elena could hope for.

"I feel guilty leaving Mia in the Tinottis' hands but I have a very healthy selfish streak and wanted my time with you."

Elena sat up now, pulling the sheet up to cover herself.

"I sent a message to William asking him to meet me at Hatchard's. He was insistent that to restrain Mia any more was a mistake. I told him that they were too much alike for him to be any judge of what was the right action to take." She was becoming annoyed all over again. "He said that was exactly why he knew it was the wrong thing to do."

"Lord William is a force to be reckoned with."

Meryon eased himself up so that he was resting against the headboard.

"Yes, but I have always been able to count on him to do right before. Mia's influence is not for the best, I'm afraid." She watched Meryon, hoping for some support.

"That is an understatement," he said, folding his arms. "The viscount should have informed you right away and let you handle the situation."

Elena laughed. "That's what I said at first, but think about William. He is a man, not a governess, and besides that, a man who is inclined to share an adventure with any willing soul."

Despite the fact that she and Meryon agreed with each other Elena could see that they were close to an argument, so she kept any further thoughts on the subject to herself. She was not going to ruin their lovely afternoon with a nonsense disagreement over something so domestic.

Meryon must have read her mind. "I know this a big bed but there is only room for two people, as far as I'm concerned. Unless you are inclined to a ménage à trois?"

"You are not serious." She could not hide her dismay.

He shrugged. "I thought you might consider it an adventure."

"I would not." He seemed to accept her vehemence. "Would you, Meryon?"

"Not today."

A MÉNAGE À TROIS was not something he'd ever considered, even after viewing some of the vignettes at the whorehouses in his youth. A threesome was too much like watching circus gymnasts, albeit naked. But letting Elena think he was intrigued by it did give him an advantage. If Elena had any idea how besotted he was, he would lose all control of the situation.

They made love again and this time the sex was as slow and languorous as it had been rushed before. Elena seduced him, touched every part of him with her hands and her mouth.

Meryon loved the feel of her against him. Like her singing, her lovemaking unleashed emotions that were beyond any of his experience, from an overpowering lust, to love, to a fury of need frightening in intensity.

Wave upon wave drove him until he could wait no longer. Once the two of them were joined by the act of his entering her, of making them one, Meryon gave in to the physical need that took control and drove them together to completion.

Each knew what the other needed, wanted, and each gave as completely as mind, body, and heart would allow. That overwhelming hunger obscured the fear that Meryon needed her more than was wise.

He fell asleep again, sated and now wanting another kind of intimacy. He had never fallen asleep next to a woman before.

Unease crept back while his eyes were closed.

25

ELENA WAS DETERMINED not to be annoyed by Meryon's snores. Not snores, but the kind of breathing that meant the man needed rest. She lay next to him awhile, feeling used in the most delicious way. Obviously he felt the same.

Had anyone ever written a poem to a sleeping lover? Elena liked to think of sleeping with another as the dearest sign of trust a couple could share. Meryon was not pushing her away.

As if he heard her, Meryon moved in his sleep, reaching out so that his hand touched hers. The little bit of physical contact was enough reassurance to send him deeper into sleep again.

Elena supposed one little touch was one more way that men and women were different. Just that bit of contact was enough for Meryon.

Physical closeness made her want even more of him. Elena wanted to know everything, from what he thought about the way the Regent treated his wife to how often he had been to Gunter's.

Elena turned her hand so that their palms touched and she could feel his pulse, the smoothness of his fingers despite fencing and his time at Jackson's. Clearly the need to use their hands and fists was another way that men were different from women.

There was no saying which was better or if either truly worked. At least she was generous enough to allow that.

As Elena moved to hold his hand, Meryon pulled his hand from under hers and tucked it beneath the bed pillow. His gesture left her feeling dismissed.

Don't be so missish. This is hardly the place for such airs, she chided herself. *Leave him alone. He is every inch a man and sleeping like this proves it.* Resisting the urge to smooth the hair back from Meryon's brow, Elena slid from under the covers and out of bed, gathered her clothes, and went into the dressing room.

Tugging the bellpull, Elena tried to ignore a feeling of awkwardness. Her shift was wrinkled and damp but she had no other with her. Who would have known that it would be a casualty of their lovemaking?

The maid came quickly and helped her dress without comment, managing to convey a sympathy that was as nurturing as it was pragmatic. The woman was comfortable to be with.

"Madame, the duke asked me earlier to have wine and cakes in the salon. He will meet you there at his convenience."

The word "convenience" rankled, almost enough that Elena considered going back into the bedroom and making sure that the duke's convenience and hers were the same. Instead Elena took her vague sense of irritation with her to the salon, sipped the wine, and picked up one of the volumes that sat on the table next to the tray.

MERYON REACHED OUT to her and found cold linen. He wanted Elena to be here, next to him. Disappointed, he rubbed the fatigue from his face, sat up. No sounds came from the dressing room. That meant Elena was downstairs drinking wine and eating cakes, waiting. Meryon took his pillow and threw it across the room, and then was embarrassed as it reminded him of Rexton when the boy did not have his way. Well, that was the truth of it. Meryon wanted her here and now so that he could play some more.

He ignored the banyan that lay on the chair and dressed as he picked up his clothes. His breeches fit tightly and he patted the fall as if consoling himself. His shirt and cravat made him feel more gentlemanly, but he could not put his closely tailored coat on without help.

If he asked her to help him, it was possible that they could put the chaise in the parlor to good use. To that end he left his cravat loosely tied and imagined using it to pull her to him. He checked the clock and decided that he had all the time he needed.

That might work today, but what about tonight, tomorrow morning, after dinner? The one thing he had not counted on was that having a lover would not be at all *convenient*.

As he pulled on his boots, an impulse struck him with such force that he almost raced down the stairs with one foot bare. If Elena Verano became his mistress, she could live in this house and be available whenever he needed her. He squelched the thought that he might as well move in here with her as he seemed to want her every minute of every day.

She had a staff that would be too big for this place, but he shoved all the practicalities aside as he pulled open the drawers of his chest and hunted for some bauble to give her that would show her how serious he was, how much she meant to him.

Damnation. There wasn't much and nothing good enough for her. A book! Perfect. He spent more minutes than he wanted to trying to decide whether to give her the one with erotic sketches or the exquisite leather-bound copy of the *Kama Sutra* that had been on this shelf from the first day of his ownership.

The *Kama Sutra,* he decided. They could read it aloud to each other. Something they could share in more ways than one.

He found paper and, by some miracle, a pen and ink that were still usable. He wrote a note. The words came easily since they came from his heart. There, he thought. The time from impulse to action had been less than five minutes. He still had to put on his other boot, so he rang for the maid.

"Take this to Signora Verano," he said, handing her

the slim volume, "and tell her that I will join her in less than two minutes."

He pulled on his boot and using the glass, combed his hair and retied his cravat in a traditional knot. He would have plenty of time with her now.

THE BOOK HAD the most beautiful binding Elena had ever seen. There was no title on the front or the spine and she admired the elaborate gilt scrollwork that filled the cover. Studying it more carefully, Elena realized the scrollwork was a vine of some exotic flower, which entwined a man and a woman in the most erotic way.

She set the book aside, curbing one curiosity for another more compelling. The note read: *For you, Elena, with thanks and appreciation for your generous spirit and in anticipation of the next weeks and months.*

The note was not signed, though there was no doubt from whom it came. Elena had never seen Meryon's handwriting before and distracted herself for a minute as she tried to see some of him in the bold black ink and the disciplined lines.

Bold and disciplined. And very much in control.

Weeks and months. That should have pleased her. Protestations of undying love would have not been the truth. She knew that, but "I love you" would have been a lovely lie.

Elena took the book up and opened it, not at all surprised by the title page. *Kama Sutra.* She snapped the book shut. How clichéd. How like a man.

Meryon found her with the book in her lap.

"Thank you, Your Grace," Elena began without preamble. "Words of affection would have been enough of a gift from you."

She watched the duke for his reaction. He was a little surprised but not embarrassed, which was a relief. Or was it? *No, it was not.*

Elena wanted Meryon to grab the book, proclaim himself a thousand kinds of fool for thinking that something so carnal could express his true feelings, and promise to show her a dozen times a day what she meant to him.

"I'm sorry. Truly I am." Meryon took her hand, kissed it, and then gathered her into his arms. "I should have waited and we could have gone to the jeweler together. That way you could choose something yourself, but I wanted to give you something right away, something that would show you what you mean to me."

Meryon kissed her, that tender kiss Elena recognized from their first meeting. It eased the frustration with his reticence, but not the discomfort with his gift. Why could he not express his feelings, even if he felt no more than gratitude?

"Elena, there is something more. I want to give you this house. It may not be styled to your liking, but you may redecorate it any way you wish." His expectant smile confused her.

"But I have a home, Meryon. In Bloomsbury."

Elena made to step out of the embrace. Before he let go of her, the duke kissed her on one cheek and then the other. "My dear, I want you closer. I want to be able to see you whenever I am free."

Elena froze, quite literally, froze. Then her whole

being shivered as if waking from a fantasy. Meryon took up his glass of wine and drank as though what he wanted was as conventional as singing *Messiah* at Easter.

The explanation that came to her mind, the words, might be too direct, even crude, but Elena asked and hoped she was wrong. "You want to set me up as your mistress?"

"Yes, yes." He smiled again, not the true from-the-heart smile. This one was almost patronizing, as though she had not understood her lesson on the first telling.

She gave him an answer. It might not have been the one Meryon was looking for but there was no other response that could fully express her thoughts.

Elena slapped him.

It was not the most destructive blow in the world, but from the duke's shocked expression Elena knew he understood the message. And was surprised by it.

She found her voice. "You are telling me you want me to be your *mistress*? Not even asking. Telling me." She made fists with both of her hands to keep from slapping him again. "I wish a woman could challenge a man to a duel."

Meryon's confusion was insultingly real. The duke was shaking his head. He looked puzzled, his mouth slightly open, though not a word or sound came from him.

"Your Grace, you are the stupidest man I have ever met. A fool. An idiot." Turning from him, Elena marched toward the door. "Take me home now." She waited there, her back to him. She could feel the duke's eyes on her and gave him his answer on the chance he had misunderstood her anger. "No, I will not be your mistress. What's more, I will have nothing more to do with you. Not after that insult."

Still the duke did not move to open the door for her. Elena would not raise a hand to open it herself, but waited for him to act as a gentleman should.

"Elena, what on earth." Meryon tried again. "Listen to me."

"Are you so used to having everyone do your bidding that you do not even understand the word *no*?" Elena made the mistake of turning back to look at him as she spoke.

The duke was composed now, except for his eyes. There she saw anger and embarrassment. Good, Elena thought; that made two of them.

"I am sorry if I misunderstood your interest." His stiff words made his discomfort clear.

"Who do you think I am? What do you think I am?" Elena knew she was shouting and wanted to do more. She wanted to shake some sense into him. Instead she closed her eyes and prayed for self-control. It came to her, some small, angel-given gift that helped her behave as the lady she was born and raised to be, not the screaming witch he had unleashed with his vile suggestion.

"Meryon, you are the second person I have been with. I have had no other lovers." Elena stepped away from the door. "For me, making love is a special connection, a giving and sharing. What does it mean to you, if not that?" Elena did not wait for the duke to answer, but spoke for him. "Is it no more than physical need?"

"Yes, it's physical need, but more than that. I thought that having you in residence here would make our lives simpler."

"My living here would make your life simpler. Mine would be in a ruin. Did you not even think of Mia and what it would do to her debut? Have you become so used to everyone deferring to you that you have lost all understanding of true feeling?"

Elena knew that was not so. Their first meeting had shown her that Meryon was capable of deep emotion and compassion. She had seen it again when the carriage wheel had come off.

Stepping closer Elena hoped he would answer as the man she knew from that first meeting.

MERYON HARDLY KNEW what to do and even less what to say. His pride rose up like an angry beast. "My apologies," he said again, with a perfunctory bow.

Elena raised her hand with that abrupt gesture she used to stop someone from speaking.

"Don't you try to stop me, Elena. You've had your say and I will have mine." The duke did not even try to control his voice, did not care how he sounded. Reason had no place in this.

"You are standing here telling me you are insulted by my offer when you clearly want the same thing I do." He raised a hand to his cheek. "You want me every bit as much as I want you. You know that is true."

"I would have been happy to know you better. To

have an affair based on affection and respect. Not commerce and convenience."

Elena was quieter, still angry but not shouting. Meryon had a mental image of a balance where when one of them shouted the other calmed.

"Know me better!" He laughed, he could not help it. "We know each other intimately. What more is there?"

Elena shook her head as if he had asked the most pathetic question imaginable. "We know each other physically, Your Grace, but now that is almost a distraction. Do you really think that to know where to touch and when to kiss is to know me completely?"

"No, of course not. If giving you the book was a mistake then surely my note gave you some idea of how I regard you." How did he explain that sex was all he could give of himself for now?

"Your note was its own insult. You appreciate my generous spirit." She picked up the note to read the words. "And the way you can reciprocate is with a meaningless thing."

Elena tossed the book onto the table and ignored it when the volume fell on the floor. "Meryon, what we could have had was never about gifts or money. Never."

"Tell me what you want." He took a step closer to her. How could things have gone so wrong so quickly? "It seems I am incapable of understanding without an explicit explanation."

"Meryon," she said, taking a step closer as well.

They were still too far apart, in every way.

"I was hoping for love." She blinked away the tears he

could see filling her eyes. "Don't you understand that what we have is about love and not power?"

"You were expecting a proposal of *marriage*?" Meryon recoiled as if punched. He did not mean to edge the word with such disdain but he was totally confused. Marriage was out of the question. As she had said, they hardly knew each other.

"Marriage?" Elena's tears were gone and the anger was back. "We are not much more than strangers. This argument is proof enough of that, of our mutual misconception despite our compatibility in bed." She bent over and picked up the note and the book from the floor, read the note again, and then crunched it into a ball, dropping it on the table.

"I would not consider marriage for even a single second, Your Grace. I am an independent lady of means. I value my freedom too much to tie myself forever to someone like you."

"Someone like me," he repeated, stung.

Elena circled the room, but there were no paintings here to calm her. She stopped after ten steps and with a sharp breath continued her diatribe.

"I was insulted that you would ask me to be a kept woman, so that my life would revolve around nothing but *your* needs, when *you* wanted it, at *your* convenience. I would be no more to you than your valet or your tiger."

"I have heard quite enough," Meryon said, reaching for his hat and gloves.

"I am not finished," she shouted as she crossed the room to stand in front of him. "If you, Your Grace, were not so afraid of laughter, of love, of so much as a smile, we could have been very happy together. Now all you have are these two days to remember me by."

The duke grabbed her wrist and pulled her close. Elena's shock at such handling barely registered. When he spoke it was through gritted teeth. "When I say that I have heard enough, signora, you are well advised to stop talking."

"Oh, is that phrase another code? Is it like telling the tiger to go look for your walking stick?" Elena yanked her wrist from his grip and folded her arms, as if that would guarantee her safety. "That makes it all the more clear that I am not part of your world."

"Elena!" Meryon could feel his temper uncoiling, like a bear too long asleep. "You are the most aggravating, self-righteous woman I have ever met." The words streamed out oh, so quietly, but with lethal accuracy, and he made no attempt to hold them back. "You can shout like a harridan and always think you are right. You may be beautiful and sing like an angel, but you lack every feminine trait save one."

Meryon so wanted her to ask what that one trait was. Of course, now she did not speak, which was just as well as he had not finished.

"You think that one night of ill-advised conversation in the dark is license to invade my life in every other way."

He could see her biting her lip and wondered where her control had been a minute ago.

"If you need to hear the words 'I love you' then you will wait a long time. I never even spoke those words to my wife." He bit the words off and looked away from her. "The truth is . . . " He took a deep breath and unclenched his fist. "The truth is, I'm not sure that I even know what love is, but if shouting and hitting are part of it then I want nothing to do with it."

"I am happy to leave it that way, Your Grace." Elena's expression was as haughty as a queen's. "Take me home. Now."

She stood straight and still, waiting for him to do what she asked. No, what she commanded.

"I will, but you will always have a special place in my memory. I have never lost my temper with a woman. Until today."

Elena said nothing, but continued to draw on her gloves.

There was no point in continuing this. He was a Pennistan and only a fool would think he did not have a temper, but he had learned with the aid of a good tutor and his father's switch to control his anger better than his brothers ever did.

With a vow of silence until he bid her farewell forever, Meryon left the room to call for his carriage. He never would have guessed, when they raced up the stairs, that the day would end like this.

26

MERYON DECIDED HE WOULD go back to Jackson's after he left Elena and find someone who wanted a fight as much as he did. Then he would go home, avoid the family, and let Magda and a glass of wine soothe his wounded pride.

Elena Verano would call that truly pathetic, but it was no more pitiable than a woman who assumed that sex paved the way to a future beyond the bedroom. This had nothing to do with his ducal title and everything to do with Elena's unrealistic expectations.

He had brought the cabriolet, thinking that with the fine weather the drive back would be a lovely way to end their interlude. Now the new conveyance would be the one bright spot on the interminable trip back to Signora Verano's home.

ELENA ENDURED THE DRIVE back to Bloomsbury as if it were a punishment she deserved, wondering in which circle of Dante's Hell a person was made to suffer for sins of carnal feeling and pride.

She stared at the dark green blanket that covered her knees, picking out the threads of varying shades of green with brown and black mixed in. As much as she tried to ignore them, the duke's words echoed endlessly in her head. *His mistress.* Meryon had asked her to be his mistress.

The thought made her feel ill. That he could reduce lovemaking to a financial arrangement disgusted her. There was no point at all in pursuing any sort of friendship with this man.

If she opened her mouth she would cry, Elena was sure of it. Heartache filled her so completely that it would take only the slightest opening for it to pour out.

It was no distraction to watch Meryon's hands. His touch on the reins to urge the horse forward or to slow him was a crude simile for the control he wanted over her. She had invited it as surely as she had invited his first kiss that night in the dark, when they had been no more than a man and woman without name, title, or expectations.

Now Elena understood that they were more than that. He was a duke. With the title came a way of life that meant everyone did as the duke wanted, as the duke wished. Oh, yes, a duke had enormous responsibilities, but those did not affect her nearly as much as his wants and wishes.

He had never told his wife he loved her. That might have been the most amazing thing Meryon had said when temper had burst from him. That was no longer something that should concern her. They had no future, and the reason why had much to do with his inability to even say the word "love."

Elena Verano was better off without him. Meryon was a duke and her world was singing, a skill, or more accurately, a gift that was worth more to the soul than the dozen titles Lynford Pennistan could lay claim to.

Signora Verano might be known as a singer. By birth she was Lady Ellen Bendasbrook, a name that she had rejected as the Duke of Bendas had rejected her. In Italy her married state had protected her from advances. Now she knew that if Elena Verano stayed in London there would always be conjecture by both men and women.

How she wanted to talk with someone about this, but there was no one to whom she could unburden herself. Perhaps she should go to Paris. Coming to England had been a mistake.

Elena closed her eyes as they filled with tears and reminded herself that it was not more than twenty minutes to Bedford Place. Surely she could keep her composure that long.

The trip took so long that it was a struggle Elena almost lost. It both helped and hurt that the duke did not seem to notice her deep uneven breaths or the few tears that tracked down her cheek. Would all her memories of him be like this, pain mixed with pleasure?

Elena opened her eyes as the cabriolet made the turn onto Russell Square and it became clear that they were, indeed, traveling more slowly than usual. Through eyes blurred by tears, she could see conveyances of all types clogging the street that edged the square. The greensward itself was filled with people.

Russell Square was a popular spot, but she had never seen so many people in one place, much less a few doors down from her own home. She pulled off a glove and brushed the tears from her lashes so she could see more clearly.

A crowd, a large crowd, gathered around a man, standing a head above the rest, addressing them. He had a booming voice, but still the words did not carry to the edge of the multitude that must number in the hundreds. The throng pressed forward and the whole group groaned.

"Where did all these people come from?" Elena bit her lip. She'd had every intention of never speaking to the duke again.

"I hope they have the required magistrate's permission."

The duke sounded more concerned than indignant.

"They must have." He answered his own question and went on looking at her for the first time since he climbed up beside her. "They would have brought a statement for you to sign giving the time, place, and purpose."

"Yes, a man came to the door but I am not the legal householder, merely renting, so I could not sign permission. They must have found others. I wonder if my neighbors realized how many more than fifty there would be." Were any of her neighbors even home? "Why are these people not at work?"

"I suspect they wish they *were* at work," Meryon answered.

They were being so calm and sensible, as if no angry words had been spoken, as if nothing had changed. It made her eyes fill all over again. *Stop*, she commanded herself, and was relieved when it actually worked.

"Since the war," he added, "there are too many people and too few positions. Think of all the soldiers who are no longer needed in the army."

Now she wanted to yell, "I am an intelligent, educated woman, not the strumpet you would make me." Instead she tried to sound civil. "I read the papers, Your Grace."

"I see. Yours was a rhetorical question." His voice was stiff.

"Yes," she snapped. She raised a hand and then dropped it, realizing how often she made that gesture. "Please do not say another word. Otherwise we will start arguing again. I have no interest to entertain the public."

"Nor do I. You spoke first."

"And of course you must have the last word."

The duke looked at her as if deciding whether to rise to the challenge. After a long pause he inclined his head. "Yes, I must. Call it a ducal privilege."

"As if there weren't enough ducal privileges without that one more." Elena bit her lip to hold back the smile at having bested him. It was petty but she would count her victories, no matter how small.

She gripped the edge of the carriage frame as the horse grew restless. The animal was strong and well-bred and responded to Meryon's calming touch despite the unusual circumstances.

No one paid any attention to them, their interest focused on the speakers amongst them. Elena could not tell if the men scattered amidst the crowd were the main orator's representatives or were taking advantage of the gathering to make their own opinions known.

The people acted as though they owned the thoroughfare and it took the duke more than a few minutes to move the cabriolet to the side of the street. Finally Meryon had a word with the tiger and Wilson led the horse around the edge of the mass of people.

Eventually the crowd grew too dense to proceed. The duke did not relax when he stopped the carriage, but called Wilson to him and sent him off to ascertain if there was another route to the house in Bedford Place.

I can walk from here, Elena thought. It would be all she could do not to run and it could not happen quickly enough. Without a word to the duke, Elena stood. Surely she could jump down without doing herself injury.

"Do not even think of jumping down." The duke took her arm above her elbow and hauled her back to her seat. "It is not far to your house but it is obviously not safe."

Safer than I am here with you, Elena thought, pulling her arm from his grasp.

Meryon spoke even as he concentrated his attention on something or someone in the crowd. "Look over there, signora. Is that not one of your servants standing on the base of that statue?"

The height of the cabriolet now proved an advantage.

It was easy to see over the throng and Elena followed his line of sight.

"Yes! Yes, it is." Elena stood up, pressing a hand to her heart. The duke's horse sidled a bit and she sat down abruptly. "It's Signore Tinotti's wife, Tina."

"Either she climbed up there to find a better view or she is looking for someone."

"Tina would never be so unladylike as to climb up on the plinth for a clearer view of that speaker."

"Then what is she doing there?"

"An unanswerable question, Your Grace." Elena was proud of herself for not snapping at him, for asking something neither could possibly know the answer to. And where was Tinotti?

"She may need help climbing down." Meryon could not make out Tina's expression from this distance.

"Perhaps. But she does not enjoy crowds, because she is so tiny." The tiger hurried back before Elena could speculate that Tina's fear of being trampled was why she had climbed up on the statue.

Wilson took a moment to catch his breath. "Your Grace, sir, the hard part is this stretch right here. The people on the edge are not riled, just curious. They will move if we do. It's simple enough once you are beyond them. You turn at the next street and work your way around."

"I will do that presently." The duke turned to Elena but seemed lost in thought, someplace else entirely. When he spoke he was as commanding as ever. "I will go help the woman, if you will promise me, Elena, *promise*, that you will wait here for us."

She did not want the duke to do anything heroic. She

did not want to see him as anything but a cad, but Tina's well-being came before her own sensibilities.

"Yes, I will wait." Elena watched her maid as she answered Meryon. She was wearing something in a bold blue. It was easier to think about that than how frightened Tina must be.

"Look me in the eye and promise. No matter what you may think of me, your safety is as important to me as your honor is to you."

WHEN ELENA TURNED her eyes to his, Meryon wished he hadn't insisted.

"I will wait, Your Grace."

Those were the words she said, but her eyes spoke volumes more. They were defeated. No, worse than that. Heartbroken. And he knew her heartbreak was his fault. He had done that. It did not matter at all that his own heart felt leaden.

"Wilson!" the duke called out as he reached for his cane. The tiger came to him immediately. "You are to stay here and watch out for the lady and the horse. Mind you, boy, the lady's safety comes first."

Meryon did not wait for more than a nod and reached for his cane. As he was about to jump down from the side of the carriage away from the crowd, Elena spoke as though the words were being forced from her. "You had best leave your walking stick here. The crowd might not welcome a gentleman among them."

"The lady's right, sir, Your Grace."

Meryon dropped the stick and decided that did not

make much of a difference. He took off his gloves, removed his stickpin, loosened his cravat, and traded his hat for the tiger's cap. The cap was what changed him the most, and Wilson smiled and raised a hand to cover it.

Meryon walked back to Elena once more and pulled himself up onto the one high step so she could hear him over the noise of the crowd. "I will have to say something that will make her come with me, to convince the Signora that she will be safe with me."

"Tell her that I sent you to look for her. I will wave to her if you direct her attention to me."

"All right." Meryon stood there a moment longer, trying to read more than heartache in Elena's eyes. The sadness faded but the disillusionment that replaced it was not any easier to see. His anger resurfaced, but this time aimed at the person who had erased his lover's smile. Elena had the right of it. The Duke of Meryon was an idiot.

With a last nod, he jumped down. Crossing the road, he searched for an opening in the press of people, well aware that he would never do this for one of his own servants. Or maybe he would. But at this moment his motivation was less than pure.

The Tinottis were more than secretary and housekeeper. They connected Elena with a life that she had left behind in order to find a new one here.

Meryon knew it was too late to undo the rift he had caused and was not even sure he wanted to. But even though he might not want her love as much as he wanted her body, in that corner of his heart where honesty never slept, Meryon admitted that he would do anything to erase the pain from Elena Verano's eyes.

So Lynford Pennistan, Duke of Meryon, Earl of Danford and Swinton, Viscount Ladislaw, plunged into the gathering of people, none of them rich, most of them poor, surely all of them as English as he was. In doing so Meryon became part of the hoi polloi for the first time in his life.

27

THE NAMELESS CROWD became people instead of rabble. A man carrying a shaking dog as though it were a babe elbowed his way toward the front. Meryon followed him through the gaps he left behind.

People would turn toward the dog-laden man, annoyed at first, but the minute they saw the puppy their irritation disappeared and they made way with words of understanding.

There were any number of women with children. Men accompanied most of them, but some of the women were on their own. None wore hand-tailored clothes, but as many had good teeth and clean clothes as did not.

Food sellers sold pies and buns at the edges of the crowd and a woman wove her way through offering to tell fortunes. A happy mood prevailed, as though a fair had outgrown the field where it was staged.

Meryon spoke only when necessary, lest his accent betray him, but he wanted to find out why the crowd had gathered as much as he wanted to rescue Signora Tinotti.

The first three he asked merely shrugged.

Finally one man gave him half an answer. "This lot is here for the fun, but the ones up front are here for the speeches. When you try to crowd in there they won't let you, lest they not hear. They'll sell leaflets and newspapers when he's done talking."

"Tell me the names of the speakers."

"There be one speaker, sir. It's a man named Carlile. He owns a print shop, and speaks so people will buy what leaflets he prints and his newspaper." The man gave Meryon the once-over. "I expect you would not like what he has to say. He wants to give all men the right to vote." With a tip of his hat, the man moved on, leaving Meryon wishing he had come to hear Carlile.

When he was near enough to Signora Tinotti, he tried to gesture to her but someone barred his way. This close, he could see that Tinotti had the air of someone doing her best not to betray her fear, but her wide eyes gave her away.

The people closest eyed her suspiciously. What sensible woman would do something as indelicate as climb onto a statue? One or two people spoke to her, but she shook her head and did not answer. She spoke English, he was sure of it.

A rousing cheer from the front distracted them and Meryon felt a wave of unrest ripple through the throng as they pushed forward again. This group could turn from amiable to ugly with the slightest ill wind. Even as he had the thought he heard a pained cry.

Meryon glanced back to see a boy helped from the ground by his mother, whose "You pig. Pick on someone more your size!" made no dent on the bully's armor.

The man took her advice and jabbed Meryon in the ribs hard enough to hurt. "Outta my way, you dressed-up coxcomb." The man rubbed his knuckles as though the jab was just the beginning.

Meryon hesitated a mere second, and then unleashed a day's worth of anger and frustration on the unsuspecting but oh, so deserving victim. Reverting to the style he and David used in the boxing ring at home, Meryon ignored all the gentlemanly rules of boxing that Jackson insisted on, ramming his fist into the bully's gut. Meryon came up under his chin with his other fist. The man went down before he realized he'd met his match.

Meryon straightened, tossed his cap to the ground, and with his hands raised, hoped the man had friends as big as the bully was. The man did have friends but they were smarter than the bully. Shaking their heads at Meryon, they pulled their leader up and half walked, half carried him away from the crowd.

As Meryon bent to pick up the tiger's cap he saw five men at his back, ready to fight on his side.

"Well done, Your Majesty," one of them called out.

Meryon laughed and shook his head, feeling better than he had for hours. "There are times when words are pointless." The men and the others nearby nodded. "I thank you for your support."

The outer fringes of the crowd began to melt away, as

if outpunching the bully was all the entertainment they needed.

Or they wanted none of the anger that was all they could hear of the speeches at the front. Anger bordering on a call to action. Meryon hoped his behavior did not spur the contagion on.

"Signora!" he called once he'd cleared the crowd and stood at the base of the statue.

Meryon did not have to call her twice. She had seen the brief spat with the bully, and Meryon could tell it had not encouraged her to trust him.

"Per favore, la vostra attenzione, signora!" he called again. When she focused on him, Meryon waved a hand behind him. She followed his direction. He saw the servant catch sight of Elena.

With a frantic nod, Signora Tinotti wasted no time in clambering down, taking shelter between his body and the statue.

She exploded in a spate of Italian that made no sense at all to the duke. One woman in the crowd glanced at her askance. "Is she French?" she asked.

Meryon ignored her, but when Signora Tinotti began to cry and babble even faster a man asked, "Is she possessed or daft?"

The duke cast him a freezing look and they backed away. If these men were given the vote the country would be in the hands of the uneducated and stupid.

"She is neither daft nor possessed. She is afraid. Which means she is the only sensible one here," he growled.

He should never have voiced his concern. A fight

broke out between two men, apparently over a young woman who stood nearby pretending hysterics.

He could have broken up the fight or taken a hand in it, but he thought of Elena waiting for him. Yes, Wilson would defend her, but the boy could not adequately protect Elena and the horse if a riot ensued.

With a word of warning to Tinotti, Meryon swept her into his arms as he would a child. With a squeaking sound, the servant pressed her face into his coat, as though trying to hide.

Making his way through the crowd carrying a frightened woman guaranteed cooperation. Meryon thanked the man and his puppy for the inspiration. When he reached the carriage he found Elena standing beside it.

"Tina," she began.

"We will walk, Signora Verano. You can tend to Signora Tinotti in a moment. Move briskly, like the rest of the crowd. If they turn mean, the cabriolet will be too likely a target."

Wilson insisted he would stay with the carriage. It made sense and Meryon hoped that both the boy and the cabriolet would be in one piece when he came back.

Meryon strode toward the edge of the square and Elena fell into step beside him. "Is Tina hurt?"

"Not at all. But she is still shaking and I think too upset to walk. Besides, if I continue to carry her, no one will question why we are hurrying away." He shifted her in his arms. "Signora, let Signora Verano see you are not injured."

Signora Tinotti raised tearstained eyes to Elena and began in Italian. *"Ah, signora, mi dispiace tonto—"*

"Tina, please use English."

"It is Mia. I do not know where she is. When she saw the crowd gathering, Mia announced that she was going to take one of the servants and see what was happening. Neither one of them came back. Tinotti and I hurried to see if we could find them. Then I lost Tinotti. I was afraid that I would be trampled so I climbed up on that ugly statue to wait until everyone left."

Elena raised panicked eyes. "Your Grace, I cannot leave until I know that Mia is safe. I must find her." Elena turned back toward the park.

"Listen to me." He felt a wave of relief when Elena did just that. "We will go to your house and see if Miss Castellano has returned. I am certain that Tinotti found her and any minute now he will come to look for his wife."

It made sense, but apparently the women did not think so. Elena and Signora Tinotti began arguing in Italian. Meryon, taking advantage of Elena's distraction, continued walking toward her home on Bedford Place. Since he still carried her servant, Elena had to follow him to continue whatever they were arguing about.

By the time Elena and her maid had decided what to do, the front door of the Verano residence was in sight and Tinotti came on the run to meet them. "Mia is home, she's safe," the secretary called, hurrying breathlessly toward them.

The duke set his burden down so she could race to her husband, then offered Elena his arm. "I will see you home."

Signora Verano held up her hand as if to ward off evil.

"My virtue is in greater peril on your arm than if I walked the street alone. Good-bye, Your Grace. I appreciate your rescue of Tina. And I am greatly relieved that everyone is safe."

Despite the small speech, she did not pull away from the duke when he took her arm.

Fatigue had replaced her anger and for the first time Meryon noticed that while her beauty would last forever, distress always took a toll. Elena looked exhausted, as though the burden she carried had proved too heavy.

The irresponsible behavior of her ward was the last straw. And he had hurt her with what he thought a reasonable proposal, one that she had considered an insult.

The girl would apologize for what should have been an innocuous adventure and all would be forgiven. There was no doubt that he too would have to apologize, though Meryon had no expectation of forgiveness.

Meryon could feel the tension in her, the words ready to burst from her. But Elena kept her counsel until they were actually inside the front door of her home.

The hall was filled with people, most of them servants, and her ward. Elena hurried to Miss Castellano. "Mia! You know I forbade you to leave the house today. What were you thinking?"

"That I do not have to do what you say. That I can make my own decisions." The girl smiled, a little guiltily, but with enough arrogance to make it unappealing. "Elena, I am a grown woman now. I can say no to your dictates and there is nothing that you can do about it."

Meryon watched as Elena stood silent, as if trying to gauge how serious the girl was.

"Go to your room."

"No," Miss Castellano said with a grin that Meryon himself wanted to slap off her face. "I will wait for you in the blue salon." Elena's ward walked very slowly into the salon. The servants needed no encouragement to leave. In a minute the two of them were alone in the hall.

"Thank you for your help today, Your Grace."

It was the most wooden expression of gratitude he had heard in a long time.

"But, sir, if you think that rescuing Tina will redeem you, then you are greatly mistaken." There was nothing wooden about Elena now. As she spoke, anger replaced fatigue. "I am a widow, with money, some standing in society, and a ward to introduce to the ton. There is nothing you can say or do that will make me reconsider your offer. You can threaten to blacklist me among the ton. You can defame my voice and my talent. If necessary I will return to Italy before I let you hurt me or the people I love."

"Madame, you wrong me." He spoke with urgency. "Why would you think so ill of me?"

"Because you have power. Because you are a duke. That is what dukes do."

"I would never do anything to defame you personally, or your beautiful voice. You must believe this." He wanted to take back the last sentence. He should have begged instead of commanded, but he went on before she could push him out the door. "Let me assure you no one will ever learn a word of our conversation from me."

"Thank you."

"No thanks are necessary."

He bowed formally and opened the door for himself since the butler had disappeared with the rest of the servants. Meryon stepped out onto the stoop and stopped. Groups, largely family groups, were streaming past the Verano residence, less than a block from where the crowd had gathered.

"There is one more thing, Your Grace." She stepped out onto the front steps with him. "There are greater issues at stake than my sensibilities.

"Your brother is right. The government has created the nightmare we sampled in the square today and the House of Lords must find a way to show us the better times that peace should bring."

With that, she went inside and closed the door. Part of him knew that Elena was angry at everything and everyone because of their argument. Everything from the color of her shoes to a government moving too slowly. But he wanted his turn to speak. Meryon hated it when people thought his ducal privilege kept him from seeing what went on in the rest of the world. He hated it because he was afraid they might be right.

He had more of a sense of it today after his brief foray into the crowd. His satisfaction over the confrontation with the bully had reminded him that there was a reason that Pennistans had fought in so many battles, and apparently not all of it was because of loyalty to the crown.

His war was in Parliament now, and that was definitely a sign that change was coming, that more battles would be fought in the House of Lords than on any battlefield. It was more likely he would be bored to death than killed by a sword.

Meryon doubted he would ever have a chance to continue this discussion with Elena Verano, to justify or rationalize or even argue what his Parliamentary responsibilities were, to tell her about his plans. It was the least of his disappointments today.

28

MERYON WALKED DOWN Bedford Place, back toward Russell Square to reclaim his carriage. A man was coming toward him down the street, a bag slung over his shoulder and a wad of broadsheets in his hand. "*The Republican,* sir?"

Meryon nodded, handing him a few coins. "Do you have any of the leaflets that Mr. Carlile prints?"

"Only these crumpled ones, sir." He reached into the bottom of the bag and showed him what was left.

Meryon took them and waved off the change the man would have given him.

"Thank you, my lord." The man smiled in appreciation and raised his customer's station as well.

Meryon found the cabriolet, with Wilson, his tiger, standing on the driver's seat, lecturing a group of interested men and boys.

"It's been in England but three years. Some frog was the first to show it off, but it is such a splendid invention that we are willing to forget that."

The audience murmured with varying degrees of interest in the speaker, the carriage, and the single horse.

"My employer purchased it when he was in France last winter and it has just arrived. Mind you, it is not the first in England, but it is the finest."

Meryon hopped up beside Wilson, who looked mightily relieved.

"Looks like a curricle," one man called out.

"Yes, that it does," Meryon answered, "but it is lighter and requires only one horse."

"An economy." The crowd laughed at the idea that someone like him should need to economize.

"In theory, yes, but in fact the horse must be well-bred and large, and it will be costly no matter what the color."

"Aye." Several in the group chorused as though they had been played that trick.

"Gentleman, I appreciate your enthusiasm, but I am expected home and if I am not on time the cook will serve my food cold and with too much pepper."

They laughed again and one or two applauded. Most of them understood that whether the cook was your wife or your servant, rank meant nothing if you were not prompt to meals.

Wilson took up his post at the back and Meryon moved off through the near-empty streets, trying not to think about what a mess he had made of things. Elena actually thought that she could find happiness in marriage, twice in one lifetime. Or, perhaps, having found it once she thought it would be easy to duplicate.

It was impossible. He did not even play an instrument. And he was sure that she had read nothing of Hazlitt, his favorite of the current writers.

It did not matter now. He had a feeling that the only person who could explain it to him would not even look at him, much less talk to him. The whole thing had ended before it began. He laughed. He did not even need wine to sound like a lovesick schoolgirl in a decline.

He was *not* lovesick, nor a schoolgirl. He was an experienced man of the world who had misread an invitation. As a gentleman he would treat her well should they ever meet.

In the meantime, he would have to write some sort of apology. He made the last turn onto Penn Square. The horse knew the way and he relaxed his hold on the reins and considered what sort of apology he should write.

A *note* of apology. Would that be too short? A letter, perhaps. A book would probably not be enough for her. A note so heartfelt she could not mistake his sincerity. If he used his blood for ink.

He would not blame Elena for what happened next. He had allowed himself to be distracted. Wilson called to him from his perch, speaking just loud enough to be heard.

"Sir, Your Grace! We're being followed."

Meryon looked over his shoulder, and sure enough a hulk of a man was trotting along the road behind them. The bully from Russell Square.

Meryon called back to Wilson. "I want no scene in

public. I will take the carriage back into the mews, to the stable. Then I will see what he wants."

"I know what he wants," Wilson called out in an aggrieved tone. "Your blood! I'll jump off and rally the boys to help."

Before Meryon could stop him, Wilson hopped down, stumbled, and took off running for the mews. By the time Meryon reached the stable, the big man was making a grab for the wheels. If that bastard ruined his cabriolet, he would find out firsthand what the Pennistan temper felt like.

The head groom came out to take charge, and Meryon stepped down from the seat and turned to face his pursuer. The groom had moved the conveyance into the stable when two men came up from Meryon's back, grabbing his arms and twisting them up behind him.

Their leader came to him with a satisfied smile, and pushed Meryon's hat off.

"Good evening to you, Duke. It's time for you to learn not to pick a fight with someone bigger and stronger than you." The smell of bad teeth and worse food made it an effort for Meryon not to turn his head.

"I'll grant you taller and bigger, you buffoon, but not smarter." Wilson must be around somewhere. Meryon rather enjoyed an uneven fight, but not this uneven. If the fools would let go of him he would match them punch for punch.

"You know who I am," Meryon said, playing for time.

"Been thinking about doing this awhile now, you stuffed-up piece of dog meat. Been following you all day,

had a nice rest while you and your whore were at that little house. Followed you all the way back to Russell
Square. When you went into the park I thought I was all
set, but those fools thought you were worth saving."

"Your first mistake."

As the bully pulled out a knife, Meryon lifted his foot
and pushed up and back, making contact with the soft
part of one of the men behind him. The man let go of
Meryon's arm with a howl and doubled over. The one who
held his other arm let go as well, smart enough to figure
out that he would be next.

Now seemed an excellent time for his side to show
up, Meryon thought. Three against one he could handle.
But not three and a knife. Someone wanted to see him
dead, maimed, or scared witless.

"You two, stay back; I can take this fop," the bully
called out when Meryon could hear the men running
away.

Better, much better odds now.

The dusk made it harder to see, but the first lunge
was impossible to miss. The man had no skill and would
rely on his larger size. Meryon risked the move to pick his
hat up from the ground and use it as shield. It lasted for
about a minute. He'd liked that hat, damn it.

The next swipe and Meryon took a cut to his coat, but
he was able to grab the bully's wrist and twist it so that the
knife clattered on the cobblestones.

"A fop, am I? I just disarmed you. What does that
make you? A nancy boy, I'd guess, and those two keep you
happy when you can convince them to stay around."

The bully roared and charged him. As Meryon stepped aside, Wilson came running from the back of the house with three of the grooms. And Magda. Meryon waved off the grooms, but Magda came charging, barking furiously.

Meryon allowed the distraction a moment too long. The bully wrapped his arms around him from behind and picked him up. The man did have size on his side. Wherever he landed Meryon knew it would hurt. Magda yapped at the bully's heels, and he raised one foot and kicked the dog so hard that she flew across the alley. With one pained yelp Magda fell in a heap.

"Magda!" Wilson screamed. "You bastard. You son of a bitch. I'm gonna kill you." Wilson ran to the bully, yelling an impressive string of obscenities. The boy jumped on the attacker's back and began pummeling him with his hands, pulling his ears and reaching around to scratch the man's eyes out.

The bully dropped Meryon and gave all his attention to shaking the boy off his back. The drop was harmless, but before Meryon could gain his feet, the sound of a pistol caught the attention of everyone except Wilson, who was getting the best of the man four times his size.

"See to Magda, Wilson. Now." Meryon used his voice of authority, and the boy dropped off the bully's back and ran over to the fallen spaniel.

Garrett came out from the back garden, one pistol smoking, the other cocked and ready.

"Your Grace, your dinner is waiting. I will take care of the uninvited."

Meryon nodded and went over to Magda. Wilson

hovered over the dog. "I don't see any blood but I think she's dead."

"No. I can see her breathing. Let me carry her into the house and we will send for the senior groom to examine her. He doesn't work in the stable anymore but he will know what to do."

Wilson stayed close as Meryon picked up the dog as gently as he could. By the time they were inside, Meryon could feel the weight of her, but Magda was still breathing.

No sooner had they reached the senior groom's quarters when Rexton caught up with them, out of breath from racing down from the nursery. The boy insisted that Wilson repeat every detail of the fight.

It took two hours to revive the dog and to calm Wilson, who kept trying to explain that the grooms had been at supper. The senior groom felt no broken bones or swelling of blood and thought that the dog might survive.

"Mind you she's likely to nip at you and growl if she's still in pain, so do not think to pet her until she comes to you."

Both boys nodded.

"And you come to me if you start to worry or anything changes."

The old man winked at Meryon, who tried not to smile as he thanked him.

Meryon had changed his clothes for dinner before the butler informed him that the meal would be late due to upset in the household. Either Cook was taking advantage of the incident as a show of power, or everyone loved Magda more than they feared the duke.

Meryon stopped in to see Magda, who was resting in

an elaborate dog bed, her eyes closed but her tail thumping every now and then. The boys sat nearby, their attention split between a game of checkers and Magda. Without disturbing them and with a word to the nurse about Wilson's presence, Meryon headed down to his study.

He prepared a pen, smoothed some paper, and twenty minutes later was still staring at the blank sheet as he thought over the attack in the mews.

Bendas was intent on doing what he had failed to do the morning of the duel, and confronting him would mean nothing but lies and public spectacle.

He would talk to the viscount, Meryon decided. It was the least he owed Lord William after his help last year.

Picking up the pen again, Meryon smoothed the piece of paper, creamy white with the Meryon crest on it. The words to the viscount came easily enough. Short and to the point. If Lord William cared at all about the future of the Bendasbrook family and fortune he would see him as soon as he returned from Kent.

Meryon still had to write to Elena, and he knew those words would not come as quickly. When Garrett knocked on the door, Meryon was relieved to have an excuse to delay the note. Meryon poured both of them a brandy and offered Garrett a chair on the other side of his desk. "It appears you found out what you needed to know without resorting to brutality."

"We talked."

Meryon waited, rolling his glass between his hands, warming the brandy.

"The grooms found the other two hiding in one of the

storage buildings. They're frustrated. Even the bully. They want work. They need money to feed their families."

"Go on."

"I told them that breaking the law and ending up in jail would hardly guarantee their families' future."

"That's the truth, Garrett. But we both know they need more than that."

"It's amazing how useful those old army skills are."

Meryon raised his glass in salute. "I take it they are more bruised than you are."

"Your Grace. I'm a man of God now." Garrett saluted his brother-in-law in return. "I offered them money if they would tell me who put them up to this."

"Ah."

"Yes, they really did not have much of an idea. They said a gentleman came to them and offered them money if they beat you up. The worse off you were the more they would be paid. He gave them one guinea as a mark of good faith."

"Bendas." Meryon was sure of it. And annoyed that he'd never considered Bendas would try something like this.

"Or one of Bendas's minions did it on his orders. The bully, whose name is Reese, described a mature man but not an old or crippled one. DeBora or Rogers, I would guess." Garrett's expression turned even more solemn. "Lyn, Reese was told that if you should die of your wounds there would be no consequences."

Meryon took some brandy to ease his anger. "That is fascinating, Garrett. This is the first clue I've had that

Bendas is fighting back. In his style, which is indirect and illegal. I should not be surprised."

"But you are."

"Yes," Meryon said.

"I warned you no good would come of this."

"Stop sounding like a Greek chorus. I am not the one contemplating murder. Bendas is."

"What will you do now?"

"Protect myself, my family, and my staff, by pushing harder to bring Bendas to justice. I've sent a note for William Bendasbrook to come see me as soon as he returns to town."

"All right. I am expected back at Pennford soon, but I can stay if it will help."

"No. No. I can defend myself if Reese and his friends come back. Wilson will be on the watch. And the boy fights. Not with any skill, but he is ferocious." He considered Wilson, Reese and his friends, and the crowds of unhappy people he had seen at Russell Square today. "What we do not need is someone like Bendas, urging attacks on the ton. That will lead nowhere but to trouble."

"Those people are not Jacobins, Meryon. They are men looking for work and a way to feed their families."

"Which, I imagine, is exactly what the French aristocrats first said about the Jacobins."

29

GABRIEL AND HIS WIFE had gone to the theater, which left Meryon and Garrett to have a late dinner together.

Meryon went to his suite determined to write the note and send it before he saw Signora Verano again. It was the most urgent charge on his time but not the most important.

Garrett had gone out as well, and Meryon would bet his favorite stickpin that Garrett would make the rounds of the parties and see what stories The Gossips bandied about regarding tonight's incident. Meryon had no doubt The Gossips would hear through that mysterious manner of communication they kept such a tight secret.

Moving as quietly as always, his valet left wine at the duke's right hand.

"Blix."

The valet turned around, his face an obsequious mask. "Yes, Your Grace?

"Did you hear of my experiences today?"

"Yes, Your Grace. The boy, Wilson, had everyone's attention at supper and made the most of his moment. He said that you single-handedly rescued a woman in distress and beat off several men who would have done her injury and, later in the mews and with Magda's help, bested the same ruffians who came looking for revenge."

"That is more imagination than truth, Blix." Meryon rubbed his forehead as he spoke.

"I do not doubt your words, Your Grace, but your clothes were in a disreputable state."

"Part of my disguise, so no one would think that I was an agent provocateur or, worse, an aristocrat."

"Very well, Your Grace."

He turned to leave and Meryon smiled. He might lose a valet tonight, but he was curious.

"Blix, tell me, do you have an opinion on the current state of the economy?"

Blix had his hand on the doorknob, but he let go of it and turned around.

"Yes, Your Grace."

"Explain it to me."

Meryon wanted to laugh out loud at the shock on his valet's face.

"You want my opinion, Your Grace?"

"Yes."

"I read the papers."

"You are the second person to say that to me since noon today. Does what you read help you form an opinion?" This was like teaching Rexton to play chess. Laborious. He was not sure it was worth the effort.

"No, Your Grace." Blix stared at his shoes for a long moment and Meryon decided his valet's answer might be worth his patience after all. "In fact, Your Grace, I was in Russell Square today."

"You were?" Now it was his turn for shock. Was that the slightest bit of bravado he heard in his valet's voice?

"Yes. I was curious."

Meryon wondered what that meant. "Tell me what you thought of the speeches."

"The crowd was more impressive than the speeches. There were so many people, and one must assume they were out of work. I had no idea there were that many people desperate for a position."

Meryon folded his hands on the top of his desk and leaned across them. "If they are desperate for work, then soon they will be desperate for food and shelter."

"Absolutely true, Your Grace." Blix took a step closer to the duke and there was definitely enthusiasm in his voice now. "Does Parliament have a plan?"

"Not that I know of, but I do. I am preparing a bill to provide food and shelter and training for widows and orphans."

"But we have the poorhouses."

"Which are woefully inadequate and tend to perpetuate the problem. Training is the important part of this proposal. Train them how to do the work that is springing up everywhere, in factories especially."

Blix nodded but did not seem willing to commit himself any further.

"Change is in the wind, Blix, and we are fools if we think that life will stay the same. We will always be a country of farmers, but the farm must learn to coexist with the new manufacturing enterprises. The best we can hope for is that we can control it before it takes control of us. My proposal for care and training is aimed at that. If I can convince those who invest in manufacturing to support the care and training, the project will be self-sustaining."

"It's an excellent idea, Your Grace. It could work. But first you have to convince the others in Parliament."

"Well, I made the first step tonight." Meryon leaned back and folded his arms across his chest. "I convinced you. I want you to know that I would welcome any further wisdom you would care to share."

"As you wish, Your Grace."

He spoke halfheartedly this time and Meryon realized he might be asking too much. Meryon watched the servant steadily and willed him to speak. Blix merely waited attentively.

"Aha, you see, Blix, it is not only the titled and wealthy who are afraid of change. If the two of us, who are practically in each other's pockets, cannot exchange ideas and information, then how am I to do it with complete strangers?"

"There is one more thing."

"Yes." It sounded as though a confession was coming, and indeed Blix squared his shoulders as though willing to take a bullet for what he was about to say.

"It was my half-day off, today, Your Grace, and I thought that I would walk, as I often do, which is how I happened to be near Russell Square. I went to Bloomsbury to acquaint myself with the residence of Signora Verano. To see her in person if I could."

Meryon waited, not at all happy with this revelation.

"I was under the impression from some conversations I overheard that you were going to be seeing rather a lot of the lady and I wanted to know what she looked like, what colors she favored, and if I should consider changing your style to complement hers."

"Quite a speech, Blix. I had no idea that such was one of the responsibilities of a valet."

Blix bowed at the rebuke. "Mr. Brummell always said that the employer was a valet's best advertisement. Your Grace, you are not the slightest bit interested in what you wear as long as it is clean and well made. A family trait, so Lady Olivia's maid tells me. If you will beg my pardon, Your Grace, it is in both of our best interests for you to appear at your best in all situations."

It was as though he had started a flood. Blix had not said this much in total in the five years that he had been Meryon's valet.

"I stand corrected. Now I will correct you. Signora Verano has made it clear that she is not interested in anything more than the most occasional acquaintance. So I do believe that your trip to Bedford Place was for naught."

"I see, Your Grace."

Yes, I'm sure he does, Meryon thought. "Tell me who told you of my interest in the Signora."

Blix gestured toward the settee. "You did, Your Grace, when you discussed it with Magda."

Meryon laughed, truly laughed. He was indeed his own worst enemy. "Thank you, Blix. Thank you very much."

Now Blix did smile, almost a grin. The valet bowed. "You are welcome, Your Grace." He closed the door behind him, leaving Meryon to wonder if that was the first time he had ever thanked the man.

Reaching for his wine, he took a sip and then a longer drink, thinking he could easily down the whole bottle. His understanding of both women and servants left a great deal to be remedied. It made him wonder who else he might have been underestimating.

The pen and paper waited. The note still had to be written.

How he wished this note was a beginning and not an ending. If Elena had agreed to live in the house on St. German Street, he would be sending her a message telling her when to expect him, along with a book of poetry with a marker at his favorite. Not one from the erotic collection, but something more romantic. Then when they were together, no words would be necessary.

If this had been the beginning instead of the end they would have hours and days and months and years to share everything.

If thoughts of what-might-have-been were his punishment, then his wrong had been colossal. As Meryon dipped the pen in ink and wrote the date, he accepted that the last few days would be all he would have of Elena Verano.

Those few hours were better than nothing at all.

30

TINA, WILL YOU PLEASE go tell Mia that if she
wants her gowns to be ready for her first ball then this had
best *not* be one of the occasions when she chooses to say
no."

"Yes, signora."

"I will wait in the blue salon."

Elena walked into the salon and right over to the
Canaletto. She refused to go upstairs, but the blue salon
was not much better. Elena could swear she could
still feel Meryon here, smell the intoxicating sandalwood scent he favored. If she went up to hurry Mia
along, Elena knew she would be drawn into her sitting
room, to her desk where the soot-stained letter awaited
her.

It was still readable. Reason had overcome her moment of anger when the thing arrived, and Elena had

pulled the letter from the fire before the paper took heat and went up in flames.

Now she had only to decide to open it. Once she had read Meryon's apology Elena could put this behind her and build a life around what she treasured the most, her music and her friends.

"I am so sorry, signora, but you must come up. Mia is in tears and begs to talk to you."

Mia crying? That was as rare as rain in the desert. Elena hurried up the stairs with unladylike speed, giving up any hope of arriving on time. There were some things more important than making a dressmaker wealthy.

When Elena went into Mia's room, the girl was well on the way to making herself sick from crying. "I am so sorry, Elena. I should never have been so rude to you and I want to tell you how sorry I am." The girl gasped the words out through tears.

Elena sat down on the bed and began rubbing Mia's back. "Stop crying and catch your breath, *cara.*"

Mia nodded and with noisy breaths controlled her tears. It took another few minutes for her distress to ease.

"It is so hard to stay home when everyone else is having such a good time and I have to sit here until after Easter." She said the last word as though it were at least ten years away instead of ten days.

"I know, Mia. Believe me when I say that I felt the same way once. But the waiting is over. Please understand that I haven't done this to be mean but because the more secure my place in society, the more invitations you will receive." Elena bit her lip to keep from laughing at Mia's expression.

"Is that why you were trying to be friends with the Duke of Meryon. For me?" Thankfully she did not wait for an answer but went on. "But that is why I was so awful. I was jealous of him. I thought that you were falling in love with him and were going to forget all about me. Oh, I am a selfish, selfish girl."

She hung her head and Elena had to press her lips together to keep from mentioning that the entire world did not revolve around Mia's needs.

"Mia, I want you to pat your face with cold water and have Tina help you dress. I will send word to LaVergne and ask if we can come in an hour. We are giving her so much business I hope she will be accommodating."

Mia laughed, a sure indication that the tear storm was over.

"I will be in my suite. Please send Tina to tell me when you are ready."

Once Elena was in her sitting room, she gave up the fight and sat at her desk to read the duke's letter. She spread the paper before her and read the note in less than a minute. It was short and she stared at the paper. It was exactly what she expected and not at all what she wanted.

She read it again. This time each word sealed his fate.

My dear Signora Verano,
My humble apologies for any discomfort I
caused you with my obviously misguided suggestion.
I look forward to seeing you socially. Hearing

you sing will be the bright spot in a Season that is
over for me even before it begins.

                                        Meryon

She ripped the note into ten small pieces, and tossed
it into the fire. It disappeared in a smoky, black curl,
which was all the words were worth.

Grabbing a handkerchief, she blotted the few traitor-
ous tears that had escaped before resolve ended them. She
was not about to let a man make her life miserable. It had
happened before and, she vowed, it would never happen
again.

When Mia came to her door, Elena's composure was
firmly in place. "We are off to the dressmaker, *cara,* and
after that the milliner, I think. There is nothing like a new
hat to boost our spirits."

"Yes, and then to Gunter's," Mia added. "Lord
William is to meet us there for an ice. By the time we are
home again, we will be ready to shine and enjoy every moment of the Season."

WHAT ARE YOU DOING at breakfast so early?" Gabriel
set down his knife and picked up a piece of well-buttered
toast.

"I did not sleep well."

"That's hardly surprising. We heard about Bendas's
bully."

"Ah, yes, the first step toward family legend. Give the
story a name. I'd prefer The Duke's Triumph."

"No, no. Everyone would have to ask which duke. Besides you are not allowed to choose the name the story is known by." Gabe asked the footman to "fetch some more hot water."

Meryon thought of Elena. "Fetch some more hot water" was the code for "leave us alone."

"Lyn, you are not going to laugh this off, are you?"

"Of course not. Steps are well under way to end this once and for all."

"Legal steps?" Gabriel asked.

Meryon did not deem that question worth answering so he nudged the subject in a different direction. "I've been debating moving the children to the house in Richmond to make sure they are safe."

"Good God, Lyn, they are safer in this barn of a house than anywhere else. It's not the castle fortress that Pennford is, but it would take weeks to go through every room and even longer to burn the place down."

"Burn it down? Thank you for introducing a whole new fear into my already too imaginative brain. The truth is that I like the house in Richmond much better than this one. I find that the Season has not even begun and I am already bored with the ton."

"You are?"

"Yes." Meryon spoke the one word but was sure that Gabe could hear what was unsaid. "And you will leave it at that."

Meryon ignored his brother's considering stare. Gabriel was debating whether to ignore the order, he was sure. Which was another reason it had been a mistake to invite Elena Verano to dinner. The whole acquaintance had been a mistake, starting with their ill-advised conversation in the dark.

A silent breakfast followed, with the rustle of the paper for company. When Meryon had signaled the footman that he was finished, Gabriel tossed the paper on the chair next to him.

"Since you are awake so early, Lyn, come with me to the gunsmith. The boys want to start to hunt and in order to do that I must teach them to use something besides slingshots. I could use your advice."

Meryon allowed himself to be talked into it and even suggested that they take the cabriolet, but stopped short of allowing Gabriel the reins. They were out early enough that the streets were not crowded.

"So, Lynford, your efforts to ruin Bendas are legal, aren't they? I did notice your failure to answer before."

"Because the question does not even merit an answer. The entire reason I am seeking justice is because of Bendas's illegal actions." He slowed the horse so a man with a stick could finish crossing the road. "Now we will talk about something else and not bring that subject up again." He thought for a moment and then smiled. "Here is something guaranteed to distract you, brother. Your insistence on the necessity of finding positions for the retired soldiers has fallen on fertile ground."

A boy ran in front of the carriage, startling the horse, and it took all of Meryon's attention to keep the horse from bolting.

"Well done, Lyn. We don't have crowds like this in the country."

"You think this is a crowd?"

"Well, more than we ever see in Sussex." Gabriel sat back again. "So my nagging convinced you it needs to be addressed."

"That and someone else who used a similar logic," he admitted. "I have a plan to aid widows and orphans but I am going to work on the problem of unemployment as well. This on a more personal level."

But more than hiring one boy at a time, he thought, remembering Elena's teasing comment.

"I've read through the proposals that David sent me and I think that six of the dozen are sound and worth pursuing. I will write to David today and instruct him to forward a letter of interest to the business representative in Manchester."

"Well done, Your Grace."

Gabriel's approval was satisfying and Meryon smiled at his brother.

"I admire you for it," Gabriel continued. "It is setting an example and showing others how it should be done. If Parliament will not take the steps that must be taken then individuals will have to."

When they reached the gunsmith, it was clear they were going to have to wait, though when Rimbaud's assistant saw that the duke had accompanied his brother he hurried to assure them that they would be seen to as quickly as possible. They were invited to look at the latest pistols from Italy, but neither one cared enough to give the display their full attention.

"What did you think of Georges's vignettes?" Gabriel

asked as he bent to look at the firing mechanism of a small pistol.

"His short plays intrigued me. They gave us all something to discuss. Georges has created an impressive following," Meryon said.

"Because he writes the truth even if his stories are presented more like fables. We congratulated him on his success and hope it lasts for a decade." Gabriel's pleased expression left no doubt of his sincerity.

"What a strange world we live in when a man like Georges can arrive on the London scene and create a name and fortune for himself, but a woman like Signora Verano is dependent on society to give her recognition, to say she is acceptable in company, and the very thought of her making money with her talent is unseemly."

"As you said, Lyn, she wishes to be embraced by the ton; Georges has no such ambitions."

"But she could have made a different choice."

"What? To sing on the stage? To become some man's mistress?" Gabriel was silent for less than a minute. "Have the two of you had a falling-out? You seemed very close the other night." He thought a little more and winced. "Lyn, you did not insult her in some way, did you?"

"I do not want to discuss it."

"Which is the same as saying yes."

"Apparently I can see change coming and make the most of it, but when it comes to women I am like a schoolboy who insults the girls he likes the best."

Before Gabriel could say anything else, the gunsmith

came up to them. Meryon hoped it was the last of the discussion but the moment they were back in the cabriolet, Gabriel brought it up again.

"I do not want to discuss it, Gabe. I have sent a written apology and hope she will speak to me when we meet again."

"That bad, is it? How unlike you, brother. You are usually the most diplomatic of men. I will pray for you and not mention a word of this to Lynette."

"If that is meant as a joke, it is not funny. I have said all I will say and ask you to forget we discussed it."

"Drop me at Gunter's, will you? I am to meet my wife and the boys there. We are off to Astley's Circus."

Meryon trusted that meant he had dropped the subject. "You are taking the boys to Astley's? I will tell Cook to prepare a supper to soothe wild children."

"And exhausted parents."

Meryon did as his brother asked and was about to move out onto the road from Gunter's when he saw that Gabriel had left a packet on the seat. His damn tickets to the circus, no doubt.

With a word to Wilson, Meryon hopped down, papers in hand, and made his way to the door. The place was crowded but Meryon saw Gabe standing by a large table filled with familiar faces. All of them laughing, full of life, with Elena Verano in their number. Of course she would fit into Gabriel's circle of friends. He and Lynette valued talent before status and Elena could claim both.

She was wearing a pale peach dress, her bonnet a

straw-and-ribbon confection, and she looked more delicious than the ices on which Gunter's had built such a
success.

Meryon stood gazing at them for a few minutes, as
did everyone else in the place, longing to be part of the camaraderie that bound them all in such bonhomie.

Elena was watching Miss Castellano, smiling, as the
young girl told a story. Lord William listened to Mia with
a different look altogether. Meryon thought a courtship
might be well along, and wished he could be amused at
his one-time jealousy of the viscount. That absurdity was
one more example of his lack of common sense where Signora Verano was concerned.

Meryon stayed by the door until Mia finished her
story and everyone laughed. They were enjoying one another, the afternoon, and their ices.

He knew the party would end the moment he walked
over. Elena would stop smiling. Lord William and Miss
Castellano would wonder why, if they did not already
know.

Gabriel would whisper to Lynette, and she would
think even less of Meryon than she already did. And
Gabe's boys were already too well mannered around him,
unless Rexton was with them.

Garrett would be his faithful boon companion, but
one out of eight did not sound like welcoming numbers to
him.

Meryon decided to leave them alone. Besides, he
needed to write to David and set in motion the ideas he
had mentioned to Gabriel. He would spend some time
with Rexton and Alicia. They always cheered him.

Having half-convinced himself he did not have time to while away the afternoon at Gunter's, Meryon handed the packet and a coin to the host at the door and went back outside to his cabriolet. Another burst of the cheeriest sort of laughter convinced him he was doing them a favor by not intruding.

31

MERYON CALLED HIMSELF a fool for having deliberately avoided a meeting with Elena Verano. Tonight.
He would find her tonight even if it meant going to each
of the five events for which he'd received invitations. It
might not be Easter yet but the entertainments of the Season had begun.

Meryon's weakness annoyed him so much that even
news that the trustees of the Bendas dukedom were beginning to ask questions did little to ease his annoyance.

His source reported that the trustees who lived in
London had two concerns, one major and the other apparently inconsequential. The trustees had asked Bendas
for an explanation of his recent investments in land,
which seemed excessive and undirected, and another
wondered at his constant hiring of new staff.

Did it not seem odd, one asked in a letter to his

fellows, that in a time of such widespread unemployment the staff at the Bendas townhouse appeared to be in a constant state of upset?

Overall the report Meryon received, from the very trustee who questioned the staff replacement, had good news, but the whole process was taking too damn long.

Even a visit to Rexton and Alicia did not cheer him as much as usual. Rexton was crushingly disappointed that he had not been allowed to go to the circus with his cousins. His whining grew so persistent that finally Meryon agreed to take him directly after Easter. That helped improve his mood, but having won the victory the boy began to nag Meryon about his longing to learn to shoot, another bit of influence from his cousins.

Alicia could have cared less about guns but she did respond most readily to her brother's mood and clung to her father's knees with "Me, me, me," her constant refrain.

As he dressed for the evening he congratulated himself on being so distracted by the children that he had given Elena Verano barely a thought for all of an hour, and swore to himself that he had never expected a response to his letter of apology.

Garrett was waiting for him in the salon. The majordomo reported a delay in bringing the carriage round because one of the horses had been injured and a new team was being readied. At Garrett's query, the majordomo assured him that the horse's injury was minor, so Meryon and Garrett sat down to wait.

In the same parlor he had shared with Elena not so

long ago. "I told Gabe today that I was considering moving the household to Richmond," Meryon began. "I told him of my concern for the children's safety but, to be honest, that was a faradiddle."

"Living at Richmond would mean a longer trip to Parliament."

"If I came in on horseback, I could enjoy the air instead of being cooped up in a carriage."

"Yes, and the children would be able to have more freedom."

"Exactly."

"However, it is not just Parliament that is farther away, Meryon. All the entertainments of London would be much less convenient."

Looking him straight in the eye Meryon told the truth. "I grow tired of them already."

Garrett sat back and thought before he spoke. "Is this still about Rowena? Do you miss her more here? She always did prefer London to Pennford. And actively disliked the house at Richmond."

"No, no," Meryon said quickly, then wished he had lied.

"Then you are leaving because your friendship with Signora Verano has not been a success and you want to avoid seeing her."

The duke went and poured himself a brandy, drank it, and poured another. He stayed by the drinks table but that did not silence Garrett.

"Meryon, I saw you come into Gunter's yesterday and leave as quickly. When the host brought the packet that Gabriel had left behind, everyone was disappointed that you had not joined us. Signora Verano looked stricken, and now I know why."

"She did? She looked stricken?"

Garrett considered his choice of words. "Stricken is all her expressions rolled into one word. She looked at once relieved, then hurt. I wondered if she thought she herself the reason you had not joined them."

The silence lengthened between them. Meryon went to the door, drink in hand, opened it, and yelled at the porter. "I want the damn carriage now!"

"Your Grace!" The porter recovered from his shock at the duke's unusual rudeness. "It is coming now. Here, let me help you with your hat and greatcoat."

"I can help myself. We don't have time to wait for the warm bricks, but be sure we have a bottle of brandy."

Garrett followed him slowly, thoughtfully, and shivered when he sat on the cold leather seat. They were well on their way to Berkeley Square before Garrett spoke again.

"So now you want to make sure all of us are as unhappy as you are. Or at least as uncomfortable."

"You know, Garrett, sometimes you talk too much."

Garrett laughed. "When Olivia says that I know exactly what she has in mind. From you I will give it a different meaning and sit quietly if you will at least share the brandy."

Meryon shrugged. He'd understood the joke but did not find it very amusing. Handing the bottle to Garrett, they shared it without cups. After his third swallow Meryon decided that the silence was a sympathetic one, or the brandy made it seem so. "I sent a note of apology for my insult, and this is the first time I will see her since she received it."

Garrett grabbed the bottle out of his hand. "Then that is enough spirits, Meryon. Stick with lemonade and save the rest of the brandy for the ride home."

Meryon snatched the bottle back, took one last gulp of the brandy, and put it back under the seat.

"Enough!"

Garrett's sharp word startled him.

"Now I see where Rexton learned to sulk. For God's sake, man, if it was your fault accept responsibility for it and move on. If you want to try again, I promise you that a drunken, petulant declaration will win you no favors."

Meryon glared at him.

"No, I will not meet you at Jackson's. I leave tomorrow and want to return to my bride without bruise or blemish."

"I miss Olivia's cinnamon buns."

"Good God, you're drunk already. How much did you have before we left?"

"Some."

"More than some." Garrett rapped on the ceiling and told the driver to take them back to Penn Square.

"No. I want to go to the house on St. German Street and drink until we fall down."

"That won't take long in your case."

"Then I will sleep in the bed there and you can sleep wherever you want."

Garrett laughed. "Not with you, Your Grace."

"No, no. Don't be ridiculous." Meryon waved away

the idea. "There are other bedrooms there. The maid will make one up."

And that was how the Duke of Meryon came to sleep in the great big bed he had shared with Elena, all by himself though his dreams were hardly lonely.

TWO DAYS LATER, as he looked for the invitation to the musicale at Baron Monksford's, Meryon decided he had made a monster of this first meeting with Signora Verano. The longer he stayed away from the social scene the more it would make The Gossips curious.

With the house to himself again, his own company bored him in the extreme and he had always found spirits an unreliable escape from the world around him.

Surely Elena had an invitation to sing tonight at Monksford's. The Duke of Meryon could join the number who crowded around her after she sang. He fortified himself with a good dinner and several cups of coffee and not one drop of wine.

If Blix thought the duke too particular about his dress, he made no comment and willingly ruined two lengths of linen before the duke announced his satisfaction with his cravat. Blix did have to ask the duke to stop advising him, as he could not contrive a proper knot if the duke would not close his mouth.

Meryon knew he could not tolerate waiting in a long line of carriages and so decided to arrive early. Still, he sat alone in his brandyless carriage long enough to have a headache from pretending that he had no worries about this meeting with Elena Verano. She might not fall into his arms, but surely she would not give him the cut direct.

No, she would not do that, if for no other reason than his rank. Small consolation but all he felt entitled to.

Neither Gabriel nor Garrett had asked him exactly how he had offended the Signora. But both knew that the offense had been his. He had no idea how. Maybe they understood as he now did that the man was always the one in the wrong. If they knew the details, Meryon knew they would be shocked by his crudeness.

Impulse. Damnable impulse. If he had thought for five minutes he would have approached her differently. Or not at all.

Baron Monksford welcomed him with his too effusive deference. His wife was as charming as he was not, and Meryon found himself happily discussing the upcoming Season and the Monksfords' daughter's bow to society.

"I recall how nervous I was," Lady Monksford said, "but Rosemary is as calm and collected as her father."

Is that how she saw her husband? Meryon thought it must have been a love match. From his perspective the baron was stolid and unimaginative. If Rosemary was anything like him, then she would be something less than a raging success. That, however was not his problem. As Lady Monksford moved on to greet another early arrival, Meryon stepped into a ballroom lined with chairs.

How did people regard him? His family understood his efforts to control his temper and knew that beneath that façade was a great deal of passion of all kinds. The rest of the world saw him simply as a duke, he decided. His title distracted them from the man he was to the man they expected him to be.

How did Elena Verano see him? She was one of the rare few who saw the man beyond the title. Other than that he would not guess or he would turn around and run for the brandy.

THE DUKE OF MERYON? He is a man with a title, Mia. I expect nothing from him but courtesy." Elena kept her tone light.

"But what happened? William says—"

Elena raised her hand to stop whatever it was William had said to Mia. She did not want to hear it.

"I suspect that the duke has left town."

"No, he has been in Parliament according to William."

Then he is a coward and he is avoiding me. She was careful to keep her face expressionless. *Or has already found another more accommodating woman.*

Tina was dressing Mia's hair so that her back was to Elena but the mirror reflected Mia's excitement.

"Well, I am sorry for you that he will not be there," Mia said with a careless shrug, "but I am so thrilled that I can hardly sit still. I have practiced both pieces that I will play until I can do them with my eyes closed and with someone humming another song to distract me."

Elena laughed and watched Tina dress the girl's hair. "No more than one of the jeweled pins, Tina." When Tina nodded Elena gave her attention to Mia again. "You are comfortable with the music I wrote for the song?"

"Oh yes," she said with disarming confidence. "The Beethoven is far more challenging and I am only accompanying you. My part hardly matters."

Tina pulled Mia's ear. "More respect for the Signora, miss."

Mia squeaked and her smile disappeared.

"Tina, thank you. Mia, I am well aware that I will never be Beethoven, but it was a challenge when I already had words and needed to find a melody that fit them and what I wanted to convey."

"It is beautiful, Elena," Mia assured her, more sincere than dutiful. "But I do wish it was happier."

Mia and Tina both were facing the mirror and, at the same time, raised their eyes to look at Elena's reflection there. They must know why she had written the song. There was no need to actually voice an explanation. So she changed the subject.

"Will you be comfortable playing before so many, Mia?"

"Oh yes." Mia's reply was easy. "And thank you, Elena, thank you so much. To have this small taste of society before Easter will make my first ball much more comfortable. What could be more perfect?"

Elena could think of several ways to make the evening better, staying home being first on the list. She was so tired of pretending that she was enjoying herself, of pretending interest in the men who hovered, of pretending that she did not care if she ever saw Meryon again.

32

I UNDERSTAND THAT YOU were in Russell Square last week, Your Grace."

Meryon tried to recall the name of the man he was talking to. He was in Commons, that much he knew. "I was there quite by accident. I was bringing Signora Verano home after a ride in the park and I found I could be of some assistance to her." God, that sounded supercilious.

"Your Grace, what did you make of the incident?"

The intensity with which the man waited for the answer signaled this was no idle question. Aha! Lord Halston. That was his name. The second son of the Duke of Hale, and, at least as important, married to one of The Gossips.

"It was no incident of significance, Halston. Most of the people there were looking for some entertainment. For some that means a fistfight. I would estimate that no more than fifty of those present actually heard what was said."

"So you do not think it was a threat?"

"Not at all. I think people's right to speak and to express their thoughts in whatever context they choose can no longer be denied. They are not demanding change beyond asking us to listen to them. Not yet anyway."

The man looked shocked and Meryon smiled.

"I think the greater threat are the unemployed and the hungry."

"Yes, well, the poor will always be with us, you know."

"Unless they starve to death." Meryon had had enough of this pointless discussion and had taken a step away when Halston spoke again.

"I am more concerned about the Duke of Bendas."

"As I have been since he collapsed in Lords years ago."

"Yes, my father reminded us of it the other day. It seems that may have affected his mind in some way. My father, the duke, says that Bendas has made some strange requests of late. He walked out on Signora Verano at the Regent's dinner, and then my wife heard that Bendas asked the Signora to come sing for him."

"The man is unstable in mind and the trustees should act if his heirs do not." Meryon was pleased that he sounded so reasonable.

"Yes, that is exactly what my father said last night at our regular dinner together. My wife asked for details and even I was dismayed at Bendas's behavior. The duel,

Meryon. His behavior shocked us all. To shoot before the count of three." Lord Halston shook his head, apparently unable to find words bad enough to convey his feelings.

"I think the death of an innocent bystander was far more deplorable, and to use money to guarantee that there were no consequences is even worse."

"Yes, but death comes when God wills."

Meryon had had quite enough of Halston's clichéd excuses. "Do tell your wife to spread the word, Halston. She is so effective at keeping the ton informed."

Meryon walked away, leaving Halston confused just as he intended, and headed for the salon where the entertainment would take place, hoping to meet Elena before they were surrounded by people.

Moving to the front of the room, Meryon chose a chair on the side aisle and put his calling card on the seat. He was about to go up and examine the pianoforte, when Elena and Miss Castellano came through a nearby door. Lady Monksford was with them and Meryon paused to gauge Elena's reaction.

Elena spotted him immediately and froze.

"Good evening, Your Grace," Lady Monksford called out. "Please come and be introduced."

"We have met, thank you, Lady Monksford." Meryon bowed to Elena, and then to her ward; he smiled at some spot between the two of them, annoyed by how tight his cravat felt. "What a pleasure to have a moment with you, signora. I am looking forward to hearing you play, Miss Castellano."

"Thank you, Your Grace." The young woman curt-sied. "I hope that you will not be disappointed."

"Impossible." He tuned to Elena and could not think of a thing to say. She looked well enough, but an unfamiliar world-weariness shadowed her.

Someone, Lady Monksford perhaps, cleared her throat, and Meryon looked at Elena and said the first civil thing that came into his head. "Have you decided what you will sing tonight?"

He wanted to take her in his arms and comfort her. He wanted to make all the pain go away. Meryon hoped Elena could hear the unspoken words that his expression conveyed as much as hers did.

"Yes, I have." Her answer was brusque.

Miss Castellano volunteered the next sally. "I was wondering if Mr. DeBora will bring the Verano violin this evening."

"I invited him to bring the violin with him but he told us he is not worthy to play it." Lady Monksford spoke with enough disappointment for them to realize it was not what she wished.

"Do you think he would allow someone else to play it?" Meryon risked a glance at Elena, again, and found he had her complete attention.

"Do you play, Your Grace?" Lady Monksford asked.

"No, my musical abilities are limited to the appreciation of music. But I imagine that Signora Verano plays. Perhaps I could prevail on Mr. DeBora to allow the Signora a few minutes with the violin, in private, of course."

Meryon could not think of a word to describe Elena's

reaction, other than "speechless." Mia, however, never failed for words or enthusiasm.

"How perfectly wonderful and generous of you, Your Grace. Elena would love it and so would I. To hold something so dear to Edward. Thank you, thank you so much."

"I do not know if he even brought it and I am not promising that he will agree," Meryon cautioned.

"Of course he will. You are a duke. He will agree, either because of your rank or because he is thrilled to be able to help you."

Lady Monksford laughed. It was the slightly embarrassed laugh common among those who did not know Mia well.

"How can I thank you, Your Grace." Elena's words were not much more than a whisper.

"Smile sometime tonight." He bowed to her. "I will leave you to prepare for your performance."

Meryon walked out of the room without looking back and through the crowded antechamber. He spent the next hour talking with almost every person in the room, happy for the first time in days, if not months. It felt so totally and completely right to do something kind for no reason other than to make her happy. He did not expect a kiss or so much as a curtsy.

Meryon's conversation with DeBora lasted all of two minutes, without one moment of negotiation.

"I am sorry to disappoint you, Your Grace, but I no longer own the Verano violin. I sold it to the Duke of Bendas yesterday."

"Tell me why you did that," Meryon demanded.

DeBora stepped back, flustered. "He—he wanted it and I sold it to him."

"He had no possible use for it. You should have asked Signora Verano if she wished to purchase it."

"Your Grace, I had no idea that the Signora could afford it."

"You fool, you should have given it to her. Do you not understand that it is one of the few true connections she has with her husband, who died playing it?" Meryon forced himself to relax his fist, more angry that he would have to disappoint Elena than at what DeBora had told him. DeBora answered to Bendas. Meryon knew that as well as he knew his name, but the old duke's interest in the Verano violin was more difficult to tease out. It struck Meryon as odd and worth investigating.

The bell sounded and the guests were invited into the ballroom for the music.

Meryon followed the crowd. His palms were sweaty, his heart would not slow. He was not nervous for her this time. His anxiety was all his own.

Of course he had to wait until the last to hear Elena. The violin, pianoforte, and voice were featured and Rosemary Monksford, who apparently had no musical talent, recited poetry at the breaks between performers.

Rosemary had a pretty voice, and she recited with confidence and insight, overall a pleasure to listen to. How interesting that the girl had some actress in her, though he would never say that aloud. And how clever of Lady Monksford to find a way to showcase her daughter's talent.

Mia Castellano played the pianoforte with more skill than luck, her ability far outshining that of all the other young ladies her age. The force with which she played Beethoven was almost shocking, but like Elena she had perfected a smile that made it seem as though the passion was part of the performance as learned as the music.

At last Lord Monksford came to the front of the room and announced that Signora Verano would sing with the accompaniment of Miss Castellano. They would perform a traditional ballad for which the Signora had recently composed new music.

The pianoforte introduction was long and lovely, the mood soul-searching. When Elena began to sing the audience had to strain to hear her, but it was not the words that were important so much as the sensibility she was conveying. As Meryon listened and watched Elena sing he realized that Elena Verano's great talent was how she shared herself.

As Elena's voice grew stronger, Mia's playing quieted and the words became clearer. They were the same lyrics she had sung as a ballad at the Regent's dinner party, but what had been sung with humor then was filled with heartache now.

Love left a heart in ruins if we did not respect its power.

When she finished there was little doubt that she knew this from her own experience. Singing this piece appeared to have taken all her strength. She curtsied, lowering her head as if exhausted and when she straightened her smile was a weak imitation of happiness.

He stood, ready to rush to the stage, thinking she was going to faint. The audience followed his move and rose to applaud with gusto until Signora Verano recaptured her good humor. She thanked them with a happier smile, then gestured to her ward, who stood and gave a small curtsy.

Meryon sat back down, as drained as if he had given the performance. The room began to empty. Elena Verano was surrounded by well-wishers and Mia Castellano and some young man played at the pianoforte while Meryon realized that he knew now why he had avoided this meeting.

To see her again reminded him of all that he had lost.

Meryon watched her as she nodded her thanks and smiled at the compliments she received. He wanted that smile turned to him. Meryon could think of nothing else that would ease his cramped heart.

She had offered that smile, more than once, and he had ignored it, abused it, and lost whatever chance he had. Now he had to tell her that he could not give her the only thing he had offered that she did want.

When the crowd of well-wishers eased, he stepped forward. Elena saw that he waited and stepped away, her face composed but unsmiling.

"I am so sorry, signora, but DeBora tells me he no longer owns the violin. He sold it to the Duke of Bendas."

"What?" Elena swayed, all color draining from her face. Meryon reached for her, steadying her with both hands at her shoulders.

Mia was at her side immediately.

"Mia, I need to go home. Now."

Elena turned away from Meryon with no further explanation of her distress. The two women left the ballroom through the little door at the back, the same one they had come through before.

It took all his ducal self-control not to hurry after her—not to find out why such news would upset her so, but to find out what he could do to help her. As quickly as those thoughts flew through his mind the answer came: Leave her alone and find a way to buy the violin for her. Give it to her as a gift, anonymously even. He never wanted to see her that upset again.

Meryon asked a footman to call for his carriage and on his way out he thanked Lord Monksford and his wife, explaining very briefly DeBora's sale of the violin.

There was one other thing he could act on. He could send another apology to Elena. One from the heart. If Elena Verano could stand before strangers and share herself through songs of love, life, and loss, then he could write a letter to her that told the truth.

At home, in his study, he poured a brandy but did no more than sip it once.

Picking up his pen, he stared at the blank sheet of paper. It stared back, daring him to be as honest as Elena Verano had been. Meryon might have no hopes for a future with her, but he could prove that he did not need a dark room and anonymity to speak meaningfully and from his heart.

He called a picture of Elena to mind. The moment before she kissed him in the carriage, her eyes alight with laughter. Never, not once in his life, had he thought of laughter and kissing in the same breath. But with Elena it had seemed natural to smile back as their lips met. He realized now that that kiss had been only the beginning.

He would write the end now, with all the feeling he could wring from his aching heart.

33

ELENA AWOKE MUCH TOO early to rise when she had not gone to bed until two. She felt as though she had not slept at all, waking groggy, confused by dreams that she could not recall. Restless sleep was rare for her. It was her blessed godmother who had given Elena the key.

"You do not have to tell people, but..." Her *madrina* would always raise her finger to emphasize the word. "You must know for yourself the truth of yourself."

Elena had lived by that rule. Alas, not perfectly, as last night's sleeplessness proved.

Why in the world would the Duke of Bendas want Edward's violin? Because he knew how much it meant to her. Because he wanted reconciliation and the violin would compel her to meet with him. Those were the two most viable reasons. Unfortunately, one did not exclude the other.

Elena could not know the answer without asking Bendas. The question she *could* answer was how she felt about a reconciliation or, at the very least, the need to approach Bendas about buying the violin from him.

She was tired. Tired of trying to understand. She wondered why her mind knew that but her heart had refused to give up.

She would reconcile with her father if it came from his heart. The "if" was too big. And that is what held her back.

Tears welled in her eyes. She had been so wrong about Meryon that she could not trust her judgment where any man was concerned. With Meryon she had come so close to finding love again, then discovered that he did not understand the concept at all.

Meryon had never told his wife that he loved her. That was a bit of honesty that told her more than all the other words between them. Now she was afraid that the Duke of Bendas was not capable of love either. Elena was not sure her heart could take that risk again.

She would live without them. Elena fell asleep, so very sorry for both Meryon and Bendas and sorry for herself.

THIS TIME MERYON had no expectation of an answer from the Signora and lost himself in the various prospectuses his brother David had sent. He had examined them

before. This time he made a list of detailed comments and
asked David to add any questions he might have, meet
with the men whose projects had been selected, and start
the contract process as soon as possible.

Meryon had completed his letter to William Wilberforce and was rereading it when there was a scratch at the
door.

John Coachman came in, hat in hand, looking embarrassed but determined. The duke acknowledged his
salute with a nod.

"You have something to tell me."

"Yes, Your Grace. I'm sorry, Your Grace."

"Tell me." Meryon could not imagine it was nothing,
not if the majordomo had allowed the coachman to come
to his study.

"It's the boy, Wilson, Your Grace. I saw him yesterday
talking to a man out in the square while he was walking
the dog. They were arguing, and the man made as if to
take Magda, and the boy ran off with the dog. That ended
it, Your Grace. But this morning he would not take the dog
out to the square, only walked her up and down the
mews, and swore at anyone who questioned him."

"I see. He has been a competent employee as far as I
can tell. And honest. Tell me if I am wrong."

"Yes, Your Grace. Happy as a lark most days except for
when he has to take his wages to his mother. He comes
back no happier for the visit home. Your Grace, I think
this is his home now. But it weren't right, yesterday. I
could see he was angry and scared, if you know how you
can tell that by the way someone stands."

"Yes, yes, I do. Thank you."

"Oh, no need to thank me for bringing what could be bad news, Your Grace."

"Yes, there is, Coachman. You could have more comfortably ignored it."

"Not really, Your Grace. This is my home too, and I like the boy and would hate to see him take a wrong turn."

"I still say thank you." Meryon stood up and nodded.

"Then you are welcome, Your Grace," the servant said as he bowed himself out of the room.

Meryon wasted no time sending for Wilson. The boy came to him, smiling and proud. Meryon wasn't sure if the livery added to his cockiness or made it less offensive. Meryon stood behind his desk, towering over the boy.

"Wilson, I can see that you like it here." He would not be angry, Meryon reminded himself, not before he knew the truth. "At the very least you like the clothes you wear and I can guess you like the food you eat."

"Yes, sir, Your Grace," the boy said, his smile fading.

"And you like Magda." He could not help but smile a little. He had seen Rexton and the boy playing with the dog, all three acting like puppies, which none of them were.

"Yes." The smile was back, a grin now.

The boy did love that dog.

"Then tell me the truth about who you were talking to in Penn Square yesterday."

Wilson's smile disappeared. He looked like a trapped animal. Meryon waited, prepared for the worst.

"I don't want to lose my job, or leave Magda. Lord

Rexton's been showing me the globes and giving me books to read. Please, sir, Your Grace."

"Explain what you did to endanger your position here." Meryon knew he sounded like an unsympathetic magistrate, but Wilson's first words were not encouraging.

"I said no, sir, Your Grace. I said no both times."

"Explain. I offer no promises until I hear the truth."

The boy seemed to shrink by inches. Wilson stared at something on the desk for almost a minute, took a deep breath, and began. "The day after I came to work, a man stopped me when I was walking back from my mother's. He asked me if I wanted to earn five pounds, maybe more. I was that suspicious, sir, Your Grace. There weren't be nothing honest that anybody would pay you five pounds for. But I said as how maybe and what did he want me to do."

The boy took a deep breath. "He said that all I had to do was loosen the wheel on the carriage."

"Loosen the wheel." The duke repeated. So it had not been an accident.

"Yes, sir, Your Grace, but I said no. As how someone might be hurt. He said that was the idea and that if someone in the carriage was to be hurt bad he would pay me ten guineas and if someone died, man or woman, he would give me one hundred."

"Man or woman. He said man or woman." *My God, Elena was in danger too.* The boy might not be dishonest but he was viciously money-hungry. Meryon's fury must have shown.

"I said no! I said no!" Wilson words came out loud

and panicked. "Don't look like that. Please. You can beat me if it will make you feel better, but I told the man no and ran away as fast as I could. Ran and ran and ran back here."

"I will not hit you. I would never hit you." There are worse things he could do, but he kept that to himself. Meryon relaxed his fist. "Go on."

"I didn't tell anyone 'cause I was afraid I would be let go and then my mum would kill me."

Meryon's anger faded to a dull glow. He did not think Wilson was lying about his mother.

"Then when the carriage wheel did come off I knew the man had found someone else to do the job."

That was easy enough to figure out. "The groom who had to stay behind when you all went for cake."

"Yes, at least I think so. He's gone now. Walked off without notice not three days after that happened."

"But you still said nothing." The question was implicit in the statement.

"No. 'Cause of Magda."

"Go on," Meryon urged, not quite understanding the connection.

"She needed me. To walk her and take care of her, especially after she was hurt. I didn't want to leave her," the boy said, the first sign of tears showing.

"Then yesterday the man came back."

"Yes, sir, Your Grace. He told me that I would do what he said or he would kill Magda for sure this time."

"So the man had a different plan. Tell me what it was." He would kill the bastard for endangering Elena, making the boy's life a misery, and threatening Rowena's dog.

"I don't know, sir, Your Grace. I ran before he could tell me. Honest. I didn't want to hear."

"I am very disappointed that it never occurred to you to tell someone."

"I thought about asking his lordship's tutor, but I was afraid he wouldn't let me sit in on the lessons if he knew. I couldn't've held out much longer, sir, Your Grace. My gut is in a knot and I can't sleep without nightmares about Magda." Wilson rubbed his stomach as if it was still aching. "For sure, I couldn't 'a kept quiet much longer," he said again.

"I assume you have never seen the man before or since."

"Oh, but I did, Your Grace. At one of the parties, the big one at the palace. He was coming out with an old man, a real important, real old man who had a carriage even fancier than ours."

Rogers. Bendas had put Rogers up to this.

"There's something else you have to tell me." When the boy looked at him with something like amazed fear, Meryon just smiled.

"Yes, sir, Your Grace. I was thinking, after the men attacked us in the mews, that maybe the firecracker weren't an accident either."

The idea had never occurred to him. Meryon prayed it was a virtue that the boy could think like a criminal. "Good thinking, Wilson. You might be right."

Wilson stood straight again, as if expecting to hear he would be transported to Australia the next day.

"You made an excellent report, Wilson. If a little late

to be particularly useful. If this happens again"—the boy looked stunned at the idea that this might be a regular occurrence—"tell someone immediately. Now, back to the stables and catch up on your work."

The boy stood in place, still waiting.

"That's all," Meryon said impatiently.

"Can I still take care of Magda?"

"Yes. Nothing changes, Wilson, except for the tongue-lashing you will have from the head groom if you are any later seeing to your duties."

"Yes, sir, Your Grace," the boy called as he raced from the room. Meryon could have sworn he heard a "Whoo-hoo!" cheer as the door closed.

The duke sat down, stunned at the boy's revelations. Elena had been a target as well. Or at the least, which was still appalling, Bendas would not have cared if she died too.

He walked over to the window and stared out into the back garden. A servant or two hurried across the open space, probably using it as a shortcut from one part of the house to another. The early flowers were in bloom and one of the gardeners was pruning and trimming. Meryon tried to let the everyday activities calm him.

Meryon knew Bendas was mad but he'd always thought Rogers was there to keep his insane ideas in check, not to abet them. He had to take action. To protect Elena and his own household.

Acting the gentleman was the last thing he wanted to do, but he would wait for an hour and if Lord William did not come he would take matters into his own hands, beginning with a visit to Elena, talking with Tinotti if she would not receive him, and then the Bendas trustees.

Meryon sat down, distracting himself with the realization that Elena could be reading his note at this very minute.

34

IN THE VERANO HOUSEHOLD, breakfast was always served late the morning after an evening performance. Usually they were all voraciously hungry and in the best of spirits, congratulating each other on the high points. After they had eaten they would talk about the weaknesses and plan further practice, rehearsals, or teaching as needed.

Elena ate what was put in front of her and listened as Mia rattled on about how successful the evening had been. But for Elena the day did not really begin until the butler handed her a letter that had arrived a few hours before.

The moment the butler gave it to her, she excused herself from the breakfast table and went up to her room, her head so filled with speculation that she walked by the door to her boudoir.

The maid had already tidied the room and Elena could hear her in the bedchamber. Closing the door, Elena then went to her desk, broke the seal, and spread the paper out before her.

She read it through four times. The salutation brought tears to her eyes, so she could not make out every word and had to read it again.

My dear Signora Verano. My dear Elena,

If it were possible to turn back time, I would. The hours and minutes would begin at that very moment when we kissed in Hyde Park, when I recognized the longing in you that matched my own.

I would also know that the first time we met, and each time thereafter, was a gift and not something to be suspicious of. Before God, I apologize for the insult I will not even name that finally made you abandon me.

There is no place to put the responsibility for these numerous insults but squarely on my shoulders, where it weighs me down as though I were Atlas bearing the world.

Perhaps any intimacy between us is unwise. I fear you would too soon grow tired of my constant need to apologize, and would look elsewhere for someone who can treasure you without limitation.

The time we shared together, as strangers and at the most intimate, is in my heart, a treasure that I can relive when I want to torture myself with what might have been.

With profound respect, deepest admiration, and

undying affection I will always be your devoted
servant,

Lynford Pennistan

The third time she read the note for turn of phrase, the meaning behind each sentence. The salutation told her Lynford Pennistan was at once a gentleman and a lover. Both and neither.

The kiss in the park was the first time Meryon had felt that yearning? He had not known it was the reason for their quiet conversation in the dark? He had not wanted it ever since their second meeting? Or had he been so caught up in his fear of exposure that he had not even noticed?

No man existed who knew what a treasure he had until she was gone. He had said as much about his Rowena. Did he think it was a lesson he had learned with her death? She supposed it was possible.

The last line she had already memorized.

The time we shared together as strangers and at the most intimate is in my heart, a treasure that I can relive when I want to torture myself with what might have been.

May it torture you always. She thought it and wished she meant it.

Elena did not know whether to laugh or cry. So she settled for a tear-filled smile. He had signed it as Lynford Pennistan. Not the duke. But they were one and the same.

This letter was Meryon at his most honest, both charming and incredibly frustrating. And he could still not say the word *love*. It would cost him.

She could never give herself to a man who could not

accept that, for her, love was at once the greatest gift and the greatest responsibility.

That was one of the things her godmother had not had to teach her in her urgings to know herself.

Elena had known that from the moment she had decided not to sing the song her father chose and to sing one that she liked better. She knew it was a test of his love, which he had failed.

The consequences had astounded her, but she could have made no other choice. Even at fourteen she had become a woman who would not compromise on the important things, and at fourteen what she would sing was as important to her as her father's votes in Parliament were to him. Now it was love that could not be compromised.

"Is it an invitation, signora? Will I need to prepare another ensemble for you?"

Elena did not turn around for fear that Tina would see tears on her cheeks.

"No. It's a personal letter, Tina, one that needs no response." She tucked it into the drawer.

When Elena turned to her maid she wore a smile with no tears behind it. "Now please, tell me that Mia understands that I must go by myself to this lesson. Signor Ponto will see her when he can fit it into his schedule."

"Lord William is coming later and I think Mia will be quite content to practice her English with him."

It was not the first time Elena wondered what "practicing English" was a code for, but she was sure it was too late to try to find out.

————

WHEN LORD WILLIAM came into the duke's study, he still wore his hat and greatcoat. His eyes were blazing. "You have done it. You have done it and I should call you out this minute." He slapped the desk with his gloves and Meryon could see that the viscount was seriously considering an insult.

"Good morning, Lord William." One of them would have to stay calm or this would end up even more of a disaster.

"It is not a good morning." He all but spat the words out.

Meryon waited, hoping that if Lord William was able to rage on he would eventually gain some control. If not, there was always the gun in his desk drawer.

"I helped you. I counted you a friend, God help me!"

"Stop being theatrical, my lord."

William stalked over to the door, threw his coat and gloves on a chair, and came back. Still seething but quiet.

"If I'm not mistaken," Meryon began in as civil a voice as he could manage, "I'm the one who sent for you."

"You sent me a summons?" William's confusion lasted a second. "Oh, I arrived home just after dark last night and have not looked at my correspondence. Mia was expecting me this morning and I thought it would keep." Having explained that to his own satisfaction if not Meryon's, Lord William went on. "Tell me, Your Grace, does your message have anything to do with why you are no longer seeing Elena Verano?"

"No, nothing at all," Meryon said, taken aback. "It was her decision, Lord William, and it is private." He leaned forward a little and waited until he had Lord

William's complete attention. "Private means it is between the two of us."

"Perhaps *you* think so, but friendship means more to me than watching a friend suffer. Before I left for Kent, Elena was happy. Now she is not. Oh, she pretends that she's enjoying herself but the only time I see her smile is when she is watching Mia have fun. I have not seen her look like this since the first months after Signor Verano's death."

"I am sorry to hear that." Meryon made himself relax his fist. He was the person who deserved to be punched. "If you see Signora Verano, please do give her my regards. She and Miss Castellano performed beautifully together last night."

"Did Mia do well?" Lord William asked, forgetting his anger. "I hoped to be back but the weather slowed me. That new song, the old ballad for which Elena wrote new music?"

Meryon nodded. It was not a song he would ever forget.

"It was a very important piece for Elena," William went on. "She told me that it was dedicated to the two men who had broken her heart. I know who one of them is but was not sure of the second. Now I can guess."

"Thank you for twisting the knife, Lord William. Though your willingness to inflict pain makes it easier for me to do the same to you."

The viscount's expression turned guarded. "Is this about Mia's flirtation with Lord Halston's son?"

"No, it is not. I would hardly call you here to discuss

an innocent flirtation. You have been spending too much time with The Gossips."

"All right." The man actually relaxed a little. "I suppose this is about my grandfather."

If Lord William meant to annoy Meryon with his tone of taxed patience, he succeeded.

"Yes, your grandfather; the lying, cheating, conniving Duke of Bendas is why you're here."

Lord William narrowed his eyes and picked up his gloves again.

Calm down, Meryon reminded himself. He sat down in his chair and thought before he spoke again. "For almost two years, my goal has been to bring your grandfather to justice, not to destroy the dukedom itself. You understand that, I know you do."

Lord William pursed his lips and moved his head as if agreement was being forced out of him.

"I wanted to prove Bendas so twisted with hate that he is mentally incapable of managing the estate. I wanted your father to petition the Regent and Parliament to allow him, as Bendas's heir, to assume control of the entailed estate and his seat in Parliament."

"Bad business judgment is hardly a proof of incompetence." William sat forward as he spoke. "You are a cold-hearted puzzle, Meryon."

"Coldhearted, perhaps, but everything I have done is legal." Meryon paused a moment. "The same cannot be said for your grandfather. I found out this morning that your grandfather, with the help of his faithful fool, Rogers, has made three attempts on my life."

Lord William was so astounded he could say only one word. "Rogers?"

"Yes. And what is worse, my informant was told that if Signora Verano were to die in the accident it would be worth even more to the duke."

"That cannot be." Lord William's face lost some of its color. "I don't believe you."

"You may not want to believe it, but you can. Remember, your grandfather is the man who had Olivia kidnapped." Meryon relaxed his fist but his anger did not fade. "Then the Duke of Bendas killed another man when he meant to kill me. It is not much of a step at all for him to hire someone to do what he failed at. And to crush, as if it were a small bug, the life of an innocent like Signora Verano."

"But you don't understand." William paused. "This is beyond belief. Bendas *must* be mad." William stopped talking and had some sort of internal debate before he said, "Your Grace, Elena is his daughter."

Meryon thought he had come to terms with that possibility. But from the way he felt his body tense at the viscount's words, he had not. "I thought she might be a relative. She made some comment once that led me to believe it."

"I was the one who told her not to tell you the truth. It was early in your friendship and I was afraid you would use it to discredit Bendas."

"I am not like your grandfather." Meryon's words were sharp and insistent. "I would never wish her ill. On the other hand, as Bendas's illegitimate child, whom he never acknowledged, it is clear Elena is no more than a potential embarrassment to him."

"Illegitimate?" Now it was William who spoke sharply and with insistence. "You are wrong, Meryon. Elena was born Ellen Bendasbrook. Her mother was the duchess."

Meryon could not hide his confusion. Bendas's legal daughter. Then he remembered the story Elena told him of being sent away at fourteen. "The story of his disinheriting a daughter is true, then. He put her out because she sang a song he did not like."

"Yes," William said, smart enough not to embellish the one-word truth.

"Her mother did nothing to stop it?"

"She had died the year before. According to my father, Elena and Bendas were always at odds. In fact, Elena disowned the family as completely as Bendas disinherited her. I would not listen to either one of them and have been her friend for these last ten years."

"My God, Bendas arranged for us to meet that night," Meryon realized.

"No, no, I was the one who told her what room to use. I knew you were there. I knew you both had lost someone and still grieved. I thought that you might be able to comfort each other."

"And introducing us in a more conventional way was not nearly as interesting." God, that was so like the little troublemaker. William might not be vindictive like his grandfather, but he did have the inclination to play with people's lives. "The single reason I am at all inclined to believe you is that Bendas never tried to use my friendship with the Signora to embarrass either one of us." Meryon had managed to do that without anyone else's help.

"But this latest discovery has exhausted my limited store of patience, Lord William. I will go to the chancery; I will contact the trustees of all the old duke's holdings. Bendas will be publicly stripped of his title, and no one with the name of Bendasbrook will ever be received by anyone for as long as the rest of his pathetic life lasts. Rogers will suffer with him."

"Let me handle this, Your Grace." William was not begging. Not quite. "I will write to my father today. I will go see the trustees who are here in London and find out what constitutes a valid reason to," he shook his head, "to do whatever must be done."

"It's too late." Meryon sat down. "My wife's death gave you months to act. But your father was too used to playing peacemaker or was too much of a coward. A man died because of it."

Lord William looked away.

"I should not have waited," Meryon admitted. "Do you think that Bendas would still have the title if I had died that morning, as he intended?" Meryon emphasized the last three words. Lord William's expression grew more stony. "Your grandfather missed me, but another man died and Bendas was able to buy his way out of the consequences. Lord William, I will not give up until I have justice."

"But it will be your definition of justice," William charged, recovering his mettle.

"So be it. I will take the one thing that matters to him

more than anything else. I want his name heaped with disgrace."

Lord William stared at him. "You are no better than he is."

"Spare me your moralizing, Lord William."

"All right, but if you do as you say, it's possible you will never see Elena Verano again."

"Do not threaten me." Meryon spoke with tight-lipped fury. "You are courting her ward. You are not in charge of her life."

"That is not what I meant," Lord William shouted, his frustration showing. "Bendas bought the Verano violin and I think he intends to use it to win her over."

"By your own admission, that will never happen. To use your words, 'she disowned him.'"

"That may be, but why did she come back to England? Mia would have been welcomed in any court in Europe. Edward's death made her see that she needed to try at least once to end her feud with her father."

"She has been here for months."

"And his purchase of the violin is the first sign that he may be willing. He must see, as The Gossips and most of the ton do, that you and Elena are no longer close. Bendas may well reconcile with Elena to show he can win her over when you have lost her. It will never end."

"Until one of us is dead." The thought of Elena as a pawn roused a protective urge that would never die. "I will not use her that way. She will make her own choice."

"You will not even try to win her back." The young lord rocked up on his tiptoes and down again. "If you will not even try, Your Grace, then you and my grandfather have something in common. You are both cowards."

Lord William picked up his gloves and collected his hat and greatcoat from the chair near the door. "Rest assured, Meryon, I will see that Elena and Mia are kept safe. Protect yourself."

He left Meryon without farewell, leaving the duke standing in the middle of his office, considering his words.

Elena would be safe—not only because Meryon knew that it was their friendship that had put her in danger in the first place, but also because he could count on Lord William to see to it. Elena was his aunt and good friend. Even without those connections, the viscount would put most anyone's protection before his own.

No one could ever accuse William Bendasbrook of cowardice.

Meryon was not a coward either. He was respecting Elena's wishes, that is, to leave her alone. Never see her or call on her again and to be civil when they did meet in public.

They had spoken at the Monksfords'. That was civil.

He had left the Monksfords' directly after the performance. That was out of consideration for her feelings.

Inspired by her song, he had written a heartfelt apology. That was definitely not cowardice. That was genuine.

He longed for a chance to dance with her again. That might make him seem like a fool or someone who believed in fairy tales. Perhaps he was too patient, too literal in honoring her wish. But not cowardly.

She was a Bendasbrook. Totally and completely. He

sat down and with his elbows on his desk, framed his forehead with his hands. The fact she was Bendas's daughter did make a difference.

Meryon wanted her as much as ever, and hated her father with equal vehemence. He and Elena were not Romeo and Juliet, so young that such love seemed beyond family feuds. This widened the gap between them. It seemed impossible to cross.

35

FOR YEARS THE METCALFES' ball had been
the unofficial opening of the Season. The Verano carriage
rolled through Bloomsbury and into Mayfair as Mia fidgeted. "Do you think the Duke of Meryon will be there?"
She raised a hand to her hair and then dropped it back in
her lap before smoothing her coiffure.

Tina had insisted that a lady never worried about her
appearance. It was always perfect, even if she had a tear
in her hem. Elena was glad to see that Mia had been listening.

Mia smoothed out her new white gloves instead. "The
duke promised to dance with me. Do you remember?"

"Yes, I do, but he did not promise it would be at your
first ball. The duke will honor his commitment, I am sure,
but you cannot know with certainty he will be at the Metcalfes'."

"Have you not seen him in all this time?"

"Mia, it has been less than a week since the Monksfords' musicale."

"But you used to see the duke every day."

"He is busy too. If he comes to half the social engagements we have accepted I will be surprised. But most certainly we will see him a few times over the next months."

"Months!" Mia was in transports. "Weeks and weeks of fetes, parties, balls, masquerades, theater, opera, musicales, and art exhibits." She sat back as if already exhausted and straightened as quickly. "Have I left anything out?"

"The occasional picnic and perhaps a trip to Vauxhall."

"We can go to Vauxhall?"

"If the right party invites us."

"My governess said that it was filled with dangerous temptations."

"*Cara*, your governess was close to incompetent. Have you ever known a governess who never says no?"

"She did speak four languages."

"Yes, but somehow all the words of discipline were left out."

"Except for 'Oh dear, I'm not sure.'" Mia mimicked the way the governess held her cheeks as she spoke, then laughed. "I loved her. She was too easy."

"Exactly why she was the worst possible chaperone for you."

"I no longer need one. I am a young lady about to make her bow to the ton." She spoke as though it was the beginning of a fairy tale, and Elena hoped it was.

As for herself, Elena was relieved to be relegated to the group who escorted the young ladies. It was the perfect excuse not to dance if she wished to decline.

Though she might consider dancing a reel. One thing she was sure of: She would never dance the waltz again.

The carriage joined the line to the Metcalfes' front door and Elena assured Mia that this was a test of patience that everyone had to endure.

MERYON WAS GREETED effusively by Earl Metcalfe and was announced, though the words could barely be heard above the din. As he walked into the largest salon he could feel the hum of excitement. Young men and even younger girls were so crammed into the house the term "crush" had a quite literal meaning.

The terrace doors were open and a number of guests walked in the garden. The sound of voices made a mockery of the music played by a small group of musicians in the corner of the large salon. From past visits, Meryon knew that the ballroom was at the back of the house, but he could see the doors were still closed so the dancing had not yet begun.

He worked his way to the stairs and a footman assured him that there were three rooms prepared for those interested in cards. That would be an ideal way to spend the next hour.

When he came down from the card room, he went directly to the ballroom. It was crowded and the dance floor was ringed with watchers, but he saw Elena immediately. She looked spectacular, wearing a bronze satin gown with feathers in her hair. As much as she might try to blend in with the mothers and grandmothers with whom she stood, her youth and beauty set her apart.

She was chatting with Lady Monksford, though both of them kept their eyes on their charges as the girls danced their way up and down the line of a reel.

Meryon caught sight of Lord William as well, standing at the edge of the floor, on the other side of the room with some of the gentlemen. He was not talking to them but had his arms folded, watching Mia dance with all the pride of a mentor on this most important of nights.

By following his gaze Meryon was able to spot Miss Castellano. Elena's ward was obviously enjoying every moment of her first ball. Meryon did not recognize her partner, an earnest young man who was agog at the beauty who had accepted his invitation to dance.

As the reel ended Meryon recalled his promise to dance with Miss Castellano. That would be the perfect opportunity to speak with Elena.

Meryon circled around the back of the crowd and came up beside Lady Monksford, her daughter, and Elena and her ward. Ah, he would earn eternal gratitude from Lady Monksford if he also danced with her daughter, a girl whose face was flushed with excitement that left her complexion mottled with red and white.

"Oh! I cannot dance like that again or I will look even worse." Miss Monksford did not seem the slightest bit upset, but laughed when Mia said that she must dance outside on the terrace so as not to become overheated.

"Oh, yes, Mama would love that!"

The two of them dissolved into giggles but sobered

the moment they caught sight of the duke standing be-hind them.

"Your Grace!" Miss Castellano's greeting was so en-thusiastic that it sounded like they had been friends since her infancy.

Meryon returned her greeting, said hello to Lady Monksford, met her daughter, Miss Rosemary Monksford, and turned to greet Elena.

She curtsied to him. Meryon bowed. Then Elena gave him a small smile. Not very meaningful but better than nothing. He wanted to ask her to dance but thought to wait for a waltz. Instead, as the next set formed, he asked if he might dance with Miss Castellano.

"You must call me Mia, Your Grace. We have known each other quite long enough."

And I am so much older than you that I could almost be your father. He thought it for her, though in fact, Mia was all smiles and charm and did not appear at all put off by his age.

They took their turn on the floor, and later he did the same with Miss Monksford and three other young ladies. They all danced creditably well, but Mia Castellano was by far the best of the group.

Finally, *finally* the concert master announced a waltz. Meryon turned to Elena and bowed. "Would you dance with me, signora?"

"No, Your Grace. This is Mia's night. I am observing."

It was not a snub, but close enough that the baroness murmured, "Elena." The one word conveyed a wealth of sensibilities, all of which could be summed up in a few more words. Something akin to "Don't be ridiculous."

Meryon knew exactly what Elena was thinking. That she wanted nothing to do with him but would remain civil at all costs. For Mia.

He was ruthless enough to take advantage of that. He had to have a few minutes alone with her. "I'm sure you would enjoy a breath of air, a sweet or perhaps a lemonade." Meryon held out his arm and, as he hoped, she could not refuse.

He smiled and she looked away, which struck him as odd until the baroness laughed. "Oh, my goodness, no wonder you do not use that smile very often, Your Grace."

He turned that same smile on the lady and she blushed. "So few occasions merit it, my lady, but this company is exceptional."

Lady Monksford curtsied to him and pretended that Rosemary had called her, leaving them alone.

Elena hesitated and then, with a word to the mother of one of Mia's friends, let Meryon escort her to the dining room. The room was empty, supper not yet announced, but one of the servants was happy to bring the duke and his guest some wine.

"Let's stand near the door so that The Gossips can see we are being civil but not secretive."

They stood quietly for a moment. He enjoyed having her near, would have been happy to stay like that for an hour, but that, too, The Gossips would have noticed and commented on.

"Elena, Lord William told me this morning that you are the daughter of the Duke of Bendas. That he is the man who disowned you at the age of fourteen and the reason you went to Italy."

"I see." She put down her glass of wine and folded her hands at her waist. "Do you know why William found it necessary to violate my confidence?"

"He thought about it before he spoke. I am sure he considered it necessary. It was."

"And why is that, Your Grace?"

"Your father—"

"The Duke of Bendas. I do not call him my father."

Elena spoke with such anger Meryon hoped it was not aimed at him. "As you wish," he said, bowing slightly. "Lord William thinks that the duke bought the Verano violin so that he can attempt a reconciliation."

She seemed to consider the idea, and then shook her head. "I do not know if that makes a difference or not. I would just as soon buy it from him. I do not trust the Duke of Bendas at all."

"Whether you reconcile with him or not, I need you to understand that I have every intention of stripping him of his title and his honors. And I want to assure you that action has nothing to do with you."

She watched him for a long while, her eyes staring into his, as if she could find what she was looking for if she held his gaze long enough.

"Where is the stranger that I met on our first evening together?" she finally asked. "The man who kissed me with a touch that was a promise everything would be all right." Elena reached for her glass and took a sip of the wine. "Almost every other time we have been together, in public, I've seen the man you are now, contained, with passion carefully controlled."

She must have felt him stiffen at this rebuke because

she went on, her words hurried now. "I am sorry. I am sorry to hurt you this way. I need you to understand."

He bowed from the neck, his face sober, but he said nothing. He understood. He understood that what he did have to give was inadequate by her standards.

"I do care about you, Meryon. I even worry." She said the last as though it embarrassed her. Then she turned practical. "That night, when the wheel came off your carriage. Did it ever occur to you that you were the intended victim?"

"Yes." It was almost the truth. "And it also occurred to me that you might have been a target as well."

"Oh, you sound like William," she said dismissively and set her glass of wine down. Holding out her hands, she raised and lowered them imitating a balance. "So, the feud between you and Bendas threatens me from both sides. There is very little comfort in the fact that if I am hurt, it is only because I am too close to one or the other of you."

"It is not something to joke about. Bendas is quite unbalanced and I am determined to keep him from harming anyone else, including you. At least the danger from me is no more than hurt feelings."

"Yes, a broken heart is so easy to recover from."

"I am forever sorry, but I have apologized before. More than once." Irritated, close to angry, Meryon turned to leave, But Elena stayed him with a hand on his arm.

"If you could ever learn to give love as passionately as you seek justice then there might be hope. If you were not so afraid to risk your heart." She stopped as if she knew that was asking the impossible.

"I will escort you back to your friends, signora."

"Of course, Your Grace." She took his arm, barely touching his sleeve and they walked down the passage. "Neither of us wishes to attract The Gossips. Soon our friendship will be a dim memory."

"Not too soon, I hope."

"Once again, you ask more than I can give. I will forget it all, Your Grace, even our first meeting."

"No, signora," he said with deliberate command. "Our first meeting was as honest as a baby's breath. It was a solace I did not know I needed and will always be grateful for."

Meryon waited to see if she would say anything else. He could not recall the last time he had waited for someone to dismiss him.

"As you wish, Your Grace. I hope the rest of your evening is uneventful."

Elena left him to return to her party. Meryon watched her out of sight, then found a footman and asked him to ensure that his carriage was brought round immediately. He left without saying good night to Metcalfe, who would hector him into going back to the card room when all he wanted was to go home.

As the carriage rolled through the streets he could not forget one line. "If you were not so afraid to risk your heart."

Meryon realized he was not so different from Lord William.

He'd watched the young viscount watch Mia as she danced her way through her first ball. His heart was in his eyes. Every time she laughed or flirted with one of her partners, he would wince as though it was a pinch to his heart.

If there was ever a man willing to declare himself, willing to share his heart, it was William Bendasbrook. And even he was afraid. *Not* a coward. Just afraid.

Meryon had seen many men who were afraid. It was not a company he particularly wanted to be numbered in but it was better than being called a coward.

The carriage came to a halt in front of Penn House. For now, he knew exactly what he was going to do: spend the rest of the evening with the one female who loved him without limit. Magda.

36

IT TOOK A WEEK to orchestrate the final confrontation with Bendas. In the meantime the Indemnity Act passed and the budget was under discussion.

Meryon had met twice with William Wilberforce and, even after frank discussion about the difficulties of even presenting a bill that would mandate care for widows and orphans, Meryon was still determined to go forward.

There had been no further attempts on his life, unless he wanted to count a particularly awful fish soup Cook had prepared.

Meryon had seen Elena Verano three times. They had bowed, curtsied, and spoken briefly, convincing no one that they were still on friendly terms.

There had been no word from The Gossips about Elena's relationship to the Duke of Bendas, so Meryon was reasonably certain she had either refused a meeting or not been approached.

Meryon was set on moving the family to the house in Richmond. His appearance at the Italian ambassador's reception would be his farewell to the ton, and to Elena if he could find a few minutes alone with her.

Meryon spent most of that Saturday reviewing the confrontation with Bendas, determined to leave nothing to chance. The ton would be well represented and would be witnesses, but Meryon had also managed to secure the attendance of two of the Bendas trustees. They would inform the others.

Meryon left time to dress and arrive early, but when the nurse reported that Alicia was ill, he hurried up to the nursery. The child was feverish and chilled, the nurse had sent for a physician, and Rexton was playing out in the stables and would not be allowed near his sister until she was properly diagnosed.

Meryon was loath to leave, but his plans had been too difficult to arrange to abandon them for what might well be a cold.

He left strict orders for the nurse to send for him if the physician's diagnosis warranted it, left the nursery, and dressed as quickly as he could.

Wilson rode in the carriage with him, if only to guarantee that his livery would not smell of horse. The boy knew exactly what was expected of him. As the duke's page, he would be at Meryon's beck and call. As the boy said, "Like I am for John Coachman or the head groom in the stable."

"Everyone will be curious about you as I never use a

page. They will stare at you, but will not talk to you. You know exactly what you are to do."

The boy nodded and they traveled the rest of the way in silence. Bringing a page, when he had never done so before, would attract the attention of The Gossips, which ensured they would not miss a moment.

The drive seemed to take forever, but that could have been because Wilson fidgeted so. Finally the coach reached the front door of an impressive townhouse, larger than the usual, with the double doors opened wide to the sight of people milling around inside.

There was no line of carriages. Meryon had arrived beyond fashionably late, and for a moment he worried that Bendas might have left already.

Meryon was greeted by the ambassador and his wife, who were still receiving guests in the hall, then made his way, with Wilson trailing him, through knots of people discussing everything from the business of Parliament to the best way to train a dog to attack.

Besides the best of society, the company was filled with foreign dignitaries and "friends of Italy." The Duke of Bendas, most likely invited because his long-deceased wife had been Italian, sat by himself and was easily the oldest person present.

The Gossips had found a spot near the door where they could see who came and went in the passage and at the entry, and still keep an eye on the main salon. At the moment they were talking among themselves, though they never stopped looking around for something of interest. Meryon nodded to the cluster and they all nodded and curtsied back.

He moved deeper into the overcrowded salon. Perfume, candle wax, and the smell of overheated bodies made it more of a crush than was pleasant. Finally he heard Elena's voice and headed toward it, determined to have a word with her before the drama unfolded.

Standing at the center of a group of gentlemen, Elena was doing more listening than speaking. She was wearing a maroon gown and an exquisite diamond necklace that called attention to her discreet décolletage. He watched for a long minute until she looked up and saw him, then he walked straight to her. The crowd stood back and he bowed.

"Good evening, signora."

She curtsied, eyed Wilson with a moment's curiosity, but did not answer Meryon's greeting.

"Take my arm for a moment."

Her eyes spoke for her, their chill freezing him to the bone.

"Please," he added hastily.

"No, thank you, Your Grace."

That was all she said, without an excuse, without a regretful smile. Then she doubled the offense by resuming her conversation, in German, with some gentleman Meryon did not recognize.

Meryon recognized a sickening mix of anger and embarrassment that he had not felt since his days at Oxford. Now The Gossips had something to talk about. With a curt nod, which Elena ignored, he moved away on stiff legs. He would have to move forward with his plan without warning her.

If she and Bendas had reconciled, what he intended

would hurt her as much as it hurt Bendas. Meryon did not care. He could not care.

When he saw Lord William come into the room, Meryon gave himself no more time to think about the consequences. He nodded at Wilson and they took their places halfway across the room but in direct line of sight of the Duke of Bendas. And Rogers.

Meryon and Wilson stood by themselves, a sea of people moving around them. Wilson did as directed and stared at Rogers, who felt the scrutiny in less than a minute. Bendas's secretary glanced around the room until he saw Wilson. They stared at each other and then Rogers pretended to ignore him.

A minute later The Gossips had noticed Rogers's discomfort and Wilson's intense stare and had begun to watch and, more unsettling, to speculate.

Meryon could see Rogers growing restless, unable to decide what to do. Short of panic, but confused. Finally he bent down to speak to Bendas, who looked over with sneering disdain at Wilson and Meryon.

Perfect. But Meryon had claimed victory a minute too soon. In that minute, Elena approached the Duke of Bendas.

No, he thought. Elena was most emphatically not part of the plan. Meryon watched as if it were happening in a dream.

Elena curtsied graciously and waited.

Bendas stood slowly, giving her a perfunctory bow, but smiled as he did.

Bendas glanced at Meryon with cold calculation replacing the smile.

Then the old duke nodded at Elena, giving her permission to speak.

Walk away. Oh, Elena, dear heart, walk away. Meryon wanted to shout, but knew that it would no more than delay the inevitable. Bendas was going to attack him through Elena. Bendas might not know precisely what Meryon had planned to ruin him, but that would not keep the old duke from taking his revenge beforehand.

Meryon did not hear what Elena said; her back was to the room as she spoke, unaware that most everyone was watching them.

Bendas must not have heard her either, because she took a step closer and spoke again.

Bendas said nothing at first.

Terror was not too strong a word to describe what Meryon felt. Acting on a moment's thought, not quite impulse, he moved closer to her to lend his support. Elena had made it clear she did not want him involved. Torn between what he knew was going to happen and what Elena wanted, he stopped six feet from her and the duke, praying that his trap had not compromised her attempt at conversation, if not reconciliation, with her father.

Bendas faced the room and spoke out loud as if he wanted to entertain, not just The Gossips, but everyone in the room.

"You want me to sell you the Verano violin?"

Meryon was close enough to see that Bendas's smile was wicked and unfriendly. Elena herself took a step back.

"I will give the violin to you, Ellen, if you admit that you were a disrespectful girl and have grown into a vain and stupid whore."

The crowd gasped, almost as one. Elena did not say a word, or not one that Meryon could hear, but she did begin to turn away from Bendas, swaying slightly.

Meryon hurried to her side, just as the old man lifted his cane and blocked her way. She reached down to move it aside and he swatted her knuckles with it.

Now Meryon did act on impulse. Whether she wanted his help or not, whether he was the reason for Bendas's insult or not. Meryon took her injured hand, kissed the red mark, and kicked the cane out of Bendas's hand.

"You are the vain and stupid one, Bendas." Meryon held on to Elena's ice-cold fingers. They were all the inspiration he needed. "You are a disgrace to your name. Everyone here is now a witness to your insanity. You no longer even know right from wrong."

Bendas narrowed his eyes and opened his mouth but Meryon wasn't finished.

"Tell us: What was your excuse when your daughter was fourteen and you disowned her?"

"She is *not* my daughter," Bendas declared

"Oh, yes, she is. Your son and heir as well as his son, Lord William, will attest to it. Lord William has been her staunch supporter for all these years." He could feel Elena begin to shake and he tucked her hand over his arm, pulling her close. "Lord William has a letter from his father swearing that you threw your daughter out of your house because she chose to sing a song that displeased you."

Meryon turned his back on Bendas, who had collapsed into his chair. Facing Elena fully, Meryon bowed to her. "I know better than to ask if you are all right. May I escort you home, my lady?"

Meryon had no idea what would come next, but was almost sure she would not refuse him. Elena did not answer or could not, but did not let go of his arm. They had taken two steps away when Bendas yelled, "Wait!"

Meryon would have ignored him if the old duke had not pulled the violin case onto his lap.

"I bought this from DeBora." Bendas's half-blind eyes radiated spite. "I was going to keep it to remind me of my child's perfidy, but I think I will give it to you so you will have a constant reminder of how much I hate you."

Elena murmured, "Why?" to no one in particular but Meryon whispered back, "Because he knows you are not afraid of him, will never bow to him. Using his title to cow people is the only sick pleasure he has left in life."

Bendas could not hear what he said. But Bendas had apparently reached his limit anyway. The old man pushed the violin case at them, and when neither one of them would take it, Bendas opened the latch and emptied the case.

The Verano violin, broken into pieces, clattered to the floor.

Elena screamed.

The crowd surged forward, and for a moment Meryon thought Elena had fainted. But no, she was kneeling, laying fingers that trembled on the ruined instrument.

Bendas laughed.

As Elena began to gather the pieces and put them in

the case, she spoke loud enough for Bendas to hear. As the room was dead silent that meant it was loud enough for everyone in attendance to hear as well.

"I am *ashamed* to be your daughter. I renounce you once and for all and will never, ever acknowledge you again."

Bendas grunted a dismissal.

Meryon bent to help Elena, his temper on the breaking point. His own hands were shaking with rage and he could not handle the pieces as carefully as Elena, so he held the case as she continued to fill it. It took all the control he had to ignore Bendas. Elena was far more important. He would attend to Bendas later.

Whether or not Meryon had ruined Elena's chance at reconciliation with her father, Garrett was right. His fight for justice was too much like revenge. It had cost too much.

He heard Bendas spit and felt the spittle land on his shoulder. It was such a vulgar insult that Meryon was sure the people watching would realize that the man was insane.

Meryon stiffened and cast Bendas a withering glance. He latched the case, gave Elena his hand, and helped her to stand again.

Then he took out his handkerchief to wipe the spittle from his shoulder.

"So it comes to a duel," Meryon said, as though it were hardly worth noting. He turned to Elena. "My lady, I love and respect everything about you and will do as you wish in this."

She was shocked. He could tell she could barely take

in what was happening. *Courage,* he said with his eyes. *You have only one more decision to make.*

"My lady, I ask you as your servant, do you want me to kill this man in a duel?"

"No, no," she said, finding her voice. Her white face was now flushed. She raised a hand to her heart.

"And so it will be, my lady." Meryon turned back to Bendas, who looked disgusted by Meryon's consideration. "He is no longer a gentleman and not worthy of a challenge."

Meryon offered Elena his arm and escorted her from the salon, the crowd making room for them, most of them edging away from the corner where Rogers was Bendas's only support.

As they left, Meryon saw William and the trustees talking together with Wilson nearby, ready to tell his story. Bendas was at the end of his road to ruin, at the gate of Hell.

37

ELENA SAT CURLED UP against Meryon in his carriage, her brain unable to take in the enormity of what had happened.

Her father's behavior had shocked her. Meryon's behavior had too. Elena really was not sure which of the two surprised her more.

She did know that next to Meryon was exactly where she wanted to be.

He hugged her to his side. "We will be in Bloomsbury soon," he whispered against her hair.

She could not face Tinotti and Tina. Mia would cry even more than she already had at not being able to attend.

"I will never be your mistress, Meryon. There is no room for discussion on that."

She could feel him straighten a little and draw in a

breath to answer her. Elena went on in a rush. "If you accept that, then I would like to go to the little house on St. German Street." She sat up and hoped she did not look as bad as she felt.

"I cannot take you to St. German Street."

"All right." Elena looked out the window, too drained to cry, though her heart ached at the rejection.

"Elena, darling, you misunderstand. You are better off without me. Please listen. I am the reason Bendas treated you so badly. If I had not pursued him for my version of justice, he would have, at the very least, left you alone and, at the most, welcomed you as his daughter again. I saw Rogers whisper to him that there was going to be trouble. Bendas saw what I had put in play and he thought to escape it through you. When that did not work, he tried to hurt you as a revenge on me."

"You take too much responsibility, Lyn." She was not going to argue with him about this.

"That could be."

Was that agreement she heard from him? She *must* look awful.

"Elena, no one knows when the man's mind first began to fail. It could have started when you were fourteen. We would have to be as mad as he is to understand why he has acted this way."

"Then we cannot let him win. Please, Meryon, take me to the little house."

"Of course I will." His voice registered his surprise. "If you are sure. It is not the seat of our happiest memories."

"It was the place of our greatest intimacy and our first

truly awful misunderstanding. That makes it as much a home as any other place where we have kissed and argued."

"Then you will have to find a Canaletto when I redo the small salon." He raised a finger and pressed it against her lips even though she had made no move to speak. "In this case I am not going to ask what you wish, but hope that I can read your mind. I will happily take you to the little house, but you must rest. I can see you are still very shaken."

"Yes." She could agree to that. "If you will rest with me." Meryon smiled and kissed her forehead, which was almost annoying. She was not an invalid.

He more than made up for it later when they were in the great lake of a bed. Elena had indeed slept for almost two hours and when she woke up, Meryon was beside her reading by the light of one weak candle.

He smiled at her, but kept reading. She decided that he needed a distraction but made a mental note that when she was ill he would take very good care of her. Whether she needed it or not.

Elena rested her palm on the curve of his hip. She loved the feel of that spot, the warmth of it and the way she could feel his body react to her touch.

She wrapped her fingers around his arousal and Meryon could ignore her no longer.

"Do you feel well enough for this?" He showed her an illustration in a book of erotic drawings.

"Not today," she said with a laugh, "but do mark the spot."

When he leaned over to place the book on the night-stand and blow out the candle, Elena wiggled closer to him, annoyed that she was still wearing her shift.

He must have read her mind because he pushed back the covers on his side of the bed and began kissing her ankle, then her calf, then her knee, raising the shift with each kiss.

When he reached her waist he slid his hand under her back and raised her a little. Pressing his mouth to her he kissed and licked until she was writhing.

"Hold still or I will leave you frustrated quite unintentionally."

"Holding still," she gasped, "is not what I want to do at all."

"All right, then." He looked up and smiled. "Let us move together, shall we?"

They found a rhythm and Elena was lost in the rocking, rhythmic, fiery orgasm too soon and not soon enough. Before she was fully aware, Meryon moved atop her, sliding his manhood into her, rubbing against the already sensitive parts of her. The orgasm did not end until his seed came into her. They stayed joined until the last of the pleasure faded.

Finally, he helped her out of another ruined shift. This time she was the one who pulled the sheet up over their shoulders. There were no fires today and, as the night shadows deepened, the room took on a chill.

"Do you want to sleep more?" he asked.

Since she knew that was what he needed, Elena agreed and, tucked together, she closed her eyes. His even breathing soon followed, and then the longer breaths that she already recognized as deep sleep.

They were lovers. They would be lovers for as long as she wanted. Elena drifted into a light doze as she calculated that forever would be just long enough.

ELENA LOOKED AROUND the salon for a place to put a Canaletto and wondered if Meryon realized that arguments would be a way of life for them.

As the maid set a tray with tea and biscuits on a table, Meryon came into the room. The maid curtsied to them and disappeared.

He watched the maid leave and nodded when Elena raised the teapot. "I took a few minutes to speak to the maid. Her name is Marcella and she says that this house belongs to her more than any of its other occupants. She is forever grateful to have been offered the post and hopes she can stay on forever."

"She does talk then?"

"Only when spoken to." He took a healthy sip of the tea that Elena poured for him. "Our conversation made me realize the difference between lonely and alone. Another bit of wisdom gained by talking to servants. Talking to them may become a habit."

"Hmm, beware awakening a beast. I love the Tinottis, I truly do, but it is rather nice to have a servant who does not want to discuss every domestic detail with you."

"That's when the ducal stare can be useful."

"Keep thinking that, Your Grace." She laughed at his expression. "Perhaps you are right. It is a way of telling them that they have encroached, but I do not see it nearly as often as I used to."

He tried to use it on her and she pressed her lips together to keep from laughing. In the end he was laughing too.

"Oh, Elena, you are such a joy. Marry me. Please say you will marry me." He must have seen her shock because he quickly amended his proposal. "Say you will at least consider it. Someday."

"Marriage." She walked to the window that overlooked the back garden and noticed that the pink and red flowers blooming matched the ones on the wall in the salon. It was easier to think about that than to consider all that Meryon's suggestion implied.

"Only consider it, Elena. I love you. More than I ever thought possible. I hope that you love me. My cowardice is in the past and you need to know what I feel. Being your lover is not all that I long for. I want you to be a part of my life in every way, not just in bed."

He kissed her. Not a seductive kiss, but one that felt to her like an apology.

"I am sorry if this upsets you, and I leave the decision completely in your hands."

I am already tired of all this obsequiousness, she thought, but was wise enough not to say it aloud. He was a man who, once he was aware and committed, did nothing by halves.

"Very well. Then I will be as honest with you." As she took a breath, she wondered if he would invite someone to Jackson's when she was done. "I do not ever want to marry again. My independence is too precious. As a widow, my world runs as I wish, and I see no reason to change that. To marry again means too big a leap of faith. Could what we have survive the change? Can we not keep our lives as they are?"

"Coward." He made the word sound like a term of endearment. "I will agree to your terms now, my darling, and save the argument for sometime when we need one. For now contentment is too fine a comfort to tamper with."

THE NEXT WEEKS were much as he hoped. Near perfect, with just enough difference of opinion to give them a fine excuse to make up.

They met at St. German Street and once or twice spent the entire night there. By June, when the session ended, they were recognized as "very close friends," and when Mia announced her engagement to William several people congratulated Meryon as though he were Mia's father.

The subject of marriage never actually came up, or not very often. Rexton had asked if she was going to become his mama and Blix had suggested Meryon consider redoing the duchess's suite.

Mia and William were, fortunately, too caught up in their own plans to nag them, but the thought of marriage came back to Meryon every time he and Elena had to say good night and go to their separate homes. He wished that she had the same feelings, but she seemed so perfectly and utterly pleased with herself, with him, with life, that he knew that was not the case.

38

LYNETTE AND GABRIEL RETURNED to town to discuss their project with their patron, Dr. Schotzko. This time they had brought all the children as far as the house in Richmond, where Lynette's mother was supervising the servants for now.

This morning Elena had come early to join Lynette, Gabriel, and Meryon for breakfast. Afterward the four adults, with Rexton and Alicia, were going to Richmond for a small family house party. Though as Lynette said, "It is doubtful that any house party with this many children can be called small."

Mia, William, and the Tinottis were to meet them there as well. Meryon thought it had the makings of a riot but found he was looking forward to the chaos.

They were lingering over the last bit of tea and toast when the majordomo came to him. "I beg your pardon,

Your Grace. This is highly unusual but Wilson insists on speaking with you before you leave for Richmond. The dog, Magda, is with him."

"Oh, show him in," Gabriel called from his end of the table. "The duke is still breakfasting and we should all like to see Magda."

"Yes, tell Wilson I will see him here," Meryon told the majordomo, and returned to his last bit of toast.

The butler was not as good as Blix at keeping his expression bland. He did answer "Yes, Your Grace," but his expression conveyed horror at the idea of a stable servant being welcomed into the private part of the house.

Alan Wilson walked into the room with a straight back and Magda under his arm. He was a little taken aback when he saw that the party was larger than just him and the duke, but he recovered quickly and gave a jerky bow.

"Good morning to you, Mr. Wilson."

"Good morning, sir, Your Grace." The boy answered with more formality than he usually showed.

"Put Magda down."

When Wilson hesitated, Meryon explained, "She knows this room well and exactly who will give her food from the table."

With a nod, Wilson set Magda down and the dog trotted to Gabriel.

"Now tell me what is so important that you must speak to me at breakfast."

"It's Magda, sir, Your Grace. If I am to go in the cabriolet I want to know who she's traveling with."

"I thought she would stay here."

Meryon heard Gabe choke back a laugh.

"She can't," the boy said firmly. "She is part of the family too. Sir, Your Grace, I came to see if she could ride with Rexton and Alicia, or even up in the box with John Coachman."

"Brilliant, my boy," Gabriel called out. "You have marshaled an excellent argument with Lord Rexton on your side."

Wilson bowed his head but did not look away from the duke.

"Yes, Wilson. I understand your concern, and Magda will certainly be included in the family outing."

"Thank you, sir, Your Grace," the boy said with a smile that was a reward all its own.

"Wilson. Could I have your attention for a moment?" Gabriel called out.

"Yes, sir." The boy walked down to the end of the table.

"Please tell me who you are."

"I am Alan Wilson, the duke's tiger, and I walk Magda and work in the stables and ride with John Coachman so I can learn to handle the reins of a coach and four."

"I am Gabriel Pennistan, the duke's youngest brother. I live in Sussex with my wife and children. I am a man of science and study the human body and spend all the rest of the time doing whatever my wife tells me."

Wilson bowed.

"You have met our sons before, have you not?"

"Some of them, my lord."

Gabe looked at Meryon and he nodded. He knew what was coming and thought it an excellent idea—which he hoped Gabriel appreciated as a hugely unselfish gesture, since Wilson was the best groom on staff. Of course that only proved he had a future beyond the stable.

"Wilson, I would like to invite you to join us in Sussex. I think the duke would be willing to let Magda come too, and you could learn a skill of your choosing."

Wilson looked puzzled and then his face cleared. "You want me to become a part of your family."

"Yes, in essence."

"Thank you, my lord, but no." Wilson answered without a moment's hesitation.

They wrangled on for another five minutes, but Meryon could see that Wilson's mind was set.

Finally, Meryon interrupted. "Wilson has made his choice, Gabriel. He wants life in Penn Square and to be head groom one day." To Wilson he added, "You can always change your mind."

The boy bowed his head, obviously relieved that the discussion was over.

"I think you have chores to do before we leave. Would you like a muffin?" The last was an impulse and he held the basket out.

"No, thank you, sir, Your Grace. It would not be seemly." He bowed to all of them, and with impressive dignity he left the room, Magda trotting behind him.

They all sat in silence. Elena was the first to speak.

"Why did he not accept the offer?" Elena's puzzlement was thorough. She searched all their faces.

Gabriel shrugged. "He is comfortable here. He likes his work."

Lynette tried. "He does not know us well enough to trust us with his life."

"Why Wilson did not take the muffin is the bigger question," Gabriel said, only half joking.

"That I have the answer to," Meryon said, thinking of his conversations with Blix. "Wilson refused it for much the same reason he refused to go to Sussex.

"Servants are as aware of their place as their betters are and will hold on to it with a death grip, because it is what they know."

The three nodded and Meryon went on. "Elena." He waited until she was looking at him. "Sussex, if not the muffin, required too big a leap of faith."

MERYON, ELENA, GABE, AND LYNETTE traveled to Richmond in the same carriage. Rexton and Alicia had left earlier so the trip would not interfere with the toddler's nap.

As a gesture of goodwill to Lord William, Meryon had allowed Mia and William to take the cabriolet, and all the way down the road he was afraid he would find them in the ditch or worse.

When they arrived at the house Meryon saw that they were safe and had already organized the amazing number of children into two teams for a game of hide-and-seek.

Gabriel, never content with contentment, had some idea that this was the time to play cricket. Meryon informed him that a duke did not play cricket after the age of thirty and that he was going to show Elena the house and then the grounds.

Or perhaps the other way around, he thought. Anything for some time alone with her. She had been unusually quiet on the drive down and he wanted very much to know what she was thinking.

He lived his dream of escorting her through every room of this much-loved spot, but made it even better by kissing her at every doorway. It took them a very long time to reach the grove of trees near the cascade.

Spreading the blanket he had asked the housekeeper for, they sat in the shade of the trees, with the front of the house filling the sky, the rare blue sky.

They could hear the children yelling, far enough away to be entertained by it. He rested his head in her lap and she brushed his hair back from his forehead.

"It is such a lovely house, Lyn. So beautifully balanced. It reminds me of some of the styles that developed from Palladio—the perfectly matched proportions, the two chimneys, and the central pediment."

"I have always liked it best of all the Pennistan properties. I have thought more than once of spending the months of Parliament here."

"I could live here." She stopped stroking his hair, but would not meet his eyes.

"You could?"

"Yes." She spoke the one word with conviction. "All it will require is a great leap of faith." Now she did look at him, and pulled his ear like a very annoyed governess. "How undeniably brilliant of you to throw that phrase back at me."

He shrugged and sat up, lest she was thinking about injuring him in a more serious way.

"I hope that Wilson changes his mind. I know I have." Elena looked him in the eye and he could see tears on her lashes. "I know that marrying is a leap of faith. But I know now that it is worth the risk."

He closed his eyes and thanked God and blessed Alan Wilson.

"Lyn, I know that whatever comes, it will be worth the effort. I would be a fool not to say yes, should you ever ask me to marry you again."

Meryon knelt on the blanket and took her hand. He would be a fool to let this moment pass. He had his mouth open, the words "Will you marry me?" ready, when Rexton came racing down to them, shouting.

"Papa, Papa! Signora!" They tried to look like something other than lovers but the boy did not notice anything unusual. "Lord William fell out of the tree trying to rescue one of Cousin Marie's cats and I think he has broken his arm."

Epilogue

March 1819

LETTY HARBISON WELCOMED the Duke and Duchess of Meryon with genuine pleasure. "We are so happy to have you make your first appearance as a married couple at our ball." She turned to Elena. "Your Grace, I will not ask you to sing tonight because I know everyone will want to wish you well, but I would very much like to speak to Signor Tinotti about a possible engagement entirely at your convenience."

"Of course, Mrs. Harbison, I would be delighted. Your ball will always hold a special place in my heart."

"Yes, our ball last year was your first singing appearance in England, was it not?"

Let her think that is why, Meryon thought. He and Elena both knew the true reason that they would always attend the Harbison ball.

"Be sure to notice the decorations this evening. They are our wedding gift to you, Duchess."

Elena glanced at Meryon, then nodded at Mrs. Harbison, not at all sure what Mrs. Harbison had done with the bit of information she had asked for. It took them a few minutes to work their way into the ballroom. Everyone stopped them to wish them the best. Meryon insisted on talking for a few moments with each one of them.

"Oh my," Elena said as they walked into the ballroom, still mostly empty. "You did have a part in this, Lyn, you cannot deny it." She gave her husband a knowing look.

The ceiling of the ballroom had been painted to look like the sky. Not just any sky, but the whispered blues and white of a Canaletto sky. The walls were an imaginative variant of Canaletto's festival scenes, with the palaces of Venice painted in such a way that the doorways to the terrace were the doors of the houses.

"Oh, this is wonderful! It is too, too kind. Much too much."

"Oh, I don't know, my dear; she could have flooded the ballroom with water and brought in gondolas."

Elena laughed. Then she squeezed his arm and hurried back to their hostess. He stayed where he was and watched as she thanked Letty effusively, her laughter making him smile at them both.

He loved her laughter, especially in bed. When he told her he had never ever laughed in bed before, she admitted that she hadn't either. It made him realize he was not the only student. They would both learn about life and love from each other.

The ball was one of the most entertaining that the

Harbisons had ever hosted. Before dinner was announced he noted that Elena was no longer in the room and made his own way down the passage he had first traveled a year ago. He found Elena standing at the window. He thought of any number of clever things to say, but when he came up next to her, Elena turned into his arms. "I am so happy you knew to come here. While I was waiting I was remembering last year, when I told Mia that one should *never* expect to find love twice in a lifetime. And I was right."

She raised her head and smiled at him. "But little did I know; what I never expected was that I would find a different, more passionate love. Nothing equals what we have."

Elena hugged him tight, stepped out of his arms, and went over to the settee, patting the seat next to her. "Tell me, Your Grace, what has been the best part of the last six months?"

He took the chair across from her. That patting gesture was one of the few things that annoyed him.

"Well, Your Grace," he began, "do you recall the time we were at the house in Richmond, walking down to the river, and it began to rain?"

She nodded with a very tolerant expression on her face. He was annoying her a little. He knew very well this was not what she meant. But she had not qualified her question. He loved the little glimmer of irritation in her eyes.

"We had to take shelter in the boathouse," he reminded her, which was completely unnecessary. He knew she remembered it as well as he did. "That game of hide-and-seek we played? I have to admit that being caught was one of the finest experiences of the year."

"Mine as well," she admitted, while still managing to sound like a condescending duchess.

"Rexton would be shocked to hear me say that losing was so gratifying, but then he is too young to appreciate a naked woman."

She was silent. A silence filled with meaning.

"I can see that you are not happy with that answer. Please, my darling wife, tell me how I can make you smile."

"Tell me the truth, my husband." If there had been a pillow handy, he was sure she would have thrown it at him.

"That is the truth, darling girl. But I will tell you what you want to hear." Now he did stand up and come to sit beside her. He took her hand and kissed it. "It is not so much a single instance as a way of life. That we always seem to be what the other needs. When I am too serious, you make me laugh. When you are ready to throw things, I hand you something unbreakable."

She laughed at that, a breathy sound that made him feel that all was right with their world. "I have long considered the ideal match to be one where each found the other exciting and calming as the need arose. Is that what you mean?"

"Precisely." He kissed her lightly. "On a practical level, I find myself happy about a number of things. That Olivia is safely delivered of a son. That David is so enthusiastic about the projects he is developing in Manchester. That

Lord William's arm has healed well. That Rexton seems to be enjoying school and Alicia is healthy."

He did occasionally think about more children, but although he and Elena talked about it sometimes, tonight he kept that thought to himself. She would cry because she was so sure she was barren, and he would have to show her that it did not matter to him at all and this settee was too small to substitute for a bed.

"You are kind not to add that my father's death has made our lives simpler," she said.

"Simpler for us and so much easier for his heirs. The man had become a caricature of his best self. That Rowlandson cartoon of him stomping on a violin was proof of that."

They sat in silence for a moment. Meryon was not sure if Elena would ever forgive her father, but he knew she prayed for him.

"And what are your favorite memories, Duchess?"

"Redecorating the house on St. German Street has been so entertaining. If one of your unmarried brothers decides to come to town it will be the perfect spot for him to be on his own."

"Yes, and close enough to Penn House that he need never miss a dinner."

"What I am happiest for occurred more than six months ago. That night that William suggested that I use this room when I needed to escape. I must admit I worry a little about whether his marrying Mia is the best match for the two of them." She was quiet a minute and he knew that meant an internal debate.

Finally she drew a deep breath. "William so deserves

someone who will love him for the man he is, not the dukedom and wealth he will inherit."

"Mia does enjoy him. They are always laughing."

"Yes, but we both know that marriage is not all laughter."

"Well, my dear, they will have to make their own leap of faith. The best influence that we can have is to set them a good example."

She put her head on his shoulder, and they sat in silence. He was wondering if the settee was too small. He had no idea what Elena was thinking.

"Meryon, does that door lock?"

"Yes," he said, proud of his foresight. "I checked when we came in."

"I was wondering," she asked very, very quietly, as though someone might be listening. "Have you ever made love in a wingback chair?"

"What an excellent idea!" He stood and lifted her from the settee, and they both began laughing.

IN THE BALLROOM The Gossips were watching the passageway.

"Where are they?"

"Could they be playing cards? You know how the Harbisons love their cards."

"Nonsense, the Duke of Meryon almost never plays cards. He might be talking about his investments. His brother is Lord David, and all he can talk about are those projects the duke is investing in."

"God, Lord David is boring."

There were nods of agreement and the group stared down the empty passage.

"The rest of the rooms are dark."

"Oh, really?" one of them said with a lascivious wink. "Well, they are newlyweds. Can we guess what they're doing?"

"Please, he's a duke. She married him for his money and he married her because she's a duke's daughter."

"I saw them laughing together this evening, more than once."

"Nonsense, dukes don't laugh, any more than they marry for love."

"Marry for love? Oh, my dear," said the wisest among them, "I think this one did."

Author's Note

Stranger's Kiss takes a close look at a duke's life: the social, political, and personal world of the most important non-royal aristocrats in Regency England.

To my way of thinking, a duke is a cross between a big-name Hollywood star and a U.S. senator. Like a Holly-wood star, a duke attracted attention from all walks of life and provided endless fodder for gossip columns. In the political realm, a duke's position in the House of Lords gave him significant influence over the legislation introduced and passed in Parliament.

From my perspective, 1818 was the lull between two dramatic years in England's march to industrial and polit-ical change. In 1817 the Pentrich Rising represented an aborted attempt at revolution, and in 1819 the Peterloo Massacre was an (over)reaction to a public demonstration in Manchester.

Both of these events took place in the Derbyshire region,

where the Duke of Meryon's family has historic roots, and in my fictional world they had a dramatic impact on how the Pennistans view the future and their place in it.

Here are a few comments that will separate fact from fiction: The Duke of Meryon's interest in proposing a bill to care for widows and orphans is far ahead of its time but reflects his awakening to the needs of the world beyond Mayfair.

William Wilberforce is one of the true historical figures in *Stranger's Kiss*. The movie *Amazing Grace* gives an entertaining and generally accurate account of his struggles to abolish the slave trade in England.

All the musicians are fictitious (except Beethoven!). The songs that Elena sings are also creations of my imagination. The Marquis Straemore and his wife, Marguerite, are characters from the series I wrote for Kensington and used with Kensington's permission. Titles are available on my website, MaryBlayney.com.

Once again I must acknowledge Lois McMaster Bujold, whose character Miles Vorkosigan is the inspiration for William Bendasbrook.

My thanks to Regina Scott, Shannon Donnelly, Meg Grasselli, Kalen Hughes, Nancy Mayer, and the members of The Beau Monde for sharing their expertise. And to Alan Wilson for the use of his name.

As always, the support and genius of my writers' group—Lavinia Kent, Marsha Nuccio, and Elaine Fox—make all things possible. The "rapid response team" of Shauna Summers and Jessica Sebor at Bantam is truly amazing in both speed and expertise. Thank you all for making this such a rewarding experience.